INHERITING MISS FORTUNE

LUCY LENNOX

INHERITING MISS FORTUNE

I was a man without a family... or so I thought.

I came to tiny Majestic, Wyoming, to escape misfortune: the loss of my brother; my parents' blame for it; the billion-dollar secret that caused it all.

I find peace in my horses, in my friends, in quiet nights alone... and sometimes in remembering a scorching-hot one-night-stand from two years ago.

But everything changes when Tully Bowman, the man behind that unforgettable encounter, turns up in Majestic bringing me the daughter I've inherited (along with her multi-million-dollar trust fund).

Just like that, my peace becomes chaos, my quiet nights are filled with little Lellie's cries for "Daddy," and the heat between Tully and me becomes more than just a memory.

Because it seems Tully's planning to stick around... at least until I prove I'm a "suitable father" and not the fortune-hunter Lellie's grandparents think I am. And the longer we spend together—the more he challenges and provokes me, comforts and calms me—the harder it is to remember why I ever thought one night would be enough.

I'm a bad bet for fatherhood, but if I choose to keep Lellie and raise her as my own, it won't be for her money. It will be because this precious girl and the man who brought her to me might be the fresh start and new family my heart has been looking for.

And because the best thing that ever happened to me might just be... Inheriting Miss Fortune.

AUTHOR NOTE

Special thanks to Amanda Boes for help with horse stuff and to Andi Privitere for a certain ringtone suggestion.

If you'd like to make suggestions that might make it into the next book, please join us on Patreon where you can read along while I write each book and get early peeks at exclusive content like NSFW artwork and mini-fics featuring your favorite characters! Join here →
https://www.patreon.com/lucylennox

ONE

TULLY

"Custody goes to *Devon McKay?*" Franklin Scott boomed. "Of *my* granddaughter? You can't be serious!"

I clenched my jaw and held my tongue. His reaction was no surprise. As Katie's parents and sole surviving family members, Pastor and Mrs. Scott might have seemed like the obvious choice to get custody of her daughter. Obvious to anyone who hadn't been close to Katie, that was.

The founding partner at my firm frowned at me from across the large conference table. "Tully, do you know this Mr. McKay?"

I opened my mouth to respond but quickly shut it. The answer to that question was... complicated. I didn't know him in the way that one knew a longtime friend or coworker. While I'd heard a little about him from Katie, I'd never gotten to know him personally outside of having spent a few hours with him once at a party at Katie's house.

Having said that... I *did* happen to know what his face looked like when he tried to keep himself from coming. What his hot mouth felt like wrapped around my most intimate body part. The way his face had turned gently against mine as he'd surreptitiously inhaled the scent of me before leaving.

I blinked and focused back on my boss. Orris Dunlevy's thick, chalk-white hair was always perfectly formed into a slight swoop to one side, regardless of how frustrated he was. Monogrammed cuffs peeked out from his thousand-dollar suit jacket as he studied me with his arms crossed and one eyebrow raised.

"No, sir," I said on an unsteady exhale. "I mean, not really. I've heard of him, of course. I did prepare the will."

The pastor clenched his fists on the tabletop while Katie's mom continued to cry and flutter an honest-to-god old-fashioned hankie near her face. "Someone needs to explain to me how this happened," he demanded.

Orris nodded but stayed focused on me. "Tully?"

"I'm unsure what you're asking exactly," I said carefully. While I was considered the golden boy of Dunlevy, Pace, and Trumble, no one in this firm was safe from the scales of justice around here... and by "justice," I meant money.

As the founders of the Church of Heavenly Victory, Franklin and Paula Scott were richer than god. And they'd moved all of their legal business to the firm as soon as Orris had hired Katie out of Duke Law. Keeping the Scotts happy was the key to keeping my bosses happy.

But I'd been Katie's friend as well as her personal attorney, and I wasn't about to let her down, especially when she was no longer here to stand up for herself or her daughter.

"I'm asking you to tell me why Ms. Scott named this... *Devon McKay*... as the legal guardian of her child," my boss clarified.

At the mention of Lellie, Mrs. Scott sobbed louder, which only made the pastor's face turn redder.

I cleared my throat and prepared for the explosion. "He's her biological father."

Orris's eyes only widened a little, but everyone else in the room, including Katie's parents, another managing partner, two associates, a junior associate, and two assistants, all seemed to lose their collective minds.

"Impossible!" Pastor Scott barked.

"Kathryn, how could you?" Mrs. Scott sobbed.

The managing partner turned to the junior associate and spoke in a low voice, "Get us everything you can on McKay."

I concentrated on breathing and reminded myself to stay calm and professional. While I understood and had expected the panic, I also trusted my good friend. Katie adored her daughter and would have never named Dev McKay Lellie's guardian if she hadn't trusted him with the girl's future.

And it wasn't like the man wouldn't be able to afford to hire help. Not once he realized Lellie's guardian would also be the trustee of the fortune her mother had left her.

Mrs. Scott seemed to get control of herself for a moment. "Wait. Isn't that... that *McKay* the boy who used to work on Daddy's ranch?"

Her mention of Dev's past brought back memories of the night we'd met. Memories of muscled shoulders and biceps, callused hands, and late-day stubble.

I could see the man as a ranch hand, no doubt about it.

"He can't have a pot to piss in," Pastor Scott said, outraged. "He mucked stalls for my father-in-law—"

His wife stopped him with a hand to his arm. "Frank, dear, didn't he end up going to Yale? Whatever happened to him? How did he and Kathryn wind up dating without us knowing?"

I clamped my teeth together. While confessing to Dev's biological involvement in this custody situation was appropriate and inevitable, it was not my place to remind the Scotts about the details of Lellie's conception—specifically, that it had been done through a fertility clinic with no *dating* involved since their daughter had been proudly asexual. I doubted my reminder would matter anyway, not when Katie had explained her asexuality and decision to use a sperm donor several times and they seemed not to have listened.

"He did go to Yale," Pastor Scott said, seeming to pick the details out of long-forgotten memories. "Thanks to me. She had me write him a recommendation for a scholarship, as I recall. What happened to him? Where the hell is he?"

Orris met my eye with a lifted brow.

"Wyoming," I said. "Apparently, he lives on a ranch there and is impossible to get a hold of. If I'd been able to find a number for him, I would have requested his presence today."

One of my peers, an older attorney named Grace, who worked full-time on the Scotts' business, leaned forward. "I believe it's obvious from his lack of interest in these proceedings that he has chosen to relinquish his interest in this case."

I stared at her. "Are you kidding? I just told you he hasn't been informed about Katie's—*Kathryn's*—passing. He couldn't possibly have relinquished his interest."

Orris turned to her. "But you *can* go ahead and begin proceedings to challenge his guardianship."

"I beg your pardon." I moved my hands under the table in case they started shaking. While I would definitely defend my client vigorously, I really didn't want to get fired in the process. "You may *not* do so. I understand the Scotts' concerns, of course, but *Kathryn* Scott was also our client. She made her wishes very clear, and we executed them carefully in the preparation and signing of her Last Will and Testament. There is no legal standing to challenge Mr. McKay's guardianship at this time. At the very least, it's premature, and moreover, it is an obvious conflict of interest coming from this firm."

Orris made a shushing gesture with his hand as the pastor began to interrupt. "Tully, I understand you're upset. You and Kathryn were close."

I nodded numbly. Even three days after her accident, I hadn't really begun to process the fact that Katie was gone. Some part of me expected to see her striding into the conference room wearing her bright, mischievous smile, and I knew that when the day was done, my fingers would twitch against the urge to text her. *Gurl, you would not believe the meeting I had today...*

"No one is accusing you of not doing your due diligence in preparing her will," Orris went on. "You're a fine attorney who would have made sure the legal preparation was airtight. But surely you can see how Pastor and Mrs. Scott would be the best guardians for their grandchild now that Kathryn is no longer with us."

I tilted my head at him, incredulous. "Surely I do not, sir. Are you suggesting a mother should not be able to choose who gets custody of her child upon her death? What is the point of preparing a will if that's the case?"

Mrs. Scott began wailing again.

Orris spoke to me as if trying to gentle an unpredictable stallion. "Mr. McKay might be a fine man, but the child is clearly better off being raised by two loving grandparents who've known her since she was born, and the Scotts have plenty of money to make sure Eleanor has everything she could ever need for her comfort and education."

It galled me to hear Lellie referred to as "the child," as though she were "the vase" or "the chair." It also irked me that I was expected to use her legal name, as if I hadn't rocked Lellie for hours when she was only a few weeks old and hadn't pulled a sticky glob of banana out of her ink-black curls only a month ago.

"Lellie is independently wealthy," I stated, moving on to the next portion of Katie's will. "As the sole heir of Kathryn's estate, she inherits even more. Whoever ends up raising her will have plenty of financial support."

I didn't add that the estate was worth at least ten million dollars because it wasn't her parents' business, but they needed to understand that basing their custody case on being the more financially stable option for Lellie was a losing proposition.

Katie's parents gasped. The surrounding attorneys typed and scribbled notes. Orris pressed his lips together.

Pastor Scott turned to Orris. "Remove Kathryn from my will and see about recouping her trust fund."

I bit my tongue to keep from snapping at him that trust funds didn't work that way. Katie had gotten access to hers several years ago when she'd turned twenty-five. Because of her lukewarm and sometimes strained relationship with her parents, we'd immediately moved all assets into a new one. When Lellie had been born, we'd restructured the trusts again.

Mrs. Scott sniffled. "It will have to go to Eleanor now."

The pastor shook his head. "She will not be listed as my heir. Not as long as that... that *ranch hand*... has custody of her."

His wife looked at him in shock. "She's all we have left of Kathryn. I won't lose her, Frank."

Orris, ever the peacemaker when tempers flared and clients became irrational, tried to calm everyone down. "There may be a middle ground here. What if we offer McKay a visitation scheme? If he's currently a rancher in Wyoming, she could be in line to inherit a spread in Wyoming." He turned to me and lifted an eyebrow in inquiry.

"Devon McKay doesn't own the ranch," I admitted. "It's my understanding he just works there." Not that there was any indication of formal employment like a W-2 or payroll records. Which meant he was most likely getting paid under the table.

Orris's white eyebrows came together. "A Yale graduate works at a ranch he doesn't own? What in the world does he do there?"

Pastor Scott threw up his hands. "See? He never did make good, even with a Yale scholarship. Do we even know if he graduated? There's no way on god's green earth that low-life is getting my money. Or my granddaughter," he added.

I thought back to the man I'd met at Katie's house. To Dev's inky-black curls and the striking hazel eyes that seemed to carry a lifetime's worth of pain in them. He'd skimmed his hands along my skin as if worshipping it with tenderness. Not only had he been quiet and kind, but he'd also been generous. By giving Katie the ability to have a child with no strings attached, he'd shown himself to be selfless and thoughtful. I hadn't realized he was the "old friend" Katie had asked to father her child until long after our hookup, but once I had, I'd understood that he hadn't let himself come that night because he'd been due at the fertility clinic to make his contribution the following day. Dev had literally denied himself pleasure in order to do well by his friend.

Low-life? Hardly.

I may not have known Devon McKay well, but I believed he was a decent person, and Katie had certainly thought so.

Grace leaned forward, drawing attention away from the blustering pastor. "Do we know whether he even wants custody of the child?"

Everyone got quiet. Pastor Scott lost a little of his bluster. Orris looked thoughtful before he spoke. "Grace, draw up papers for him to voluntarily relinquish custody to the Scotts. There's no conflict of interest in that," he added, in light of my earlier objection. "And we have several options in case he fights it."

"What kind of options?" I asked, though I already suspected.

"Offer him whatever it takes," the pastor insisted. "We're getting custody of our grandchild, even if we have to pay for it."

While Pastor Scott turned to speak with Grace about the details, Orris turned to me with piercing eyes and spoke too softly for the Scotts to hear. "How much is it going to take?"

I knew what he was asking. If the Scotts wanted to bribe Dev to sign away custody of Lellie, they'd have to offer more than he'd gain by keeping her and her inheritance.

"Over ten million," I said in a low voice.

His eyes widened in shock. "Kathryn's trust fund was only worth two."

"She made good money here, and she was good at investing," I said, not willing to be specific. "Plus, she came into some money a couple of years ago from another source."

"What source?"

"She didn't tell me. I only know about it because she placed it in trust for Lellie, so she needed me to draw up the papers."

"That's what you meant when you said she was independently wealthy," he said. "I thought you were referring to the savings account the Scotts had set up for her when she was born."

"No."

He sighed and ran a hand through his previously immaculate hair. "Mr. McKay isn't going to turn down custody of this child when he learns she comes with a fortune. Even if he doesn't want her."

I didn't want to believe that, but I had to admit the truth. "No, sir. Not many people would."

Katie hadn't talked much about Dev. I knew they'd been close in high school but had drifted apart after college, at least in part because Dev hadn't moved back to Texas... or stayed *anywhere* for very long. When I'd confessed to Katie what had happened between us the night of her party, she'd laughed, but I'd seen concern flicker in her eyes, too... until I'd quickly explained that it had been a onetime encounter with no expectations on either side. "Good," she'd said with a soft smile. "Because Dev's one of the best men I know, Tully, truly. But I don't get the feeling he's interested in commitments right now. To *anything*."

I hadn't understood what she meant by that cryptic comment, but I hadn't felt like I could press for clarification without letting her know how often I'd replayed the events of that night, even when I'd tried to forget it.

When Lellie was born and Dev hadn't initiated any contact—something I knew Katie didn't expect from him but would've been open to—or even called to congratulate Katie, I'd figured I had my answer. Dev was a drifter. A wanderer. A kind man, sure. A beautiful man, without a doubt. But not necessarily a dedicated or responsible one.

As much as I hated to think of sweet Lellie being brought up by the influential Scotts in their hateful megachurch, I also wasn't sure if a drifter—no matter how kind or beautiful he may be—was the ideal parent for her. And if he was an underpaid ranch hand, might he be tempted to keep custody of her simply to have the kind of financial security he'd never known before?

It was definitely possible.

I wanted to see Katie's final wishes carried out—of course I did. It was the last tangible thing I could do for my friend. But as I thought over Orris's words, a little bit of doubt crept in over the best way to achieve that.

Like most young, healthy parents, Katie had written up her will to protect her daughter against a theoretical worst-case scenario. In her case, though—my throat burned with unshed tears—it had become reality far more quickly and suddenly than Katie could ever have predicted. She'd probably chosen Dev as Lellie's guardian because she'd wanted to assume the best of him and had thought he'd mature or settle down at some point, becoming the kind of person she'd actually want raising her daughter.

Maybe he *had* become that person. But maybe he hadn't.

I loved Katie and Lellie enough to make sure that whoever became Lellie's guardian would do right by her. Lellie deserved to have the kind of safe, stable, comfortable childhood I'd never had. One unburdened by worries about whether there would be food in the fridge tomorrow, or if the mortgage had been paid this month, or if, after celebrating the windfall of a rare cattle sale at the local bar, her father would come home in a roaring temper... or not come home at all. She deserved to have adults in her life who made her needs a priority and to be loved as much as Katie had loved her.

And, though I hated to admit it, that kind of stability was something the Scotts could give her... even if it wasn't the situation Katie had wanted.

"You'll bring the child to Wyoming, Tully," Orris pronounced. "Along with the custody documents Grace will prepare."

I started. "Me? Surely we should send someone else," I tried, suddenly panicking at the idea of confronting Dev with a child he'd never met.

"The nanny can't make the trip," he reminded me, "and you're the only person in the firm who knows the child personally. Would you prefer I assigned a junior associate to handle the matter?"

The thought of Lellie traveling so far with a stranger when she still called out for her mother in the night made me sick. "No. Definitely not."

He nodded as though he'd expected no less. "Didn't think so. You care about the child, and I trust you to do what's best for her." His eyes bored into me once again. "Do whatever it takes to prove Devon McKay is unfit, Tully. Beg, bribe, or bully him until he gives up custody. Do you understand?"

I could tell from his expression that there were words he'd left unsaid. I felt the weight of them regardless.

Your job depends on it.

I swallowed hard. "Yes, sir."

TWO
DEV

I'd heard about the Final Night celebration for months. The street festival was a Majestic, Wyoming tradition—a chance for Majesticans to enjoy the final days of the low season before the hiking, fishing, and mountain climbing tourists took over the area around Memorial Day—and so far, just being here for it tonight had made me feel like a true local.

And I guessed, at this point, I was. Majestic had been my home now for almost a year. When I'd arrived to help my friend Silas and his new husband, Waylon Fletcher, with roundup on the Fletcher family's ranch, I'd never expected to stay for long. But the wide-open space, the scent of horse and hay, and the utter lack of anyone other than Silas who knew my sad story had made it a kind of unexpected sanctuary. So I'd bought some land and put down roots for the first time in years. After the last thaw, I'd broken ground on my first house, and now I rode my horse, Trigger, over there nearly every day to oversee construction and bask in the natural beauty of the site.

For the most part, I had everything I'd ever wanted. A beautiful outdoor playground with never-ending trails to ride. A purpose in improving Fletcher Ranch's horse breeding program and helping care for the herds. Good friends who reminded me to laugh and enjoy living in the present rather than stewing over the past. A secret billion dollars in the bank—a number that still terrified me sometimes but meant I'd never go back to my hardscrabble childhood. And soon enough, when construction was finished, I'd have a place on Earth to call my very own.

But despite all of that, as I made my way through the late-afternoon crowd of revelers on Poke Street, I was half-inclined to head back to the ranch and call it a night. Way's sister had announced her pregnancy earlier in the evening, and seeing the Fletcher family's excitement over the news was bittersweet. There had been times in the past year when I'd envied their close family dynamic, but other times, like tonight, it had made me uncomfortable. They weren't *my* family—not that I had much of one anymore—and being around them sometimes reminded me of my loss.

Watching Silas and Way fall in love and build a life together sometimes hit me the same way. I was glad for Silas, of course. More than glad. After a decade of being the rock and the fixer for the tight-knit group of college friends we referred to as our "brotherhood," he deserved to soak up every bit of happiness he could find, and it was clear Way loved him deeply. Watching the pair together, though, I'd started to feel that maybe I didn't have *everything* I wanted. The winter nights out here were long and cold, and I'd often wondered if they'd be better spent with a warm body and kind soul sharing my bed. While Majestic was a wonderful place to live, it wasn't exactly brimming with what Way jokingly referred to as "casual encounters," much less potential life partners.

Not that I had any interest in one of those anyway.

"Devon, get over here!" Way's Aunt Blake called from the nearby Love Muffin booth, where she was busy passing out her famous toffee bars and honey garlic chicken skewers. Big vats of lemonade weighed down a table behind her, and coolers full of ice were stacked underneath. My arms twinged at the reminder of the heavy lifting I'd helped her with earlier.

"Congratulations," I said, offering her a smile after hearing Sheridan and Bo's news. No one would spoil that baby more than Jolene Blake. "I just saw Sheridan and Bo."

Her face lit up as she handed me a skewer. "Gonna have us a baby, Dev. Best be prepared, especially since Waylon is going to take a little warming up to the idea."

That surprised me. Silas's husband seemed like the quintessential family man. "He doesn't like kids?" I understood the aversion. Babies and I didn't really get along, mostly because I didn't know what to do with them. As a single man, I mostly spent my time with other guys. I hadn't spent much time around kids at all.

"It's not that. He just doesn't have experience. It's okay. He'll get over it real quick, don't you worry."

I nodded while thinking, *Better him than me*. I liked my life just the way it was. Being able to take a long trail ride whenever the mood hit, having the option of eating cereal for dinner five nights in a row, and barking out the word *fuck* when it was called for were all freedoms I wouldn't have if I'd ever chosen to raise a kid.

No, thanks. Not for me. It was one of the best-known benefits of being a gay man. No one assumed kids were part of my life plan.

"I'm sure he'll be a doting uncle," I said politely before pulling a piece of chicken off the skewer with my teeth.

She gave me an assessing glance. "You'll make a good father, too, one day."

I nearly choked on the chicken. "No, thanks."

"I can see it. Maybe now's not the right time, but you find the right man, and it'll happen."

Jolene Blake was a force to be reckoned with. She'd decided early on to adopt me whether I liked it or not. Most of the time, I liked it fine. She brought me dinner, made sure I was included in family meals, and introduced me to various townsfolk. Her attention to me had started as an intense matchmaking scheme trying to connect me with her son, Foster, and she was still hell-bent on getting the two of us together.

I'd avoided her schemes for the most part—only because he was Way's best friend and unavoidable in Majestic—on the chance things between us became awkward.

But one night in the dead of winter and after one too many drinks at the Old Oak, Foster and I had come close. We'd stayed late at a corner table, sharing intimate confessions about previous hookups and life regrets. When I'd asked him if he wanted to come back to the ranch with me, no strings attached, he'd offered me a soft smile.

"Would it be better than the last guy you were with?"

I'd huffed out a laugh. "My memory hardly goes back that far, Sheriff."

This was a lie. My memory of the last man I'd been with was crystal clear. I'd been back in Texas a couple of years ago, doing a favor for an old friend. She'd invited me to a party, where I'd met one of her coworkers.

He'd been drop-dead sexy and just the right amount of cocky, not to mention buttoned-up, slicked-down, and urbane in a way that made me want to put my hands on him, if only so I could mess up his perfect exterior. It had been memorable, alright. So memorable I hadn't bothered hooking up since then because it would most likely be a disappointment in comparison.

Foster must have seen the wistful look on my face. "Uh-huh. Why don't we table this discussion for another time?" Foster had said with a low laugh. "Maybe a time when we both aren't feeling the effects of the weather and whiskey."

We'd never made another attempt. Instead, we'd become good friends, creating the kind of relationship I didn't dare fuck up with sex.

But his mother liked to think it was just a matter of time. Even now, she nodded toward where Way and Silas were still joking around with Sheridan and Bo and said coyly, "Looks like Foster found the fun crowd. You should join them. Let loose a little. Tell my son to do the same while you're at it." She shot me a wink, and I returned an eye roll.

"Stop meddling," I mumbled around my last bite of chicken. She reached for the empty skewer to toss in the trash.

"Stop avoiding happiness," she said. This time, her expression cut right through me. "It's time to move on, Dev. Embrace your life and enjoy yourself. Live a little. Hell, live a lot. You already know summer in Majestic is magical. Maybe this can be your hot girl summer."

I couldn't help but laugh. "You think?"

Her smile was easy and genuine. "I know."

I leaned over and kissed her cheek. "I love you, too."

As I made my way back through the crowd to where my friends had congregated, I returned a few friendly greetings from people I knew. Mr. Shandy from the hardware store tipped his hat, and Millie Turner waggled her fingers at me.

Foster shot me a grin as I approached. "Did my mother send you over to spy on me?"

"More like she sent me over here to seduce you. I told her I don't swing that way."

His deep laugh helped me relax, and I was grateful they were no longer talking about babies and family stuff. "You told her you weren't gay?"

"Nah. I told her I didn't go for bossy assholes."

As Way and Silas laughed, Foster wrapped his arm around my shoulders and yanked me into his side before pressing a kiss to my hair. "Just for that, I'm going to start some rumors—"

"Devon McKay?" a cold voice clipped from somewhere behind me. I turned to see who was asking when I froze in place.

There, in an opening in the crowd around us, was a man I'd never expected to see again. The drop-dead sexy, just-the-right-amount-of-cocky guy I'd hooked up with in Texas over two years ago.

Tully Bowman looked every bit as urbane and citified as he had that night...

Only this time, he was scowling and appeared not to even recognize me.

Silas stepped closer. "Who's asking?"

Before the semi-stranger could say another word, I noticed he held a baby on his hip. Did he have a child?

I glanced around for a partner, woman or man, someone who might also lay claim to this little family pair in front of me. But then the little girl lifted her head from his shoulder and gazed at me.

"Holy fuck," Silas breathed, taking the words from my spinning head and giving them a voice.

It was easy enough to dismiss her curly dark hair as a coincidence, but there was no denying those hazel eyes. I knew them well.

I'd spent over thirty years looking at them in the mirror.

For a split second, I had the crazy thought that I'd somehow gotten this man pregnant during our one-night stand. Then I remembered it wasn't biologically possible for him to get pregnant, and certainly not from a one-sided blowjob.

But then I remembered the reason I'd been in Texas the night we'd met. The favor I'd done for my friend Katie.

And nearly fainted dead away.

"W-why are you here?" I asked, hoping against hope that I was wrong. That there was another explanation—*any* other explanation. But that hope died when he opened his perfect lips and spoke again.

"To bring you your daughter."

THREE
TULLY

I was exhausted and heartsore. Nervous to the point of numbness. And now I was angry enough to spit fire.

Lellie had been an angel on the plane. Thankfully, Orris had approved our travel on an executive jet, which meant we'd had plenty of space for her to move around and play, but the minute we'd landed, her patience had gone from limitless to hard-limited in about ten seconds flat.

My assistant at the firm had offered to come with me to help take care of Lellie, but I'd explained she was going through a "stranger danger" phase and would probably be more comfortable with just me.

Mistake number one.

Then, I'd arrived at the pre-arranged rental car and noticed there was no car seat. I'd lucked out, and a pleasant staffer at the tiny airstrip had offered to run into town to get one for me from a neighbor of hers. Once she'd arrived back and installed it for me, I'd gone straight to the nearest place that sold car seats so I could return the loaner.

Mistake number two.

Not only was the car seat twice as expensive as it would have been back in Dallas at Walmart, but the only place for miles around that sold them was the Mercantile, located right in the heart of some kind of street festival in Majestic. An overly chatty cashier inadvertently helped me out by indicating my target would most likely be found in said street festival.

I'd asked for directions to Fletcher Ranch since I knew from experience GPS could be spotty in rural locations. The cashier had shot me a big grin and expounded at length on the way to get there, ending in, "'Cept I'm sure they're all here for Final Night. Try at the Love Muffin table. Jo Blake'll know where to point you."

I'd thanked her and headed back out to the rental to throw the car seat inside and change poor Lellie's diaper for the tenth time since arriving in Wyoming.

Mistake number three. Well, I probably should have called that one *number two*.

"Gurl," I muttered, trying to keep her from rolling off the tailgate of the SUV. "You only had puffs in the past several hours. Take out the veggie dust, and all that's left is air. How is this the third dirty diaper since we landed? Explain yourself."

Renata, Lellie's nanny, had packed me with plenty of supplies, acting like Wyoming didn't have such modern conveniences as diapers and wipes, pediatric meds, clean outfits, or age-appropriate toys. At that moment, I would have much preferred she help me remember the car seat.

By the time I got us both cleaned up and found a garbage can to dispose of the waste, I let out a breath and decided to find us both a cold bottle of water before hopping back in the car. In the meantime, I'd search for the table the cashier had recommended and ask around for anyone who might know where to find Devon.

The crowd was too much, and live music was blaring from a makeshift stage halfway down the block. Lellie alternated between screaming and tucking her face in my neck to whimper. I rubbed her back and tried to soothe her. When I finally found the Love Muffin table, we were both covered in splashes of water from where she'd flung her arm out when I'd offered her the bottle.

"Do you know where I could find Devon McKay?" I asked.

The older woman behind the table eyed me up and down. "Who's asking?"

"An old friend here visiting from Texas. The lady at the Mercantile said you might save me a trip out to the ranch by pointing me in his direction."

An attractive young man in a black cowboy hat sidled up and shot me a grin. "You looking for Dev? Just missed him. He just headed over that way. Standing next to the sheriff. Tall fucker, erm... 'scuse me. I meant... tall guy, the sheriff. See him?" He pointed in a direction where I definitely saw a tall man in a sheriff's uniform shirt and well-fitting jeans.

Smiling at Devon McKay like he'd just discovered a diamond mine.

I let out a grunt.

The man next to me nodded. "Wouldn't mind bein' the PB&J in that man sandwich, if you want to know the truth. Ain't neither of them bad-looking with their shirts off."

The woman behind the table whipped a tea towel at him. "Taza Daggett, put your tongue back in your mouth and fish in a pond that's more your own vintage. You hear me? Those men are old enough to be your uncles."

"Wouldn't mind either one of them being my Daddy," he murmured, shooting me a wink. I schooled my face and returned his flirt with a scowl. If he thought he could clock me as gay, he could think again.

I was the king of straight-passing when I was in a mood, and I was for damned sure in a mood tonight. My nerves were shot, I was hot in the remnants of this morning's work suit, and I was about to have to tell the man who had a starring role in my nocturnal fantasies that he was the lucky recipient of a lifetime's worth of work and worry.

"Wish me luck," I muttered to Lellie. She burst into tears and pressed her face back into my neck as I strode in the direction of the man I hadn't seen in over two years. The man whose silhouette was just as familiar to me now as the night I'd traced it with my tongue and hands.

Before I made it through the last group of people between us, I saw the sheriff pull Dev against his side and press a kiss to his hair. My whole body jolted in surprise.

While my rational brain knew Dev could be in a relationship with someone, my stupid fantasies couldn't even fathom it.

"Devon McKay?" I snapped before losing my nerve.

A man I didn't recognize stepped closer to Dev. "Who's asking?"

Dev turned to me before his eyes flared in recognition. He looked from me to Lellie before his face lost color. He seemed to look behind me as if expecting someone else... which made sense when I realized he'd be looking for Katie.

"Holy fuck," someone said.

Dev seemed to sway on his feet. "W-why are you here?"

Despite his shock, his voice was warm and solid. It carried the same mesmerizing quality I'd been drawn to that night at Katie's place.

I swallowed and tried not to lose focus. "To bring you your daughter."

The sheriff wrapped a supportive arm around Dev's waist to keep him upright, showing he was closer to Dev than I'd ever been or ever would be. "Dev?" he asked softly. "Do you know this man?"

Dev didn't answer immediately, but his eyes were wide, and his jaw hung open in—there was no way to put it nicely—horror—and my gut twisted.

I realized with painful clarity I'd come here with a hidden agenda so foolish, so utterly ridiculous, I hadn't consciously acknowledged it to myself until that moment.

Deep down, I'd been hoping Dev would take one look at me, and his face would light up with recognition and joy. I'd wanted him to push through the crowd toward me and instantly wrap me in an embrace so tight it would erase the two years we'd been apart. I'd wanted him to confess—possibly on his knees—that he'd thought about me every day, been haunted by me every night, and had deeply regretted not exchanging contact information. I'd hoped he'd tell me he'd missed me desperately all along.

I'd wanted him to *want* me.

And while I was wishing for impossible things, I'd also hoped he'd provide me with an honorable, logical, unassailable reason for agreeing to father Katie's child that made sense of his decision to stay out of Lellie's life. I wanted an explanation that would reveal a depth of thought and feeling, and possibly hinted at a profound love for his daughter, even if it meant loving her from a distance. I hoped for words that would bridge the gap between his choice and my under-standing and show that he could, in fact, be the sort of loving, respon-sible father Lellie needed.

But the look of stark terror on his face when confronted with his child was enough to make it all clear.

Not only did Dev not want me, but he also didn't want his own child.

And I could never forgive him for that.

The worst part was I still had to offer Lellie to him. I still had to tell him that he was, at least for the moment, not only her father but her legal guardian and the trustee of an obscene amount of money.

I wanted to scream. I selfishly wanted to yank the stranger's arm away from Devon and seek a quiet place where we could talk, where I could explain everything as quickly and stoically as possible. Where I could break the devastating news of Katie's accident to him in peace. And then follow it up with the offer to relieve him of his parental duties.

Instead, Lellie chose that moment to lose her ever-loving mind. "Mamaaaaa! Ma-*maaaa!*"

The words cut through my chest like dull cleavers, taking chunks out of me with each desperate syllable. Hot tears flooded my eyes, and I suddenly realized I'd reached my own breaking point for the day just as surely as Lellie had.

"Sorry," I said quickly. "I have to go."

And I turned around and hotfooted it back to the rental SUV as fast as I could.

FOUR

DEV

I stared after them in shock for several moments until I realized everyone around me was talking at once. I focused on Silas. He knew me well enough to know how hard the news would hit me.

The only problem was he hadn't known I was a father.

To be fair, I hadn't been certain, either... and I hadn't wanted to be. Only my friend Katie and possibly my assistant, Kenji, who I'd asked to coordinate certain legal aspects of the matter, would have known for sure whether my "contribution" had resulted in a child.

My child.

"Dev, take a breath," Silas said. I could tell by the tone of his voice it wasn't the first time he'd said it.

"I'm breathing. Jesus," I said, sucking in a giant gulp of air.

"Who was that man? Do we know him?"

I loved that Silas assumed anyone I knew would be someone he would know also. I shook my head. "He's from Texas. Friends with Katie."

The brotherhood knew about Katie. They knew she and I had been close in high school, that she'd helped me find a way to afford

Yale, and that I'd stayed with her for a few nights when my parents wouldn't let me in their house after Matt died.

"That... that little girl looked like you, Dev," Silas said hesitantly.

"Yeah," I croaked.

She really did. She had my eyes. She had my hair. And seeing her —my "contribution" to help Katie achieve her dream of motherhood, my payback for all the ways Katie had helped me—had suddenly morphed into an actual, tangible human being.

My *daughter*.

Good god.

I felt everyone's eyes on me. The loud music seemed to batter my skull, and the few sips of margarita I drank earlier sat like a boulder on my stomach.

"We can't just let them go," Silas added. "If that's your daughter..."

I heard Foster curse before he took off after them in the crowd. Foster was protective of people he perceived as family, and I was definitely one of those people. He would scare the hell out of that poor child if she saw him chasing them across Poke Street, not to mention Tully—

"*Dammit*," I said, turning and racing after them. When I caught up with Foster, I barked at him to let me handle it.

"Like hell I will," he said, barely slowing down.

I grabbed his arm and glared at him. "Back off, Sheriff. This is my private business."

His eyes narrowed. I could tell he wanted to argue with me, to protect me and support me, but he also knew me well enough to know privacy was important to me.

His jaw clenched. "You text me to tell me you're okay. You hear?"

I reluctantly nodded before I picked up speed again in the direction of the little girl's shrieking.

When I finally found them, I only saw Tully's shapely ass in a pair of stylish suit pants as he was bent over trying to strap the little girl into a car seat. Her screams didn't let up.

"T-Tully, wait," I said, reaching out to touch him but pulling my hand back before I could. Saying his name out loud for the first time since that night felt strange.

He straightened up and banged his head on the doorframe. When he turned around to face me, his eyes were red-rimmed and wet, his hair disheveled.

I stepped closer and reached out to cup his head where he'd hit it. "Take a breath," I said without thinking. It was something Katie's grandmother had always said in situations like this one—a reminder not to say something you'd regret in the moment of pain.

Tully's chin trembled, but his eyes glared at me, the same bright, vibrant eyes that had attracted me from across the room two years ago. "I'm fine."

"You're not," I said softly. "You're hurt."

He jerked out of my grasp and nearly banged his head again. The little girl continued screaming. He turned back to her. "I know, baby. Here. Take another sip of water. That's it." She took a sip but then pulled her head away and cried even louder. Scrambling to figure out what else he could offer her, Tully yanked a well-loved stuffed horse out of a backpack. "Here. Here's Trigger. You love Trigger."

The horse seemed to calm her down immediately until all that was left were a few hiccups.

But I had the opposite reaction as I stared at the stuffed animal. Katie had named her baby's toy after my horse. The gesture clutched at my heart.

"Where's Katie?" I asked, knowing deep down he wouldn't be here without Katie herself unless something terrible had happened.

A tear ran down his cheek, followed by another. It took all of my self-control not to wipe them off his face. "I'm sorry."

I felt my back teeth grind together as my nose began to sting. "How?" I managed to ask.

He grimaced and shook his head as if he didn't want to tell me.

"How?" I asked again, dreading the truth.

"Car accident," he whispered.

I tilted my head back and squeezed my eyes closed. My mother's words came back to me from the aftermath of my brother's accident.

This is your fault, Devon. If you hadn't bought Matt that car. If you hadn't let him go out. This is all your fault.

I had tried not to believe her, of course. My friends, if not my rational brain, had explained that he'd made his own choices that night—choices that had included drinking and driving—but now, hearing that someone else I'd loved had died the same way... it was hard not to think fate was trying to tell me something.

"When?" I asked.

Tully's hand absently brushed damp curls from the girl's face. "Four nights ago. She was driving home from the airport, from a business trip, and another vehicle swerved into her, knocking her car into a barricade. At least, that's what witnesses said. She... she died instantly."

The raw grief in his voice drove the truth home, and I felt my tears come. I wanted to run. I wanted to race back to the barn and lock myself away so I could mourn the loss of my friend. Of another part of my past.

But I stayed where I was, tethered in place by the small being in the back seat.

"What's her name?" I breathed, nodding in the little girl's direction.

Tully's face softened. He turned to unbuckle her and pulled her out of the seat to rest on his hip. With his fingertip, he gently lifted her chin. "Eleanor Kathryn Scott, meet Devon McKay," he said in a gentle tone. His eyes met mine. "We call her Lellie."

She had Katie's button nose and the same little divot of concentration between her tiny eyebrows.

"Hi, Lellie," I said softly. "I'm..." I swallowed around a lump. "I'm Dev. Can I..." Emotion swamped me. I took a breath and tried again. "Can I hold you, sweetheart?"

I reached out my hands to her. Tully and I both held our breath as she considered it for a beat. But then she turned and buried her face in Tully's neck.

I closed my eyes and ducked my head. Her reaction wasn't surprising—weren't babies, like horses, supposed to sense which people were the right ones to care for them?—but it was disappointing.

Suddenly, a warm hand grasped mine and pulled it up to rest on Lellie's back. I opened my eyes to see Tully's apologetic expression.

"Don't take it personally. It's a phase," he said. "And she's exhausted from a very long day."

"And she probably misses..." *Her mom*, I mouthed.

He bit his lip and nodded. "She's had a rough week."

I got the sense that was an understatement, for both of them.

I rubbed Lellie's little back through the soft cotton of her yellow T-shirt. She sucked in a shaking breath and let it out. I couldn't imagine what the past few days had been like for her. My heart broke all over again as the reality of her loss hit me.

"Oh god." I met Tully's eyes. "Who's going to...?"

But I was pretty sure I had an idea, and he confirmed it a moment later.

"That's why I'm here," he said carefully. I could tell by his expression it was a complicated issue, but he wouldn't have traveled all this way with her if I wasn't at least partially responsible for the girl—*Lellie*—moving forward.

Anxiety spiked through me, making my heart beat faster, but I kept my voice calm. "We have a lot to talk about, I imagine," I said.

Tully nodded. The motion revealed Lellie was falling asleep on his chest.

"You'd better come to the ranch." I nodded toward the car seat and waited for him to buckle her in before asking. "Do you want me to drive or navigate?"

He turned to me in surprise. "Didn't you drive here yourself?"

I shook my head. "I rode with friends."

He hesitated before handing me the keys. "If you don't mind."

I got into the driver's seat and buckled up without letting on how relieved I was at Tully's decision to allow me to drive. I didn't usually do well with other people driving me, but it was something I was actively working on.

As we pulled out of town, I glanced at him. His hands were fisted on his lap and his gaze fixed out the window. With his hair mussed, his shoulders slumped, and his expensive button-down wrinkled to hell and covered in any number of unidentifiable stains, it was clear he was out of his element... and that he'd been through the wringer today.

"How did you get picked to bring Lellie?" I finally asked.

He exhaled as if he'd been waiting for the question. "I'm Katie's attorney," he said tightly. "I wrote her will."

I knew Katie was... *had been*... an attorney and that she and Tully had been coworkers, but it was clear from his earlier tears and the way he knew Lellie that they'd been friends, too. "I'm sorry for your loss. I know she thought highly of you."

He nodded but remained silent, discouraging any further discussion on the topic.

Because I understood that feeling all too well, I didn't press.

The sun was setting behind the peaks of Three Daughters, sending golden light across the summer pastures. This was my favorite time of day. I rolled down the windows, and the scent of wildflowers and green grasses, pine and sage billowed in on the breeze.

Tully closed his eyes and inhaled. "It's beautiful here."

"Prettiest place I've ever been," I agreed.

"That what brought you?" he asked suddenly. "Looking for a pretty place to stay awhile?"

"No." I frowned. "A friend needed help. So I came."

He was quiet for a minute. Then, "The sheriff, you mean."

I glanced over at him. "No, the other guy." My lips twitched. "The one who looked like a feral hellcat ready to strike."

Tully didn't say anything, but for some reason, I suddenly couldn't shut up.

"His name is Silas. We went to college together. He accidentally married a cowboy and called me in to help last summer on the cowboy's family ranch."

His head turned at this. "Accidentally?"

"Long story."

"And you stayed?" His eyes fixed on me. "You settled down?"

I shrugged. "Didn't really have a place to go back to. Besides, I like it here. It's nice and quiet. Plenty of room to be by myself."

I sensed the tension in his body. "So you prefer to be by yourself?"

Since I hadn't been born yesterday, I knew this wasn't a casual question, and I merely grunted in response.

The truth was, I did like being by myself... mostly. And the alternative—the crushing disappointment of letting down someone who relied on me, of not being enough for someone I loved—was terrifying.

I had my brotherhood and other friends, like Foster and Jo Blake, who understood my boundaries. They loved me but allowed me privacy and a small amount of necessary distance. I had no plans to change that.

A small movement in the rearview mirror caught my attention, and when I looked up, I saw Lellie, still fast asleep with her head tilted uncomfortably to one side. Her wispy ringlets danced in the blowing wind.

But sometimes things don't go according to plan, a voice that sounded like Katie's reminded me.

"What do you, ah... what do you do for work?" Tully asked.

The awkward attempt at small talk was at least better than talking about Katie's passing or the orphaned daughter she'd left behind, and I seized on it gratefully.

"I oversee a breeding program at a horse ranch. Silas's husband Way's ranch."

"Is... that what you studied in college? Animal husbandry?"

I glanced over at him and registered a discomfort I hadn't noticed before. "No. I studied business in college," I said, being deliberately vague. I'd learned a long time ago that mentioning Yale to someone I didn't know well was like dropping a bomb into a conversation. It had a tendency to change things, especially if the person didn't know me very well.

"I guess a horse breeding program is a business," he ventured, as if trying to connect the dots.

"I grew up around horses," I said finally. I didn't owe him an explanation, but for some reason, I didn't want him to think I was completely inexperienced at what I did. "More accurately, I grew up working on a ranch. They bred quarter horses used in ranch work. I guess I got the animal husbandry vibe there."

Tully nodded and turned back to the window, but there was still a coiled tension in his body that was hard to read.

"What about you?" I asked after an awkward moment of silence. "What kind of law do you practice?"

"Trusts and estates, mostly. I do some real estate work as well if my clients need it. Contract review, too, from time to time."

"Sounds... lucrative," I said for lack of anything better. It sounded boring as hell, to be honest, but I didn't want to offend him.

"It is. Stable, too." Tully straightened slightly and smoothed a hand down the remains of his crumpled dress shirt. His voice was a little starchier as he added, "I'm very grateful for my position at Dunlevy, Pace, and Trumble."

"Glad to hear it." It took all kinds, I supposed.

He hesitated. "What about horse breeding? Does it, um... pay well?"

Ah. This wasn't "small talk" but an interrogation into what kind of life I had, what kind of financial stability I might be able to provide for Lellie. For my... daughter.

Disappointment flared hot in my gut. I'd hoped... well, I guess I'd hoped Tully was actually trying to get to know me. That the one night we'd spent together had been decent enough to make him give a shit about me as a person.

The encounter had stayed with me for a long time and kept me company through hundreds of lonely nights. I'd had fantasies about Tully Bowman—imagined what it would have been like if I could have pursued something real with him if he hadn't been so closely tied to the life I'd had to leave behind. But it looked like that was well in the past for him and nowhere near his radar now.

The man was here for one reason and one reason only: to judge me on behalf of a little girl I'd never met and hadn't even known existed. And it seemed like Tully Bowman was eager to find me wanting.

Which, let's be honest, wouldn't be that difficult.

FIVE
TULLY

I knew I'd fucked up the minute Dev's face had gone blank. In my haste to get answers, I'd pushed too much too soon, and I silently cursed myself.

I'd been enjoying our talk—or, more accurately, I'd been enjoying the subconscious twitch of his lips whenever something amused him, the scent of sandalwood as the wind ruffled his dark curls, and the competent way his big hands gripped the steering wheel as he maneuvered us down the road.

When I'd realized I was relaxing a little too much in his presence, I'd panicked and scrambled to get my brain back on track. I hadn't been as subtle as I should have been, and now Dev was entirely closed off.

Which wasn't a thing I should feel upset about, I told myself firmly. Lellie was my priority here; that wasn't in doubt. I needed to determine whether Dev was a fit parent or the kind of person who might take advantage of Lellie's wealth. I didn't want to think ill of him, for Katie and Lellie's sake, but I also knew this world was harsh, and sometimes desperate situations made people... desperate.

I cleared my throat. "I'm... ah... sorry to just show up here with no warning. It's just that I couldn't find a phone number for you. I tracked you down to the ranch, but I didn't want to contact the owners and potentially get your employer involved in a private... situation."

His jaw ticked as he pulled off the highway and onto a gravel road and under a wooden archway that read Fletcher Ranch. "Appreciate it."

The awkwardness deepened again as he made his way slowly past an old sprawling ranch house and acres of horse pasture.

"It really *is* beautiful here." I winced at the repetition. It had been years since I'd felt this wrong-footed. "I should have asked before we left town, but is there a place I can get a room for me and Lellie, after you and I talk? A bed-and-breakfast or something? I expected to find a hotel or motel on my way from the airstrip, but I didn't see anything."

"There's an inn off Poke Street that probably has room, but you're not taking Lellie."

He pulled up to a large barn and pulled my rental next to a dust-covered but very expensive-looking SUV and several late-model horse trailers. Fletcher Ranch must have been doing very well to be able to afford high-end equipment.

It took me a minute to realize what he'd said, and Dev was out of the car before I could respond. I jumped out and scrambled around to face him, but he'd already pulled open Lellie's door.

"Okay, hold up. I'm not leaving her with you," I said, feeling the culmination of stress, exhaustion, and annoyance ball together in a dangerous simmer. "You saw how she reacted when you tried to hold her."

"Then you can sleep on my floor," Dev said gruffly. "Because if I'm reading you right, and I think I am, I just inherited my own... my own daughter." He turned to pin me with a familiar hazel stare that swirled now with an explosive mixture of hurt, confusion, sorrow, and yearning. "I don't know exactly how that will work going forward... but if you mean to take her away one minute after I learned she existed, you can think again."

"Learned she existed?" I shot back unwisely. "You just go around donating sperm for the hell of it? She's been alive for over a year, Devon. You never *bothered* to learn she existed until now."

The anger radiating off him told me I'd made a mistake even before he leaned closer to me and bit out, "Because she had a mother until now. And I wasn't aware I owed you an explanation for my choices, Tully." Something in the firm set of his jaw, the determined intensity of his gaze, and the soft but commanding tone of his voice made my heart hammer.

I was torn between respecting the hell out of him for taking up Lellie's cause and panicking at the thought of him fighting to keep her without knowing any of the details or having the capacity to give her the life she deserved.

"I'm not leaving her," I said again. "If that means I have to stay on your floor, fine. You don't even know what a toddler needs, do you?"

"And you do?" he snapped.

"This particular toddler? Yeah. I do. A hell of a lot better than a perfect stranger, anyway. Which is what you are," I added unnecessarily. "No matter what DNA you share." I felt my back teeth grind together. "I was there the day she was born. I held her when she couldn't sleep for teething. And I've changed her diaper more times than you can count. She knows me."

I didn't mention that I also had carefully detailed care instructions from the nanny, a brand-new paperback copy of *What to Expect the Second Year*, and my own mother on speed dial, just in case.

He grunted and nudged me out of the way, pulling open the car door and leaning in to unbuckle the car seat.

Lellie was still fast asleep, her head dangling to one side and her hair blown every which way from the open windows. I didn't realize I was holding my breath until Dev successfully extricated her without waking her.

He straightened and pulled her to his shoulder, murmuring

words too soft for me to hear. As soon as she settled against his chest with her messy dark curls next to his, I saw him close his eyes and take a deep, slow breath.

I was the opposite of religious. Had hated every minute of being dragged to church growing up and hated people like the Scotts even more. But witnessing that moment of Dev settling his daughter in his arms for the first time washed over me like a prayer being given divine light.

All the fear and tension bled out of me, and for a split second, I felt like I was standing on hallowed ground... until Dev opened his eyes and exhaled.

"Right. Let's get inside, then. You got a bag or something for her, or do I need to call someone to pick something up?"

It took me a minute to snap into gear. "No, I've got stuff. I'll just... I'll just grab it."

I moved to the back of the rental and began unloading the bags, first pulling out the folded umbrella stroller and then yanking out my small business carry-on, followed by the two very large rolling suit-cases the nanny had sent with Lellie.

I felt Dev's eyes on me while I struggled with the bags, but he made no move to help. He stood holding his daughter and rocking slightly from one dusty cowboy boot to the other.

He looked completely at home in front of a barn. His form-fitted jeans showed off lean muscles and long legs, and a cowboy-style snap-front shirt was tucked neatly behind a worn leather belt with a simple buckle. His skin was sun-warmed and golden. Crinkles next to his eyes indicated he worked in the sun and/or laughed a lot. I got the feeling it was the first.

Devon McKay was still the most beautiful man I'd ever met. Tousled curls lifted lightly in the evening breeze, late-day stubble was just beginning to cast a shadow on his face, and his lips were cherry red like he'd been eating or drinking something with tart berries in it. If anything, he was more tempting than ever.

I'd had plenty of hookups in the time since that night, but none of them had compared. Which was ridiculous. Our night together hadn't been long or full of heartfelt confessions. We'd barely learned each other's names, and we hadn't even exchanged contact information to get together again.

Though I'd wanted to. Desperately.

So why had it stayed with me? And why now could I think of nothing I wanted more than to get the man naked again?

"You coming?" he grumbled.

I blinked at him and then down at the luggage. "You're seriously not going to help me with these?"

He wrapped his muscular arms around Lellie's little body. "I've already got my hands full."

I rolled my eyes and stumbled after him, yanking Lellie's two suitcases and leaving the rest for another trip. When Dev walked through the large open doorway to the barn, I finally realized what was going on. There was no house visible out the other end of the large structure, only a horse ring and paddocks.

"Wait. You live in a barn?"

"Mm-hm."

He moved down the aisle, across a wooden-slatted floor scattered with fresh straw. The old, familiar scents of horse and hay filled my nostrils. Curious noses poked out from above stall doors and peered in our direction.

"Nothing to see here, ladies," Dev called softly before we turned left through a doorway and began climbing a narrow wooden staircase.

I yanked the giant bags up behind me as best I could, straining my shoulders and arms while trying not to make enough noise to wake Lellie.

When we got to the top of the stairs, Dev opened a door that led into a residential space. I immediately noticed the cleaner air, thanks to a cool mountain breeze blowing through several open windows. The apartment was small but quaint and comfortable. The living space, kitchen area, and a dining table—currently in use as a desk—

were all in one big open room with large windows on two sides and french doors opening to a balcony on one end. Through the french doors was a jaw-dropping view of the mountains set off with fading pinkish-purple streaks. I wondered what the sunset would have looked like if we'd gotten here even twenty minutes earlier.

On the opposite end from the balcony was an open doorway that seemed to lead to a bedroom.

Thankfully, the sofa in the living area was extra long and deep. It wasn't the ideal place to sleep after the hellish day I'd had, but it would be way better than a hard, wooden floor.

"Where do you want me to put Lellie's bags?" I asked, trying to keep things friendly. While I felt incredibly territorial about Katie's daughter, I definitely didn't want to run the risk of angering him and possibly even getting kicked out of his place.

Legally, Lellie was Dev's. Once he fully understood that, he would realize he didn't need to allow me access to her, much less a place to stay.

He tilted his head toward the bedroom. "In there, if you can find room."

I pulled the bags into the bedroom and flicked on the light. The space smelled like a mix of clean laundry, sandalwood cologne, and the faintest remnant of horse and hay from downstairs. A faded quilt lay neatly spread on a queen-sized bed. Strangely, the rest of the fittings and furnishings looked incredibly high-end, like the ranch owner had brought in a professional decorator to fix it up, not as a place for a drifter cowboy with shallow pockets to hang his hat but for a gentleman rancher who enjoyed equestrian sport and could afford to pursue it in luxury.

Dev had lucked into a good situation here, and it made me even more curious about what his income was like. I couldn't help but wonder about the Fletcher family, too, if they could afford this type of stuff but still chose to pay Dev under the table for his work on the ranch.

I wheeled the cases to an empty corner and laid them down

before returning to fetch the rest of our things. As I passed back through the main room, I realized it was decorated in the same high-end way. Stainless steel appliances in the small kitchen area and high-quality furnishings throughout.

"It's a nice place," I said, finding him ensconced in an oversized leather chair next to the sofa with Lellie still sacked out on his chest. "Thanks for letting us... *me*... stay."

He glanced at me as if to assess whether I was speaking the truth or not, and then he reluctantly nodded an acknowledgment. I rolled my eyes once I was safely in the stairwell on my way to get the rest of our things.

It was going to be a long night.

———

Three hours later, Dev was still sitting in the leather chair, but now his eyes were closed, his head was resting on Lellie's, and a steady, light snore was coming from his direction. I'd stashed the rest of the luggage away in a corner, kicked off my shoes, helped myself to a glass of water, and taken a spot on the sofa to catch up on work emails on my laptop. Thankfully, Dev's Wi-Fi password had been scribbled on a piece of scratch paper on the side of the fridge.

If I glanced at Dev from time to time, it was only to check on Lellie. Not to drink in the sight of the man, assess his face for clues as to what he'd been doing the past two years, or admire the way his work-callused hands remained gentle as they periodically smoothed down his daughter's back or brushed sweat-damp curls from her neck or forehead.

It was after midnight, and I knew if Lellie woke up, we'd all be up for hours, trying to get her resettled. I'd considered encouraging Dev to wake her when we'd arrived—she needed to eat and get changed into pajamas at the very least—but I hadn't had the heart. The break from her screaming, coupled with the heart-clenching image of a father holding his child for the first time, had combined to make the decision fairly easy.

But now, all I could do was wait for the inevitable moment when all hell broke loose.

It happened at almost one in the morning. I caught her opening one eye and glancing around without moving her head. A telltale crinkle formed on her forehead a split second before she let out a whimper. I leaned forward to try and get her attention before she screamed and woke up Dev, but it didn't work.

He jumped at the sound of her cry. The panic on his face before he realized what was happening was startling.

"Baby, baby," he said quickly in a sleep-roughened voice. "It's okay, sweetheart. D-Dev's here."

I wondered at his avoidance of the other D-word. Was he going to claim her, to be her father? His shocked terror at first seeing her suggested *no*, but his insistence on her staying at his place and the way he'd held her tenderly since we'd arrived said *yes*. I wished I could peer into his brain and know what he was thinking.

Frankly, I wasn't sure which outcome I was hoping for. I definitely didn't want her to be raised in her grandfather's church against all of Katie's hopes and wishes unless it was absolutely necessary. I wanted Dev to be the kind of man who'd do right by Lellie. But I wasn't convinced he was.

Lellie struggled to get out from his hold and finally slithered down off his lap, leaving only one tiny hand on his knee. "Mama," she said clearly.

Dev's face fell. "Mama's not here, baby." He glanced up at me. "But Tully's here. You know Tully, right?"

I set the laptop aside and held out my arms. "I'm here, Lellie. Are you hungry? Do you want some apples?" Offering her a favorite might have been a dirty trick if her favorite didn't happen to currently be a healthy choice.

Her face screwed up as she sniffed. "Ap-puh?" Then she nodded and toddled into my arms.

Dev shot me a worried look. "I don't think I have any fresh apples. Just throwaway ones for the horses downstairs."

"They're in the fridge. I unpacked our cooler earlier. There's also some leftover chicken and pasta in a plastic container. Can you microwave it a bit while I change her diaper?"

He looked a little spooked, like I was speaking another language, but he nodded and moved to the kitchen. I found the blue backpack that held her changing supplies and laid her out on a blanket on the sofa to change her. Once she was in soft pajamas and a clean diaper, I set her down and pointed to where Dev was spooning out food onto a paper plate.

"You hungry? Dev has dinner for you."

She hesitated before toddling over toward him. "Ap-puh?"

He squatted down and handed her an apple slice. "Here's an apple to start with."

She kept her eyes on him while she shoved the slice into her mouth and chewed. I moved to the kitchen before rinsing out and refilling her water bottle and setting it on the kitchen table at the place I'd made for her earlier.

Lellie made her way over and let me set her in the chair.

"Clever," Dev said, nodding to the stack of towels I'd stolen from the bathroom earlier to form a makeshift booster seat. "I guess I need to get a few things."

He set the plate in front of her, along with a fork. I quickly grabbed the fork and replaced it with a spoon. "We don't need her scratching your boss's nice table," I muttered under my breath.

I felt Dev's eyes on me, but I ignored them. "I didn't bring the travel crib thing. I figured we'd be staying at a hotel and they'd have one. We'll have to make her some kind of bed tonight, and then tomorrow—"

"She can sleep with me for tonight," he said. "I have extra pillows. I'll make a little barricade or something to keep her from falling out."

"You can definitely try that," I said dubiously. "I'm afraid it's going to be hard to get her back down after this."

He gazed at her, as if studying her features for more clues to her heritage. I wondered if he noticed she had Katie's dimple or her turned-up nose. I wondered if he cared.

"She'll do fine," he said firmly.

Famous last words.

SIX

DEV

"Careful," Tully warned before I tripped over the curb and nearly face-planted on the sidewalk. "Curb," he added belatedly.

"Fuck," I muttered, glancing at Lellie in the stroller to make sure I hadn't accidentally tipped her out.

"Language," he said for the millionth time in the last twelve hours.

"Fuck off," I hissed, hoping it was too low for Lellie to hear. "I didn't get much sleep last night, in case you didn't notice."

"Didn't notice," he lied. "I slept soundly once I put the earplugs in. Thanks, by the way, for insisting that you handle everything yourself."

I knew he was lying because I'd caught him peering at me from under dark lashes several times throughout the night as I paced back and forth with a fussy baby in my arms. Tully had stripped down to a pair of athletic shorts and an undershirt before grabbing my spare pillow and blanket and making a nest for himself on the sofa.

Thankfully, the blanket had slipped off after the first half hour, and I'd been able to distract myself from Lellie's fussing by studying every available inch of Tully's exposed body.

He hadn't changed from the man in my memories. If anything, he was more tempting, more off-limits than before. Which made me feel like I was going to jump out of my skin.

"Is the Mercantile the only place around here to get kids' stuff?" he asked as he held the door open for me. "There's no Target or Walmart?"

I shook my head. "Nearest one's several hours from here. I'm hoping to avoid that. Might have to order online, though."

As soon as I entered, Natana Whiteplume appeared. "Hey, Dev," she began with a smile before noticing the stroller. Her forehead creased in confusion. "Who's this?"

I should have expected to get the third degree once we set foot in town, but my sleep-deprived brain wasn't exactly running on all cylinders at the moment. "Uh..."

"Hi!" Tully said from slightly behind me. "I'm Tully Bowman. Do you work here? I'm desperate to find a travel crib." He smiled big and nodded toward Lellie, who was busy looking around at all the various items on display.

Natana's confusion cleared as she seemed to reassign Lellie to someone else—an outsider—in her mind. "Oh, ah, no. I don't work here. But I know the kid stuff is back in the left-hand corner. And Connie—the lady over there with the flower on her shirt—she can help you if you can't find anything."

Tully thanked her and nudged me out of the way, grabbing the stroller and taking off toward the back of the store. I blinked after him.

"Everything all set for roundup?" Natana asked.

I turned back to blink at her. "Roundup."

She grinned. "I know it's been a full year, Dev. But roundup is when we get all the horses ready to—"

My brain flicked back online. "Roundup! Of course. Yeah. Uh... yeah. I guess? Way said he hired a new hand to help us out because I guess Taza went back to Jenks' dairy."

She rolled her eyes. "Finally. Took Jenks long enough. I'm happy for Taza. He deserves to take over the operations there. But I know you lost a good hand."

"The best. I'm happy for him, but to leave before roundup..." I sighed. "Anyway, please tell me you're still up for helping out? After what happened to Way last year, Silas is going to be a total pain in the ass."

Her eyes danced as she laughed. "He definitely is. Way will be lucky to sit a horse. Yes, I'm still planning on helping, but I'm glad you guys hired someone. You've got your hands full since I know you probably have several mares close to foaling, too."

While we spoke, she glanced back in the direction Tully and Lellie had gone. I could tell Natana was curious about why I'd walked into the Mercantile pushing a stroller, but she was too polite to ask outright.

We talked for another minute before I managed to extract myself from the conversation. On my way to the back of the store, I had to exchange polite greetings with Connie, Hanson Sandoval, and Clayton Spilling. All three of them glanced curiously at Tully, and though none of them asked me about him directly, either, I knew they'd be wondering and talking it over the minute I left. I had a reputation in town for valuing my privacy, but there was no such thing as privacy in Majestic, and I realized belatedly another night without a crib might have been a decent price to pay to keep everyone's curious stares away from me.

"You want the fold-up kind or—" Tully glanced at me and abruptly stopped speaking. "What's wrong?"

"Nothing. Why?"

He glanced over my shoulder toward the front of the store and back to me. "You have a look on your face."

"What look? I don't have a look."

He hesitated, like he was going to say something, then nodded and turned back to the shelves. "Fine. What kind of bed—"

"What look?" I asked again, because apparently, curiosity really wanted to kill a cat.

He frowned and glanced back toward the front of the shop. "Annoyed. Or... I don't know. Bothered? Whatever. I'm sure it's none of my business."

"I..." I started to agree—it really *was* none of his business, and I hadn't forgotten that Tully's questioning yesterday had an ulterior motive—but my mouth refused to follow that plan. "I don't know what to tell people," I admitted. "About Lellie," I added in a lower voice.

Tully's eyes narrowed. "I guess that depends on what your plan is. If you're keeping her, you're going to have to tell people. If you're not keeping her—"

"We're not fucking discussing this here," I snapped, glancing around to see if anyone might have overheard.

In fact, I wasn't sure I wanted to discuss the situation with Tully at all.

"Language," he singsonged, turning back to the shelf.

I fought to keep my temper. Tully wasn't wrong. In the past year, I'd mostly spent time around cowboys like Taza, who was an excellent hand but was also young and crass. Hanging out with Way and Silas was hardly better. But the last thing I needed was Tully pointing out how utterly unsuitable I was to raise a kid.

I was already well aware.

And I'd been going back and forth over what to do about that fact all night as I walked Lellie across the floor. She was a helpless baby, a motherless child, *my daughter*, and she needed someone to care for her. But the thought of me being that someone, of me letting her down...

"Can we just pick something?" I muttered. There weren't many crib options—only a simple wooden crib and a foldable travel thing. Since there was no way I could keep Lellie, the foldable one was the obvious choice.

I grabbed it and set it on the ground next to the other items we'd selected. "What else do we need?"

Tully sniffed in a way that expressed disapproval of my choice...

or maybe my attitude... or possibly my entire existence. "That depends on your plan, too, Dev. Are we just visiting long enough to discuss things? Or is Lellie staying with you for longer than that?"

I opened my mouth, then shut it again. "I don't know yet, okay? And she's sure as shit not going back to Dallas with you until I do."

"Okay, then I guess we should at least get enough stuff for... a week?" Tully began ticking off items on his fingers at an alarming rate. With every additional item he mentioned, my blood pressure spiked higher.

"Enough," I finally snapped. "Let's start with the most important stuff. Food, water, shelter, clothing, sleep."

He smiled. "Maslow's Hierarchy of Needs. Except you forgot breathing."

"She seems to be handling that okay on her own." I took a breath myself and exhaled. "Thank god," I muttered.

"I brought two water bottles, but you might get a small plastic cup," he suggested, moving down the shelf to the area with toddler supplies. "And you want some of these plastic spoons and plates, I think."

We grabbed a few things. "What's her clothes situation?"

"More than fine," he said with a laugh. "Katie barely let the girl wear the same outfit twice. She's good for a while until she goes through a growth spurt."

I wondered when that kind of thing happened, but I didn't dare ask and expose my ignorance. "Sleep stuff? Does she brush her teeth or...?" I noticed all the different offerings on the shelves and began to get overwhelmed. "Do I need gripe water? What the heck is a bath spout? Doesn't my bathtub already have a spout? And what's this for?" I pulled a silicone spatula off a rack and held it up.

Tully leaned in and squinted. "Uh. I admit, I don't know, either. Is that for cooking? Like they have their own little baby spatula?"

I heard a feminine snort from somewhere behind me. Tully and I turned and saw someone shopping in the row behind us. I recognized her as one of Way's friends, JoJo Reynolds, who seemed to always be surrounded by kids.

"Do you know what this is?" I asked.

"Diaper cream spatula. Do *not* waste your time or money on that crap. Use your fingers like a normal person."

My eyes must have gotten wide because she laughed again. "Relax, Dev. Your friend's daughter is probably too old to need diaper cream." She leaned around me to Tully. "How old is she? Eighteen months?"

My gut tightened uncomfortably, and I felt the sudden urge to declare Lellie as my own rather than let people continue to think she was Tully's. I opened my mouth to answer before he could.

"She's..." I began, but then I stopped.

I didn't know how old my own daughter was. I knew when I'd done my part, but had no clue about how long the rest of the process had taken.

Jesus. As if I needed more proof I wasn't cut out for this shit.

I gestured at Tully to answer, but to my surprise, he seemed just as hesitant. "She's, ah..." He glanced at me with wide eyes.

"Her birthday...?" I prompted. He'd said he'd been there when she was born, right?

"Oh." He nodded. "February."

"Not this February," I argued. That was impossible. Lellie was way too big... wasn't she?

Panic stirred in my gut. If we couldn't come up with something, JoJo was probably going to call the cops.

"No, the February before. So she's... yeah, fifteen months," Tully finished lamely. "You nailed it."

I nodded as if adding weight to his statement.

Thankfully, JoJo didn't seem to notice our bumbling. She made a sympathetic noise. "That's a challenging stage, isn't it? They want to walk on their own, but they fall down at the drop of a hat, and they cry over the strangest things. I remember when JJ was that age. Total nightmare. But then you'll look at their fat little hand and remember holding them as a newborn..." She sighed. "Next thing you know, your husband gives you a third glass of wine and talks you into another."

I blinked at her. "That's..."

"Probably not going to happen," Tully finished quickly. "But thanks for the info about the spatula."

She waved her hand. "Sure. Dev here knows if you have any questions about kid stuff, you can come to me. I'm JoJo, by the way."

"Tully Bowman," he said with a genuine smile. "Thanks."

"Anytime." She looked from me to Tully and back again, and I could tell from her delighted expression that she was adding up one and one and getting... the absolute wrong answer. But she didn't ask for clarification any more than anyone else had. Instead, she turned around and headed to a different section of the store.

"Are we done now?" I murmured, focusing on the shelf full of brightly colored baby stuff. "Surely one small human can't require more stuff."

"February seventh," he said in a soft voice. "I blanked on it when she asked, and I hadn't done the age math in a while, but it's February seventh."

I glanced over at him as my brain slotted his words into place. Lellie's birthday. "Oh." I couldn't help but smile. "That's..." *My brother Matt's birthday, too.* I didn't know how that coincidence had come to be, but it felt like another layer of connection between me and the wide-eyed little girl in the stroller. "Thanks."

He studied me for a beat before nodding and turning back to the shelves. "So, no butt spatula. But we probably need more diapers."

We moved down to the diaper selection. There were rows and rows of packages with numbers and various descriptions on them. It reminded me of the time my grandfather had first taken me to the hardware store and asked me to get a hex bolt. I'd looked at the rows of open bins of screws and fasteners with complete overwhelm. How was I supposed to know which one was the one my grandfather had needed?

"I don't suppose we could just close our eyes and point," I said under my breath.

"I think... I think the ones she uses come in a blue package."

I looked at three different brands in blue packages. "Sky blue? Navy blue? Royal blue?"

"That one," he said, pointing. "I think?"

We moved down to the row of sky-blue packages. "What size?"

"She's like... yea big." He held out his hands several inches apart. "Like... her hips are this wide."

A sudden bubble of laughter fought its way up my throat. "We're going to get arrested," I said in a low voice. "We cannot go up there and say we need diapers for someone with a butt about the width of a cantaloupe."

Tully reached forward and picked a package off the shelf and rotated it until he found a size chart on the back. "Okay, says here she might be a... oh hell. This is by weight, not age. How the fuck are we supposed to know?"

We both turned to look at Lellie, who was glancing around with big eyes while still clutching the leather halter she'd wanted to hold when I'd introduced her to one of the horses earlier this morning.

Tully snorted. "When we get arrested, I'm telling them that's your harness, not mine."

I rubbed my face with both hands and tried to hide my smile. I was so fucking tired. "This is ridiculous."

After reaching down to unbuckle her, I pulled her out of the stroller and hefted her up and down, trying to determine how much she weighed.

"She weighs a little less than a bag of fertilizer," I said.

Tully blinked at me. "That's... a strange comparison."

"And those are twenty-five-pound bags."

He closed his eyes and exhaled. "Fine. Then I'm getting the size three, and we'll make it work. What else do we need?"

"I'm already worn-out," I admitted, shifting Lellie and her leather harness to my hip.

"You good with the bed situation?"

I forced myself not to think about Tully Bowman and *bed* in the same sentence. It was too tempting, and I was tired enough for my defenses to be scattered all to hell.

"Yes. Let's go."

As we headed to the cashier to buy the supplies we'd grabbed, Lellie reached out and yanked a package of candy off a nearby display, causing several other packages to scatter on the ground. Tully and I both jumped to grab it out of her hand and clean up the mess, knocking heads in the process.

When we finally got to the cashier stand, Connie eyed the three of us as if trying to do the same relationship calculus JoJo had done. Were we brothers? Friends? Coworkers? Babysitters? Actors in a poorly executed farce?

"You need anything else? Wipes?" she asked.

I glanced at Tully, who looked unsure. "Uh..." I swallowed. "Yes?"

She nodded and moved out from behind the counter to fetch the wipes from the area where we'd found the diapers.

"Can we go home after this?" I asked in a low voice. I wasn't sure how many more townsfolk encounters I could handle.

"Not unless you have a safe place for her to run out her energy," Tully responded in the same low voice. "I was thinking we should take her to a playground or something first so she'll nap afterward." He looked over and met my eyes before adding, "And we need to have a conversation about why I'm here."

I gritted my teeth. The last thing I wanted to do was have a conversation in which I'd have to spend more than half a second confronting the loss of Katie and the new reality of being a parent to her... *our*... child. But he was right. I'd been avoiding the conversation since his arrival, and I could no longer put it off. The sooner he laid out all the facts, the sooner he could leave...

And let me focus on finding a good family to raise Lellie.

"Fine," I said just as Connie came back with a thick pack of wipes and plonked them on the counter next to the other items.

"How old is your...?" Connie asked Tully as she scanned the barcodes.

"Fifteen months," I blurted.

Connie looked confused at my participation in the conversation. "What's her name?"

I opened my mouth to answer her when Tully jumped in. "Eleanor," he said.

"Lellie," I added, feeling my face heat.

Connie glanced between the two of us before murmuring. "What a lovely name." She told me the total of the order and waited while I pulled out my wallet. I hesitated for a moment, remembering belatedly that Silas had mentioned something about the Mercantile preferring card payments over cash for security reasons. I pulled out my credit card and handed it over.

Tully looked like he was going to say something but then clamped his mouth closed. We took our purchases outside and loaded them and the baby in the rental car before heading to the park a few blocks over.

Before I could exit the vehicle, Tully turned to face me. "You don't have to worry about money. Katie left money to cover Lellie's expenses."

I blinked at him. "Worry about money?"

He looked even more uncomfortable than he was making me feel. "I saw you hesitate back there when you heard how much the total was. I was going to offer to cover it, but I didn't want to make a big deal in front of the cashier. I know this is a small town, and people talk. But I can pay you back from Lellie's—"

"I got it," I said with an incredulous laugh. The very idea of him thinking I couldn't afford to pay for the diapers was ludicrous.

I could understand why he might think that, of course. In Tully's eyes, I was a ranch hand living over a barn. The reality was I was a billionaire who had the kind of money that sometimes made me want to vomit. But my wealth, and that of the other guys in the brotherhood, was a closely guarded secret. And Tully Bowman was the last person I would ever tell about it.

"I didn't mean to insult you," he said. His cheeks had flushed deep red with discomfort. "I just wanted to let you know, since we haven't had a chance to talk about the details yet…"

"I have a job, you know," I said, opening the car door. "I believe I mentioned it earlier." What I didn't mention was the fact that Way didn't actually pay me. It was more like we had a partnership, sharing the profits of our breeding program equally.

He sighed and opened his door. We worked together to get Lellie and her stuff out of the vehicle before making our way to a bench beside a small collection of toddler climbing structures. Several other kids were playing with attentive parents or minders nearby.

I wasn't sure of the etiquette of this kind of situation. After glancing at the other adults and kids, I turned to Tully. "Do we just… release her into the wild?"

He bit his lip as if fighting a grin. "Yes. And then we watch to make sure she doesn't get eaten by bears or coyotes."

I nodded and took a seat on the edge of the bench, leaning forward to be ready for any rescue needed. A little boy with several cowlicks sticking up around his head looked particularly prone to misbehavior, so I kept an eagle eye on him as Lellie began toddling toward the structure.

"She'll be fine," Tully said softly as he took the bench next to me.

"Mpfh."

We sat in silence for a few minutes while Lellie navigated her way around the large plastic turtle, patting it and testing it with one knee before finally climbing onto it next to another little girl.

"Can I speak about Katie's will?"

His question was spoken in the same soft tone. No one was sitting close enough to be able to eavesdrop, and I was ready to get this conversation over with.

I took a breath and prepared myself. "Yes."

SEVEN

TULLY

I watched Dev carefully as I explained Katie's wishes.

"She left full custody of Lellie to you. All of her financial assets were left in trust to Lellie, and as Lellie's guardian, you will be the trustee. That means if you keep her, you can use whatever money you need from those funds for her expenses." I took a breath. "Lellie also has her own trust that predates Katie's death. Between the two trusts, there is... quite a bit of money."

Dev refused to take his eyes off Lellie as she explored the large climbing shapes. He didn't speak for a few minutes. "Why didn't Katie leave her to someone else?"

Good question.

"I'm not sure. I mean... I can tell you that she wasn't particularly close to her parents. They had some... ideological differences."

He huffed out a breath. "I'm very clear on why she wouldn't want *them* to raise her. I just thought... a friend, maybe."

Again, he didn't look at me while he spoke. His attention was completely fixed on his daughter, and his entire body was coiled as if to spring up and bolt toward her at any moment.

Memories of his muscular body tried worming their way to the front of my brain, but I refused them. It was hard enough keeping my distance from the man as it was. The minute I replayed our night together two years ago, I would be in serious trouble. *Lellie*, I reminded myself. *You're here for Lellie.*

"Katie's closest friends are either single with no kids or already have as many children as they can handle," I explained. "And I... well, she knows I'm focused on my career. I plan to make partner in the next year or two, and the firm I work for has incredibly high standards. Katie had the same ambition, but she wanted a family, too. It became clear after she had Lellie that the firm wouldn't trust a single parent to be able to handle the demands of a partner track."

Dev's jaw ticked, and when he spoke, it sounded more like he was talking to himself than me. "I just don't understand why she would have thought *I* was a good choice."

"You're her biological parent," I said carefully. "Her closest living relative. As her only surviving biological parent, you have prima facie right to custody, which means you're basically the default choice even without her will. If someone wanted to challenge the will, it would be much more difficult going up against that."

He finally took his eyes off Lellie long enough to meet my gaze with his dark eyes. "*Does* someone want to challenge the will?"

I could tell he already knew the answer to that question. I nodded. "Katie's parents are definitely not happy."

His jaw ticked again as he returned his attention to the playground. "They can fuck off."

While I agreed with him on a personal level, I knew better than to say so. They were Lellie's grandparents, not to mention one of the largest clients at my law firm... and unlike some people, they knew for sure that they not only *wanted* to raise Lellie, but they had the capability to do so.

"I'd make a terrible father," Dev said. Again, this was muttered almost under his breath, and I wondered if he even realized he was saying it out loud.

Part of me—probably the same part that couldn't stop noticing

Dev's large, callused hands and the sandalwood scent of him—wanted to disagree. To comfort and reassure him that he could handle it. It wouldn't even be a total lie because after watching him with her last night, I felt like his heart was in the right place.

But at the same time, Devon McKay was still too much of an unknown. Being intimately familiar with the oddly square-shaped mole low on his left hip and feeling my heart go pitty-pat at the sight of him snuggling a baby wasn't the same as knowing whether or not he paid his bills on time and was likely to be around when his daughter needed him.

"Say what you want about Katie's parents, but they do want to raise Lellie," I ventured. "She could do worse—"

"*No*," he barked. A young mother from a few benches down glanced over at us in surprise. I winced and shot her an apologetic look. Her eyes remained suspicious as she glanced between the children on the playground and the two of us.

After a moment, Dev spoke in a much lower voice. "I'm not leaving her with those righteous homophobes."

"So, then..." I hesitated before continuing. "It sounds like you don't want to keep her yourself..."

He snapped his head around to glare at me. "Of course I want to keep her myself. Jesus Christ. Lellie's my daughter. She's *Katie's* daughter, and I'd want to be there for her for that reason alone. But I'm not stupid, Tully. This isn't just about what I want. It's about what's best for Lellie. And I'm definitely not what's best for her."

His words surprised me, but more than that, they concerned me. If Dev didn't take her, and he didn't want the Scotts to have her, what did that mean for her future?

Out of the corner of my eye, I saw Lellie begin to tumble off the turtle, but before I could move a muscle in that direction, Dev was already up and sprinting across the playground, scooping her up before any part of her could land on the rubberized mulch below.

"It's okay, baby," he cooed, holding her close to his chest and rocking from side to side. "D-Dev's here."

The woman who'd been eyeing him suspiciously before now gazed at him with a soft expression in her eye before glancing over at me and smiling. She clearly thought we were a couple, and more than that, she seemed to think we were adorably overcautious new parents since Lellie's fall from the turtle would have been a simple two-inch drop onto a soft surface.

I probably should have corrected her. I didn't.

Because the soft and gooey look in her eyes was exactly how I felt at the sight of muscular cowboy Devon McKay gently cradling his baby girl on a playground. It was enough to make *me* want to have his baby.

He rocked his way over and glared down at me. "We're leaving. This place is a danger pit."

I bit my lip against a smile. "Why don't we try out the swings? They have the ones for babies over there." I pointed behind him where there were several kinds of swings in a long row near a statue of a cowboy riding a bucking bronc. "They're practically impossible to fall out of."

He eyed the swings for a moment before reluctantly agreeing. I grabbed the backpack and followed him over.

It took both of us to wrangle her wriggling legs into the leg holes, but then she squawked out a happy noise and pumped her legs in excitement. I was relieved to see her retaining her usual cheerful mood despite her bad night. But then again, Katie had always said that babies were resilient creatures.

Dev pushed the swing gently to get it started. "Who's managing the money right now?"

It took me a moment to change gears and realize what he was asking. "Oh, ah... Katie had a wealth manager. I notified him of her passing and let him know I was notifying next of kin."

He nodded. "I imagine it's mostly in the stock market?"

"Not all of it. The trust also includes her house in Dallas, her SUV, and some jewelry." I deliberately didn't share the value of her estate with him. Not here and not right now. The very fact he was asking me about the money made me uncomfortable.

Nothing he'd said should have felt like a red flag—it was smart to determine whether you could afford a child before deciding to have one—but I could hear the Scotts' voice in my head and Orris's, too. Could they have been right about him? Would he change his mind about keeping Lellie when he learned just how much money she brought with her?

"But you trust this wealth manager? The money is in good hands?"

I crossed my arms in front of my chest and tried to keep my tone neutral. "If I had any wealth to speak of, I'd hire him."

He scoffed. "You're an attorney at the same firm where Katie worked. You can't tell me you're not raking in some cash."

His words and tone set my back teeth on edge. "And you're a Yale graduate. Should I make assumptions about how much money you have?"

Dev's eyes widened. "You saying you don't make a good living on the partnership track at one of Dallas's most prestigious firms?"

"I'm saying I'll be paying off school debt until I retire regardless of how well I'm paid, and I have... things... I need to pay for."

He looked me up and down, from my high-end haircut to my brand-name clothes. "I see."

Dev didn't see, not at all, but I wasn't going to explain that I was paying for my brother Nolan's college tuition or that my father's greatest talent was his ability to misspend and/or drink away every dollar he earned. It was none of Dev's business how I spent my salary, and I didn't care what he thought of me.

At least, I *shouldn't*.

I set my jaw. "Can we stop talking about money, please?"

He shrugged and continued to push Lellie. "You're the one who brought it up."

"Because I wanted to explain Katie's estate and Lellie's trusts, not because I wanted your commentary on my life."

Dev was silent for a moment. "I'm glad Lellie's protected financially," he said finally. He turned to me. "Do you think that's why the Scotts want custody? For the money?"

I shook my head. "Definitely not. They have more money than god, for one. And secondly, they were demanding custody before they learned about her wealth."

"But they did learn about her wealth?"

I started to nod but hesitated. "Well, they don't know how much she's worth, but the will obviously revealed Lellie as the sole beneficiary of Katie's estate. Which I'm sure most people would have assumed anyway. And the Scotts most likely knew Katie still had a good portion of her own trust fund. They..." I thought back to the meeting. "They did express a desire to try and reclaim her trust fund money. But it's not something they'll ever accomplish."

"Assholes," Dev muttered.

"Yeah." I reached out to touch his arm but stopped before making contact. "But they really seemed to care about their granddaughter, Dev. I don't think that was fake. They seemed to want to raise her and make sure she was loved and cared for properly. If you don't plan on keeping her..."

He didn't say anything for a little while. I thought he might be done with the conversation, but then he spoke up again, surprising me.

"Did you know that Katie tried to tell them she was asexual in high school, and they sat her down and explained there was no such thing? And then they actually worried that the purity pledge she'd taken in middle school had somehow caused her to fear relationships?"

I hesitated but nodded.

"So then they pressured her to date, and she ended up with a string of total assholes." Dev pushed Lellie through a few more swings before continuing. "She tried telling them again in college after she joined an LGBTQ student group, but her parents said she just hadn't met the right man yet. They tried to get her to change colleges to get away from that 'woke propaganda.'" He shook his head. "Thank god she had a strong personality."

I knew how much her parents' rejection had pained Katie. But I also knew she'd been rock solid about her own sexuality by the time she'd decided to become a single mom. "When she told them she was pregnant, they freaked," I said with a grin. "She said it was kinda fun, actually. She told them in a coffee shop near their church where there were people from the congregation around."

The edges of Dev's lips turned up. "I would have liked to have seen that."

"At first, she said she'd gotten drunk on a trip to Miami for a friend's bachelorette party and slept with several men in the same night. She told them she had no idea the names of any of them and wouldn't even know where to start searching for the father. They lost their minds. Then she admitted that it had actually been a very planned and careful decision made over the course of two years, which had included extensive counseling. She'd selected the kindest, smartest man she knew to donate his sperm, and then she'd used artificial insemination in a well-respected clinic. Pastor and Mrs. Scott calmed down a little, but not by much. I, ah, don't know if they entirely believed the Miami thing was a lie," I said, thinking of their reactions earlier this week.

He glanced at me. "Did she tell them it was me?"

I shook my head. "No. They didn't find out until they learned you'd been given custody of Lellie."

"They must have flipped."

I gave him a look, confirming his assumption. "They remembered you as a ranch hand."

He scoffed. "Hell, I'm still a ranch hand. They'd love that. I can't imagine them allowing someone like me to raise their precious grandchild. Their only grandchild. I can guess how upset they are."

"Take that and multiply it. They're also big clients of my firm, which means my boss is keeping a close eye on this situation." I hesitated. "I represent Katie, which includes Lellie now, but the managing partner, my boss, represents Pastor and Mrs. Scott. Needless to say, it's a little... tricky."

Before I could explain further, Lellie began fussing and wriggling to get out of the swing. Dev stopped its motion, allowing me to lean over and pull her out. "She's probably hungry," I said. "We should head back and feed her and then see if she'll nap."

While I was secretly enjoying playing happy family with Dev, I knew my time in Wyoming was short, and we needed to have some serious conversations about Lellie's future. Whoever ended up with custody would have to decide what to do with Katie's house and set up a new will for themselves stipulating custody of Lellie in case of their own death. I owed it to Katie to make sure her daughter's future was fully protected, but those conversations wouldn't be easy... and I wouldn't attempt them while Dev was distracted with his vigilante toddler surveillance.

We loaded her up in the car and made our way back to the ranch. When we pulled up outside the barn, I heard a muffled curse come from Dev and noticed several unfamiliar vehicles parked out front. I glanced at him, but before I could ask what was going on, he threw the rental into Park and hopped out.

When I got Lellie out of the car seat, she immediately fussed to be put down so she could walk on her own. By the time we approached the barn doors at toddler pace, two of the men from last night were heading in our direction with a frustrated Dev in their wake. Thankfully, the sheriff wasn't one of them.

"I'll explain later," Dev called to them, but it was clear no one was listening.

"Hey, sweetie," a friendly-looking blond cowboy said, squatting down to meet Lellie on her level. "How're you doing? I'm Uncle Waylon."

A gorgeous man with short brown hair and an intense vibe gazed at the cowboy fondly. "Don't get too close in case fatherhood is contagious, baby. First your sister, and now this."

Lellie's arm wrapped around my leg as she moved closer to me.

"You're scaring her," Dev said, shoving the brown-haired man back and nudging the cowboy. "She's not fond of strangers."

"Then introduce us," the brown-haired man said, but he was looking at me instead of Lellie.

Dev's annoyance was palpable. "Tully, this is Silas Concannon and Waylon Fletcher. Silas and Way, Tully Bowman. He's... ah..."

"The attorney," I said, holding out my hand to shake.

Dev let out a breath and looked up at the sky as if praying for patience. What had he expected me to say, exactly? *I'm a onetime hookup and the man who's never forgotten the taste of your friend's skin...*

"Attorney," Silas repeated, as if trying to decide what exactly that meant.

I bit my lip against giving him a snarky response. For some reason, the idea that Dev was surrounded by beautiful gay men at this ranch made me want to punch something. Hard.

Dev's eyes flicked between me and Silas before settling on the latter. "Can you please back off? I don't have the energy to explain this right now."

"Do you want me to call Kenji?"

Dev took a deep breath and let it out slowly. "That's... probably not a bad idea."

"Who's Kenji?" I asked.

The cowboy, *Waylon*, crouched back down and asked Lellie about the halter she was still holding. "Looks like you have Buttercup's halter. Do you like horses? She's right over there. Can you see her?" He gestured to a paddock off to the side of the barn, where a mare was standing.

"Foss!" She let go of my leg a little and pointed with her other hand. "Foss!"

Waylon held out his arms. "Want to go meet her?"

Dev shifted on his feet. I couldn't interpret the expression on his face, but I could tell something was bothering him. Silas noticed also, reaching out to put a staying hand on the man's shoulder. "Way, baby. Let Dev take her."

Dev crouched down next to Lellie. "Do you want to see the horse? Can D-Dev take you?"

We all stood and watched as Lellie reached her arms up for Dev to pick her up. Something tightened in my chest as I noticed the relief on his face. He carried her over to the paddock, out of earshot from the rest of us.

Silas turned back to me. "What's the deal with the kid?"

Waylon rolled his eyes. "Easy, tiger."

Silas ignored him and crossed his arms over his chest. "It's clear she's Dev's daughter. And if he'd known he had a daughter, *I* would have known, too."

"Not my story to tell," I said. "You'll have to ask him."

"How long is she staying?"

"That depends on Dev," I admitted.

"Are you..." He hesitated. "Are the two of you... Is this baby yours, too?"

Heat flooded my face and neck. "No."

"So the two of you don't have a history together."

I hesitated too long before stumbling over my response. "I'm not... Not the way you... I'm Kathryn Scott's attorney. Her friend."

Silas's eyebrows rose. "Ohhh."

Waylon rubbed a hand over his face. "Can you butt out of Dev's business for one freaking minute and let him decide how much to tell you?"

Silas looked offended. "I'm Dev's best friend."

"One of several," Waylon muttered.

"Fine, I'm *one* of his best friends. And I'm entitled to—"

"No, my love, you're not," Waylon said with a laugh. "And I think it's time to go and give these guys and little lady some space."

"Who's Kenji?" I blurted again. Because ever since they mentioned calling him, I'd wondered if maybe Dev had a current relationship, possibly in addition to... whatever he had going with the sheriff. And if so, that would have implications. To... to the custody situation.

The cowboy shot me an understanding smile. "Their Girl Friday."

"He'd tell you he's more like Q," Silas muttered.

Waylon shook his head. "That would make one of you James Bond, sweetheart, and I hate to break it to you. Bond would be Bash in this scenario, not you."

Silas scoffed. "He wishes."

Waylon turned back to me. "Anyway, Kenji keeps their lives organized. He's like an executive assistant on steroids."

"Who's 'they'?" I asked, annoyed at how little I knew about Dev. "Why does a ranch hand like Dev need a personal assistant?"

Silas and Waylon both looked at me before exchanging some kind of silent message with each other. "We've gotta go," Silas said and yanked his partner toward one of the vehicles before I could stop them.

Once they were gone, I headed over toward the paddock just as another man sauntered out of the barn, heading in the same direction. He was college-aged with sun-streaked, shaggy hair and was wearing a half-open Hawaiian shirt, loose linen trousers, and flip-flops. "Hey, my dude. Are you Devon McKay?"

Still holding Lellie, Dev looked toward him in confusion. "Uh... yes?"

"Cool, cool." The man hitched a thumb at his own chest. "Indigo."

Dev stared at him. "I... don't understand."

"Indigo. Your new hand? You know, for, like, roundup? Way got me all set up in the bunk room—massively chill vibe in there, dude. Magnificent energy. Like, seriously, *all* the good feels—and he said to find you to get started on whatever you need."

"Your... name... is Indigo?" Dev scowled like he was trying to translate a foreign language. "And you're... here for ranch work?" he guessed.

I pressed my lips together to keep from laughing. This kid looked about as handy on a ranch as a squid... if that squid was prone to smoking dope out of a homemade bong.

Dev glanced at me, and we shared a look of unspoken understanding, similar to the one Silas and Waylon had exchanged a moment before. This guy was an added complication Dev definitely didn't need right now.

"I can help," I offered stupidly. "With ranch stuff. If you need me to."

Dev's frown intensified. "You?"

He made it sound like this was slightly less believable than the stoner kid helping.

I straightened to my full height and tried to ignore the fact that I was still shorter than Dev. "I'm from Texas, in case you've forgotten."

The edge of his lip twitched. "And that's your ranching resume in its entirety, is it?"

I shot him a look that hopefully said, *I'll bet it's a better resume than this guy's.*

He sighed. "I could use your help, Tully... Watching Lellie."

For some reason, his rejection of my offer to help with ranch work stung. I'd sworn long ago never to return to boots caked in horse shit and long days in the saddle, but I felt the need to prove something to Dev. The fact that a day on horseback with Dev seemed like something I would enjoy was neither here nor there.

Belatedly, it occurred to me that I didn't know when roundup was or whether or not I'd still be in town. That thought reminded me I needed to check in with the office to let them know I'd found Devon McKay.

I excused myself to make a phone call while Dev asked Indigo a few more questions.

And that was when I learned that Pastor and Mrs. Scott had officially filed a petition for custody of Dev's daughter.

I was torn between the very fine view of Tully's ass as he walked away and the need to keep an eagle eye on Lellie as she patted Buttercup's nose.

"Foss," she repeated happily. The hippie stoner Way had stuck me with smiled at her.

"You like horses, dudette?" he asked in a gentle voice. "My sister loves horses, too. She's a tiny nugget, not much bigger than you. How old are you, sunshine?"

Why in the world did everyone need to know the age of random kids they had no relation to?

"She turned one in February," I said before changing the subject. "Tell me about your experience working on a ranch."

Indigo's eyes blinked twice before he took a breath. "Well, ah... I don't have *ranch* experience, per se, but I know horses. Like, me and horses... we vibe on the same wavelength, if you feel me."

I fantasized about throwing a bucket of ice water on Way and Silas early the next morning while they were still comfy-cozy in their bed. "Do you know how to cut horses?"

"Cut!" His eyes went wide. "Oh, my dude, *no...*"

"I mean wrangle," I snapped. "Cut one horse from the rest of the herd in order to move that horse to a different pasture."

"Oh, *that*." His shoulders dropped, and his goofy grin reappeared. "Sure. I know how to capture and lead a horse. Our polo ponies were, like—"

Polo? I blocked out the rest of his words. I played polo, too, but comparing it to ranch work was like saying that experience painting walls meant you'd be talented at painting pictures.

Was it possible to find anyone less qualified than Indigo in all of Wyoming? Surely if I went into town tomorrow and threw out a handful of pebbles, I'd hit several locals who knew more about ranching than Indigo. "Tell Way to get you on a horse and show you a few things before Friday," I barked over my shoulder as I turned and walked away. "And meet me back here at four thirty for the afternoon feed."

"Sick. But, like, what should I do in the meantime?" he called after me.

"Find a pair of boots and muck some stalls... *dude*," I called back.

I refused to look toward the rental car in search of Tully. Instead, I headed straight up to my apartment in hopes of finding food I could serve a toddler. Was Lellie allergic to gluten? Would she choke on strawberries? Could the internet possibly help keep me from accidentally killing her with lunch?

Thankfully, Tully was already there, and he'd unpacked the little booster seat we'd bought for the kitchen table. After I set Lellie down and she toddled over to him, he picked her up and got her buckled in. "Your new hand seems like a helpful guy," he began. "*My dude.*"

I saw the twinkle in his eye and grunted in response. "Helpful if you need to lose track of your herd, maybe. Or find spiritual enlightenment with the help of exotic mushrooms." I closed my eyes and exhaled. "It's my own fault."

"How's that? I thought Waylon hired him. Waylon's your boss, right?"

"Sort of. Yes, Way owns the ranch with his siblings. And yes, he hired the guy without consulting me. But..." I finished washing my hands and opened the cabinet with the bread and peanut butter. "It's complicated."

Tully's voice held a hint of annoyance. "Complicated? Gee whiz, Professor. I can't imagine little ole me would be able to understand something *complicated*. I barely graduated top of my class in law school."

I looked up at the ceiling, but there was a noticeable lack of patience up there. I'd have to find my own.

"Way's been trying to hire more ranch help all year. I pushed back. Hence, the stoner."

He took the seat next to Lellie and used a package of wet wipes to clean her hands. "Were you touching the horse, sweetie? Was she soft? Yeah, I bet," Tully said as she babbled happily in reply. "Let's get those hands cleaned off before you eat, though, okay? No yucky germs. And let's get your bib on so we don't ruin your pretty shirt." He glanced up at me, which was when I realized I'd been staring at him. "Why didn't you want Way hiring more help?"

"We had a guy here named Taza. He was good. *Is* good. But he got a better opportunity. It took me a long time to get used to him, and the man's a talker. I didn't want to have to break in someone new."

Tully nodded thoughtfully as he cleaned his own hands with the wipes and smoothed down the front of his shirt. "Which would be fine if you didn't have a couple hundred head of horses to manage, right?"

I didn't want to appreciate the firm abs under the shirt that probably cost more than my entire wardrobe back in high school, but I couldn't deny how sexy he was. I simply didn't have time for that temptation. "Right. There's no way that kid can wrangle horses."

"I told you I can help. When is roundup?"

The last thing I needed was this city boy attorney with his styled hair and germ-free fingers trying to play cowboy. "Friday. And you'll be a big help if you keep Lellie safe and entertained, like I asked."

He huffed out a breath. "Fine. But stop complaining about

needing experienced riders when you're not willing to listen to me and you're not willing to give your boss the benefit of the doubt about hiring someone capable of doing the job."

I ignored him to focus on finding the jelly in my fridge and fixing lunch. After finishing the stack of sandwiches, I cut one of them up into tiny bite-sized pieces and added it to one of the new plastic plates I'd washed, alongside some cut-up strawberries. I brought the plate to the table and handed it to Tully before returning for the other stuff.

When I placed a plate of sandwiches, chips, and fruit in front of him, he glanced up at me in surprise. "What's this?"

"What's it look like? Peanut butter and jelly sandwiches." I frowned. "Unless you're allergic?"

"Not at all. I just haven't had anyone make me a PB&J in..." He laughed lightly. "I can't remember how long. Maybe ever."

Yeah, for all that he claimed not to have "wealth," I could easily imagine that Tully Bowman wasn't the peanut butter-on-white-bread type. But he gamely reached for the sandwich anyway.

"Can you tell me more about Katie's will?" I asked as I took my own seat. "What else do I need to know?"

He took his time before answering, wiping his mouth with a paper towel and then taking a sip of water first. "Her parents are suing you for custody."

"Wait. You mentioned they weren't happy. You didn't say..."

"I just heard the news from my assistant. They've officially filed suit. My assistant said they're pressuring my office for your address so they can serve the papers."

I bit back a string of curses. The news shouldn't have surprised me. And maybe it didn't, exactly. But it sat heavily in my gut none-theless. "Oh."

Katie's parents were controlling, sanctimonious assholes, but I couldn't fault them for fighting for custody of their own grand-daughter over a single dad they'd only ever known as a scruffy high schooler from the poor side of town.

I felt Tully's eyes on me, but he didn't say anything. Not for the first time, I wondered exactly whose side he was on. Was he trying to protect Lellie's best interests? I hoped so. He didn't need to be on my side necessarily, but I sure as hell hoped he wasn't on the Scotts' side either.

Lellie finished eating and started fussing. Tully wiped her down again with wet wipes, which were beginning to seem like a miracle product. I understood now why Connie had suggested them.

Once she was clean, I took her into my bedroom and laid her down on the bed, cuddling with her and reading a picture book from her suitcase. Thankfully, her eyes began to close at the sound of my voice about halfway through the short book, and before long, I felt comfortable moving her to the portable crib and escaping back to the main room. Tully had finished cleaning up after our meal and was sitting on the sofa with his phone in his hands.

He glanced up when I entered. "So. What are you going to do?" he asked abruptly.

I didn't pretend to misunderstand. I needed to make a decision, for Lellie's sake. "That's a very good question. She needs a good home. Better than the Scotts. And better than me."

Our eyes met. As much as I hated to admit it, I really wasn't the pathway to happiness for Katie's beloved daughter.

"But I'm accepting custody... until I can find the best situation for her," I went on. "Custody of my daughter will be on my terms, and the Scotts are not in the running."

"I'm not sure that's how it works, Dev. Anyone can make a case for custody, and biological family gets an automatic serious consideration, especially in Texas. The Scotts have excellent attorneys."

I eyed him. "I guess I need a good attorney, too, then. Can you recommend a family lawyer in Texas?"

"I know a woman who's passionate about LGBTQ family law," Tully said slowly. "She's the one..." When he trailed off, I shot him a questioning look. He sighed. "She's the one I recommended Katie use for a contract when I learned she was using a sperm donor."

"But we didn't have a contract."

"I know. I thought that was..." He ran his tongue over his teeth as if searching for the correct word. "Ill-advised."

I bristled at the implied insult... which was foolish, considering Tully and I hadn't even met at that point. "I told Katie I'd never wanted kids. I wouldn't fight her for custody. She trusted that."

"Clearly. But people change their minds." He shrugged. "It's fairly common. Enough to make it worth protecting against. Trust is all well and good in theory, but sometimes the people you think you can trust are the least trustworthy of all." He smiled without humor. "I wouldn't put my future in someone else's hands like that, still less my child's future."

"And in the end, Katie trusted me with her child's future anyway," I said hotly.

Tully looked troubled, but he nodded. "She did," he agreed reluctantly. His gaze caught mine. "But you don't want her." The words *which shows I was right* remained unspoken, but I still heard them.

I narrowed my eyes. He made it sound so easy. "I told you, it's not a matter of *want*, it's a matter of what's best for Lellie, and I'm not the right person—"

"So *be* the right person," he shot back.

"You don't know what the fuck you're talking about."

Tully rolled his eyes. "Then for god's sake, explain it to me."

"Explain that I have family issues I don't want to saddle my child with? That I never want to repeat the same mistakes my own parents made? That I could never forgive myself if I—" I broke off and ran a hand through my hair.

What the fuck was I doing? In my anger, I was giving him evidence to use against me in the custody case.

I tried to soften my words and my tone. "Anyway. That was before I met Lellie, when Katie was around to be a better parent than I could ever be. I care enough to make sure Lellie finds a good situation with a loving family."

Tully seemed to be making a supreme effort to keep his own

temper under control. "Do you have the resources for this fight? It's not something you'll be able to use Lellie's money for—"

"I wouldn't." I gritted my teeth. "Don't worry about the money."

Tully's eyebrows lowered even more. "I'm just saying—"

I knew what he was saying. That I was a simple ranch hand living in someone else's apartment, sleeping on my boss's furniture, barely making ends meet. There was no way for him to know I'd fixed up this place myself, had made sure it was professionally decorated and fitted out so it would increase Way's property value as my way of thanking him since he wouldn't let me pay rent. But I didn't owe Tully any explanations. As long as I could pay my legal bills, it was nobody's business how.

"I get what you're saying. And I'm telling you, it's none of your business. Can't make it clearer than that, Tully."

"Fine," he bit out.

"Fine," I repeated. "And while we're at it, I'd like to see a copy of Katie's will, please. Along with any other documentation I'm entitled to, including trust documents, bank statements, et cetera."

Tully's fingers flexed like he wanted to hit something—possibly me—but he didn't argue. He simply got up and retrieved his computer bag before returning with a large legal-sized folder full of paperwork.

After handing it to me, he returned to his spot on the end of the sofa and watched as I began to go through it. I felt like I was a bug under a microscope and he was recording every tiny tic or change in my expression.

I spoke without looking up. "Feel free to take a walk."

"You're kicking me out of your apartment?" His tone was light, but his words carried a definite edge of hurt.

I blew out a breath. Tully didn't deserve my anger. He'd been looking out for Katie's interests two years ago and was looking out for Lellie's now. I had no right to be annoyed that I instinctively wanted him to be on *my* team.

Hell, I wasn't sure *I* was on my team.

I finally glanced up and met his eyes. "No. I'm not. I'm just having a hard time figuring out whether you're here to gather evidence for *them* or whether you're here to successfully transfer custody to me according to Katie's wishes."

Tully's shoulders slumped slightly. "That's fair." He paused. "I'm here to transfer custody. But it's my job both as Katie's attorney and her friend to make sure that Lellie is in good hands. Transferring custody to you just to have you give her away to strangers wasn't exactly what I had in mind." He hesitated. "I know not to believe what the Scotts say. I know they're biased against you. I know there's... bad blood there—"

I snorted. "No shit." I felt like we were saying things that had already been said. "I know you think they're an option for Lellie because they'd *love* her. Well, forgive me if I don't think their idea of love is all that great."

Tully set his jaw. I could practically see steam rising off him as the things he wasn't letting himself say boiled behind his closed lips.

I refocused on the pages in my lap. Katie's will was straightforward, and her wealth didn't surprise me since I'd known she had a trust fund. What did surprise me was discovering she had several rental properties, including one with a very familiar address.

"Is she fucking kidding?" I murmured, flipping through the pages in search of any additional information.

"What?"

"Did you know she managed rental properties?"

He looked surprised. "Yes. She invested some of her trust fund in them as a way of transferring the money away from her parents' reach at first. That was before she met her wealth manager and let him move it into various financial instruments. Why?"

I handed him one of the pages. "That's my parents' house. She owns my parents' house."

More accurately, *Lellie* owned my parents' house, which meant I, in effect, was now their landlord. And the reminder of my parents served to completely ruin my day even more than learning that the Scotts might have a strong case for custody.

I tossed the rest of the papers on the sofa and stood up. "I'm going for a ride."

Anger sparked under my skin, and I couldn't get downstairs and out of the barn fast enough. Because it suddenly occurred to me that Pastor and Mrs. Scott weren't the only biological grandparents who might decide Lellie was better off with them than me.

There was no doubt in my mind my own parents would fight me for her tooth and nail.

NINE

TULLY

As Dev stormed out of the apartment over the barn, I let out a long groan, partly of frustration and partly of relief.

His moodiness was getting to me.

All morning, I'd felt like I was standing in a pasture under a wide-open sky back in Texas, watching the clouds roll in and feeling that same silent tension gather around us that charged the air before a lightning strike. I'd known a storm was brewing but not when it would hit.

One minute, I'd felt a connection growing between us, the kind where we could at least be friends for Lellie's sake, and the next, he closed off, retreated like I was the enemy, and glowered at me over a peanut butter sandwich. One minute, he was introducing his daughter to the horses or reading her a book before nap, and the next, he'd lit out of the apartment, leaving me to watch Lellie without even asking if I minded.

I *didn't* mind, of course. But if he was going to be her guardian, for however short a time, he needed to know that he couldn't simply storm off when he was angry.

I bit out a curse as I looked at the papers strewn across the couch.

What was so upsetting about knowing that Katie had owned his parents' place, for heaven's sake? The man was incomprehensible sometimes.

Which probably made me a fool for constantly wishing I understood him.

Before I could berate myself too much, my phone rang with a call from my boss. Thankfully, my assistant had already warned me about the custody suit when I'd called to check in earlier, but I still wasn't prepared for the aggression in Orris Dunlevy's voice.

"I'm going to need that address for Devon McKay," he began.

I didn't pretend not to understand him, but we both knew his pressing me for Dev's address was shady as fuck. My firm might be handling Pastor and Mrs. Scotts' case, but I was not their attorney. I was representing my client Kathryn Scott and, by extension, her daughter.

"Feel free to have whoever is handling the case reach out to me," I replied, trying to remain calm. "How are things proceeding with the Hernandez trust? Jay said—"

"Fine, fine. It's all in hand. But I need you to talk to me about the Scott case. Did you make contact with Mr. McKay?"

"Yes. I arrived yesterday."

"And? Has he agreed to release custody of the child to the Scotts?"

"Definitely not." I stretched my neck from side to side. "He does not want them having custody of Lellie."

He made a discontented noise. "So he plans on keeping her."

Not exactly.

Thankfully, Orris continued without waiting for my confirmation. "Good thing they proceeded with the lawsuit, then. Brock Lois is handling the case. He's the best. I'm sure he's already working on getting as much dirt on the man as possible, but I don't have to tell you that anything you can offer him in support of the Scotts' suit would be greatly appreciated."

I clenched my back teeth. "Sir, respectfully, I'm not going to do that. My client was very firm in her decision against leaving custody of Lellie to her parents, so I will not assist a suit to go against her wishes."

"Tully, I understand your conflicting emotions here, but there are things you don't understand—*can't* understand. Sometimes there are misunderstandings between an adult child and her parents that become meaningless when something as terrible as the child's death occurs. You wouldn't understand that, since you're not a parent yourself. What's clear is that the Scotts love their granddaughter very much and would make a stable and loving home for her. Any judge in town will side with Pastor Scott, whose church is a fixture in the community and who's been in a forty-year committed marriage, over a single father who's never even met the child. The Scotts are going to win their suit, and if an associate of Dunlevy, Pace, and Trumble hinders their efforts to gain custody of their granddaughter, we stand to lose millions of dollars of their legal business from our books. I won't stand for that."

"I am not suggesting we hinder them, Orris," I said. "I'm only stating that I will not *aid* them by betraying my own client. I have an ethical obligation to represent the interests of my client and her child—"

"Surely you believe the interests of the child lie with the Scotts." Orris's tone conveyed that this was not a question but a clear statement of what I was expected to believe, whether I actually believed it or not. If I disagreed with it outwardly, I would receive a harsh and immediate black mark on my record as a potential partner at the firm.

"My opinion is irrelevant, sir," I hedged. "It's not my place to have an opinion here. It's my job to represent my client."

I felt a trickle of sweat slide down my lower back.

"As it's my job to represent mine," Orris said firmly. "Franklin Scott is my client. The Scotts' business is worth way more to this firm than Kathryn's ever was, make no mistake. If it comes down to having to choose sides here, Tully, I expect you to choose the right one. Do I make myself clear?"

My jaw began to ache. There was no point in accusing him of pressuring me into unethical and unprofessional behavior unless I was ready to get fired. And I definitely was not. "Yes, sir."

"Good. I'll have Brock's people get in touch with you to get these papers served. Meanwhile, I need you to stay there and keep an eye on McKay in case he gets the idea in his head to take the girl and run."

I thought about the work I was already missing. "Stay here for how long, exactly?"

"As long as it takes, Tully."

After ending the call, my hands and jaw ached from clenching them so hard.

How the fuck am I supposed to handle this?

I knew what I owed Katie, and I felt that responsibility keenly. But Katie knew my career was my life—the dream I'd worked toward since I'd been a poor-as-fuck kid in Texas squirreling away every penny I'd earned as a ranch hand to put toward my tuition as a down payment on a better, more stable future. Being a partner-track attorney at a firm like Dunlevy, Pace, and Trumble wasn't the sort of job where you could easily transfer your acquired skills and contacts to a new firm, either. If I had to find a new position, it would mean starting over from scratch, with a massive loss of money, seniority, and career security.

I didn't even want to contemplate it. Hard fucking *no*.

Which meant I had to make sure it didn't come to that... somehow.

I paused in the bedroom doorway to check on Lellie. She was still sleeping peacefully in the travel crib with her little arms flung out beside her head and her rounded cheeks pink from heat. I moved close and pulled the cotton blanket down until it was only covering her lower legs and feet.

The room smelled like sandalwood. Like Devon. I closed my eyes and indulged in a few deep inhales. Memories that were never truly far off cascaded behind my eyelids. The scent of his faded cologne as

I brushed my nose along his neck and behind his ear. The salty taste of the skin there. The sound of his deep voice as he encouraged me to *feel good, just like that.*

I shook my head and quickly grabbed the video baby monitor so I could go downstairs to the barn and get some distance from Dev's scent and his surroundings.

I was here to give this man custody of his daughter and to make sure that Lellie would be safe in his care. That was all—and after that conversation with Orris, that was going to be more than complicated enough—so it didn't matter how often I'd fantasized about doing much, much more to him these past two years.

Indigo was busy filling troughs in the nearest paddock with fresh water while listening to something on giant headphones. At some point, he'd managed to swap his flip-flops for mucking boots, but he'd stuffed his linen pants in the top of them, making them balloon out comically.

When he saw me, he jumped. "Whoa, dude. Warn a guy."

"Sorry. I was just stretching my legs and having a look around," I explained. "My name is Tully."

"Dope. Indigo. I'm here to help out with the horses for a bit. You, too?"

I reached out to offer my knuckles to a nearby gelding for a sniff. "No. Just here for a visit. Up from Texas. What about you?"

"I'm from Utah, originally, but I went to school in Colorado. Just graduated last week, so I'm probably heading back to Utah in a couple months to get, like, a real adult job," he said sadly. "When I thought about going back *now*, though, I was totally bummed. So I told myself, 'Nah, Indigo, you need a summer adventure.' But, like, also gotta make money, right?" He shrugged. "Mostly, I wanted an excuse to climb Three Daughters, so...here I am."

I hoped that wasn't as creepy as it sounded. "Three Daughters?"

He tilted his shaggy hair in the direction of a triple-peaked mountain vista in the distance. "Three Daughters. Killer climbing, bro. Big water, too, if you're into it. Mountain biking. All that. You know

AdventureSmash? They're holding their GrandSmash race here this summer."

I wasn't sure I spoke the same language as this guy, but he seemed friendly enough. "Sounds like fun."

"Oh, yeah. Gonna be lit," he agreed. "Some friends of mine are already heading up the mountain. Hope to connect with them again next week, maybe, but I needed the rest. Did a climb last weekend that was a total muscle-fuck. Totally flashed it, but fuck, man. *Intense.* You know?"

I definitely did not know, but I nodded anyway. "So, you're going to be able to wrangle the horses during roundup in a few days?"

His affable smile didn't dim. "Yeah, dude. Easy-peasy, lemon-squeezy. No stress, lemon zest. I've been playing polo forever, so like... how hard can it be?"

I imagined Dev's response to this attitude. Since it was possible his reaction would cause local law enforcement to show up, and since I definitely didn't want that sheriff turning up anytime soon with his proprietary attitude toward Dev, I decided to do a little proactive crisis management.

"Well, that depends," I told Indigo. "In order to separate herds, you need to understand herd dynamics. From what I know about the Fletcher Ranch, these are primarily trail horses used on dude ranches. They spend the winters here being taken care of, and then when the summer tourist season begins, they get sent in smaller batches to their respective ranches for the summer. That means those large herds you see in the pastures will need to be picked through to separate out each individual horse."

Indigo's smile had finally faded. "Why don't they just keep 'em organized all winter? Like the Johnson ranch horses live in this pasture and the Smith horses live in that one? Seems like it'd make it easier come summer."

I nodded. "It might. Except there are other reasons to separate them differently. Pregnant mares need special care. So they might get put together closer to the barn where Dev can keep an eye on them.

Older horses more sensitive to the winter weather might need to be kept in a pasture that's more protected from the wind. Certain animals might have special dietary needs, and keeping them together would make daily feeds easier."

My information about Fletcher Ranch had come from an internet search on the plane yesterday, but I'd done some additional research on my phone since hearing Dev describe his job as managing the ranch's breeding program.

"It's probable that many of the programs that lease horses from the ranch don't need specific horses as much as they need a specific *kind* of horse. Like ones trained for trail riding or ones trained for carrying packs. So at roundup, maybe Dev needs to pull ten trail riding horses of varying sizes for a particular dude ranch program, and then he needs to pull eight packhorses for a different program. And let's say all of those horses come out of a large herd in the same pasture. He needs to be able to separate out the right horses to load up in the trailers for those contracts."

Now there was actual concern on Indigo's face. "Whoa. But, like, can't I just clip a lead to each of their harnesses and walk them out?"

"Not when you need to divvy up a hundred horses in a day. But if you're comfortable in the saddle... do you ride western?"

"Yeah. Been riding since I was little. Only started polo in high school cause of this hot dude..." His cheeks turned pink, and I wondered if he knew he'd tripped and fallen into the gayest ranch in rural Wyoming. Lucky bastard.

"Uh-huh. Well, I suggest asking Dev or Way to take you out before roundup and show you how cutting works. Be honest with them about your abilities and tell them you're willing to do what it takes to be ready in time."

Indigo eyed me. "You seem to know a lot about this. You going to help, too?"

I shook my head. "I need to stay here and look after Lellie. The little girl you met earlier."

His face softened, and his smile returned. "Now, see, I'm much better at wrangling kids than horses. You should switch places with me and let me do the baby thing while you do the cowboy thing."

I wish, I thought and then immediately dismissed it.

I didn't actually *want* to be a ranch hand. Not ever again. Dev could side-eye my nice clothes and haircut, but those were the trappings of a life I'd built on my own terms and the way I told the world that Tully Bowman was worth something. I wouldn't trade that for all the muck boots and saddle leather in the world.

"One of us was hired for the cowboy thing," I reminded him with a grin. "And it wasn't me. But you'll do fine as long as you can get some practice in before the big day."

He inhaled through his nostrils. "Thanks, Tully. 'Preciate it."

A squawk from my pocket reminded me about the baby monitor. I pulled it out and saw Lellie waking up. After throwing a "Later!" over my shoulder, I bolted back up to the apartment to grab her before she tried climbing out of the crib herself.

She woke up cranky, whimpering, and wriggly. I did a quick diaper change and spared a moment to wonder at the vast turn my life had taken in the past week.

My clients at Dunlevy, Pace, and Trumble were wealthy power players with high expectations and limitless influence. I was invited to fundraisers and galas, high-stakes wealth-management discussions, and meetings about tax shelters for people who didn't think twice about purchasing a second yacht.

And here I was, trying not to get poop on me while crouched on a bed over a barn in nowhere Wyoming with a toddler who wasn't even mine and was every bit as moody as her father.

I felt the uncomfortable pinch in my chest as I remembered Orris's earlier words.

If it comes down to having to choose sides here, Tully, I expect you to choose the right one.

One of my law school professors had spent an entire lecture on various ethical dilemmas, all relating to the concept of conflict of interest. That professor loved to quote Camus. *A man without ethics is a wild beast loosed upon this world.*

It was clear that I was being pressured into a conflict of interest here, and my boss was unwilling to recognize it as such. That was wrong. Obviously, it was.

But it was one thing to defend Dev's right as Lellie's biological father to retain custody of her and another to defend his right to give her away to a stranger instead of allowing her to stay in her own family. Was *that* worth derailing my entire career?

I hadn't heard a single compelling reason why Dev was so hell-bent on refusing custody of Lellie himself. He was affectionate and sweet with her. He had a support system and a family-centered place to live. With Lellie's money, he'd be able to afford a proper house and plenty of childcare. So if he didn't care enough to try to keep her, should I really risk my job to help him keep her away from the Scotts?

I gathered Lellie up and nestled her against my chest, inhaling her sweet, clean scent as she babbled against my shoulder.

The answer should be simple, but like everything else in the past two days, it felt anything but.

Why didn't Dev want to keep his daughter?

And why did his rejection of her cut *me* so deeply?

TEN

DEV

After leaving Tully and Lellie, I made my way downstairs to saddle Trigger. The stoner was singing at full volume while mucking out stalls. A pair of large, expensive headphones covered his ears. Thankfully, the kid's distraction meant I could avoid an awkward conversation.

Once we got away from the barn and paddocks, I gave Trigger his head and let him tear across the open pastureland toward my home site. Even though it seemed weeks in the past, I'd been to the site as recently as yesterday morning, and I certainly didn't need to check on it now, but I craved being on my own land. There was something about it that centered me and made me feel more... myself.

When I crossed the invisible boundary between the Fletcher Ranch and mine, I skirted around the jobsite and made my way into the trees leading up the hill behind the house. I knew the builders were finishing the insulation and beginning to hang drywall, so there wasn't much to see from the outside, but just knowing I would soon have a home of my own always gave me a sense of happy relief. Of rightness and belonging.

I waited for that feeling to come over me now, but it didn't.

Instead, as I looked at the house, I felt... *lonely.*

I'd built the place with space in mind. Multiple large bedrooms, several large gathering areas, plenty of room for the brotherhood to come and visit without us tripping over each other. But how often would they come, really? And what would I do in that big house the rest of the time?

For a second, I let myself imagine having Lellie with me. Hearing her baby-babble to the horses as she had with Buttercup earlier. Showing her the wildflowers in the pasture. Teaching her to ride, when she was older. Taking her to Final Night and all the other town events—because obviously, I'd force myself to stop isolating so much, for her sake. Making sure she was safe and healthy. Giving her a home she could always, *always* come back to. Reminding her every day that she was loved unconditionally, no matter how bad she fucked up or how many choices she made that I didn't agree with.

But that wasn't right, either. That was about *me* wanting her with me, and as I'd told Tully repeatedly, me wanting her wasn't the issue and never had been. Lellie had already lost her mother. Was I really going to saddle her with a father who had no idea what he was doing and, as my parents liked to remind me, a really shitty track record when it came to taking care of his family?

It wasn't right to do that to an innocent child. I couldn't expect her to fulfill me when it was a parent's job to *give* rather than take.

I loved her too much to keep her.

The sun made its way through the trees in warm golden shafts as Trigger picked his way along the deer trail. Fat bees hummed nearby on golden lupine, purple bellflowers, and a patch of deep coral flowers that might have been Indian paintbrush.

There wasn't a question about whether I wanted to settle here in Majestic—I'd already made that choice. But inheriting Lellie and realizing I couldn't keep her was causing me to question myself in a way I hadn't before.

Something about this town had felt like home to me from the beginning, and having the easy friendships with Silas, Way, Foster, and their family gave me a support system that grounded me just like my brotherhood did, but in a more immediate way. And still... I'd held myself back. I'd insisted on solitude and distance. I'd clung to my privacy.

I needed to tell them the whole story about Lellie.

With roundup only a few days away, I'd have to find someone I trusted to help with her. Tully had agreed to watch her, but I couldn't rely on him. His life was back in Dallas, and I didn't want to keep him from it.

And part of me knew that the longer he stuck around, the more tempted I'd be by his presence.

After calling on the radio to confirm Silas was home, I turned Trigger around and headed for the Fletchers' farmhouse. Trigger was used to hanging out in the small fenced area next to Way and Silas's garage, and he immediately went to work picking at some weeds with his teeth.

I jogged up the steps to the ranch house and let myself in. "I'm here. Put your clothes on," I called, heading automatically to the large kitchen in the back, where I could hear the familiar rumble of Silas's laugh.

As soon as he saw me, Silas shoved a cold glass of lemonade in my hand and gestured for me to sit next to Way at the large kitchen island. Thankfully, both were fully dressed... which wasn't always a guaranteed thing.

Silas nodded toward a pile of ingredients and supplies on the counter. "I'm making a crumble with some blackberries Sheridan picked up at Final Night. Way decided to come home from work early to supervise me."

Way reached out and stole a fat berry from the basket. "Not true. I came home to check on Indigo and make sure he knew what to do since Dev was obviously busy with other things."

"Where the hell'd you find that guy again?" I asked before taking a sip of the lemonade. The cold, sweet tang was exactly what I'd needed after the dusty ride.

"University of Colorado at Boulder," Way said with a straight face. "He's in town this summer to take advantage of the outdoor adventure sport and wanted a place to crash."

"If I catch him smoking pot around the stock—"

Silas caught my eye. "He's vegan, for fuck's sake. I don't think he smokes."

My friend had obviously forgotten about two of our friends at Yale who'd made smoking pot and plant-based eating their entire personalities.

Way nodded. "He's a health nut with a college degree in education, and his references were pristine."

That was reassuring, but it wasn't why I'd come. I waved the topic of the new ranch hand away. "I need some help with Lellie during roundup."

Silas kept his intense gaze on me while he mixed the ingredients in his mixing bowl. "Uh-huh. You going to tell us how you ended up with a kid?"

Way looked back and forth between us. "I think you should get the guys on the phone before you have this conversation."

I shook my head. "I can't handle Landry right now, and Zane's busy with tour stuff."

Silas shot his husband a look, and Way immediately dialed his phone before propping it up so we could all see the screen. Within moments, Kenji's face appeared. "Silas, don't forget you have a call with Bash and Rowe in the morning to go over quarterly earn— *Oh*." He looked up and noticed me. "Hey, Dev. I'm scheduling a call with a family law specialist, but they're going to want to get copies of any paperwork you have. I need to know what your goal is."

It was his professional way of asking if I intended to pursue custody or not.

"I…" I began. "I can't keep her, but I can't let her grandparents have her either."

Silas raised an eyebrow. "Your parents are pushing for custody? Did *they* know about her?"

I shook my head. "I mean Katie's parents. They're awful, and they're challenging me for custody in Dallas. I just learned that they officially filed suit."

As usual, Silas's eyes were pinning me with the heat of a thousand suns, silently demanding explanations.

"I... helped out a friend a couple of years ago," I began. "A friend I grew up with. Remember me telling you about Katie? I owed her a favor—a big one—and she called it in. She wanted to become a mom but didn't want a relationship. I donated my sperm, but I made it clear I didn't want to have anything to do with any baby that resulted. I... I didn't even want to know if there *was* a baby. I asked Kenji to sort out some legal aspects, and I... I didn't let myself think about it after that."

"Until this week," Silas prompted.

"Yeah." I stopped and ran my fingers through my hair. Silas moved to the sink to wash the berry juice from his hands before coming over to stand near me while I continued.

"I guess Katie didn't have anyone else, and she trusted me to choose the right alternative," I said with a shrug. "Or... I don't know. Maybe she thought I'd change my mind."

Silas watched me for a long moment. "And have you?" he asked softly.

"No." I rubbed my face with both hands. "You know I can't. I'm a wreck, Silas! I can't bring a child into whatever the fuck my life is. I can't be trusted to keep her alive, and we all know it."

"Bullshit," Silas hissed. "If you're talking about your brother, you can stop that right now. Matt's death was *his* own fault, Dev, not yours. You didn't tell him to speed. You didn't tell him to drink before getting behind the wheel of that car. You didn't—"

I threw up my hands. "I bought a half-million-dollar sports car for an irresponsible kid. Who does that?" The words were a direct quote from my mother, and whenever I said them aloud, I heard them in her voice, complete with the heartbroken little crack on the word *does*. It would never go away. Like my shame and guilt, her words lived just under my skin like invisible tattoos. "It was my fault for giving him the temptation."

Kenji's soft sigh came through the phone. Way's eyebrows crinkled in concern. I could tell by his expression this situation wasn't news to him, which meant Silas had informed him at some point about the story of my brother's death.

"My point is," I continued, trying to shake off the pity party, "I can't take her. But I can't let the Scotts have her either. They're small-minded fearmongers who care more about status and their family reputation than they do about giving a child what she needs. I saw firsthand how they treated Katie, and I won't let them do that to Lellie." I took a deep breath. "I need to find a good family to raise her. Someone who wants a daughter and will take excellent care of her. Love her and..." My voice trailed off as emotions threatened to overwhelm me.

Silas's arm slid around my shoulders as he pulled me into a hug. "You'd be an amazing dad. No one would love her as much as you would."

Way stood and wrapped his arms around both of us. "And she's sure as shit not alone in the world. Not anymore. Not ever again. Neither of you are. We'll do whatever you need... no matter what you decide."

After a moment in which I simply allowed myself to receive their support, I pulled back and swallowed. "Right now, what I need is some help. First of all, roundup. I need someone we trust to watch her in case Tully can't stay. Way, do you think your aunt Blake would do it, or will she be too busy at the cafe?"

He laughed. "She'd drop anything to get that sweetheart in her arms. I'll call her as soon as we're done here and line it up. I'm sure Sheridan can cover her at the cafe. What else?"

"Kenji, I need you to find someone to start researching my legal options. Is there a way for me to decide who gets custody? Or if I don't keep her, does that mean the Scotts will automatically get preference?"

"On it," he said, already typing on his keyboard.

Silas and Way exchanged a look but didn't say anything out loud.

What did that look mean? Were they considering offering to take Lellie themselves? If so... how would I feel about that?

I knew Silas and Way were the real deal. They were passionately in love with each other and dedicated to Way's family and our friends. They would have tons of support, and Lellie would grow up here on the ranch surrounded by love and adventure. Any child of theirs would be incredibly lucky.

I couldn't deny that a sliver of unease curled through my gut at the idea of them raising her, though. Of having to give her up while still having her so close. Of trusting anyone else to raise her.

I'd have to get over that because I couldn't have it both ways, but I decided to let it be for now. That might not have been what their look was about, anyway. Deciding to raise a child wasn't something you did on a whim or with a silent look.

"I need to get back to her," I said. "But you'll ask Jo about watching Lellie?"

"Of course," Way agreed.

I let out a breath. "Thank you. All of you."

When I turned to leave, Silas reached for my arm to stop me. "Don't do anything rash," he blurted.

"Like what?"

"Like... give her up without talking to the rest of us. Let us help you through this, Dev. Don't make any important decisions in a vacuum. Okay?"

Maybe he did want her. Maybe he just needed time to discuss it with Way. If that was the case, it suddenly seemed like taking my time to consider things was a good idea. Not rushing such an important decision would be the prudent choice.

"Okay."

Silas let out a breath and gave me another hug before slapping my back and shoving me toward the door. "Go get your girl. And don't think I'm done asking you about that hottie who brought her."

Way sputtered. "Excuse me? Hottie? What the fuck?"

Silas waved his hand over his shoulder. "Not as hot as you, sweetheart. Obviously. I just mean there's obviously some kind of tension between Dev and his *attorney* friend... and I'd like to hear that story at some point."

"No story," I said, lying through my teeth.

Silas knew me all too well. "Sure, babe. And I'll believe you when you can say that without turning the color of an overripe tomato. Which, incidentally, is the same color Tully turned when I asked him about you."

I flipped him the bird as I headed out the door.

After riding back to the barn, I untacked Trigger and pampered him for a bit before turning him out for the night with the other personal stock. Someone had already filled hay nets and ensured there was clean water for everyone, which meant someone else must have taught Indigo how to do the afternoon feed.

Just when I was ready to head upstairs to the apartment, lecturing myself about the need to apologize to Tully for disappearing like I had, I heard Lellie's little giggle come from around the corner of the barn. I followed the sound and found her and Tully sitting in the grass with a pile of dandelions between them and several yellow blooms shoved in Tully's hair. He was making a funny face at her as he pretended to wonder what she was laughing about.

The sun shone down from a deep blue sky, and the gentle scent of horse, hay, and new plant growth floated on the warm breeze. I stood and watched them for a few moments before Lellie noticed me. Her entire face lit up, and she made a happy noise.

"Dah!"

ELEVEN

TULLY

The look on Dev's face when Lellie attempted to say his name could only be described as shock. I knew her well enough to know she was attempting to say "Dev" because she didn't know him as anything other than that, but the way she said it could definitely be interpreted as a toddler's attempt at saying "Dada."

I quickly tried to ease the tension. "That's right. Dev's here. Maybe Dev needs some flowers, too."

"Dah!" she said, grabbing a handful of flowers in her fat fist and standing up to approach him. By the time she reached Dev, the flowers were more of a yellow mash, but he received them as if they were the Crown Jewels.

"Thank you, sweetheart. What beautiful buttercups. Do you know these flowers have the same name as the horse you met yesterday? Her name is Buttercup, too."

She ran back and threw herself down with abandon. Dev followed, lowering himself carefully to the ground beside me. I tried not to appreciate the intoxicating combination of horse and clean sweat coming from him, but it was nearly impossible.

He began to tie the flowers together into a chain, narrating the process to Lellie, who pranced around us, babbling and pulling at random clumps of grass. When he finished the chain, Dev leaned over and lowered his voice. "I'm sorry I left earlier without asking you to watch her. It was rude and presumptuous."

I blinked at him in surprise. "Thank you."

"No, thank *you* for watching her for me. I was upset and didn't want to be around her while I was feeling that way." He hesitated. "Let's chalk that up to another reason I'm not exactly parent material."

I appreciated his gratitude, but his self-deprecation rubbed me the wrong way.

"What will you do when I'm gone?" Because if he decided to walk out every time he got upset around a toddler, he was going to spend a lot of time alone.

His hazel eyes met mine. "You leaving?"

My heart rate ticked up the way it always did when I was the sole recipient of his gaze. "No. Uh... I mean...Not right away. Not anytime soon."

Something in his face softened. "I'll have to stop behaving like an ass, I guess."

"Always a good strategy," I murmured, looking away in hopes of getting out of the damned tractor beams that wanted to lure me somewhere I had no business going.

The crunch of tires on gravel alerted us to a visitor. The SUV was emblazoned with law enforcement symbols and lettering, and sure enough, out stepped the tall fucker from the night before.

The sheriff came bearing gifts.

"What'd you just say?" Dev asked.

I blinked at him. "Me?"

"Yeah, sounded like you muttered, 'Fucking great.'"

My face heated. "Did I? I... I'm just embarrassed because my hair is full of flowers and dirt." I quickly brushed some of the flowers out of my hair to support the lie.

Dev's eyes narrowed. "Are you trying to impress him?"

I stopped and took a deep breath. "Please. Pretty sure that's your job, Dev. The man's not interested in a random lawyer from out of town."

"Says you."

"Says the guy who saw exactly how protective the asshole was of *you* last night," I hissed as the sheriff got closer.

"We're just friends," Dev said defensively.

"None of my business. And I hardly care," I shot back.

Wow. Apparently, it was true what they said about lawyers. They really did lie all the damned time.

The sheriff's grin was almost as big as his wingspan when he reached us. "Hey, Dev. I thought you might appreciate a home-cooked meal to celebrate the new addition, so to speak."

"You cooked?" I blurted.

His smile dimmed as his eyes flicked from Dev over to me. "Don't be ridiculous. I stopped at the cafe and picked up Dev's favorite."

Dev smiled. "You brought me your mom's Thai power bowl?"

The sheriff nodded. "And she threw in some penne pasta with marinara for the princess. Hope that's okay."

Dev took the large paper bag with reverence. "That's perfect. Thank you so much."

Awkward silence landed like a harsh bellyflop.

"So..." Foster gave me a cool-eyed stare that marked him as law enforcement as surely as the shiny badge and the holster at his waist. "I'm Foster Blake. And you are?"

Dev shook himself. "Sorry. Foster, this is Tully Bowman. Tully, Foster. He's the sheriff of Majestic."

As if that wasn't obvious.

Foster held out a giant hand to shake. For a split second, I wondered if I could get away with pretending I hadn't seen it, but I didn't want to cause trouble for Dev with his friends, so I shook the man's hand. And nearly felt my bones pop in his grip.

I gritted my teeth before pulling my injured hand back.

Dev sensed the tension. "And this is Lellie," he said, gesturing to where she was still denuding the general area of all things that came close to being classified as flowers.

Foster moved closer and crouched down near her. "Hi, baby. Are you picking flowers for your da—"

Dev and I both squawked out a sound to keep him from finishing that sentence. Foster glanced at us in surprise. "Ix-nay on the ad-day," I said without thinking.

Dev bit his lip and shifted from foot to foot. "It's just that I'm not... I don't know if I'm... We're not doing that right now."

Foster looked between me and Dev. "Oh-kay...?"

I walked over and picked Lellie up. "Why don't I take her and the food inside so the two of you can talk?"

Dev's forehead crinkled. "There's no need—"

"That'd be great," Foster said with a shallow smile, taking the paper bag from Dev and shoving it at me. "Thanks, man."

Lellie chattered unintelligibly while I carried her and the food inside the barn. I mentally mapped the apartment to determine which window might give me a view of their private conversation, but when I arrived in the apartment, I forced myself to stay away from *all* the windows lest I be tempted to turn into someone I could hardly respect.

But it galled me knowing Foster was out there asking Dev about Lellie. About Katie.

About me.

I sat Lellie and the food on the kitchen counter before pulling the flowers from her fists and collecting them in a little pile I promised to preserve. Then, I moved her to the sink to wash her hands.

I was so surprised by the sound of Dev entering the apartment a minute later I nearly sprayed water everywhere.

He seemed to be alone.

I cleared my throat. "Did your *friend* leave already?"

Dev shook his head and moved around the kitchen island to wash his hands, too. "I invited him to join us for dinner. He's just running up to the big house first to talk to Way about work stuff."

"Oh. Well. I guess I could head into town and grab dinner myself to give you two a chance to..."

Dev glanced up with a frown. "There's plenty of food. Why would you leave? Unless you don't want to be here?"

"No, I... I just assumed that you and the sheriff would want some privacy."

The divot between his eyebrows deepened. "Why?" Suddenly, his forehead smoothed. "Ahh, you think there's something there. Between me and Foster."

"I don't think it, I know it," I said without thinking. "Which is fine. Obviously. I'll make myself scarce."

Dev stepped closer until our hips brushed together. "I'd rather you stayed." His voice was low and made my muscles feel warm and loose. "I told you, Foster and I are just friends."

"I think you're being naive."

He laughed softly under his breath. "I didn't say we didn't give it a try. His mother keeps trying to push us together. But—"

"What do you mean by give it a try?" I blurted before snapping my mouth closed and wishing I could cut out my own tongue.

Dev turned and studied me. "We ended up out late together. Drinking. I asked him back to the ranch. He asked if it would be better than the last guy I was with. And the answer to that was an unequivocal no. Nothing could possibly be better than the last guy I was with. So Foster and I decided we were better off as friends."

My heartbeat could have rivaled a wild stallion's. Who'd he hook up with last? "Oh," I said, doing my best not to look interested. The heat of his stare stood all of my body hair on end. "Must have really been something."

His hand moved to my hip as if nudging me aside so he could reach the kitchen towel, but instead of pushing me away, he pulled me closer. Dev's face was close enough for me to see the honey-brown striations in the green of his eyes.

"It was definitely something," he murmured, eyes lowering to my lips. "I wasn't allowed to come. Never done that with someone before. Can't imagine what it would be like if I got to do it all over again. I sure as shit wouldn't hold back like I did the last time."

Before I could fully process what he was saying, Foster let himself into the apartment, and I jumped away.

Dev's words echoed in my head and in my gut the entire time Foster was there. Dev hadn't been able to come when the two of *us* were together. I'd learned later, of course, that he'd had to save himself for the visit to Katie's clinic the following day. If he'd never done that before his last hookup, that meant... that meant *I'd* been his last hookup. How was that possible? We'd had one night together two years ago.

Two years.

He hadn't been with another man in two years? Why?

Could it have something to do with what he'd admitted to Foster the night they'd almost given it a try? That none of the opportunities he'd had since would compare?

Surely not.

My stomach tightened with need as I watched him. While I'd had plenty of hookups in the past two years, Devon McKay had been the gold standard since that night. It was true nothing I'd done since then had come close to the one night I'd had with him.

Now, as I watched him with Foster, I tried to see their relationship as just an affectionate and trusting friendship, but it was hard to see Foster's protectiveness and possessiveness as the behavior of someone who only regarded Dev as a friend. Surely, Foster wanted more.

Who wouldn't?

"Dev tells me you're from Dallas," Foster said, jerking my attention out of the clouds.

I was sitting on the sofa enjoying a cold glass of white wine while Foster sat on the floor with Lellie and a few empty Tupperware containers and a wooden spoon. He was alternating between pretend cooking and pretend drum playing.

I tried to focus on being polite. "Yes. I grew up halfway between Fort Worth and Abilene. Little town called Gordon."

Foster's eyebrows lifted. "And you ended up practicing law at a fancy firm in Dallas. Must have busted your ass to make that happen."

While I wanted to interpret his comment as snide, I chose instead to give him the benefit of the doubt. "I did. What about you? You from here?"

He nodded. "Born and raised. My mom owns a cafe called the Love Muffin. Way's sister and her husband work there, too. I basically grew up in the center of the town's gossip mill."

Dev chuckled as he lowered himself to the floor near Lellie and handed her several plastic bottle caps he'd rescued from his recycling bin and washed in the sink. Her face lit up as she dropped them one by one into one of the Tupperware containers and began to stir with the spoon.

Dev spoke without looking up from Lellie's play. "Foster's mom is definitely the hub of gossip in town and the local matchmaker. You'll meet her on Friday. I think she's going to help out with Lellie."

Foster grinned at me. "If you're not careful, she'll set you up. Expect her to ask you all your preferences as soon as you meet her."

He kept his eyes on me as if waiting for me to add to the conversation by going ahead and informing him of my preferences.

I didn't.

Dev cleared his throat. "Tully's not here for that."

Foster glanced at me with dancing eyes that seemed to see right through me. "That right? You sure?"

I stood. "Anyone ready for a refill?"

Foster's low laugh made me smile, but I'd be damned if I'd let him catch it. Instead, I headed to the fridge and leaned my head into the cool space to give my hot cheeks a break. Dev's murmured warning for Foster to "lay off" was answered with another low laugh.

"This the guy?" he asked.

I didn't hear a response. Instead, I imagined Dev shooting him a glare in hopes of silencing the teasing.

As I grabbed the wine and returned to the living area, I tried to remind myself that I was here for Lellie. I was not here for any reason connected to my dick. And even if I was, Dev himself had said I wasn't here for that. He obviously had plenty on his mind right now without a one-night stand—even a best-ever one-night stand—showing back up in his life begging for a second, third, and possibly fortieth night.

The rest of the evening was fine. Foster talked about the challenges he faced in organizing law enforcement coverage for the influx of tourists in the summer season and how the needs would be much greater considering the large adventure races Majestic was hosting.

While listening to them talk about the town and its people and events, I learned a great deal about the place Dev had decided to call home. I could see the appeal. Unlike in the small town I'd grown up in, the townsfolk here in Majestic seemed open-minded and eager for new opportunities. It sounded like a charming small town, which I had to admit could make it a good place to raise Lellie.

If only Dev wanted her.

As the evening wore on, I couldn't help but notice what a natural Dev was in caring for his daughter. He was gentle and attentive. Even though he didn't know much about babies, his affection for her was obvious. And he couldn't take his eyes off her. At first, I'd thought it was out of concern for her safety. And there was that, for sure. But he also watched her with a sweet kind of fascination. I caught him smiling tenderly at her when she tried and failed to balance a piece of pasta on her spoon all the way to her mouth and grinning like a fool when she stacked three containers in a row without them falling over.

He was fucking adorable with her... and it was winding me up in unexpected ways.

First and foremost, I still couldn't understand why he didn't want to keep her. He'd said he wasn't what was best for her, and then he'd implied he had trouble controlling his temper. Or... well, that wasn't actually what he'd said. He'd said he hadn't wanted to be around her when he was *upset*.

Was he seriously implying a parent couldn't be upset around their children?

"Foster," I said, remembering a story from earlier in the evening about the age difference between the sheriff and his little sister. "When you were a teenager and Anna was younger, did you ever get upset around her?"

He looked at me like I was cognitively impaired. "Uh... is this a trick question? Of course I did."

I glanced at Dev before looking back at Foster. "You don't think being upset around little kids can be detrimental?"

Foster looked between Dev and me as if searching for the catch. "I guess it depends on what you mean by upset. Are you talking about abuse?"

"No. I just mean being disappointed or angry. Losing your temper when they're in the vicinity."

"That's... standard fare for a teenage boy, isn't it?" He scratched the back of his neck. "At least for me. One of the reasons I wanted to be a cop was because injustice got under my skin so badly. Still does, obviously. I remember one time I learned a few kids in Anna's class had stolen her new snow boots. I wanted to beat the shit out of them."

"Did you take it out on Anna?"

"Of course not," he said at the same time Dev said, "Tully, what the fuck?"

I waved my hand in the air. "So you're saying that it's natural. It's not detrimental to be your regular self around a little kid, even if that means ups and downs in your mood."

Foster seemed to understand there was subtext here. "I would say it's necessary. How else do you model proper self-control to your kids? If they never see you upset, they'll think it's not natural to get upset. And if they don't see how you handle it, they—"

Dev stood up and lifted Lellie off the ground. I could tell he knew exactly what I was doing, and he wasn't happy about it. "Sorry to cut your visit short, Foster. It's time to get this girl in bed."

Foster's easy grin was the exact opposite of the tension I felt. "Yeah, no worries. Thanks for including me tonight. I had a good time getting to know this little one." He cupped the back of Lellie's head and leaned forward to press a soft kiss to her forehead. "Lellie-girl, will you let me come visit again sometime?"

She leaned her head against Dev's neck and peeked at Foster with a shy glance before giving him a smile. Foster beamed at her.

I couldn't help but realize he would make a good dad, too. In fact, the two of them would be a dream come true for Lellie.

I didn't realize I was holding my hands in fists until I felt the bite of fingernails in the tender skin of my palms.

"Nice to meet you, Tully," he said to me before clapping me on the shoulder.

I hoped I managed to mumble something polite in reply.

After he left, Dev muttered something about giving Lellie a bath and disappeared into the bedroom. I busied myself by cleaning up both the makeshift toys and the remains of dinner. It wasn't until Dev never reappeared that I wondered if he was avoiding me.

I finally peeked in to see him dead asleep, curled up next to Lellie, who was also out like a light. Three picture books were spread out around them as if Dev had fallen asleep mid-story. Dev had changed into a soft T-shirt and baggy knit shorts, and the sight of his long muscular legs stopped my breath.

My hands remembered the feel of those muscles, of rough hair against soft skin. Of the contours, the curve of his inner thighs.

My tongue remembered, too.

I stood there staring at him, drinking in every inch of him since he was safely tucked away from my hungry attention in the escape of sleep.

He was the sexiest man I'd ever known. Even Katie had called him sexy. One night, we'd been out to dinner at an Italian place after work, and she'd pointed out a man across the restaurant.

"That guy looks like my friend Dev," she'd said only a couple of months after the night of her party and my hookup.

My eyes had raced across the space in hopes of seeing her elusive friend. When they'd landed on the man she referred to, I realized it wasn't actually Dev, just a guy with the same dark hair and similar hazel eyes. "Not even close," I'd said without thinking.

Her bubbly laugh had indicated her delight at my response. "Dev's gorgeous as hell. I'd set you up with him if I thought he'd ever make his way back here. But I think..." She'd stopped and rubbed her barely there pregnancy belly with a wistful smile. "I think he's not going to have much reason to come around anymore, now that the fertility stuff is done."

I'd knocked over my wineglass, which had then spilled into her purse. She'd jumped up, tipping the table and knocking several pieces of flatware onto the floor in a noisy clatter.

Once we'd finally gotten everything cleaned up with the help of a nearby server, I'd fixed her with a stare. "Dev is your baby's father? *Dev* is?"

"Yes? Why do you look so freaked-out by this?" she'd demanded. "Is it because I wouldn't take your advice about putting a legal agreement in place? I told you I was asking an old friend to donate, and we don't need—"

"You didn't tell me *which* old friend," I'd groaned. Finally, I'd confessed, "I... I slept with him. With Dev. The night of your party. We hooked up."

Her eyes had gone wide as she'd leaned across the table. "Oh, my god! Really? That's excellent! But... wait, I thought he wasn't supposed to, you know, engage in those kind of activities right before the donation—"

"He didn't," I'd blurted. "*He* didn't."

She'd lifted a perfectly shaped eyebrow at me before laughing out loud. "Did you?"

When I'd answered with a comically manic nodding of the head, she'd laughed even harder and asked me to spill the details. I hadn't been able to stop myself from gushing about how we'd started talking out back on her patio, how we'd spent hours teasing and flirting, and how I'd begged him to sneak back to my place.

When she'd looked a little concerned by my enthusiasm, I'd forced myself to backpedal and play it off as nothing more than a hookup... and I'd been glad I had when she'd explained Dev wasn't interested in commitment. It was probably better she didn't know I'd also begged him to let me see him again, to give me his contact information, to at least admit that a connection like ours didn't come around often.

It was definitely better that she hadn't known how many nights I'd spent wondering why he'd been so reluctant and simply mumbled that he had to go.

Now, I was beginning to connect his reluctance to claim Lellie— or any child of his—with the reason he'd been so quick to bolt and never return.

I just didn't understand *why*.

I knew plenty of men who never wanted to become parents. Hell, I knew plenty of women who felt that way, too. But if your own child was placed into your arms and was as lovable as Lellie was... wouldn't that change things?

As I watched the two of them sleep, I realized he'd done me a favor by walking away after that night.

Because I wasn't so sure I wanted to have a relationship with someone who could reject Lellie.

In fact, watching her sweet face relaxed in sleep with a chubby fist wrapped around her little stuffed horse's mane made me start to wonder.

If Dev didn't want this precious girl... maybe I did.

And maybe I'd decide to fight him for her.

TWELVE
DEV

The next few days passed in a blur.

Ever since the night Foster had come over, Tully had been acting strangely. At first, I'd wondered if maybe Tully had developed an interest in the sheriff, but then we'd gone to the cafe for lunch, and Tully had completely brushed off Foster's friendly greeting.

I'd tried to talk to Tully about it, but he'd brushed me off, too. In fact, he'd treated me like a necessary article of clothing or piece of furniture, seeming entirely neutral about my presence. There'd only been a few times when I'd thought maybe I was wrong—that maybe he was affected by me, but he was just damned good at hiding it—but I hadn't been sure.

We'd been civil with one another for the most part—discussing his job and my horse breeding program, sharing stories about Katie, even chatting about the weather. But the only times he'd really seemed like himself were when he was with Lellie and when he was on his laptop, catching up on work.

I'd wondered if he was itching to get back to the office, but when I asked him about that, he'd assured me his job was to stay right here in Majestic to assist in Lellie's transition, but I hadn't felt assured.

His strange behavior was like a burr under my skin, making me feel on edge and stressed.

But that was far from the only thing stressing me out. I also couldn't find good parents for Lellie.

I'd gotten up the courage to approach Silas about it, and he'd very quickly disabused me of the notion that he and Way had been considering it.

"No offense, Dev, but we have our hands full as it is with the ranch, Way's job in town, and my consulting work. It's not that we don't want kids, exactly… I'm just not sure we're ready for them anytime soon."

He'd eyed me with that intense stare before adding, "Besides, I'm pretty sure you already know who the best parent is for her. You're just too damned stubborn to see it."

I'd walked away. Silas was wrong. While I was definitely falling head over heels in love with Lellie—who wouldn't?—I also knew I wasn't the best parent for her.

Meanwhile, Silas wasn't the only one giving me hell about it. Jo Blake had heard all about the situation from Foster and had decided to donate her own two cents to the cause.

"You don't need a man," she said as she held the door open to the kids' resale shop she'd insisted on taking me to. Roundup was almost here, and I'd taken Lellie to town to find some sturdier shoes than the more fashionable ones Katie had seemed to prefer. After finding the right pair at Lake Sports, I'd stopped by the cafe for a muffin and some juice before we tackled the grocery store.

That's when Jo had lit up and insisted on taking her "favorite girl" shopping.

"Correct," I said, leading Lellie over the threshold by the hand. She was in an anti-stroller mood, so I'd decided not to fight it. "I'm glad you finally realize that and will stop pushing me at Foster."

Jo waved her hand. "Oh, I still have hopes in that direction, don't you worry. I'm just saying you don't need a co-parent to commit to keeping Lellie. We'll all help you."

She led me over to a rack of clothes in Lellie's size. "I'm thinking she needs a cowgirl getup."

"She has more clothes than Zendaya."

"Are any of them roundup-themed?" she asked with a sniff.

I pinched the bridge of my nose and inhaled. The industrial scent of laundry detergent and sanitized toys tickled my nostrils. "I'm not going to fight you on this as long as you help me get a few bath toys. Tully keeps giving her my measuring cups and spoons, which is not great when it comes time to make coffee in the morning."

She eyed me. "Foster told me about him, too."

"Tully?" My voice had a strange, squeaky tone, so I corrected it. "Tully?"

"Mm. Seems like there's a story there."

I ignored her prompt and instead led Lellie to the toy section, where her entire face lit up at the brightly colored plastic haven.

Jo followed me over, clutching a pleather outfit with fringe that I didn't want to look too closely at. "She needs that octopus," Jo said. "And the little table and chairs."

"I don't have room for a table and chairs," I explained.

"You will at the new house. We should go ahead and get it. Store it in the barn."

I tried to keep calm. "Jo, I already told you. I'm not keeping her. I'm hoping to find a good family and—"

"Pish. Don't be ridiculous. I can see how you are with her, and Sheridan couldn't stop talking about how excited she was that her little peanut will have a built-in friend right out of the gate."

"She's like ten minutes pregnant," I muttered. "They'd be at least two years apart in age."

"And when the house is ready, we'll decorate a big-girl room all for her. Maybe giraffes and other safari animals. I saw a fantastic Pinterest board when I was looking for nursery ideas for Sheridan."

I let her continue to babble about what a wonderful, albeit fictional, life my daughter would have here in Majestic. The conversation made my stomach hurt because it *did* sound wonderful. She made it seem like the perfect life for Lellie and me.

But she was leaving out the imperfect parts. The painful parts. The inevitable moment where I'd make a critically poor decision that would lead to disaster. I had a proven track record, and I was sick and fucking tired of people thinking they knew better than I did.

"Can we move on from this topic, please?" I finally asked. "Do you think we should get her a sun hat for when you bring her outside during roundup?"

I didn't expect them out in the far pastures, but I knew Jo would want to bring Lellie outside to watch the horses being loaded into trailers near the barn.

Jo's face lit up. "I'm on it. I saw one back by the dresses that would be just the thing."

As she turned to make her way back toward the front of the store, I let out a breath and returned my attention to Lellie.

One of her dark curls was sticking out at a funny angle from the way she'd slept. Even though I'd tried to wet it down and fix it, it still stuck out and up. I didn't know how to do hair without making Lellie scream bloody murder. There was probably some trick to it that Katie had learned from her own mother. But my mother wasn't about to show up here and teach me how to raise a daughter.

I glanced back to see Jo chatting happily with a man near the checkout counter. She would teach me anything I needed to know about raising a daughter. I knew she would. But it wouldn't be the same.

There'd been times since my brother's death when I'd felt inside out with grief. More recently, it had faded into a duller pain but one that was still achingly persistent. It was at times like this that the dull pain turned sour. I missed things I'd never even had. Parenting advice from my mother was an unexpected one.

The sour feeling in my stomach persisted throughout the day, even though I tried my best to ignore it and enjoy the mother figure I did have. Jo spoiled us, taking us to the little shop that sold handcrafted granola and trail mix and treating Lellie to a cookie while she got a much-needed coffee for herself and me.

"You know," she whispered once we'd settled at an outdoor table in front of the shop. "Brady Kurt is gay."

It took me a minute to recall the name of the friendly man who'd sold us the treats. I lifted an eyebrow at her. "Is he? I would have given him the secret handshake had I known."

She waved her hand dismissively. "I just mean if you and Foster aren't going to give it a try, maybe you could ask Brady out. He's good with kids, too. He helps out with his niece and nephew."

"Are you trying to find me a babysitter or a husband? I'm a little unclear at this point."

Jo held Lellie on her lap as Lellie shoved pieces of the cookie in her mouth. Crumbs covered both of them, but Jo didn't seem to notice or mind.

"And I happen to know he's single. Apparently, he was seeing a guy up in Billings, but the drive was too much for both of them."

I savored a sip of the coffee before replying. "I seem to recall earlier today, you told me I didn't need a man. What happened in the last half hour to change your mind?"

Sometimes Jo reminded me of Silas. She had a way of looking right into your soul as if determining your eternal fate. "I don't think you were meant to be such a loner. I think you hold yourself apart when what you really want is to love and be loved. And this little girl needs your love, Devon McKay. So whatever you have going on up in that head of yours... well, you need to get over it. And I happen to know from experience that parenting is much easier when it's done with a partner."

Her reference to her ex surprised me. She rarely spoke of him. All I knew about Foster's dad was that he'd left Jo when Foster was eleven and Anna was still in diapers. His leaving had shaped Foster's protective tendencies and had led to Jo's fierce independence.

It was unusual for her to imply she'd lost something good and decent when he'd left.

I couldn't help but let out a soft laugh. Jo looked up in surprise from where she'd brushed off some of the crumbs. "You're laughing?"

"Yes. Because you're making my point for me. Parenting is easier with a partner. I don't have a partner. Therefore, maybe Lellie would be better off in a two-parent household." Not that my reasons were related to my single status.

Jo scowled. "Is that what her mother would have said?"

I sighed. "I don't want to argue with you. I just want you to respect that I know what's best for Lellie."

Her scowl turned into a knowing grin. "Ah. Just like a true parent."

I closed my eyes and inhaled. Was I sure I missed having the "well-meaning" advice of a parent?

———

Later that evening, Tully's recent distraction and distance resolved into a bizarre passive-aggression that took me by surprise.

"Thanks," I said after Tully lifted Lellie out of her seat at the dinner table and offered to take her to see the horses before bedtime.

"Might be a good chance for you to make some decisions," he said.

I glanced at him. "Decisions?"

We'd spent some time discussing my breeding program earlier in the meal, so it took me a minute to realize he wasn't asking me about equine bloodlines.

He looked pointedly at Lellie before flaring his nostrils at me. "Unless you plan to keep her in flux indefinitely."

"If you're referring to her guardianship," I said. "I'm working on it. Finding a good family for a child isn't exactly the same thing as asking someone to water your houseplants."

He grunted and walked out, leaving me staring after him in surprise and annoyance.

Everyone seemed to have an opinion about my custody situation, but Tully's unreadable reaction got my back up in a way no one else's did.

Did he agree with me that she'd be better off with someone else? It had seemed like he'd originally encouraged me to keep her, though maybe it had only come from supporting Katie's decision. Had he changed his mind? And if so, was it because he'd been around me for a few days? Did he see something in me that indicated I wouldn't be a good parent?

Why did it matter if *he* believed it when *I* already knew it to be the truth?

I forced myself to clean up our dishes and tidy up the apartment before preparing Lellie's bedtime routine and setting out her pajamas. The tiny cotton tee and shorts set smelled like my laundry detergent now since she had very strong opinions about which pajamas she wanted to wear each night. For some reason, pulling her little clothes out of my laundry basket had stopped me in my tracks earlier this afternoon.

What if her adoptive parents didn't let her wear her elephant pajamas whenever she wanted? What if they insisted on her wearing girly stuff when she wanted to wear something else?

Questions like this were constantly floating around in my mind, keeping me from deep sleep and messing with my head.

Anxiety was my new normal now.

Kenji had scheduled a conference call with my attorneys, including the Texas lawyer Tully had recommended, but there wasn't much they could do until I was officially served with papers about the custody petition. When I questioned why that hadn't happened yet—an associate from the same legal firm was sleeping on my sofa, so the Scotts' attorneys must know where to find me—the lawyers had explained that there would be an "ethical wall" preventing Tully from sharing information with other attorneys at the firm.

I simply had to hope that Tully's ethical wall was sturdy enough to buy me the time I needed to find a good solution for Lellie.

I'd briefly considered asking one of my polo player friends from New York if he and his wife would be interested in adopting her. They'd talked about starting a family by adopting a child rather than pursuing a pregnancy, so I'd thought of them right away. But then I'd remembered some of their casual comments about forcing their children to play polo "whether they liked it or not." The other people in the conversation agreed and said that pushing your kids into extracurricular activities was the only way to guarantee them a good future at a good school. The whole conversation had seemed pretentious and stifling.

That wasn't what I wanted for Lellie, and I knew it wasn't what Katie would have wanted, either.

But if I intended to micromanage the kind of upbringing Lellie would have, it would make finding the perfect parents even more impossible than it already seemed.

It had been less than a week, and I already felt like giving up. Not only had I racked my brain to come up with people, but I'd also asked the brotherhood to do the same. Zane had mentioned a gay couple he knew in Atlanta who might be a good option, but as soon as he'd opened his mouth to tell me more about them, Kenji had abruptly ended the video call.

The sound of tires on gravel filtered through the open window. I looked out to see Foster's SUV. Instead of waiting for him to come up, I made my way downstairs and met him out front of the barn.

"Hey," I said with a smile. His visit would be a good distraction from my stormy mood.

His usual wide smile was noticeably absent. "Unfortunately, I'm here on official business. I need to serve you papers." He held out an envelope. "The request came into my department a little while ago. I thought I'd bring it out myself instead of sending a deputy."

Tully came around the side of the barn with Lellie in hand. He seemed to realize what was happening sooner than I did.

I glanced over at him. "Did you know this was coming?"

"I told you they'd filed suit." His voice carried a tone of defensiveness, but I could hardly blame him.

He was right. He'd warned me. But holding the actual notice made it very real.

I opened the envelope and pulled out several documents. The official petition for guardianship was there, as well as several other documents requesting information.

I bit out a curse under my breath and handed the papers to Tully before leaning down to pick up Lellie. "Did you visit Trigger today?" I asked, shifting her onto my hip.

As I walked toward the paddock to take comfort in my horse, I heard Tully speak in a low voice to Foster.

"This is going to be a hell of a battle, especially if Dev's not firmly committed. I wonder if he'll decide to let them have her," Tully said.

"Like hell he will," Foster snapped back. "He said the grandparents weren't a good choice."

"They're not ideal, but they're family. They'll take care of her and make sure she never lacks for anything. They'll love her."

I ground my teeth together and forced myself not to shout at him over my shoulder.

Foster's low voice was barely intelligible. "Not like he will."

I closed my eyes and inhaled the familiar, soothing scents of horse and hay. Lellie's hand had snuck into my hair and clasped a hank in her fist.

Foster was right. I was beginning to realize that no one but Katie could possibly love this precious baby as much as I could.

Because I was falling for her faster than I would have believed.

And giving her up was going to be damned near impossible.

As I greeted Trigger and guided Lellie to feed him some peppermints, I couldn't help but simmer with anger toward Tully. It was obvious, now that he was ready to take Lellie out of my hands, that he was no longer on my side—if he ever really had been—which meant his fucking "ethical wall" was probably thin as tissue.

The idea that he'd prefer for the Scotts to take her made my blood boil.

After giving Trigger a few final pats, I took Lellie upstairs and got her ready for bed. I heard Tully moving around the apartment, but I ignored him and focused on my daughter.

When she was finally asleep in her portable crib and I couldn't avoid returning to the main room to grab a cold glass of water, I saw Tully at the kitchen table with his laptop and the stack of legal documents Foster had brought.

"Guess someone gave the enemy my address," I muttered under my breath.

Tully turned to me and narrowed his eyes. "Guess someone has his mail delivered to this address," he snapped back. "I found you easily enough. It's no surprise the Scotts' attorney did, too."

"If you think the Scotts are the right choice for Lellie, then I'd like you to leave," I said flatly. "Lellie is currently legally my child, and you have no right to work for her fucking grandparents to change that."

He stood up and stepped closer. I tried not to notice the bare feet sticking out of his worn blue jeans or the fact that the Wyoming sun had turned his forearms and hands a honey gold in the few days we'd spent time outside with Lellie. "I'm not working with the Scotts," he hissed. "In fact, I've put my job on the line by refusing to help them, so you can fuck right off with your accusations."

I was in no mood to be appreciative, or even rational, for that matter.

"I heard what you said to Foster, so it's clear you think she'd be better off with them than me."

Tully stepped closer and poked a finger into the center of my chest. "What I *think* is that you are willfully fucking ignorant." *Poke.* "What I *think* is that I've tried everything to convince you to keep your daughter, and you're the one who insists you're a bad bet, not me." *Poke.* "What I *think* is that you'd be as good a parent to her as

Katie would have been. But you know what's more important than any of that bullshit? A good parent actually wants their child."

He met my eyes with heat and thunder rolling heavy and unpredictably. "So you're right, Dev. That makes you a shitty fucking choice."

I grabbed his wrist to stop him from poking me again. His skin was warm, and the faint prickle of body hair against my palm reminded me of the most sensual night of my life.

"Don't you realize how much this is fucking killing me?" I asked, hearing way more anguish in my tone than I'd hoped.

Tully's face softened. I still held his wrist in my hand, and his body was close enough for me to feel his warm exhales on my cheek.

"You say that what you want isn't important. I say it's the most important thing of all." His gaze held mine. "So what do you want, Dev?" he breathed.

You. Lellie. All of it.

The dream.

I gritted my teeth. Those words, however truthful, would never pass my lips. Instead, I chose a different truth.

"Know what I want?" I growled to keep my voice from breaking. "You on your fucking knees, choking on my cock. Maybe then I could escape this fucking pressure for ten goddamned minutes."

Our eyes locked as the shock of my words fell heavily around us. His nostrils flared, and the hand of the arm I held curled into a fist.

But instead of fighting me, instead of pulling away and telling me to fuck off, Tully Bowman dropped to his fucking knees.

THIRTEEN

TULLY

I was a slut for him.

I'd been a slut for him for two years now, though I wouldn't have put it into those words.

But hearing him throw his anger at me in an uncontrolled mess of accusations and knowing it did absolutely nothing to diminish how badly I wanted him made the truth quite clear.

It took laughably little to make me get on my knees for Devon McKay.

I never took my eyes off his as I lowered to the floor. "This what you want?"

A dare. A challenge. I wouldn't be the one to blame for this ill-advised detour between us.

His eyes searched mine before his chin dipped.

"Say it," I ground out, moving my hands to his hips and tucking my fingertips under his waistband just so I could feel the bare-skin warmth of him. "Say the words, Dev. Tell me again *exactly* what you want right now."

"Please," he breathed. "Suck my cock."

As I moved my hands to his belt, he took a breath and added, "Remember, you owe me."

The words should have stung. They should have hit me like an offensive gauntlet, an unfair quid pro quo from our first night together. But they didn't. We both knew his completion had been a very long time coming.

I owed him because I *wanted* to give it to him. I'd spent two long years wondering what he would have looked like if I'd made him lose control.

My fingers made quick work of his buckle. Dev's long fingers threaded into my hair. "Seeing you on your knees for me is going to make me come before you even see my dick," he murmured.

I would get on my knees for you any day of the week.

I remained silent, opening his jeans and reaching inside to free the bulge behind the layers of cotton. His cock was long and uncut. The masculine scent of him already filled my nose, but I inhaled hungrily anyway. There would never be enough of Devon McKay to satisfy me. I knew this was my only shot at getting my hands and mouth on him. As prickly as he'd been all week, there was no telling how he would respond to me after this.

And I wasn't about to lose my shot.

I rubbed my face against the warm, silky skin of his shaft before tasting the salty tip. A low rumble of approval vibrated through him.

His fingers tightened in my hair. "That's it."

I took the head of his cock into my mouth and sucked gently, wrapping my tongue around him. I wanted to drive him absolutely crazy, edge the fuck out of him until he finally admitted just how badly he wanted me.

Not an orgasm. Not stress relief.

Me.

My tongue wanted every inch of him, to learn and own.

To possess.

"So good," he murmured. "So fucking good. Just like that. Just like that, Tully."

The sound of my name in his deep voice went straight to my dick. I reached down to adjust myself before moving my hand back up to grasp his balls. I used my other hand to work his pants down lower, but he quickly took over and shoved them down around his knees.

Dev's muscular thighs begged for my hands. I wanted all of it. This quick blowjob in the kitchen would never be enough.

I moved my hands around to squeeze his ass cheeks and pull them apart. His groan gave me enough confidence to seek out his hole with a finger and tease the rim a little—not enough to actually penetrate, but enough to make him wonder if I would.

"Fuck," he gritted out, his hands tightening even more in my hair. "Driving me fucking crazy. Take it."

His hips pushed forward, sending his cock to the back of my throat. I gagged and pulled off before surging forward again to swallow him. This time, I was prepared. I relaxed as best I could so he could feel my throat. The resulting deep moan made it worth it.

He was losing control. The Dev I was coming to know would never admit to needing anything, would never admit to being at someone else's mercy. Even the night we'd hooked up had happened according to his strict rules. He'd orchestrated how far and fast we went, who'd gotten off and who hadn't.

Tonight was different. We were playing by *my* rules. He would climax when I wanted him to, as often as I wanted him to.

"Gonna make me come," he said.

I immediately pulled off to catch my breath and wipe my mouth with the collar of my T-shirt before yanking it off and dropping it on the ground. Dev made a surprised, disgruntled sound before trying to pull me back onto his cock.

I glanced up at him. Instead of doing what he wanted, I opened my pants to give some relief to my own erection. "In a hurry?"

His eyes were dark and commanding. "Yes."

"I mean to make you beg," I admitted.

"I've waited a long time to feel your mouth around my cock."

I was going to come right there on the floor. "That right?" My voice didn't sound very steady. I swallowed and tried again. "You sure you don't want something else around your cock?"

What the fuck was I doing? I decided I didn't care.

His eyes darkened even more until it became hard for me to swallow. His hand moved from my hair down to my face to clasp my chin. His touch was deceptively tender, and his words were the same.

"That what you want, Tully?"

I closed my eyes as desire swept over me. My head felt like it was a billion tiny bits of dandelion fluff all trying to pretend to be something solid and capable.

"I want you," I admitted softly. "So fucking badly. However you want me. However you need."

He leaned down and kissed me, gentle at first. But then he pressed harder, and the kiss became more desperate, hungry. I lost my breath in wanting him, craving more of him. Bits and pieces of words tumbled out of me between biting kisses. *Please* and *god* and *anything*.

Eventually, Dev grabbed me up and manhandled me over to the large sofa before shoving me down on my back, stripping the rest of my clothes, and climbing on top of me. Our bare cocks pressed together as he crushed his mouth to mine again. My hands were everywhere... touching, caressing, grabbing. It wasn't enough, but I kept trying.

I wanted to take. I wanted to give. I wanted to fuse us into one unrecognizable shape of lust and desire until all that remained was an empty husk and the echo of gasping breath.

How was it possible to want someone this much?

"Let go, dammit," he growled.

I pulled my hands away a split second before realizing that wasn't what he'd meant. He wanted my orgasm. He wanted to make me come.

"Don't want it to end," I confessed raggedly.

He made a noise in his throat and shook his head before

muttering something about buttoned-up city boys needing to get dirty.

And then he moved down my body and swallowed my cock. Within seconds, it was over. My body thrust up into that delicious heat. My fingers scrambled for something to hold on to. My legs came around him in hopes he wouldn't pull away.

The dandelion fluff scattered to the wind.

And I remained quite solidly in Dev's orgasm debt.

FOURTEEN

DEV

It was a mistake. Of course it was a mistake. But I couldn't bring myself to regret it.

Touching Tully—tasting him, teasing him, making him come—was worth any amount of complication it would cause between us in regards to Lellie.

I'd fantasized about him too long and too often to chastise myself for taking what I wanted one more time.

The scent of him surrounded me as I pulled off his softening cock and resisted pressing a kiss to the tender skin of his inner thigh.

Tully's hands gentled in my hair as his breathing settled. "*Fuck,*" he said in a voice hoarse from blowing me earlier.

But I didn't want his gentleness. Not now. I needed to get the hell away from him before taking everything he was willing to give me.

I was still smarting from his implication I was a poor choice of parent for Lellie. I understood it came from his anger and resentment toward my decision not to keep her, but it still cut deep.

It still mingled with the existing insecurities I had... and it festered.

"We should get some sleep," I said, pushing off the sofa, away from his tempting bare body.

"W-what?"

I didn't dare look at him. "Morning comes early around here," I mumbled, grabbing up my clothes and shoving my legs into my boxer briefs.

"What about you? You didn't—"

"Nah. I'm good."

"Dev."

I ignored the confusion in his tone, the hurt. "Good night, Tully."

His silence battered me as I walked away, feeling like the worst kind of asshole on the planet. But he was too tempting, and I was too mixed up in my head to stay with him, skin-on-skin and vulnerable. Surely, he'd be able to feel from my touch, from the noises I made, just how much I wanted him and just how much I'd be willing to sacrifice for more time with him.

But it would be like pouring oil on an already slippery slope.

I quickly hid myself in my bed, trying my hardest to ignore the sounds of him eventually sneaking past me to visit the bathroom and returning to the living room a few minutes later. After what seemed like hours of tossing and turning—silently, so as not to wake the sleeping toddler in her crib—I finally couldn't stand it.

I made my way to the bathroom and locked the door. My cock hadn't been able to stop replaying the taste and feel of Tully in my mouth, the sounds he made, and the salty-sweet scent of his skin. I grabbed the body lotion on the counter and shoved down my boxer briefs. The sound of my fist shuttling over my slick cock was obscene and desperate. My cheeks burned with embarrassment, but I came to the image of Tully on his back for me.

After, I cleaned up quickly and snuck back to my bed. Sleep came easy after that, and morning came way too soon.

Once again, I snuck out, only this time, it was for ranch chores. Thankfully, Indigo was already up and mucking stalls, cheerfully humming along to music only he could hear.

I got to work checking and feeding the pregnant mares first. Then I moved to the other horses in the barn who needed special care. Indigo periodically asked questions, but he seemed to follow directions well enough, seeing to the regular ranch horses out in the near paddock.

Things would most likely go back to being awkward between Tully and me after last night, but maybe that was for the best. It was getting harder and harder to keep my physical and emotional distance from him, and I needed to. He was going to head back to Texas and his career sometime soon.

One night this week while making dinner, we'd had a conversation about his job at the firm and how hard he worked. The passion in his voice when he'd spoken about the intellectual challenges of structuring large estates had been palpable. There'd even been a point during which I'd almost wished I was back living in Texas, just so I could hire him to manage my legal business.

That was ridiculous, of course. I wouldn't move back to Texas for all the money in the world—not that I needed money. Being so close to my parents geographically would make their absence in my life unavoidable. And if I already felt their blame and disapproval from this far away, I couldn't imagine how suffocating it would be if I was back in Dallas.

Not that Tully would want me there anyway. He was more likely to join my parents in shunning me.

As I worked, I let the thoughts and feelings hit me without trying to dismiss or brush them off. My friends had forced me into therapy after Matt died, and I'd learned the best way to get through grief and pain was to let the emotions come, but I had to admit I didn't always feel capable of it.

It might work... but it was sure-as-shit uncomfortable.

After finishing my chores, I told Indigo I was heading to the main ranch house for a bit to talk to Silas before coming back to help feed the rest of the stock. It was early enough that Lellie was probably still asleep, but I knew Way and Silas would be up.

I took the utility vehicle down the dirt track to their place, imagining the thousands of times Fletchers had traveled the same path between home and the main barn. When I arrived, Way and Silas were on the front porch drinking coffee.

Silas took one look at me and turned to whisper something in Way's ear. Way nodded, waved to me, and headed inside.

"You didn't have to send him away," I said after joining him on the porch.

He ignored my comment. "You want coffee?"

I raised my travel mug. "Just refilled it before coming over."

"You finally going to explain what's going on with the hottie?"

I kept my eyes trained across the land I'd just driven over. The large bulk of the old barn was visible through a stand of trees in the distance. "We hooked up."

"Last night?"

"No, I mean..." I realized that was a lie. "Well, yes. That, too."

Silas quirked an eyebrow.

I took a sip of coffee and savored the flavor before swallowing. "Two years ago. When I was in town to help Katie get pregnant. She had a party. He was there. We hooked up."

Silas nodded. "Okay. Is it making things awkward? Is that the problem?"

I shrugged. "It's definitely not making things easy," I admitted.

"Ah," Silas said knowingly. "You have feelings for him."

I looked out again, this time glancing west toward the triple peaks of Three Daughters. This land was so beautiful, so peaceful, it still stole my breath sometimes. "Big feelings," I finally said.

His eyebrows lifted. "Wow. I can't believe you just admitted that out loud."

I glanced at him and let a smile tug at my lips. "Me neither."

"You must really need advice," he teased.

I simply nodded.

Silas took a breath. "Dev, last year, when I came here after Way... I thought I had it all figured out. I had my career, my friends, my home back in New York. Above all, I had my pride. I was in control."

I let out a soft snort.

Silas grinned and pointed at me. "Exactly. That's exactly right. I didn't have anything under control because the minute I met that sexy cowboy at a bar in Vegas, my future was suddenly and irrevocably out of my hands. And everyone knows I wouldn't change it for anything."

"My situation is hardly the same. It's not like Tully is my... Waylon."

"Who says he's not?"

"For one, he lives in Dallas."

Silas flapped his hand dismissively. "I lived in New York. Apparently, there's such a thing as a cross-country move."

I shook my head. "Not for this guy. His identity is all wrapped up in making partner at a big-city firm. He does trusts and estate law. It's not like there's work for him in Majestic. And you know I won't go back to Texas."

He shrugged. "I never thought I'd move to rural Wyoming, but never say never, right?"

"He's also angry with me about the custody thing. He thinks I should keep Lellie."

Silas's gaze sometimes felt like a boat anchor. "We all think that."

I opened my mouth to argue with him, but he held up a hand to stop me.

"Don't," he said. "It's a load of bullshit, and we both know it. I get that you're still mourning Matt's death. It was awful. But it was an accident. And the idea that you might let an accident keep you from giving Lellie the most loving future possible pisses me the fuck off. You want to know why? It's not even because I care about her, though I do. It's because I care about *you*. And I know you need that girl of yours. You need her to teach you how to be a family again, how real families are supposed to be. How true parental love is unconditional."

"I already have a family, and it's you assholes," I said, speaking of him and the rest of the brotherhood. Even I noticed how petulant I sounded.

Silas nodded. "Definitely. And we'll always be your family. Which means we'll always be here for you and Lellie. You won't be doing this alone."

"Doesn't she deserve a mother?"

"Absolutely. And she had one. You'll make sure she knows all about Katie as she grows up. That's something you can do because you knew her. It's not something a random couple from Atlanta can do for her. Besides, you implied you might be okay with Way and me taking her, and we certainly can't provide her with a mother. So that's clearly not a true concern." He bumped his arm into mine. "Now, get your head out of your ass and commit to your daughter so we can let Jo Blake loose on decorating Lellie's room in your new house."

I had to admit that sounded fun. And thinking about being there for Lellie's milestones was even more exciting. But I also knew from some of the things Tully had said about Katie that being a single parent could be exhausting, nerve-racking, and isolating, even if you had plenty of money.

"I'll think about it," I said, standing up and stretching. "Thank you for being here. For helping me feel like I could do it."

Silas stood up and yanked me in for a hug. He wasn't usually demonstrative, so the gesture took me by surprise. Thankfully, my travel mug was empty, or I would have sloshed coffee all over both of us.

"You have a lot of love to give, Dev. Anyone would be lucky to have you as their dad." His voice was gritty with emotion and hit me right in the solar plexus.

"Thanks," I managed before pulling away, nodding awkwardly, and heading for the utility vehicle.

"Hold up," Way called, jogging down the porch steps. "Mind giving me a ride? I told Indigo I'd help with the morning feed so you can get back to Lellie."

I nodded and climbed into the driver's seat before turning the vehicle around and heading for the barn. When we arrived, Way took off with Indigo toward the farther pastures while I headed up to the apartment.

Tully had Lellie on one hip while he scrambled eggs with his free hand. He was shirtless and sleepy-faced. His hair stuck up on one side, and his voice was scratchy as he murmured to her about breakfast.

My heart took a wild detour toward fantasies of domestic bliss for a split second until I reined it in.

"Mornin'," I called. "Thanks for getting her up."

His eyes met mine but then skittered away as he made a sound of acknowledgment. I walked over and took her out of his arms. "You ready to get dressed while Tully finishes up?"

She tucked her head against my chest and melted my heart. I gave her a quick hug, then chuckled as she squirmed out of my hold and demanded to be put down. Jo Blake said she'd never seen a child so determined to stand on her own two feet at this age. "Stubborn," she'd said. "Like her father."

I'd dismissed it at the time, but maybe she was right.

Maybe Silas was, too.

Once Lellie was dressed, I brought her to the breakfast table, but as we ate, the silence between Tully and me grew excruciating. I considered ways to break the tension, but I couldn't come up with anything that wasn't offensive or ridiculous. He all but ignored me, speaking happily to Lellie and only engaging with me when absolutely necessary.

I scrambled for a way to get us all out of this. "I'm taking Lellie to Three Daughters for a hike. Would you like to come?"

Maybe if we could get away from the ranch, get outside in the summer sun, and move our bodies, we'd find a way to get past this awkward discomfort. And maybe I could ask Tully's advice about what Silas and I had discussed.

Tully cleared his throat and refused to meet my eyes. "Thanks for including me, but I have a couple of important calls and a ton of work to catch up on. Maybe you can enjoy the day together, just the two of you."

His rejection of my invitation stung, but I understood. Why would he want to spend the day with someone who ran hot and cold like a temperamental faucet?

After we finished eating and cleaning up, I packed up enough snacks, drinks, and supplies for an army before moving Lellie's car seat from Tully's rental to my SUV.

I headed into town first to Lake Sports, where I'd seen a hiking backpack that Lellie could ride in.

Jackson Painter greeted me as soon as I walked in. "Hey, Dev, who's this?" His smile was wide for Lellie. I introduced her by name, avoiding explaining that she was my daughter. I didn't want to have to explain the situation or deal with future questions about her when... or, okay, *if*... she didn't end up staying with me.

"I came for one of those hiking backpacks I can put her in. We're going to do that flattish trail at the base of Maude unless you have a different suggestion."

He directed me toward the right side of the store. "No, that's perfect. It's only a mile to Newton Lake, and you can picnic there. Show her how to skip rocks."

"She's not quite sixteen months," I told him, as though that number would have meant a damn thing to me even a few short weeks ago. "More likely to eat rocks than skip them."

Considering her size again, he wrinkled his nose, then nodded. "Fair point. Maybe show her how *you* skip rocks and let her plonk them in the water."

When I pulled down the backpack to check it out, Jackson squatted down to distract Lellie. He was all charm and sweet smiles.

"You're good with her," I observed. "Did you and Lake ever think about having kids?"

Jackson and his husband had been together a while, and I'd always admired their relationship.

"We're in the process of trying to adopt," he said, smiling back at

Lellie as she waved around a colorful set of webbing straps she'd pulled off a nearby rack. "It's not easy."

We continued talking as I tried on the backpack and decided to buy it. It wasn't until I was halfway down the highway toward Three Daughters that I put two and two together and considered that Jackson and Lake could be potential parents for Lellie. I admired both men and knew them to be kind and loving people, dedicated to their business and the town of Majestic. They were generous, attentive, and warm. I couldn't imagine anyone better suited to becoming parents once I started thinking about it.

But when I made the logical leap between realizing they'd be great parents and imagining myself handing Lellie over to them, my gut roiled.

I pulled into the small parking area by the trailhead and rearranged the necessary supplies into the pockets of the backpack before pulling Lellie out of her car seat and trying to load her into the pack.

She heartily rejected the offer.

We started out with me carrying an empty backpack while Lellie toddled at her usual drunken-sailor pace down the trail.

The day was beautiful, warm and sunny without any humidity. There were wildflowers along the edges of the trail and Lellie even noticed a brightly colored butterfly. Several other visitors shared the trail with us as we made our way toward the lake. Lellie's legs tired fairly quickly, and she allowed me to put her in the backpack so we could pick up the pace. Thankfully, the little baggie of apple slices I'd brought kept her busy long enough to get used to being in the pack.

Unfortunately, by the time I reached the lake, she was dead asleep. I carefully pulled the pack off and stood it on the grass, pulling out the old beach towel I'd brought as a makeshift picnic blanket and setting out the supplies for our lunch and a diaper change.

Once everything was set up, I carefully pulled her out of the pack and held her close as I settled onto the towel and gazed out at the lake. Another family played at the edge of the water, and their three kids alternated between laughing together and bickering.

A teenager farther down the lake shore played music from their phone while an older woman sat on a small camp chair and read a tattered paperback.

I looked down at Lellie's face. Her dark lashes were curled against the tops of her cheeks, and her rosy lips poked out almost like a pout. Her skin was impossibly flawless and soft. I ran a thumb across her cheek and jaw to her tiny ear. What had she looked like as a newborn?

Part of me now regretted missing it. Getting to know her now with her funny personality quirks had begun to make me realize what I'd missed. She was obsessed with flowers and frogs but had a clear aversion to birds for some reason. She was obsessed with apples but detested apple juice. She loved to dance, but her version of dancing was just swaying her body without ever moving her feet.

What had she experienced in her short life that had contributed to her idiosyncrasies?

I tried to imagine her growing up within the loving embrace of Jackson and Lake. They would be the fun kind of parents who nurtured a fierce love of outdoor adventure. They'd teach her to ride a bike and swim. They'd take her to the rodeo and introduce her to everyone in town. Jackson would be the kind of parent who volunteered at school, and Lake would most likely throw himself into making adorable Halloween costumes.

What would *I* be like as a parent?

I was quieter and less social than they were. Yes, I loved being outside, too, but I'd be more likely to teach her to ride. To meander through the large ranch property in search of deer tracks and signs of elk. I'd spend cozy nights curled up on the sofa in front of the fire, reading books with her. Maybe it would be boring.

But maybe it would be exactly what she needed.

My brain whirred with options and various imagined scenarios until Lellie began to stir in my lap.

When she woke up, she happily ate her new favorite—PB&J—while stumbling back and forth to the water's edge. Every time she reached the edge, she tried to lean over to pat her hand on the cold water, and every time, I had to rescue her before she fell in.

I couldn't hold back my grin. She really was stubborn...

Like her father.

It wasn't until we were a quarter of a mile back down the trail that she lost her good mood and dissolved into a tantrum. I tried not to take it personally, as a sign of my failure as a parent, but it was hard not to feel like I could have somehow prevented it if only I'd been more experienced.

When we got back to the vehicle, she fought me at every turn. She didn't want the car seat. She wanted "ap-puh" and "Dah." I tried explaining that I was out of apples, and I couldn't hold her while I drove.

My attempts to explain things rationally weren't well received.

Lellie cried without pause the entire ride home. My nerves were completely shot by the time I pulled off the highway and onto the ranch road. I selfishly hoped Tully would be up for taking a turn with her, or, at the very least, I hoped his familiar presence might calm her.

But when I pulled up to the parking area, Tully was hopping behind the wheel of one of the ranch trucks, completely oblivious to my arrival. It wasn't until he pulled past me that I noticed he was hauling a trailer with a horse in it.

My horse.

Trigger.

"Hey!" I shouted, throwing my truck door open and jumping out. "Hey!"

He didn't hear me but continued driving away, the tires from the truck and trailer throwing up dust in their wake.

My heart was in my throat. What the hell was he doing with my horse, and why hadn't he bothered to stop and explain?

"What's happening?" I asked when I noticed Indigo standing near the large open doors to the barn.

He looked shaken. The whites of his eyes were huge. "I-I don't know, man. Tully said... something about colic, I think? Asked me about where we keep the medicine, but I didn't know. I'm sorry!"

Colic?

Trigger had seemed just fine last night. He was only nine years old, in his absolute prime. The gelding was my baby. He was more important to me than anything in the world, with the very recent exception of Lellie. The idea of him suffering made me nauseous.

I opened the door and unbuckled Lellie, taking her in my arms to soothe her cries. "Does he know where to go?" I asked Indigo.

Way pulled up on a utility vehicle and thumbed in the direction of the dust plume. "Hey. If the two of you are here, who was that in the truck?"

Indigo looked like he was about to throw up, himself. "Tully. He said one of the horses was sick. I think he's, like, taking him to the vet? He said he knew where to go."

I explained what he'd said about Trigger and suspected colic.

Way met my eyes. "Go after him and make sure he gets there. I'll call Pete to give him a heads-up."

I hesitated, taking a step toward the truck before remembering I had Lellie in my arms and then doubling back. *Shit.*

I needed to go, but I also needed to stay.

Indigo reached for Lellie. "I can take care of her."

I was afraid she would freak if I tried handing her off to anyone else. What kind of parent left their kid when they were upset? "Maybe I should take her with me."

Indigo opened his mouth to speak but seemed to second-guess himself. Way didn't show that much restraint. "No. Leave her with us, Dev. She'll be fine. Go."

I pressed a long kiss to her dark curls before attempting to hand her to Indigo. "Can Indigo hold you while I go find Tully, sweetheart?"

Thankfully, she didn't fight me and went right to him, murmuring, "Tuh-wee."

My heart cracked.

After thanking them and jumping back into the truck, I lit out after him. A million questions tumbled through my head. How did Tully know what to do? What made him react so quickly? How did he even recognize the signs of colic in a horse?

And how hadn't I noticed them myself?

I thought back over my movements this morning and realized I'd never gone out to the paddock to check Trigger. I'd taken care of all the high-needs horses first and then run up to the ranch house.

Fuck. This was my fault.

I sped up enough on the highway to catch sight of the burgundy trailer ahead. He slowed down before the edge of town and hung a careful left at the large sign for Majestic Animal Hospital. I silently thanked Pete for making sure the signage was large and clear on the highway. Tully must have noticed it when driving between the ranch and town earlier in the week.

The large building was surrounded on one side by a fenced paddock and on the other by another fenced area for dogs.

I pulled in next to Tully and hopped out, going straight to the trailer door latch to check on Trigger.

Before Tully had a chance to say anything, Pete himself came striding out of the front door. "Way called. Let's get him checked out."

I appreciated his calm demeanor when all I wanted to do was scream. A nervous lump in my throat kept me from speaking, but Tully found his voice just fine.

"I saw Trigger out the window pawing the ground, turning to look at his flank, and just acting off."

I moved up next to the horse, murmuring reassuring words as Tully continued. "When I got downstairs to take a closer look, I realized he was doing that thing where it looks like he's trying to urinate, but nothing came out."

As he described all the typical symptoms of colic, my heart began to beat faster with panic. We worked together to back him out of the trailer and help get him through the open bay doors on the side of the building and into Pete's large animal exam room. Two vet techs met us. One immediately began helping Pete, and the other gently led Tully and me out of the exam room and into a quiet waiting room off the lobby before returning to help the doc.

"I should be in there with him," I said, immediately pacing to the other side of the room.

"No. You shouldn't." Tully sat down on one of the chairs and rested his elbows on his knees. I realized he was dressed in the outfit I'd taken off the night before.

I stared at him. "You're wearing my clothes."

He looked in confusion down at the blue jeans. "Oh shit. I'd just stepped out of the shower when I glanced out the window and saw Trigger. I grabbed the nearest clothes and went running out to check. I didn't think. Sorry."

I waved away his concerns. "How did you know what was going on?"

He glanced up at me without smiling. "I grew up on a ranch. I've been around horses since I was Lellie's age and riding since I was three."

The words jangled between us like an old rusty can filled with bottle caps. "What?"

He rubbed his face with both hands as if he was exhausted already. Considering the recent spike in adrenaline, I wasn't surprised. "Can we not do this right now? You're going to say, 'Why didn't you say something?' And I'm going to reply, 'I tried. Several times.' And then you're going to act like even though I grew up on a ranch, I still probably don't know beans about horses. And that's just going to piss me off. So... can we just wait in silence until your friend has something to tell us?"

I opened my mouth to argue with him. To tell him he didn't know me well enough to predict what I would or wouldn't say.

But then I realized he was right. In fact, I'd done the same thing with Indigo.

I dropped into the seat next to him. "I'm grateful you noticed and acted quickly. Thank you."

He leaned his head back and sighed. "I hope I overreacted."

"You didn't."

"Okay, I hope it's not colic or anything else serious."

I closed my mind against all the possibilities and tried to distract myself. "Your family owned a ranch?"

He inhaled through his nose. "My dad ran a small cow/calf operation. Failed at it, mostly."

There seemed to be a story there, but it sounded like one he didn't feel like sharing. "He still around?"

Tully glanced out the window toward the road, keeping his gaze away from mine. "As far as I know. We had a falling-out when he strongly suggested I should stay home and work the ranch instead of accepting a scholarship to college. He doesn't keep in touch with me or my little brother."

"You have a brother?" I asked, careful not to make it sound accusatory. I could hardly be upset that he hadn't mentioned his brother when I hadn't mentioned my own, but it blew my mind how much I didn't know about Tully. How much I hadn't asked.

"Nolan," Tully confirmed. "He's a junior at Texas A&M. Studying animal science." He darted a look at me. "He said one person in the family who wore thousand-dollar suits was enough."

I barked out a laugh before I could hold it back. "I dunno. You make them look damn good."

Tully released a breath. "Thanks."

"And you made the right choice," I offered. "Taking the scholarship."

"Agreed."

Hearing the two of us had something in common intrigued me. Hearing him open up made me think I needed to do the same. Maybe that would bridge the distance between us.

I cleared my throat. "Money was always tight when I was growing up, so my dad helped me get work at a nearby ranch when I was fourteen. That's how I met Katie. It was her grandparents' ranch."

Tully nodded, clearly familiar with this story. "She loved being on the ranch. Her grandparents still have the land, but they've sold off all the stock."

I let out a sigh. "They were wonderful to me. Gave me every opportunity to learn and grow. Made me feel capable and important. Delmar and Biddy... they were like my surrogate grandparents. Have you met them?"

Tully finally turned to me, a soft smile edging up his lips. "Yeah. I complimented Biddy on her banana pudding once, and now she makes it for me every year at Fourth of July." His smile faded. "Katie's death nearly broke them."

I felt a band around my chest at the thought and leaned over to cover my face with my hands. "Fuck." That girl had been everything to them. They had probably ten grandkids, all told, but she was the closest one to them and the light of their lives. "Are they supporting the Scotts' bid for custody?"

"I haven't heard. They adore Lellie. But Delmar has pretty serious arthritis, and Biddy is losing her memory. I can't imagine they could offer to help care for her or be anything other than moral support."

I used to touch base with them once or twice a year, but I hadn't spoken to them since I left Dallas two years ago.

"If they were younger, I'd consider them as guardians," I said, feeling the now-familiar pinch of discomfort in my gut at the thought of giving Lellie to anyone.

Tully looked away from me again. "Maybe they know of someone."

"No."

He turned to look at me. "No?"

Before I could say anything, Pete came in. And the look on his face wasn't good.

FIFTEEN

TULLY

Instead of watching the vet, I watched Dev. His face was pale, and his hands shook.

"Is it colic?" he asked as he stood quickly and approached the doctor.

The man was smaller than Dev and had to look up to meet his eyes. "We're pretty sure it is, but I'm going to put in a nasogastric tube to do more investigation. I just need you to sign the consent first."

Dev quickly strode across to take the electronic tablet before scribbling his name and handing it back. "Whatever you need to do. You know that."

The vet nodded and turned around, not wasting another moment on small talk. Dev returned to the seating area but remained standing for a beat before pacing across the small space.

"You trust this guy?" I asked. "Because we could find someone in a bigger city if we needed to. I could—"

He shook his head. "Pete's great. I've worked with him for a year now. He's been out at the ranch for some difficult deliveries and various situations with the trail horse stock. He's as good as any large-animal vet I've worked with."

I'd noticed the man hadn't mentioned the cost of treatment. Since this was Dev's personal mount instead of a ranch-owned animal, the treatment burden was probably on Dev. "It could be expensive."

"Yeah."

"No, like... it could be *really* expensive. Sometimes colic requires surgery, Dev."

He stopped and furrowed his brows. "I know. It's okay. Pete knows I'll pay whatever it takes."

Dev worked on a ranch. Yes, he was in charge of the breeding program, but even a ranch manager job in rural midwestern areas only paid around fifty grand a year. It wasn't the kind of salary that could easily swallow a ten-thousand-dollar surgery.

He went back to pacing. After a few minutes, he stopped and glanced at me. He was obviously nervous.

"I've been thinking about keeping Lellie."

I blinked at him.

"Because of the money?"

It was his turn to blink at me. "What?"

The timing was too coincidental. Anger crackled under my skin. "You're going to keep her so you can afford to take care of your horse? Are you kidding?"

"What are you talking about?" he snapped. "What does one thing have to do with the other?"

"We were talking about how expensive Trigger's treatment might be, and then you suddenly decided to keep custody of your daughter and her fortune! What do you expect me to think, Dev?"

He curled his hands into fists at his side. "I expect you to think I'm better than the lowest scum on the fucking planet. I expect you to understand that while I love that fucking horse and would do anything for him, I wouldn't use my daughter that way. I expect you to... to... to care about me even the smallest amount, just enough to give me the benefit of the doubt. Jesus fucking Christ. Is this what you think of me?"

My body went cold, and I realized in an instant what a huge mistake I'd made. I'd seen how much he cared for Lellie. I knew that whatever decision he made about her, it would have nothing to do with her money. Didn't I know better than to make assumptions about him like the ones he'd made about me?

I stood up to reach for him, to make a physical connection, but he whipped away from me and strode out of the waiting room.

I stared at the empty doorway, frozen in shock and regret. What had I done? How could I fix it? Should I go after him?

Before I could make a move, his phone pinged from the chair he'd been sitting in before the vet had come in. Way's golden-boy face appeared in the contact image on the screen. Since I knew he and Silas had Lellie, I answered it quickly.

"It's Tully. Dev went to stretch his legs. You want me to find him?"

"First, how's Trigger?"

"They suspect colic. Starting a nasal tube first. Dev's stressed, but he says he's in good hands."

Lellie's happy chatter in the background made my shoulders drop.

"Pete's great," Way confirmed. "He's been looking after our stock for years. He and my sister Sheridan became good friends in Girl Scouts growing up, and then the two of them ran their scout group like a couple of pampered dictators. JoJo Reynolds still looks intimidated whenever Pete and Sheridan get together." His warm laughter helped relax me even more. I was happy to hear Pete was a trusted professional and a good friend of the family. Hopefully, that meant he'd go above and beyond in caring for Trigger.

"Dev will probably be here for a while. Is Lellie okay, or did you need me to come back and put her to bed?"

"She's fine. Aunt Blake came to drop off some food from the cafe, and it's looking like she's not going to leave. We were thinking of bringing the portable crib over to the house and setting her up here. Would that be okay, do you think?"

I thought it sounded like a great idea, but I also knew it wasn't my decision to make. "Let me find Dev and ask. I'll call you back."

After ending the call, I made my way outside and recognized the back of Dev's wide shoulders as he leaned against a fence and peered eastward. Darkness crawled across the flat land like a slow incoming tide while the sun set behind Three Daughters in the opposite direction.

He had to have heard my boots churning up the dusty gravel, but he didn't turn around. Instead of calling out, I walked right up to him and pressed myself against his back.

His body tightened, and I waited for him to elbow me away.

He didn't.

"I'm sorry," I breathed before dropping my forehead onto his shoulder. "I'm so sorry."

"I can afford to care for my horse without touching Lellie's money," he said, voice gruff with emotion.

"I know you wouldn't do that. I was just surprised. And maybe still angry," I admitted.

Dev hesitated. "I have money, Tully."

"Okay."

He reached back and put his hand in my hair, pulling my face closer to his neck. "No, I mean... I have a *lot* of money."

His confession sounded nefarious, like maybe the money came from an infamous bank heist. "Okayyy?"

Dev sighed and turned around, placing his hands on my hips. "I can't tell you more than that, but I just need you to know not only would I never make my custody decision based on money, I wouldn't ever need to."

"I understand. Thank you for telling me. And I'm truly sorry for implying the worst. I honestly don't think you would be mercenary like that; I just didn't understand why you wouldn't be more worried about the expense. It makes sense if you've..." I couldn't help but be curious and also tease him a little. "Started an OnlyFans? If so, slide me that link when you get a chance."

His smile was fucking beautiful. It made my heart speed up in my chest. "No porn. Unfortunately, it was a fairly unsexy business deal. All legal, by the way. I can tell you're low-key wondering if you should call the cops."

I placed a hand on the center of his chest, still half-afraid he'd shrug me off. "Shame about the porn," I murmured, catching sight of his lips and wondering if he'd let me taste them again.

I had a hammering need to be close to him, to touch him and connect to him.

I'd thought of him a million times in the past two years, though I'd damned myself for a fool every time.

I'd tried to convince myself I'd barely known Dev. That all we'd shared was a casual hookup, not the deep, instantaneous connection I remembered. That a couple of hours' acquaintance was too short a time for the amount of rent-free space he took up in my brain.

But now, being here with him and seeing what he was like day to day, I realized there was something to be said for instant chemistry. Something undefinable had attracted me to him back then—something more than simple physical attraction—and that was why I hadn't been able to forget him. Dev was someone I wanted to spend more time with.

And our story wasn't over yet.

Dev's body was still tight with anxiety. "Would you mind going back to the ranch to make sure Lellie's okay?"

I realized I'd forgotten to tell him about the missed call. "Way called. Your phone was on the chair, and since I knew he had Lellie, I answered it. Hope that's okay?"

"Of course." He shifted on his feet but didn't take his hands off my hips. "Everything fine?"

I quickly reassured him. "Way's Aunt Blake is there. That's Jo, right?" When he nodded, I continued. "She's going to stay. They wanted to know if they could move the crib to the house for the night.

I said I'd ask you. Would you rather me go back and keep her at your place?" I didn't want to leave him, but I also wanted to do whatever would give him the most peace of mind.

Dev brought a hand up to cup the side of my neck. His fingertips moved into the hair on the nape of my neck. "I selfishly want you to stay here with me, but I should let you go get some rest."

I swallowed. "I want to stay."

He moved closer, until I felt the metal of his belt buckle catch against my clothes. "I trust Jo. Silas and Way would probably be fine, but if she's there, too, I'm sure Lellie's in good hands. And if she'll let them move the crib over, that's even better. I'll call and let them know."

Neither of us made a move to exchange his phone. Instead, we locked eyes. The setting sun bathed his face in a warm, rosy gold, setting off chestnut streaks in his dark hair.

"Stay," he said in a low voice. "I'd like you to stay."

My head felt airy and empty. There were words I wanted to say to him, but I couldn't for the life of me come up with any. All I could think about was kissing him again.

As soon as I leaned in, he met me halfway, crashing his lips into mine and causing me to hitch in a breath in surprise. I grabbed his head, threading my fingers into his hair and holding him while we devoured each other's mouths.

His aggression surprised me, but I was a hundred percent here for it. It was a relief to know the strong pull I felt toward him wasn't one-sided. We kissed for long minutes, and Dev's hands moved down to grab my ass and pull me closer until I felt the thickening ridge of his cock against mine.

"Fuck, wait," I said, pulling away. "We're in a parking lot."

He glanced past me at the vet building, the parking lot, and then the road. "No one's around."

"Still. I don't want one of the vet techs to come out and find me nutting in my pants."

His huff of laughter surprised me. He stepped back and ran his hands through his hair. "Fair." His eyes flicked down to the bulge in my jeans and back up to my face. "Why can't I stay away from you?"

My heart flitted around my chest like it was untethered and at risk of escaping. "Do you want to?"

He closed his eyes and inhaled. "I *want* to want to."

I took a step back, feeling slighted and stung. "Why?"

Dev's eyes opened and met mine. "Because it's complicated. Because I don't just want a quick fuck with you. Because you live in Texas, and I'm never going back." He sighed. "Because I don't even know if you want me anymore."

"I w-want you," I said, hating how quickly the words came stuttering out. "I've wanted you for two years, Dev. I wanted to finish what we started. Get to know you better. Hell, I just fucking wanted to lay eyes on you again. And now I'm here, and I feel like my presence annoys the fuck out of you. I can't tell whether you want me close or you want me to fuck back off to Texas."

He reached out and snatched a tiny piece of my shirt between two fingers and his thumb, clasping it lightly down by the bottom hem and tugging it so I would step closer again. His eyes were serious, but the corner of his mouth curled up. "Can't I want both?"

I stepped close again, noticing the familiar combination of faded sandalwood cologne mixed with hay and horse. The world's most comforting and provoking scent.

"What are we doing?" I murmured before pressing a kiss to his stubbled jaw.

"Dunno, but when you're touching me like this, I find I don't care overmuch."

He kissed me again, and I wondered idly if he realized his voice got Texas-soft with me more than others. We kissed again, featherlight and teasing, until Dev moved to pull me into a tight hug.

"Sexy as fuck, *and* he can sit a horse," he murmured under his breath. "How are you still single?"

Laughter bubbled up. "That's all I needed to do to get your attention? Find me some cattle, and I'll really impress you. I can rope a steer, too."

He pulled back and smiled. There was obvious worry in his eyes about all the things weighing on his mind, but it was nice to see him smiling.

"If you're too good in the saddle, I'll have to recruit you away from that law firm."

"You can't afford me, McKay," I teased before remembering what he'd said about having a lot of money. I wanted to ask him about it, find out more about whatever business deal he'd been involved in, but I didn't want to risk spoiling the ease between us.

The sound of someone exiting the building caught our attention, and we moved away from each other.

Dev cleared his throat. "Better call the guys back and check in."

I fished his phone out of my back pocket and handed it to him. "I'll go back inside in case they have an update on Trigger."

He grabbed my hand. "Stay. They'll come find us when they have something."

I watched the last golden edges of the sun disappear from the outline of the mountains, I listened to him greet his friends and ask to tell Lellie good night.

"Hi, sweetheart," he said with a big goofy smile. "You ready for bedtime? Do you have your horse and your books?"

His smile faded as he listened to her babble. "I don't remember the words exactly... okay, okay... Nate was an ordinary wolf who lived in the forest," he began.

The story was familiar. It was one of Lellie's favorite picture books, the one she insisted on him reading each night since he did all the animal voices. I was sure he was ad-libbing tonight, but when he got to the scene where wolf and bear argue over spaghetti, she was still in stitches on the other end of the phone, shrieking and giggling the way she always did. Her laughter made him break character and laugh, too.

I closed my eyes and breathed in the sound of their joined laughter. *Katie, you would have loved seeing him with her.*

Memories of my best friend during various moments of her too-short motherhood floated through my mind as the night air swirled around us. What would she say to Dev about the custody situation? What would she advise me to do about my own conflicting priorities?

"You okay?"

I blinked open my eyes to see Dev peering at me with a divot of concern between his brows. He must have ended the call and put the phone away while I'd zoned out.

"Yeah," I began before realizing I wasn't actually all that okay. "I was thinking about Katie."

Dev studied me. "I haven't had a chance to ask you... that's not true. I haven't wanted to hear more about how she died. I guess I've been avoiding thinking about it. I know the two of you were close. Do you want to talk about it?"

He looked awkward as fuck, but that only made me appreciate the gesture more. "I wish she was here. I wish she could see you with Lellie."

Dev looked down at the tip of his boots while he kicked at a stubborn weed. "What was Katie's favorite part of being a mom?"

I took a minute to consider. "It surprised me, actually. When she first told me she wanted to have a baby, I thought she was crazy. She was incredibly dedicated to her career. It was one of the things that bonded us early on. We were both workaholics and hell-bent on making partner. But she said motherhood was her dream, too. She wanted to have both, and she was determined to prove she could."

I met his eyes. "As soon as Lellie was born, it was like a softer side of her emerged. I wasn't there for the delivery—her friend Renata was her birth partner—but I got to the hospital about an hour after Lellie was born. I remember Katie had this quiet confidence... like... an unexpected calm. She wasn't nervous or awkward with the baby. Don't get me wrong, she definitely didn't know what she was doing with a newborn, but she wasn't afraid. *I* was afraid, but she wasn't."

Dev smiled. "I can't picture you holding a newborn. Lellie must have been tiny in your arms."

I suddenly realized he'd never seen pictures of her as a baby. After pulling my phone out of my pocket, I opened up the photo app and scrolled way back until I saw the hospital photos. Then I scrolled further back to find pictures of Katie pregnant.

We spent a while going through photos. Talking about Katie was emotional but good.

"I got the call about her accident from Renata," I said when we got to the worst part of the story. "She lives next door to Katie and is... *was* Lellie's nanny. You might have met her when you were there."

"I met so many people that night, it's hard to remember. I, ah, might have been distracted by one person in particular, and it definitely wasn't Renata."

My face heated under his gaze. "Right, well... she's younger. A grad student at UT Dallas. It's actually her parents who live next door to Katie, but she and Katie were closer in age. I would have suggested her as a potential parent for Lellie, but she's dating a guy Katie and I really don't like. And she's just... too young, honestly. She's a wonderful nanny, but I'm not sure she's mature enough to be a full-time parent yet."

"Are any of us?" Dev teased.

"What about your parents?" I asked.

His emotional reaction to discovering Katie held the deed to their house indicated that there was a story there. The way he tensed up at the mention of them confirmed it.

"What about them?" he asked.

"Would they want her?"

He hunched his shoulders a bit and looked back down at his boots. "Probably."

Sometimes getting information out of this man was like trying to get a cat to come when called—impossible and infuriating. "And that wouldn't be a good thing?"

He straightened back up but didn't look at me. "They'd be better than the Scotts, but not by much."

"Is that why you didn't move back to Texas? Katie never said."

Before he could answer, two things happened at once. A tech came out of the building to call Dev inside, and my phone buzzed with a message.

As Dev began walking toward the building, I glanced down at the text.

My assistant had forwarded me a demand for one Eleanor Kathryn Scott to appear at a specific lab in Dallas for lab testing by the end of the following week. Attached was the subpoena for the paternity test from the Scotts' attorney... signed by a judge I knew was a member of the Scotts' congregation.

My heart dropped into my stomach.

Dev's staunch declaration that he'd never return to Texas had lasted all of a handful of minutes. Even if Dev's attorneys wanted to fight the ridiculous demand to travel a thousand miles to go to a specific lab, they would lose.

Dev may not have realized what he was up against in the Scotts' legal custody challenge, but I sure did. And it would take a limitless well of money to fight it. I could only hope Dev's mysterious "business deal" had netted him enough wealth to go up against a system clearly biased against him.

Regardless, I wasn't going to tell him about the subpoena now.

Because the vet clearly had news about Trigger.

SIXTEEN

DEV

When I returned to the waiting room, Pete was waiting.

"Okay. The tube seemed to provide quite a bit of relief, and I'm cautiously optimistic we can treat Trigger without surgery." He went on to explain his diagnosis and treatment plan. "And, of course, if anything unexpected happens, I'll call and discuss it with you. But I think you caught it early. Best-case scenario, he can go home tomorrow under close supervision."

"Supervision." My stomach dropped. "I've got roundup in two days."

Tully opened his mouth but then closed it.

"What?" I prompted. "Say what you're thinking."

"You can still bring Trigger home, and I can watch him. Or I can help with roundup and let you watch him. Or we can take turns."

Pete looked back and forth between us. "Either way. You know he's in good hands here if you need to leave him longer. We have someone keeping an eye on everyone around the clock anyway since we have high-risk breeding animals on-site." He patted me on the shoulder. "We'll take good care of him, and I promise to call. Go on home and get some rest. If you need more help with roundup, let me know. I have a high schooler who works part-time as a tech. She'd love to help and has experience loading trailers. She's been doing hunter-jumper shows for years. Runs our supply closet like a drill sergeant."

My brain was sluggish. I was overwhelmed with relief at the news Trigger wouldn't need surgery.

Tully stepped forward. "He'd love that. Would you mind sharing her contact information? I can give it to Way."

Pete nodded. "Will do. I promise to take care of your baby, Dev. Go get some sleep."

I shook his hand and thanked him before turning back to Tully and tilting my head toward the door. It wasn't easy leaving Trigger, but I also knew I didn't want to see him sedated. It would agitate both of us if I went back there to say good night.

We left the ranch truck and trailer in the lot and loaded up in my SUV. The silence on the drive was comfortable. Trigger's prognosis was a relief, and I took a few minutes to allow it to sink in. Darkness had finally settled, with only the barest slim band of faded copper outlining the triple peaks of Three Daughters in the distance. Warm night air came in through the open truck windows, and the scent of sage carried hints of cattle grazing nearby.

"I love it here," I murmured. Tonight was one of those rare moments of feeling like I was exactly where I was meant to be. I'd arrived in Majestic almost a year ago exactly, and I'd felt right away that it was a place where I could find contentment.

"I can see why you do," Tully agreed. "It suits you."

"The people here are good. Loyal and kind. I assumed they'd be closed-minded and prejudiced, but I've been pleasantly surprised."

I felt Tully's eyes on me. He was probably wondering where I was going with this.

My hands stretched around the steering wheel as I pointed us home. "I'm building a house."

Why was I so nervous? Suddenly, it felt like a decision I'd known was right for me was up for debate. I wanted him to approve. I wanted him to tell me it was a good idea.

"Here?" he asked. He shook his head. "Stupid question. Of course it's here, your job is here. Is it in town?"

"Not in town, no." I explained how I'd selected the home site adjacent to the Fletcher Ranch. I didn't explain that it was a multi-million-dollar parcel of land located on a hundred acres with over a thousand feet of frontage on the Majestic River.

"That makes more sense," he said after I described the views and the peaceful setting. He hesitated. "Is there room for Lellie?"

"Plenty. It, ah… it has several bedrooms." I didn't explain that I'd specifically designed it with a bedroom and full bath for each member of the brotherhood and Kenji, plus an additional guest suite. Even though I'd told him I had money, I wasn't about to explain that I was building a seven-bedroom house for a single man. It was ridiculous and extravagant, the only obscene splurge I'd made since buying the Bugatti for my brother.

I cleared my throat. "I worry that she'll be isolated, though."

Tully surprised me with a soft laugh. "Dev, we've barely been alone in all the time I've been here. Your life is full of people. Silas, Way, Jo, Way's sister, that damned sheriff, Indigo or whoever else is helping out around the ranch, and every single person we come in contact with in town who seems to know who you are, even if you haven't met them yet. I can't imagine her growing up isolated in such a small town. Your friends wouldn't fucking allow it. Even if it was what you wanted."

That last sentence seemed almost to be a question, as if he was wondering if that was what I *would* want.

"I can see your point."

I pulled off the highway and onto the ranch road. The familiar curves and dips welcomed me to the only place that had felt like home in years.

Tully's features were hard to read in the dashboard lights, but I could see his bright eyes as he looked at me. "All she needs is security and love, Dev." His voice was soft but firm enough to make me believe him.

I parked the SUV by the barn. My mind was twisted in knots, wondering whether I could simultaneously convince him to put his hands on my body and also continue to reassure me with his words that I wouldn't make a horrible father.

Either way, I was grateful Lellie was up at the main house so I could have Tully to myself for the rest of the night.

But before I could fully exit the vehicle, Indigo was there, wringing his hands and stammering. "H-how's Trigger? Please tell me he's good, dude. I've been legit freaking out thinking he's sick and it's totally my fault. I—"

"He's fine," Tully said quickly, hopping out and closing the door behind him. "It's colic, but they're treating him without surgery, and the prognosis is good."

Indigo's eyes shot between Tully and me. I could tell he was terrified about my response, but until I discovered whether his actions had contributed to the colic, I was withholding the loving reassurance Tully seemed eager to give him. Instead of speaking and potentially saying something I'd regret, I remembered what my father used to say and took a breath, simply nodding to agree with Tully's words.

I could tell Indigo wanted to press me, but he must have read my body language. Instead, he turned to Tully. "What can I do to help? Just say the word and I'm on it."

Tully glanced at me before answering. "You can make sure to check with Dev or Way before feeding any of the stock. Colic isn't always caused by ingesting something bad, but it can be, so we need to be extra careful. Make sure you speak up if you see anything around the horses that shouldn't be there. Trash, shoe nails, sand, dead animals or bugs... anything at all that seems like it's not right. I'm not sure the vet knows the cause yet, so relax. It's not always preventable, even if it is caused by something he ate."

I appreciated Tully's levelheaded response when all I wanted to do was pin Indigo against the barn wall and interrogate him about everything he'd ever fed our stock. But I knew Way had already talked to him and checked everything related to the feed. There'd been no sign of anything out of place. Tully spoke the truth; it was very possible it was simply bad luck.

I scraped my upper lip with my teeth before deciding to put Indigo at ease. "Tully's right. I appreciate your concern. Best thing you can do is help us keep an eye out. And get some sleep. We've got roundup day after tomorrow. Gonna kick all our asses, so be sure to get some rest."

The kid let out a breath and shook his shaggy head like a dog who'd just gotten out of a pond. "Yeah. Cool. Okay. Shaking off the bad vibes. Gonna do some moonbathing before I crash. A buddy recommended it once for grounding before a big final. Crushed it, bro. Lunation, like, totally realigned me, you know?"

I stared at him for several beats while my brain tried to sort out what he'd said. Tully grabbed my elbow and steered me toward the barn. "Happy bathing," he called over his shoulder.

"What the fuck?" I griped as soon as my apartment door was safely closed behind us. Instead of answering, Tully shoved my back against the door and kissed me, his strong body pressed fully against mine. His firm warmth covered me from neck to thigh, and his tongue invaded my mouth.

I was here for all of it.

I yanked his shirt up and over his head before fumbling between us to open his pants. "Boots off," I ordered against his mouth.

The following thirty seconds were a chaotic mess of bumped elbows, the thunk of dropped boots, and the clink of belt buckles, all interrupted by more kissing and grappling. I wanted to get him naked without having to take my mouth and hands off him.

"Bed," I said at one point, which only served to spread out our shucked clothes across the space between the door and my bedroom. Tully tripped along behind me, hopping out of his jeans while simultaneously grabbing at mine.

We fell together on the bed in our underwear before yanking them off and groaning as our bare bodies finally collided.

"Fuck, you feel good," he said. "You're all muscle."

His hands moved over my arms and shoulders, squeezing the curves and dips of my biceps and delts. His body was plenty fit, but I could understand why he saw a difference between us. I spent most of every day outside, moving and lifting, riding and wrestling large animals while he spent that time sitting and typing, planning and negotiating asset management.

"You're gorgeous," I admitted. "I've..." I stopped my mouth before saying something I'd regret.

He pulled back from where he'd been sucking on my neck. "What? What were you going to say?"

I sighed and leaned over him, brushing my hand through his short hair. "I've thought of you an embarrassing amount of times since we were together. I..." I took in a large breath before letting it out. "I stopped hooking up because everyone was a disappointment compared to you. I told you, that's why Foster and I didn't..." I shrugged.

"Devon McKay, you sweet-talking son of a gun." Tully's lush lips widened into a huge grin. "I can't deny it's kind of a rush knowing I cockblocked the sheriff."

"You're very prickly about Foster," I observed, enjoying every minute of this.

His grin faded. "The night I arrived, I thought the two of you were a thing. And you're already like a son to his mother. Everyone wants the two of you to get together."

"Except me." And Foster, but I didn't say that part out loud. Foster had known before I did that we were better off as friends, but he loved to be provoking when given a chance. Supposedly, he'd done the same thing when Silas came to town. "Whoever ends up with Foster will need to have a spine of steel."

"And you don't?"

I shrugged. The slight movement reminded me my dick was very happily nestled against his. "Can we stop talking about other men?" The rough edge to my voice betrayed my desperation.

Tully arched up into me and grinned again. His hands moved down my back to squeeze my ass. "Not if it lights your fire."

I kissed my way down his throat to his chest, moving to the side to drag his brown pebbled nipple into my mouth. He sucked in a breath. "My fire is always lit when you're around," I murmured.

He lifted my chin until I met his eyes. They were the color of the Gulf of Mexico on a clear summer day when the water was an incredible turquoise. I wanted to dive deep down and swim in there forever.

"You going to bolt if we do this?" Tully asked softly.

Not yet.

The words were there, but they remained unspoken. I knew this couldn't turn into anything other than a short-term string of hookups. There was too much going on in my life, not to mention he lived a thousand miles away. But I wanted to take as much from him as I possibly could this time. And that sure as hell included an orgasm.

"You're so fucking beautiful," I said instead, not paying much attention to the words but knowing they were the truth.

Tully's eyes narrowed. "You've barely looked at me since I arrived."

I let out a huff of laughter before sucking the skin below his ear. "Liar. All I do is drink you in."

Why was I being so honest? I didn't want him to know how much I felt for him when anything beyond the short term was impossible.

I cleared my throat and added, "I can appreciate an attractive man as much as anyone."

He tilted his head, unsure. "Good to know."

I leaned in to press my lips to his. They were irresistible, soft and firm at the same time. His fingers dug into my scalp as if making sure I didn't pull away. I wondered if he'd meant what he'd implied the other day, about me fucking him. The thought of being inside the hot clench of his body made my cock even harder than it already was. Which seemed impossible.

But I didn't need to be inside him to come. If I simply remained pressed against his bare body with his hands on me and the warm rumble of his voice vibrating against my chest, my release was inevitable.

"Tell me what you want," Tully murmured against my lips. "My mouth. My ass. My hands." I felt his grin. "Dirty words? A few spankings?"

I couldn't help but laugh. "You'd like that, wouldn't you? A chance to enforce a little discipline."

He moved his hands down to squeeze my ass. "You have a very delectable ass, cowboy. It might look pretty with some pink on it."

Being with him like this was just like I remembered, easy and hot. But this time, I wasn't anxious about getting back to Katie's before she noticed I was gone. We had the whole night.

I leaned down to kiss him again, too lightly to satisfy. Every time I pulled away, he sucked in a breath and let out a grumble of frustration. "I want you." I breathed against his neck. His stubble abraded my lips and tongue as I licked and teased the sensitive spot under his chin. "So fucking much. Any way you want."

He moved his hands into my hair and tugged. "Want you to fuck me. I've wanted it for a long time."

I moved down his body and took his cock in my mouth, giving it a few licks and pulls before lifting my head off and making a point of wetting my fingers where he could see. His eyes, that impossible color that reminded me of private islands and fruity cocktails, tracked my movements.

After shoving a pillow under his ass, I moved my hand down between his legs, shifting slightly to the side before leaning back down to lick a thick stripe along his shaft. The hair on his legs tugged on my dick, and the musky scent of his arousal filled my nostrils.

He was tight and hot around my fingers. I wondered how long it had been since he'd bottomed for another man and how much prep he'd need before I could feel the squeeze of his body around me. Just the thought of it made me groan around his cock.

"Dev," he said, inhaling a noisy breath and yanking my hair to pull my head away. "Please. I want to make you come."

I wasn't done stretching him, but I moved to kiss up the trail of hair on his stomach and latch onto one of his small nipples as I continued exploring his hole with my fingers. His torso wasn't as pale as I would have expected in someone who spent his days at a desk, and though I knew how the rest of him had gotten tanned from being in the sun this week, I knew for a fact he hadn't been outside without his shirt.

I would have noticed.

Hard.

I moved farther up and sucked a mark onto the base of his neck, low enough to remain hidden under a shirt collar but high enough I might get a peek of it if I knew it was there.

Tully shoved me away. "Enough. Where's the lube?"

He turned to find my bedside table, fumbling into the drawer and finding the bottle immediately.

He also found a dildo.

Tully's eyes glinted. "You want to bottom for me, Dev?"

"Not right now," I said, reaching for the lube. As I pumped some onto my fingers, we had a quick exchange about our status and preference for condoms.

"Want to go bare," he said as my slick fingers entered him again. "That good?"

I nodded and leaned forward, giving my cock a cursory pass with my lubed fingers before lining myself up at his entrance. His face was flushed and his eyes bright. His hair was a mess from my greedy fingers when we'd kissed earlier.

The buttoned-up city boy was nowhere to be found in the ruggedly disheveled man with the semi-feral tangle of hair currently splayed out on my bed, and I found myself wishing I'd be the only one to ever see him like this, sex-mangled and well-loved.

As I pushed into his body, into the stranglehold of his channel, I closed my eyes and prayed for patience. Tully let out a long, slow sound of surrender, which caused me to open my eyes again and watch his face.

His eyes were half-lidded, and his top teeth pegged his bottom lip for a split second before he opened his mouth in an O shape.

"Good?" I whispered.

He closed his mouth and nodded, using his hands to pull my hips in closer. I moved slowly, back and forth, until I struck the right spot inside and Tully's head arched back. A low curse escaped his lips on a groan.

My balls ached with the need to come, but I also felt a strange tingling in my upper chest as I watched him take his own pleasure. I wanted him to feel good. His experience was exponentially more important than mine, and I felt like if I could just make him happy, he'd want to do it again. And again.

"You feel so fucking good," I murmured before kissing him. His body was straight fire, and his strong hands traveled all over my ass and back and into my hair as I moved in and out of him. With every thrust, he let out a small whimper, which was probably why I felt like I wouldn't be able to hold out much longer.

I reached for his cock but noticed my hand was shaking. I felt out of control and wrecked. My orgasm was being held at bay by the barest whisper of a silent plea.

"Tully," I begged. "Need you to come."

His hand closed around mine and squeezed. Our combined grip shuttled over his cock at the speed and pressure he chose while I leaned my forehead against his shoulder and watched. The rhythm of my hips began to slip as my release roared toward me like an arrow shot from a bow.

It was too late to hold back, but thankfully, Tully cried out, and just as I felt the giddy relief of my orgasm, I also sensed the warmth of his on my hand.

As I thrust once more into him, his legs came around my back and held me close, locking us together. His chest heaved with deep breaths, and his tongue came out to lick his lips.

"Fuck," he breathed. "Fuck."

I shifted to the side a little so I wouldn't crush him as I lay down. My arms were no longer capable of supporting my weight. My entire body felt like a bowl of overcooked noodles, and my brain was happily absent, frolicking in a field of daisies somewhere out of sight and mind.

"Worth the wait," I murmured against the skin of his chest.

A puff of air hit my hair as he laughed. "That was a hell of a wait."

"Too long," I admitted.

"Way too long," he murmured. His fingers moved into my hair, toying with the strands. Between his gentle caresses and the orgasm, I could have fallen asleep right there, but I knew better than to fall asleep covered in jizz.

"Stay here," I said, shoving away from him. I felt like I weighed a thousand pounds.

I cleaned us both up and nudged him over to one side of the bed before sliding in beside him and pulling the blankets over us. Tully moved toward me and threw a leg over mine before settling his head on my bicep. "This was all part of my elaborate scheme to get a good night's sleep in a decent bed."

I wrapped my arm around his back. "Devious but vastly over-played. You could have offered to show me your dick in exchange for swapping beds, and I would have done it in a heartbeat."

He barked out a laugh that made me smile. "Slut."

"Mmhm."

We lay together in comfortable silence for a while. I assumed we'd drift off to sleep eventually, so I was surprised when I felt Tully's body stiffen in my arms.

"I forgot to tell you something," he said.

It was clear I wasn't going to like what came next.

SEVENTEEN

TULLY

Telling Dev about the subpoena and the requirement to go to Texas for the paternity test was a shitty way to end our night together.

But it was also necessary.

Dev's expression shut down just like I knew it would.

I sat up and wrapped my arms around my knees so I wouldn't have to look at him. "Don't shoot the messenger," I said under my breath as he cursed and reached for his phone, flicking on the bedside lamp and throwing the covers back.

As soon as my words were out, he stopped blustering. There was a beat of silence before he let out a breath. "You're right. I'm sorry." He leaned over and cupped the back of my head before gently turning me around to face him. "I'm not upset at you. I'm just... upset."

"I am, too." I hadn't meant to say that, exactly. I'd intended to say, "I understand." But when my words came out, I realized they were true.

Dev looked surprised. "Why are you upset?"

"Because I don't like to see you so worried, and hurt, and frustrated. And because I don't want Lellie to have to go through this. It's also unnecessary since anyone with functioning eyeballs can see she's your daughter."

He sat down on the edge of the bed and turned toward me, reaching for my face. Before he could say anything, I added, "And because I know you don't want to go back to Texas."

Dev's large hand on my face was warm and gentle. I closed my eyes and leaned into it, wishing I could turn back the clock half an hour and put us back in our intimate little bubble.

"You'll come with us, though," he said, sounding calmer than he had in a while. "And while we're there, we'll go to Katie's and see what needs doing."

"What about Lellie?" I could tell he knew what I meant. Would he keep her?

His jaw firmed, and his eyes hardened. "I'm sure as hell not letting the Scotts raise her. I care about her too much to allow them to shape her beliefs into the hate they preach. As for whether I'm going to keep her... the answer is yes. I told you I'd been thinking about it, and it really hit me today that I... I can't stand to give her up. Maybe that's selfish of me—"

"It's not."

"Yeah?" Dev's eyes met mine, their hazel depths pleading for reassurance. "There might be people out there who know more about parenting than I do and are maybe even better suited to it than I am, but... there is no one in the whole world who loves her as much as I do."

"I know." I said the words with my whole chest, believed them to the core of my being. "I'm so happy for you. Both of you."

"I'm scared shitless," he admitted. "I have a lot of things to think through. Hell, I don't even know what the schools are like here. And I'm going to have to hire an amazing nanny who loves her as much as I do. I can't do it myself, and I don't want to rely too much on my friends when they have lives of their own."

My heart warmed to see him finally turn this corner. "I'll help."

Dev leaned in and pressed a kiss to my cheek. "You already have. Thank you for not letting me run away from her."

I held him close and moved the kiss to our lips. "Are you saying I shouldn't let you run away from me, either?"

There were clearly plenty of things going through Dev's head, but he chose the easiest route. "Not tonight anyway."

I let the words stand without challenging them. Instead, I indulged myself in pushing him back on the bed and climbing on top of him to kiss him again and again. We made out like horny teenagers, hands everywhere and lips not far behind, until we ended up sideways on the bed in a sloppy sixty-nine. My obsession with his foreskin was a little unhinged, and I kept pulling off him to slide it back and forth before leaning back over him to tease it with my mouth. Every time I did that, he made a strangled sound in his throat that made my cock throb.

When we were finally empty and trembling, sweaty and gasping, I reached for his hand and tangled our fingers together.

We didn't speak, but I felt miles closer to him than I had before. Dev seemed to finally be dropping some of his walls with me, and I was grateful for it. After a while, we got up and shared a quick shower before drying off and slipping into bed together again.

The windows were open, and the night air was cool. It was a pleasant change from Dallas, where I wouldn't have dared open my windows in summer.

We settled back down so I was lying on my front with my head turned on the pillow to face him. Dev was on his side, trailing lazy fingertips along my back.

"What changed your mind about Lellie?" I wondered. "Spending the day with her? I would have thought that much alone time with a toddler would do the opposite."

The low rumble of his laugh made me smile. "No. Don't get me wrong, it was a good day... until she had a meltdown in the car on the way home. But before we went to the mountains, I stopped at the sports store to get a hiking backpack to carry her in. It's owned by a couple I've gotten to know fairly well. Nice guys, both of them." He paused. "I was surprised to find out they're trying to adopt. And they're having a hard time of it. They're the world's most perfect couple. Smart, hardworking, kind. They're super involved in the community and well-loved by everyone. They'd be the perfect dads for her, but..."

He trailed off, and I waited patiently while he gathered his thoughts.

"It made me nauseous to think about handing her to them," he said roughly. "And if I can't imagine giving her to them..." His lips tightened, and his nostrils flared. I could tell he was overcome with emotion. His voice came out in a whisper. "How could I give her up, Tully?"

I shifted over to give him a hug, holding him tightly and hoping it made him feel supported and less alone. His arms tightened around me as he tucked his face into the side of my neck.

After a few moments, he pulled back and met my eyes. "If I can't give her to Jackson and Lake, then I sure as hell can't let the Scotts take her from me. They probably think they're dealing with someone who can't afford to fight them, but they're wrong. And I will spend every last cent fighting for her."

We talked about the necessary visit to Dallas, about dealing with Katie's house and personal effects, and about the most likely methods the Scotts would use to try to discredit him. Surprisingly, Dev didn't seem worried about them succeeding. I got the feeling from a few things he said that he had friends in high places, as well as deep pockets and never-ending commitment.

What he didn't seem to realize was that the playing field wasn't always fair, especially if judges were old friends with the plaintiff or biased against single parents and/or gay men. I'd seen plenty of situations where the legal system didn't adhere to the principles of justice and fairness.

I refrained from mentioning them to him—Dev needed all the

encouragement he could get, and he needed to stay focused—but there was nothing to keep me from doing a little legwork in the background. I'd made a name for myself in law school for my ability to research the hell out of things very quickly.

I knew his attorney in Texas would be glad to receive any relevant case law research I could find. Susanna was known for being smart, focused, and relentless. Her brother Tomas was a friend of mine from law school, which was why she'd been willing to take Dev's case on such short notice.

Susanna charged what she was worth, though, and I found myself wondering again about Dev's financial situation. He said he had a lot of money... but how could a ranch hand, even one who was careful with money, save up enough to save his horse *and* his daughter in the same week? I knew I couldn't ask, but I worried about it anyway.

What I wasn't going to do was worry about my own situation right now. Technically, doing research on Dev's case was in my purview as Katie's attorney, but I was pretty sure Orris wouldn't see it that way. Which meant I would simply make sure he didn't find out.

Despite mentally preparing arguments against the Scotts in court over and over—a futile practice since I wouldn't be making them—I managed to fall asleep quickly. As usual, morning came early on the ranch, and I was awakened by Dev's attempts at sneaking out of bed.

"Fuck," I grumbled. "It's still full dark."

"You sure you grew up on a ranch?" Dev's sleep-roughened voice was sexy as hell, especially since I could hear the smile in it.

"I left it for a reason," I grumbled into the pillow.

His warm hand caressed the back of my head and down between my shoulder blades. "Go back to sleep."

I shook my head and stretched. "Nah. I'll get up and help." But when I stood, I felt the residual soreness of the previous night's amazing sex. "Maybe no horse riding, though," I muttered.

Dev looked back over his shoulder and grinned at me. "Yeah?"

"Don't look so smug. It's just because it's been a while." I moved toward the living room, where my stuff was heaped in a corner.

"How long?" he called from the bedroom, where he was pulling clothes out of a dresser drawer. My eyes lingered on the pale muscles of his ass.

I thought back. "God. Probably three years? I dated a guy a few years ago, but we'd been broken up for a while before I met you." I didn't add that I hadn't liked anyone enough since then to do more than swap quick orgasms before going our separate ways.

Dev came out of the bedroom dressed in jeans and a wash-worn T-shirt. The faded logo indicated it was from his days playing polo at Yale. I pointed to it and snickered. "Are we representing our troubled youth today? Our checkered past? I didn't get the memo. Let me change shirts. Pretty sure I have one from Jimbo's Feed and Seed somewhere around here." I pretended to rifle through my suitcase.

He glanced down at his shirt and then grinned up at me. "You mean my chukkered past."

I stared at him, forcing myself not to snort. "You did not just make a polo pun, you snotty diva."

He sniffed and adopted a highbrow accent. "I'll have you know the Yale Polo program began in 1903. For almost a hundred years, it was played in the Armory, which was used as a cavalry training center during World War I. In fact, the first polo at Yale was recorded in 1886."

"You tell a story almost as good as my grandpa, and he's been dead for thirty years." I made a fake snoring noise.

Dev's grin was adorable. I could tell he was passionate about the game. "Polo started two thousand years ago. It actually has a fascinating history. It's one of the oldest recorded sports and has even been used for military training."

"Know what the actual oldest sport is?" I asked. "Besides running, which was more of a survival thing than an actual sport."

"Don't say it," he said, rolling his eyes as he headed to the kitchen.

"Two men wrestling. And thank god for that. Cave paintings showing this glorious invention date back fifteen thousand years in France, and I, for one, am an avid fan."

We continued teasing each other while Dev moved to the kitchen and pulled out ingredients for smoothies. He dumped a mountain of frozen fruit, fresh spinach leaves, protein powder, and greek yogurt into a massive blender before turning it on.

He quickly poured the concoction into two travel mugs before handing one to me. "Coffee's downstairs. Let's go."

We made our way downstairs, where Indigo was already pouring coffee from the large carafe in the tack room into a travel mug with rainbow and cartoon stickers plastered all over it. Dev moved over to a desk against the wall and swiped the laptop's trackpad to wake it up. "Tully, while we're riding out to feed the stock in the pastures, you can go through this tutorial video on the stock management software we use. Basically, today, we're going to do a final check on who's going where and whether everything's up-to-date in their record. If they need vaccines, shoes, et cetera. Everything should be in order, but we want to make sure. Then tomorrow, you can help us manage the orders and double-check everyone's going where they're supposed to before updating locations and status for the stock being moved."

I was relieved he was allowing me an important role without any further encouragement. For a moment, I was disappointed he hadn't wanted me to mount up and join them on horseback, but then I realized he trusted me more than Indigo on a stock management software program. "No problem."

He met my eyes. "And if you get done before we return, you can go up to the big house and check on Lellie."

My heart went soft. "Want me to do that first?" I asked in a low enough voice Indigo wouldn't hear.

He shook his head. "Hopefully, they're already up, and I don't want to look desperate." He winked at me, which made my heart speed way back up.

After grabbing coffee and swallowing down half the smoothie, I followed the two of them out to the main aisle of the barn and watched as they fed and checked on the high-needs stock housed inside. Once they were done, Dev scribbled some notes on a scratch piece of paper and handed it to me. "Once you learn how to update stock records, you can add these notes from this morning, okay?"

I agreed and headed back to the tack room while they left to feed the horses in the farther pastures.

The computer work went by quickly. The system was easy enough to learn, and I finished everything Dev needed before taking off to the ranch house to find Lellie.

"Tuh-wee!" she said when Way led me into the kitchen from the front door. She was sitting in Jo's lap at the kitchen table, waving her milk cup at me. I wanted to run to her and pull her into my arms, inhale the baby scent of her, and... take her back into my keeping.

It wasn't right. It wasn't fair. But for some reason, she felt a little bit *mine*, and it was going to be nearly impossible to say goodbye when the time came.

"Hi, babygirl," I said, shoving the strange swell of emotion down. "How'd you do on your sleepover?"

She chattered at me without her usual intelligible language. I understood about a quarter of her words at best, but I was overjoyed to see she was plenty comfortable and happy with Silas, Way, and Jo.

I declined Silas's offer of coffee but accepted the offer of bacon from the leftover slices resting on a paper towel.

Way glanced my way from where he was finishing his breakfast at the table. "Dev giving Indigo a hard time?"

I swallowed the salty bacon and reached for another piece. "Don't think so. He calmed down last night after we got home." Suddenly, I realized what I'd said. "Back! After we got *back*."

Way tilted his head at me, Silas made a funny noise in his throat, and Jo looked up from where she'd been helping Lellie with her cup.

I played it cool by choking on the bacon and gasping for breath.

They all continued to stare at me until I calmed down. I made sure to keep my eyes averted. From everyone.

"The two of you slept together!"

Shockingly, the exclamation came from Jo. Silas, Way, and I swiveled our heads in her direction as I tried not to choke again.

"Aunt Blake!" Way cried with a laugh.

"Jesus," Silas muttered before turning to me. "She's right, though, isn't she?"

"Don't answer that." Dev's voice was cool and collected, coming into the room like a serene tide. "And I apologize for my friends." He said the last word with a hiss as he shot each of them a glare.

None of them looked repentant in the least.

Silas studied him. "You're looking relaxed," he said dryly. "And if I had to guess, I'd say you're looking more relaxed than you've looked in... oh, say... two years?"

Bacon shot up my nose, and I tumbled off the stool. Thankfully, Dev grabbed my elbow to keep me from hitting my head on the counter as I coughed.

"Cut it out," he snapped at his friends. "Or I'm about to tell Jo what really happened in Vegas."

"What happened in Vegas?" Jo and I asked at the same time.

Way's cheeks turned pink, but it was Silas who held up a hand. "Fine. Save the details for later if you insist, but if you won't tell me, you'll sure as shit tell Landry."

"Give me more credit than that," Dev said, reaching past me for the last slice of bacon without removing his hand from my elbow.

Way shook his head. "Even I know that man can get any gossip out of anyone. He has magical methods."

"It's called tequila shots, and it only works on Silas," Dev said before muttering, "And Kenji."

He squeezed my elbow before walking toward Lellie. As soon as she noticed him, she squawked. "Dah!"

"Hi, precious girl," he said with a big smile, leaning over to pull her out of Jo's arms. "How's my favorite tiny human today?" He pulled her close and pressed a kiss to her messy curls. She shoved her cup at him proudly, causing him to praise her for drinking her milk like a good girl.

As he took her over to the large kitchen window to show her what a pretty day it was outside, I noticed I wasn't the only one staring. Way, Jo, and Silas were all watching him intently.

"She belongs with him," Silas said softly so only I could hear.

"Yes."

"How do we convince him?"

I opened my mouth to say he was keeping her, it was already decided, but then I snapped my teeth closed. It wasn't my place to say, and I knew firsthand how critical it was to keep someone's confidence in private matters. "We give him the support he needs to see he can do it," I said instead. "We help him see it's possible."

Silas turned and met my eyes. The man's gaze was intense. It would have been intimidating if he'd held any power over me, but he didn't. "You're on his side," he said as if the news surprised him.

Technically, I was supposed to be on Lellie's side. But I'd come to realize that was the same thing.

"Yes," I said softly.

He tilted his chin down before looking back at Dev.

"Good."

———

The two days of roundup passed in a whirlwind of activity. Somehow, the morning after Trigger's emergency visit, Dev managed to talk to Indigo enough to learn he was better with kids than ranch horses. After a quick shift in duties, I saddled up and rode with Dev, Way, and Natana while Indigo and Jo watched Lellie and Silas and the new hire from the vet's office checked out stock and loaded trailers.

It was crazy busy, exhausting, and wildly entertaining. Natana was a trick rider in the Majestic rodeo, so she had stories and stunts for days. Somehow, I'd missed that Way was also the mayor of Majestic, and a national news organization had caught wind of it and came out to do a feature story on him. The photographer and reporter had stayed to get some coverage during roundup, which ended up bringing other Majesticans out of the woodwork as well.

The ranch was bursting with guests. Way's sister Sheridan brought out tables loaded with food and cold drinks, and several of their neighbors started asking questions about who Lellie belonged to.

It didn't take Dev long to claim her. In fact, all it had taken was one confused older man glancing between Lellie and Sheridan and saying, "I thought you weren't due for a while yet?"

Dev had hopped down from the saddle, grabbed Lellie from Sheridan's arms, kissed her on her fat cheek, and said, "She's mine, Mr. Jenks. This is my daughter, Lellie."

The older man had looked just as confused as before, but Lellie's adorable smile had won him over in no time.

If only she had that smile now.

Roundup had ended only Saturday, and here we were on Monday, already on our way to Dallas in a private jet Silas had somehow arranged, though it felt like the sun had barely risen.

And Lellie was not a fan of this change to her routine.

"I think we should give her something to chew on," I suggested again over the sound of her screaming. "It's probably her ears."

Dev shot me a look while Lellie continued to thrash in her car seat. The plane had only been in the air a few minutes, but Lellie had been screaming for at least a half hour.

"Fine," he said, shoving the backpack at me. "You figure out what to give her, then. Everything we brought is mushy."

He was right. As I rifled through the bag, I found overripe bananas, cut-up strawberries that had softened in their own juice, pumpkin bread squares Jo had packed, and little fingers of peanut butter and jelly sandwich. "Shit," I muttered. There wasn't anything that would help her work her jaw to pop her ears.

"PB&J," I said desperately, pulling out a piece of the sandwich and saying a silent thank-you to the universe when she shoved it into her mouth. Fat tears rolled down her cheeks, and her eyelashes were spiky-wet. I reached out a thumb to wipe them away, but before I could reach her other cheek, a pristine white cotton handkerchief appeared.

I glanced up at the stranger who'd arrived with the plane before murmuring my thanks. Kenji was slender and poised, dressed immaculately in designer suit pants and a crisp Oxford shirt. He looked like a Japanese cover model who'd been recruited by Brooks Brothers to make business attire look sexy and chic at the same time.

He hadn't cracked a smile since I'd met him last night.

We'd made our way up to the main house for dinner after showering the dirt and sweat of roundup off and had been introduced to Kenji, who'd arrived sometime during the afternoon.

"He's here to accompany you to Texas," Silas had said before whisking Dev away to his study, where the three of them presumably talked about things they didn't want me to overhear.

I'd wanted to ask Dev about it when we returned to the apartment, but he'd excused himself to check on Trigger as soon as we'd gotten Lellie down for the night.

Roundup had kicked my ass, so I'd fallen asleep on the sofa before he'd returned. Thankfully, he nudged me awake just long enough to move me into his bed with him before I fell right back to sleep.

And now I couldn't ask him because Kenji was right here.

After wiping Lellie's face of tears and now peanut butter and jelly, I glanced apologetically from the ruined handkerchief to Kenji. He waved my concerns away. "It happens."

"Thank you for arranging for the plane," I began, shifting on the soft leather sofa situated across from the one Kenji sat on. "I was going to ask my firm to send theirs. It was generous of Silas to do this for Dev."

Kenji opened his mouth to speak, glanced at Dev, and closed it again. Something seemed off, and it made me uneasy.

"Is this Silas's plane?" I asked, looking between the two of them.

And if it was, what the hell did Silas do for a living? I'd thought he was a business consultant.

Dev shifted in his seat. "It's owned by a company the group of us co-founded."

I attempted to glare at him while keeping an eye on Lellie. He was part of a group of friends who *owned a plane?*

He cleared his throat. "Technically, it's the company's plane."

"And you and your friends own the company," I prompted. Kenji remained conspicuously silent.

"Yes."

I closed my eyes and counted to ten, trying desperately to remember none of this was any of my business. When I opened my eyes, Kenji was gone. Thankfully, Lellie had stopped crying and was now reaching for the bag of strawberries. I helped her pick them out of the bag one at a time while Dev decided how much to trust me.

Finally, I sensed him lean toward me. When he spoke, his voice was lower. Softer.

"I met the guys at Yale. I think you knew that. We worked on a project together that went very well." He leaned over and ran a wet wipe over Lellie's hands before continuing. "After college, we started a company together. A business consulting firm that specialized in taking ideas to market and finding financing."

"Venture capital."

"Kind of. Also like an incubator. Technically, I still own part of it, but corporate stuff wasn't really my wheelhouse. I don't love working at a desk in a high-rise. That was more Bash and Silas's thing. Landry had his modeling, and Zane had his music."

I glanced at him. "What did *you* have?"

"At the time, I was working with the Yale Animal Resources Center, following up on research I'd done before graduating. I was considering applying to vet school, but I didn't want to leave the project while it was still underway. And then my brother died. And everything changed."

I knew his brother had died in a car crash a few years ago. Katie had told me that much. I moved closer to him and took his hand in mine. "Will you tell me about it?"

He glanced back over at Lellie before finally meeting my eyes again. "It was my fault. The accident."

My stomach dropped. "You were behind the wheel?"

"No. But I gave him the car."

It took a minute for the words to make sense because they didn't actually make sense at all.

"You... gave him the car? How does that make a car accident your fault?"

He closed his eyes and held his breath for a beat, pulling his hand out of mine to rub his face. "It was a fancy sports car. He was too young... too immature. He begged me for it. I should have never listened to him. He wasn't ready for that kind of responsibility."

"How old was he?"

"Twenty."

I blinked. What was I missing? "Dev. He was old enough to vote. Old enough to be in the military and get deployed in a war zone. To drive tanks. And you're blaming yourself for how he drove a car? I don't understand."

He ran his hands down his jean-clad thighs. "You don't need to understand. Just know it was my fault. I blame myself, and my parents sure as hell blame me. It was enough for them to kick me out of the family and tell me they wouldn't take a dime of my 'tainted money.' They turned to their religion, which would have been fine, except they ended up going to the Church of Heavenly Victory. So instead of getting comfort from their faith, they learned how to be extra hateful and intolerant. Pastor Scott apparently made it very clear to his congregation around that time that greed and covetousness were the root of all evil."

"That's rich," I murmured, thinking of the sprawling mansion Katie's parents lived in with their retinue of servants to support it.

"Agreed. They thought I'd gone to the evil Northeast and been turned into someone they no longer recognized. An 'Ivy Elite,' even though I was literally working for free while wading knee-deep in horse shit every day. They figured I'd gotten my money gambling with rich kids, and nothing I said could make them change their minds. It took me a long time and a ton of therapy to realize it was easier for them to blame me than themselves or, god forbid, my brother, Matt."

"So, did the therapist help you come to terms with the fact his death wasn't your fault?"

I already knew the answer based on the way he spoke about it.

"Not really. He tried, but I figured he didn't have the whole story." He surprised me by smiling. "Don't worry, I can hear how that sounds now that I'm saying it out loud."

"Good."

"I've spent a long time blaming myself," he admitted.

"Sounds like it."

He reached for my hand and held it between both of his. "It was why I didn't want to know about Katie's baby."

It made a strange kind of sense. He was obviously fearful of getting close to a new family member and possibly losing them, too.

He took a breath. "But in avoiding it, I lost out on more time with Katie. I lost out on seeing her as a mom and meeting Lellie earlier. I missed things that would have enriched my life... made it immeasurably better."

I nodded, suddenly feeling the sting of his regret in my own eyes.

"Life's too short, Tully," he said softly. "I don't want to miss any more of it."

I pulled my hand out of his so I could put my arm around his shoulders and pull him in tight to my side on the lush leather sofa. Lellie had fallen asleep with her mouth and hands coated in sticky strawberry juice.

As the sleek jet continued to rocket us toward the challenges that awaited us in Dallas, I considered how I'd felt the day I'd left Dallas with Lellie in tow.

I'd been overwhelmed with anxiety at the prospect of seeing Dev again, concern that Katie had been misguided in her choice of guardian, worry for Lellie, and reluctance to leave my work at Dunlevy, Pace, and Trumble even for a few days.

It was hard to believe how much had changed with just a short time in tiny Majestic, Wyoming...

In a short time with Devon McKay.

And I began to realize that going back to Dallas now didn't feel at all like I was going home.

EIGHTEEN

DEV

I felt raw and strange after telling Tully about Matt, but it had helped me process the guilt I still felt. For the first time since Matt's death, I had the promise of a family again. I had someone depending on me. And I felt okay about it.

Maybe better than okay.

Lellie slept with her head against the side of the car seat. Kenji had returned to his seat after Tully had walked back to use the bathroom and let him know it was safe to return up front.

"She's beautiful, Dev," Kenji said with his usual calm voice.

Our trusty assistant rarely delved into personal commentary. He was the most professional person I knew and took pride in keeping our lives in order and his role clearly defined. While he wasn't officially one of the brotherhood, he was an invaluable member of our group, and I wished he took more opportunities to own his place among us.

"Thank you. I agree."

"You're keeping her."

Kenji had an uncanny way of knowing what was up before the

rest of us did, so I wasn't surprised he'd been able to figure out my change of plan.

"Yeah. I couldn't stomach allowing someone else to raise her. She deserves to be loved and nurtured, valued and encouraged. I know I can give her that." I smoothed back a wayward curl on her head. "And I'm lucky enough to already have the support of an incredible group of friends and family."

He nodded. Glints of his ebony hair caught the sunlight slanting in from the window as he tilted his chin toward the back of the plane where Tully had gone. "He going to be able to give her up?"

I was confused by the question. "He doesn't have a stake in this."

Kenji pressed his lips together and nodded but didn't speak.

I tried explaining. "He was never on the list of possible parents. Katie faced career challenges as a single mom, and she knew that no matter how much Tully cares about Lellie, making partner at his law firm is his priority."

Kenji's eyes narrowed so slightly that if I didn't know him well, I wouldn't have noticed.

"What?" I asked, throwing up my hands. "Jesus, just say it."

"He loves her."

There was no doubt about that. "Yes. Definitely. And he's welcome to continue loving her. Visiting her. Keeping in touch with how she's doing." I looked back at Lellie.

Kenji's only response was a thoughtful "Hmmm," but it made me scowl in response.

"If you have a point to make, you're going to have to give me more than a disapproving hum," I said.

"I was just thinking about how priorities change, that's all. And that it's a good idea to give the people you care about *options*."

I shook my head. "Still not getting it."

Kenji studied me for another minute before retrieving his tablet, tapping on it a few times, and handing it to me.

I looked at an email app. "What is this?"

"The email account Katie and I set up when she found out she was pregnant."

I stared at him. "What do you mean?"

"You asked me to coordinate any legal situations that might arise," he reminded me. "So I got in touch with Katie to make sure she had my contact info. When she learned she was pregnant, she kept me in the loop. She knew you didn't want to know... but she thought there might come a point you changed your mind. I kept in touch, checking in regularly and ensuring all was well. She sent these sweet updates, sharing ultrasound photos and anecdotes since we'd sort of become friends at that point. So I set up an email address where she could chronicle things for you in case you ever wanted to see them someday. This is everything she ever sent."

There were at least a hundred emails here, if not more. "Kenji..." I whispered.

"There are photos and her birth story. I know that for sure. And then there are a few she marked for your eyes only, so I didn't read them."

I couldn't believe what I was seeing. The scope of it, the sheer number of messages and photos she'd sent, was overwhelming. Why in the world had she done this? I didn't deserve it.

Kenji's voice was soothing. "Katie wanted you to know you were Lellie's father regardless of where you were in the world or how you felt about it. She wanted to make sure you didn't miss it if you ever wanted to claim her."

"She was right," I breathed, staring at the screen. "I *do* regret not being involved in Lellie's life. I hate that I missed all these milestones."

"Katie gave you a choice, even though you were really adamant about what you thought you wanted," Kenji said pointedly.

"She did," I agreed, and the knowledge made my heart squeeze with a bittersweet combination of gratitude and grief.

Kenji huffed out a breath like I was missing whatever point he was trying to make. "Dev..." Before he could say whatever it was he intended to say, Tully reappeared.

He glanced between Kenji and me. "Want me to sit in the back and give you some time?"

Kenji lifted an eyebrow at me, but I shook my head. "Sit," I said. "Kenji just told me about an email account Katie sent messages to about Lellie. Did you know about this?"

I could tell from the frown lines this was the first he was hearing about it. "No. What kind of messages? Was she trying to get in touch with you?"

"No, no." I explained how the account had come about and pointed at the screen with all the messages.

"That doesn't surprise me," he said with a soft smile. "She was very grateful to you for helping her."

The guilt gnawed at me. "I owed her a favor. When I applied to college, she got her father and grandparents to write me recommendations, not only for admission but also for scholarships. And she's the one who found scholarships for me to apply to. Without that, I never would have been able to go to Yale. Katie changed my life."

I tried not to think about how that single decision had led to the death of my brother. It was impossible now to wish for things to have changed. If they had, Lellie might not have been conceived, and how could I ever wish for that?

"Do you want time to read through them?" Tully asked, nodding at the screen.

"Not now. I'm not..." I let out a huff of laughter. "I'm not feeling strong enough to go down that rabbit hole."

I handed the tablet back to Kenji, knowing he would send me the credentials to take ownership of the email account.

After clearing my throat, I changed the subject slightly. "Did you schedule a meeting with the trusts and estate attorney about changing my will?" I asked Kenji. "I need to make sure Lellie is protected."

"I can look over whatever they come up with," Tully offered. "And you might want to continue using Katie's wealth manager or find your own. Eleven million dollars would be a lot to handle by yourself."

Kenji and I exchanged a look. "Uh... yeah," I agreed. "Good call. Definitely someone will have to manage it."

Tully narrowed his eyes and glanced between us. "What? What am I missing?"

I opened my mouth to tell him it was nothing when I caught another of Kenji's judgmental looks.

I sighed. He was right. There was no good reason why I couldn't admit the truth about Lellie's trust fund. I'd gotten to a point after Matt's death where I was afraid of my wealth and the damage it could cause, ashamed of the damage it had done. But I knew Tully wouldn't feel that way. I wasn't sure I felt that way myself anymore.

"I already have a wealth manager," I admitted slowly. "Lellie's trust fund came from me."

Tully's surprise was colored with confusion. "But I thought you didn't know about Lellie."

"I didn't. But I knew there might be a baby, and I wanted to contribute to their financial security. That was one of the reasons I put Katie in touch with Kenji."

Tully glanced at Kenji. "You arranged it?"

He nodded. "Dev instructed me to set up a trust for any child or children that resulted from the arrangement. Once Lellie was born, the money was transferred over."

Tully was clearly shocked. "So... millions of dollars were transferred out of your account and into Lellie's trust."

Kenji and I both nodded.

"And you didn't notice and say, 'Ah, there must be a baby'?" he demanded, looking at me.

I shook my head.

"Holy shit." Tully ran a hand through his styled hair. "You weren't kidding when you said you had money."

I felt Kenji's eyes on me, so I shook my head as subtly as I could. "No, I wasn't."

I could tell Tully wanted to know more but was too polite to ask. Part of me wished I could explain that the source of my money and the sheer size of it were secrets that weren't only mine to share. After Matt's death, the brotherhood had agreed to put a lid on the wealth we'd made from selling the emergency traffic control system we'd developed in college. I'd put a lot of it into charitable trusts and endowments, but there was so much of it, the money I had left continued to grow at a rate I studiously ignored.

Tully moved his hand like he was going to reach for mine but stopped when he remembered Kenji was with us. I quickly reached for his hand anyway and squeezed it. Kenji didn't seem surprised by the intimacy.

Tully's cheeks were a little flushed. I couldn't tell if he was hot, frustrated, or embarrassed. I hoped it wasn't the latter because I took comfort in feeling his hand in mine right now.

"That was good of you," he said softly. "To make sure your daughter was taken care of that way."

I snorted. "I think a good parent would have been involved in his daughter's life from the beginning. Setting up a trust fund was the very least I could do for my child."

Tully and Kenji exchanged a look, and both laughed out loud.

"Remind me to have words with my parents," Tully said.

"Same," Kenji added, shaking his head with mock severity. "Setting up a trust fund was the very least they could have done."

I kicked his shiny and probably very expensive shoe with my boot. "I meant for *me*. Obviously. In my situation."

"I know." Kenji patted my arm. "We were just teasing."

After a few moments, I asked, "Do you think Katie resented me for not wanting anything to do with the pregnancy and the baby?"

Tully immediately shook his head. "Nope. She was grateful to you for giving her Lellie, and she wanted you to have the option of getting involved because she cared about you, but Katie was also grateful that she was able to solo parent her. One of our coworkers dealt with constant co-parenting stress after a contentious divorce, and Katie definitely didn't want to have to deal with that."

I knew he was right. Katie had explained to me how seriously she'd taken the decision to become a single parent. But I still worried I'd let her down.

Kenji added his own reassurance. "You'll see when you read her messages. She was grateful. She was also happy, Dev. Very happy."

"It couldn't have been easy," I murmured.

"No," Kenji said. "I'm sure it wasn't. But she had resources. That's more than a lot of single parents have."

Tully agreed and added, "And you'll obviously have the same."

Kenji clasped both of his hands together over the tablet in his lap. "You might consider hiring Indigo."

"Right," I said with a laugh. "Stoner kid?"

Tully's hand tightened around mine. "Kenji's right. That kid has spent the past three years working part-time at a preschool as part of his early childhood education program."

"Wait, Indigo got his degree in early childhood education? You're kidding."

"He's not," Kenji said. "You know I did a full background check on him before letting Way bring him onto the ranch. He graduated with a degree in early childhood education. His references from the preschool were stellar. They love him and have tried to hire him permanently."

That was surprising. I would have thought Indigo was more likely to find himself a VW bus and tour the country following a Grateful Dead cover band... but if there was one thing I was learning this week it was that it was really shitty to judge people based on what you *thought* you knew about them.

Tully explained what he'd learned about Indigo's love of outdoor adventures and how much he appreciated the opportunity to live close to so many mountain sports. "Besides," he continued, "Lellie likes him. The other day, he sang her songs about mushrooms that made her giggle."

I snorted. "Were they 'special mushrooms'?" I teased.

The edge of Tully's mouth lifted. "Maybe."

Kenji grinned.

I blew out a breath and considered it. He was a nice, easygoing guy who definitely cared a lot about doing the right thing. His stress and concern after Trigger's incident proved it. After a few minutes, I muttered, "Songs, plural? Who knows *multiple* songs about mushrooms?"

Tully huffed out a laugh. "A vegan with an agenda?"

Kenji said, "He also plays guitar. Or so Silas says. Which reminds me, Zane told me to tell you that he's thinking about performing with some friends at the Factory in Dallas in a couple weeks, so maybe you can catch up with him there. He was hoping to see you when he's in Majestic for the AdventureSmash concert, but I told him you might not be back by then."

"Shit. I forgot all about the concert." Zane was scheduled to headline the event, which had been planned to coincide with one of the AdventureSmash races taking place near Three Daughters. "I thought Zane was planning to visit family in Georgia after that."

"He was, but when he found out you might miss him in Majestic, he decided he'd come to you in Dallas if he had to."

"Wow," Tully said, eyebrows lifted. "You said your friend Zane had his music, but I didn't realize he was good enough to play at the Factory. What does he play?"

While I tried to figure out how to tell Tully my friend Zane was a famous musician without sounding like a douche, Kenji tapped his tablet and handed it over. It showed the Wikimedia page for Zee Barlo, which featured a photo of him from the Billboard Music Awards.

Instead of the usual reaction of widening eyes and some form of "You're friends with Zee Barlo?" Tully seemed to shut completely down.

"Oh," was all he said before releasing my hand and turning to look out the window.

I glanced at Kenji in hopes he might understand why Tully's reaction had been so strange, but Kenji looked just as confused as I was.

"So..." I began. "If we can make the timing work for one of those events, I'd love for you to meet him, Tully."

Tully nodded at the clouds outside the window. "Sure... Maybe."

I glanced at Kenji again, who took it as a silent request to vacate the premises. Once he was gone, I moved to kneel on the floor in front of him before reaching for his hands. I tried to be as gentle as possible, watching him closely for any hints of what he was thinking. "Hey. What just happened?"

He glanced over to Kenji's empty seat before responding. "I just feel like I don't know you at all, Dev. And it makes me feel ridiculous. I had this... idea in my head of who you are, and now I'm discovering things about you that make me feel like... maybe you're a completely different person."

"I'm a different person because I have a famous friend?"

"No. It's not that. I don't care that you're friends with Zee Barlo. It's really great, actually. I'd love to meet him. But you've never talked about him. I've lived with you for almost two weeks now, and you... you're like a fucking puzzle box with latches and locks. I thought you were this smart, quiet ranch hand, but every time I turn around, I feel like I'm accidentally finding out big things that change my perception of you. I thought you were a scholarship kid like me, and now I discover you're a millionaire."

"I *was* a scholarship kid. And Tully, I hate to break it to you, but you're a high-powered attorney at a big Dallas law firm."

"Yeah, I get it. But I don't have enough money to give someone millions of dollars without even knowing I did it. Jesus fuck. And it's not the money. It's not. It's..." He pulled a hand out of my grip and waved it around. "It's the not knowing. It's the fact I've learned all this shit unintentionally. Like you don't want me to know anything, and I feel like I'm intruding by learning it anyway."

I reached for his fluttering hand and brought it to my lips. I hated seeing him agitated, but most of all, I hated that he was right. "It's not about you," I assured him. "I started realizing this week that I've been keeping people I care about at arm's length for a long time. I figured the fewer close attachments I had, the easier my life would be. You know that Silas, Zane, and our friends Bash and Landry are the nearest thing I have to family, right? But I didn't even tell them I'd agreed to help Katie conceive until a few days ago." I shook my head ruefully. "I don't want to do that anymore. So if you have questions, ask them, and I'll answer..." I thought about my agreement with the brotherhood and added, "...as long as the answer doesn't involve other people. What do you want to know?"

Tully's cheeks were deeper pink now, and I was beginning to realize he'd been upset since before the subject of Zane had come up.

He took a breath and exhaled slowly. The edge of his lips turned up, surprising me. "I want to know if you like... *like* me, like me."

I blinked at him.

His cheeks darkened. "I want to know if I'm the only one who..."

I lurched forward and kissed him on the lips. Hard. "Fuck no," I breathed against his lips. "Not the only one."

He moved his hands up to clasp my face so he could kiss me more. I could taste a hint of cheddar Goldfish crackers on his tongue, which made me laugh. I pulled back from the kiss. "Lellie didn't have anything crunchy to eat earlier because you stole her fucking snack, you shit!"

"They're made with something nefarious, Devon," he said earnestly. "It's like... crack or meth or something, I don't know. It's not my fault. Blame the fish."

I leaned in and kissed him again before murmuring in his ear. "I want you in every way. I'll do better at trying to be open with you. I promise."

He shuddered and leaned closer. "Just talk to me. I want to know you—the real you, not the one in my head."

"Talk to you..." I tried to think of how I could prove myself to him, show him I was willing to open up more and allow myself to be more vulnerable. "I'm... I'm terrified of my parents finding out about Lellie, but I also want them to meet her. I think part of me imagines they'll suddenly forgive me for Matt's death and want to be part of my life again if they learn they have a grandchild."

Tully took a few moments to consider it. "What would your ideal scenario look like moving forward? If they accepted her... and you... would you change your mind about moving back to Texas?"

I shook my head. "Definitely not. I'm building the house in Majestic, and I know it's the right place for Lellie and me."

"So then you'd visit. And they could visit. You've already established money isn't an issue for you. But your money *is* an issue with them. How would that work?"

We continued to talk it through until Lellie began to stir. Tully stood up to unlatch the buckles of her car seat while I searched for the backpack with her diaper supplies.

"One more thing," Tully said. "If you do decide to work things out with your parents, pay attention to whether you're doing it because it's what you actually want or because it's what you feel like you 'should' be doing. My mom spent a lot of years begging me to reconcile with my father. She used to say, 'He's your father,' as if that was enough reason to put up with his bull..." His eyes slipped to Lellie. "Malarky. It took me a long time to figure out that being a father was more than donating DNA, and if he wasn't going to act like a father, I wasn't going to treat him like one."

Tully's words stayed with me as we landed and made our way to Katie's house in Uptown. It was an adorable historic home that she'd taken great pride in fixing up after law school. I wondered if I should try to hang on to it for Lellie or sell it. Tully would probably have good advice on the subject, but it was definitely too soon to bring up the idea of selling her house.

Kenji managed to bring half the suitcases in without breaking a sweat, whereas I felt like a soppy mess. My shirt was covered in sticky handprints, spilled coffee, and sweat, and I was desperate for a shower.

"We need to leave for the clinic in an hour," Kenji reminded me. "I'll arrange for a pickup."

Tully nodded toward the driveway. "There's a garage in the back. Katie's Range Rover should be in it. We can use that."

Kenji allowed Tully to show him around upstairs so he could deposit the luggage accordingly. Meanwhile, I was dealing with a sudden and unexpected situation.

"Mama!" Lellie cried as soon as she realized where she was. "Mama!" She squirmed to get down and surprised me by running immediately to a toy box in the corner of the living room instead of somewhere she expected Katie to be lurking.

She busied herself with her toys, pulling out a brightly colored plastic music keyboard and a wooden sorting box. One by one, she brought them over to show me, chatting happily, if unintelligibly, about each one.

I let out a sigh of relief for the temporary reprieve, even though I now realized I'd need to expect more moments of confusion like this.

Tully returned to the living room and asked how I was doing.

"I feel so stupid. I should have known she'd wonder where Katie was when she came here," I said before lowering my voice. "But I don't know how to help her. I don't know what's appropriate to say to her about Katie's death."

"The attorney I recommended is going to meet us at the clinic. Susanna might have some good resources."

I blew out another breath, feeling exhausted and overwhelmed. Before I could ask Tully to watch Lellie while I cleaned up, Tully grabbed me and pulled me into a hug. "You're doing well. I promise." He pressed a kiss to my ear. "It would be hard for anyone. Just keep caring about her the way you do and go easy on yourself."

I fought back the sting of emotions for the millionth time that day. "Thank you."

When he pulled away, I suddenly realized he'd left his luggage by the front door. "Oh... are you... I guess..." I scrambled to figure out how to act casual and still beg him to stay. "You'll want to go to your place?"

"I assumed I'd go home, yes."

"Right." I cleared my throat. "Of course."

His bright eyes took on a teasing glint. "Unless you want me to—"

"Fuck, yes. Yes, please," I blurted before he'd even finished the sentence.

He laughed and leaned in again, teasing me with the barest brush of his lips on mine. I grumbled and lurched forward, demanding more for a few precious moments before pulling away. "I'm filthy. Would you mind keeping an eye on her while I shower?"

Kenji walked in, looking as crisp and fresh as always. "I'll watch her while both of you shower. Think she'll let me brush her hair?"

"No!" Tully and I both barked in unison. Lellie hated the hairbrush.

Kenji held up both palms. "Okay, fine. It's just that I suspect the Scotts are going to take this opportunity of showing up so they can put eyes on her. We want to make sure there's nothing they can point to as evidence you're not a good parent."

"You're welcome to try," I said, telling him where to find what he needed. Then I grabbed Tully's hand and dragged him up the stairs and into the guest room.

The shower was quick but very productive. When I returned downstairs in clean clothes, I not only felt refreshed but also relaxed. Tully and I had gotten each other off before scrubbing each other down, a regime I recommended with a full and hearty five stars.

When we entered the living room, Lellie's hair was immaculately combed. The curls were adorable instead of haystack-esque, while Kenji appeared to be serenely scrolling through his cell phone.

"How in the world..." Tully murmured.

"Yeah, what's your secret with the hair?" I demanded.

Kenji looked up. "I told her it wasn't time for Lellie's hair brushing but that her stuffed tiger would look extra special if I brushed its hair. And then I made a big deal about how much Tiger loved having her hair brushed and how she looked so beautiful she would probably get to bring one of her toys in the car when we go for a ride. By the way, Lellie is bringing Tiger *and* the music toy, so don't praise me too much."

While we loaded up the car, I realized I was feeling much better about the trip to the clinic. Even though I dreaded seeing the Scotts, I was looking forward to getting one step closer to proving I was Lellie's father and the best person to raise her.

It only took half an hour before my optimism died a quick and sudden death.

When it wasn't just the Scotts waiting outside the paternity clinic but my parents, too.

NINETEEN

TULLY

I sensed Dev's tension the moment I pulled the car into the parking lot of the clinic. There was some barely perceptible change in his breathing, or maybe he made a low sound in his throat. Either way, my eyes flicked to his in the rearview mirror.

Dev's eyes carried a world of pain. I'd seen that emotion in his expression before, and I was desperate to understand it so I could try to ease it in some way.

"Nervous?" I asked.

"It's my parents. I don't know why they're here, or—"

Kenji muttered a curse under his breath and began tapping on his tablet from the passenger seat next to me.

"The Scotts must have told them," I said. "You said they go to the Scotts' church, right? I wouldn't put it past Pastor Scott to use that to his advantage."

Kenji remained calm, which seemed to be his superpower. "You don't have to speak to them. In fact, I can get a protective order started…"

"No," Dev said firmly. "I'll talk to them, but not until after the test. I want this over with, especially while Lellie is in a good mood. But if... if things go bad..."

After throwing the vehicle into Park, I turned and met his eyes. "Kenji and I will get her out of here. You can get a ride back to the house."

He reached out and squeezed my shoulder. "Thank you. That would make me feel much better. I don't want her caught up in the middle of this."

Neither do I.

I didn't say the words, but I felt them just as strongly as he did.

We got out of the car. Dev unbuckled Lellie while Kenji and I stood behind him, blocking them from view. I'd chosen a parking spot on the other side of the lot, but I could see the cluster of people with the Scotts heading our way.

I also saw Susanna waiting for us near the entrance. After waving her over, I met her partway and skipped the pleasantries. "Those are the plaintiffs, as well as Dev's parents, who we didn't expect. We think the Scotts might have recruited them to their cause."

"Got it. I'll handle them. You get everyone inside. The clinic is good about taking patients back to a private room and making everyone else stay in the waiting room. They'll only allow the plaintiff's attorney to send back a witness to observe silently and sign paperwork to that effect. If there's any misbehavior, they won't hesitate to kick people out."

She turned to greet the Scotts with a friendly smile while I turned back to Dev. He was ghost-pale but determined. His biceps and shoulders bulged against the fabric of his shirt as he held Lellie on his hip. He was wearing a pressed button-down shirt with the sleeves rolled up, and the dark hair on his exposed forearms was giving me thoughts wholly inappropriate for this moment.

I rapidly blinked my eyes as I turned away. Pretty sure Kenji caught me at it.

As we approached the group Susanna was trying to hold back, Pastor Scott approached me, all smiles. "Tully, there you are. Great to see you again. And let me get a look at my granddaughter. Hi, Eleanor, sweetie. What a big girl you are!"

Lellie immediately clung onto Dev more tightly and leaned her head against his shoulder. She wasn't great with people she didn't know well. While Katie hadn't been estranged from her parents completely, she hadn't spent much time with them and Lellie.

"Like I said," Susanna said, stepping between Pastor Scott and Dev as we continued to move toward the clinic's entrance, "you are welcome to wait out here or in the waiting room, but we simply ask you to allow my client to proceed straight to the appointment first. I'm sure you agree it's in our best interest to collect this evidence as quickly as possible."

"Of course, of course," Pastor Scott said.

I recognized the attorney standing next to him and gave him a cool nod. Brock Lois was an attorney with his own practice who occasionally worked with Dunlevy, Pace, and Trumble. I assumed Orris had been the one to refer the Scotts to him since he was well-known at our firm as a bulldog in family law cases. I didn't trust Brock for shit, but I was grateful the case was no longer causing a potential conflict of interest with my own firm.

Then I noticed the man behind Katie's dad.

Orris Dunlevy stepped around Pastor Scott. "Tully! Good of you to come. Thank you for escorting everyone here safely. I'll take it from here."

Heat filled my face as a swell of embarrassment twisted my stomach. Before I could say anything, Dev broke his silent, stoic act. "He's here at my request. Until this situation is settled, I believe it's in everyone's best interest for Lellie to have as much support as possible, both legally and personally."

It was enough to stop the Scotts and their attorneys in their tracks and allow us to continue into the clinic without further interference.

"Well done," I murmured as Susanna stepped forward to check Dev and Lellie in for the appointment.

Dev turned and shoved Lellie into my arms. Thankfully, she

came willingly and clung to me as tightly as she'd clung to Dev. "If you're her representative at this appointment, they'll let you back with us," he murmured.

I glanced up and saw the nerves in his expression. He was terrified, and I couldn't figure out why.

Thankfully, a nurse called us back very quickly, and I followed Dev while Susanna held the door and ensured no one else followed us other than a nondescript junior attorney from Brock's firm who had been sent as the eyewitness. Kenji settled himself in a chair in the waiting room and remained unruffled.

Orris shot me a final glare as the door closed behind us.

When we got to the exam cubicle, I reached for Dev's arm. "Hey. You know it's not a blood test, right? It's a cheek swab."

"I know."

I lowered my voice. "Why are you shaking?"

"What if this is it? What if she's not really mine?"

I wanted to bark out a laugh, but I could tell he wasn't joking.

"Devon," I said, making sure my voice was still low but also firm. "This child is your clone. Look at her. Look at her eyes. They're the color of southern pine and sweet tea." I flicked one of her dark curls and then reached out to wrap one of his thicker waves around my finger before tugging. "I wish you could see it like the rest of us do."

Susanna must have realized what was happening because her expression softened, and she grinned at him. "He's right. Anyone who saw you holding her out there knows how ridiculous this performance is. She looks more like you than my twin brother looks like me."

Dev inhaled a shaky breath. "Thank you. I know it's silly. I just got here and suddenly worried that they would find a way to take her from me. The fact I'm her biological parent is the only thing on my side."

I wanted to tell him that wasn't true, that there were a million other things about him that made him Lellie's perfect choice, but a lab tech walked in before I had a chance to speak.

After briefly introducing himself, the tech had everyone sign the necessary consent forms before getting down to business. It seemed to take forever to gather multiple samples and line them up carefully in a tray with barcoded labels indicating Dev and Lellie's names and birthdates. We even had to sign the envelopes the samples were being sent in. And then, just when it looked like we were done, we each had to sign off on witness statements to ensure proper chain of custody of the samples, too.

Lellie was good throughout most of the long, boring process, only making a break for it once while Dev and I were signing the last few items. Susanna stepped out to take a call, and Lellie tried to follow, but fortunately, her toddler stumble was unsteady enough that we noticed her escape attempt immediately. I headed her off while Dev swooped in from behind, scooped her up, and tickled her.

"Not so much different than cutting horses," I teased so only Dev could hear.

"True." Dev gave me one of his genuine, devastating smiles. "And easier with teamwork," he said softly, making my heart race.

The tech produced a lollipop for Lellie, ensuring her continued cooperation, and we returned to witness the tech slide the samples into the labeled packages, seal them, and sign the final couple of forms without incident before making our way back out to the waiting room...

Where everyone and their damned brother was waiting for us.

My happy mood immediately soured, and I could sense Dev's anxiety rising again.

I'd spotted Dev's parents as soon as we'd pulled into the parking lot. His father had the same head of dark hair, and his mother had something of Dev in the shape of her face or the set of her mouth. They'd stayed quiet up to now, seeming to wait to be called on by Pastor Scott before asking to see their only grandchild.

My boss approached as soon as we came from the back into the larger waiting room. "I think it would be a sign of good faith to allow the Scotts to take Eleanor for the night."

I tilted my head at Orris while holding Lellie tighter. "I'm not sure I understand what you mean by 'good faith' in this case."

He frowned. "They're her grandparents. It's only right to allow them a visit while all of this gets sorted out."

Dev's mom was clearly listening because she nodded her head emphatically, her eyes never leaving her granddaughter.

I felt Dev move behind me. His hand brushed gently across my lower back where no one could see it before he came around me and reached for Lellie with a murmured thanks.

He stepped forward into the center of the small crowd. "Mom, Dad, this is Lellie. My daughter."

I wondered later if their quick glance at Pastor Scott for permission to approach had anything to do with what happened next. To be fair to Dev, he tried to ignore it at first.

Pastor Scott approached from the side with his arms out. "Come to Grandpa, sweetie. We sure are happy to see you, yes we are."

Mrs. Scott was already crying while Mrs. McKay clutched her hands together in white-knuckled control.

Dev glanced at Katie's father. "Pastor Scott, respectfully, since you've already met Lellie, I'd like a few minutes with my parents. I'm sure you can agree they have some lost time to make up for."

Again, the McKays watched Pastor Scott for his response. He frowned. "And whose fault was that? Kathryn obviously didn't feel that a relationship with any paternal relatives was necessary."

Dev remained calm. "Until she gave me full custody of Lellie in her will. And given that I will now be her full legal guardian, I'm sure you can respect my attempts to honor my father and my mother by allowing them to meet their grandchild. I will ask you again politely to move back and allow me to have a moment with my parents."

Pastor Scott's nostrils flared, but he finally tilted his chin down and allowed Dev to move to the side where he and his parents could have a moment. After a significant look and head tilt from Orris, I followed him to the opposite side of the room.

"Don't worry," he said in a low voice. "The McKays know what to do."

I glanced over at Dev, who seemed to be involved in an awkward introduction between Lellie and his parents. She clung to him and resisted all of his parents' attempts to reach for her.

"What do you mean?" I asked. "What will they do?"

"They've given John's team plenty of information to help prove he would be an unfit parent. Their loyalty is well-placed as they've been members of the Scotts' congregation for quite a while now."

My stomach dropped. "What kind of information?" I looked for Susanna, who caught my glance and crinkled her eyebrows.

"He has a history of wild spending—they suspect gambling may have been involved, suspicion of reckless endangerment, and he's neglected to communicate with his parents for over five years. Apparently, he's not what you'd call a family man."

I nodded along as he continued to tell me that John had the case fully in hand and that Orris appreciated me keeping such a close eye on the Scotts' "precious treasure."

"Now, we could really use your help. The Scotts would like some alone time with their granddaughter. Do you think the best way to go about it would be to arrange for the McKays to take her overnight? McKay might be more amenable to his own parents' request, and I'm sure Franklin and Delaney would be happy to host them at their house so they can all enjoy some quality time with her."

I wanted to be petulant. To ask him why the *fuck* he would imagine Dev had any intention of allowing any of them to take Lellie for the night considering how they were treating him, but I held my tongue. Not only was it not my place to fight Dev's battles for him, but it was also a waste of time.

Even if I wanted to try, there was nothing I could say to convince Dev to hand Lellie over to the Scotts, even just for one night. And I couldn't imagine he was keen to allow his parents to take her after they'd refused to speak to him for over five years.

Because I knew the truth of the "neglect to communicate" situation, and it wasn't Dev's decision. He'd told me how much their rejection had crushed him, and I knew he would never have been the one to shut them out the way Orris implied.

"I think we should leave it up to Brock to handle," I said as neutrally as possible. "He's in the best position to manage it without anyone accusing our firm of a conflict of interest."

Orris watched Dev interact with his parents. I could sense Dev's discomfort in the stiff line of his spine and the protective way his arms curled around Lellie's little body.

"He seems off to me," Orris said in a low voice. "What was he like in Wyoming?"

"He's a great father, Orris," I said. "He cares about her very much and has a stable life there with plenty of friends and family to support him."

Orris turned to me. "I thought the McKays were his only living family?"

I realized my mistake. "I meant he has close friends there who are like family. And he's been embraced by the family who owns the ranch where he lives and works. They all love Lellie and want to help him raise her. It's a small town that's very family-centered, and he's been established there for over a year with friends he's had for a decade."

He clapped me on the shoulder. "We'll figure it out. Just keep doing what you're doing by keeping an eye out. Anything you find, you just make a note of it in the case file, and I'll take care of the rest."

I stared after him in shock. From the very first meeting after Katie's death, he'd bent the ethical rules to support his friend and client and made all sorts of implications about what he expected of me, but stating it outright like this was something else entirely. "Sir, with all due respect, I will not be a party to breaking client privilege. Surely that's not what you're implying here."

I'd joined Dunlevy, Pace, and Trumble because of its reputation for excellence, its impressive client list, and its strong leadership in the legal community. Were the founding partners typical good ole boys sometimes? Absolutely. Had Orris pushed some ethical boundaries this week? No doubt. But until now, I'd always felt like he was careful to toe the line and act within the bounds of legality.

He widened his eyes in surprise. "Absolutely not, Tully, and I'm offended you'd imply such a thing."

"I'm sorry. Please explain it to me so I can understand what you meant."

"It's very simple. Devon McKay is not our client. Quite frankly, neither is Eleanor. Not technically. Her current legal guardian is Mr. McKay, who does not have an agreement of representation on file with our firm. Hence, we are not bound by any privilege."

He was right. My head swam with the realization that while *I* felt bound to Lellie's best interests as an extension of Katie, who had been my client, the firm wasn't actually legally obligated to anyone other than Katie now that Katie no longer held legal custody of Lellie.

"I see," I said weakly.

Orris nodded. "It is not our responsibility to educate Mr. McKay on how the law works. We can leave that up to Ms. Botero over there," he said, tilting his head toward Susanna, who was sticking close to Dev but didn't seem to be interfering. "In the meantime, if Mr. McKay happens to give us information that can help us with an ongoing case one of our *actual* clients is involved in, I don't see the problem with that."

While it may not have been illegal, it was certainly shady as fuck. I did my best not to show my boss how disappointed in him I was. Instead, I ended the conversation as gracefully as I could by mentioning a need to speak to Susanna about something.

After making my way over to her, Dev caught my eye. His expression was haggard and full of pain. I wanted to approach him and pull him into my arms, carry him far away from here where he, Lellie, and I could hide out and be safe and happy together.

Instead, I gave him a reassuring smile and asked if he needed anything.

"Tully, I'd like you to meet my parents. Mom, Dad, this is Tully

Bowman. He was a good friend of Katie's, as well as her attorney." As he finished the introductions, Lellie hurled herself out of his arms and into mine.

"Tuh-wee." She said my name with a whine that I was rapidly coming to recognize as a precursor to a meltdown.

"Are you hungry, baby?" I murmured. "Thirsty?"

"Wah-guh."

Dev immediately pulled her water bottle out of the backpack and handed it to her. She sipped it greedily while laying her head on my shoulder. I could feel the heat of everyone's eyes on me. I could also feel it on my cheeks as my face flared with embarrassment.

We looked like a married couple. Like a family. And while it might have been very much like some of my most secret fantasies, it definitely wasn't something I wanted any of these people to witness or misconstrue.

I shot Dev a look that he must have correctly interpreted because he quickly pulled Lellie back out of my arms and set her down on the ground before taking her tiny hand in his. "Want to walk outside a little bit? We can go look at the tree with the pretty pink flowers on it."

Thankfully, everyone allowed them to walk out unmolested. Then, we all followed them like a little trail of highly litigious ducks.

As soon as Dev had reached the little patch of lawn with the big crepe myrtle in bloom, the Scotts finally approached again. Just like with the McKays, it was awkward and strained. I could tell Dev was doing his best to allow them a moment to interact with their grand-daughter, as if he was honor-bound to act the gentleman.

I wanted to rip everyone away from him and his precious baby girl and hurl obscenities at them until they fucked all the way off. My temper was holding on by the barest gossamer thread.

You don't have to do this, I kept thinking. *You're a better person than they are.*

And it was right then, as I watched him bite his tongue against overly intrusive and downright insulting questions from both his parents and the Scotts, as I had to clench my own fists from riding in on a white horse to save him, that I realized I was falling in love with him.

No... that wasn't quite right. I wasn't falling. I'd fallen a while ago. Maybe even two full years ago.

But right now, watching him try his best to allow Lellie to know both sets of grandparents, despite their being complete assholes, I realized he was the best of men.

He was generous and kind, patient and loving, loyal to a fault, and also sexy as fuck. He crouched down to be at Lellie's level, which pulled the seat of his trousers tight across his ass and thigh muscles, and I was faced with just how inappropriate a paternity clinic boner was.

"Fuck," I said under my breath.

I heard a soft snort from behind me and turned to see Kenji. My cheeks burned again.

"You'll have to keep a close eye on him if you come to Zane's concert," he said with a knowing smirk. It was so different from his usual neutral expression I blinked.

"What do you mean?"

"He's a chick magnet. And god forbid they find out he knows the lead singer of the band. It gets a little crazy sometimes. But don't worry. Zane has security. I'll let Ryan know to arrange an escort for us in case we're able to make it back to Majestic in time for the concert." He pulled out his phone and tapped away without explaining who Ryan was.

Raised voices alerted me to trouble. Kenji's head popped up just as I began striding closer to find out what was going on. Susanna held up her hand and stepped between Dev and Pastor Scott, who was suddenly berating him.

It happened in a split second. Mrs. Scott swooped in and grabbed Lellie, causing the poor girl to yelp in surprise. The McKays stood motionless while Mrs. Scott turned and hotfooted it toward a dark blue minivan.

Dev immediately lurched toward them, but Pastor Scott held his arm. Dev's father stepped to the other side of Dev and looked like he was trying to reason with him while holding him back with a palm to his chest.

I raced across the parking lot without thinking, hell-bent on preventing Mrs. Scott from absconding with Lellie. There was no way to know what her intention was, but I knew enough to fear that this would escalate an already tense situation into a criminal case of some kind.

Mrs. Scott threw open the sliding door to the van and climbed inside. I caught sight of someone already in the driver's seat.

"Kenji, call 9-1-1," I barked over my shoulder while fumbling with my phone to try and get a picture of the license plate in case they managed to leave.

I heard Dev's terror as he screamed for them to stop. Just as the van began backing out of the parking spot, I grabbed the door handle and yanked, nearly face-planting when it opened. I dove inside, noting the car seat with a screaming Lellie halfway buckled into it. Thankfully, she was fighting Mrs. Scott every step of the way.

"Baby, I'm here," I said, reaching for her and elbowing Mrs. Scott out of the way. Lellie's eyes swam with tears, and her little chubby hands reached for my shirt, fisting the material and grabbing some of my chest hairs in the process.

"Tuh-wee," she wailed, nearly breaking my fucking heart. "Tuh-weeee!"

Once she was free from the straps, I pulled her close to my chest and tucked her face into my neck before wrapping my hand gently around the front of the driver's neck and growling, "Park this car right this minute before you are charged with felony kidnapping. The cops are on their way."

Mrs. Scott was fretting behind me. "It's not kidnapping! That's my grandchild, and you have no right to keep her from me. All I wanted was a visit. I have a right to a visit with my own grand-daughter!"

I ignored her and tightened my hand around the man's throat just enough to remind him it was there. "Do it now. I am an officer of the court, and my location is actively tracked. You will be caught and punished if you do not stop this insanity before leaving the property."

There was no need to inform him that my location was only really tracked by my Find My iPhone app. I was sure law enforcement would be able to access my location if needed since I had my phone and watch, as well as an AirTag in my wallet due to a small and incredibly unimportant habit of leaving my wallet in various locations across town by mistake.

He threw the vehicle into Park. I yanked open the door closest to me and hopped out, walking quickly away while holding Lellie close.

Running footsteps approached, but I could tell they were Dev's. As soon as he reached us, instead of grabbing Lellie out of my arms, he threw his arms around both of us and held on tight. "Oh god. Oh fuck. *Tully.*"

I tried to reassure him, even though my heart was thundering. "She's okay, just scared."

As much as I loved the embrace and wanted to wallow in it as long as possible, I quickly pulled away and handed Lellie to Dev, sending an apologetic look to him as the rest of the party approached us.

He closed his eyes and exhaled, nodding slightly in understanding. My boss was here watching everything. The Scotts' asshole attorney was here. Susanna. Pastor Scott, who wanted any excuse to declare Dev an unfit parent. And lastly, the McKays, who seemed shell-shocked altogether.

Lellie was hiccuping, her eyes wide and bright with tears. "It's okay, sweetheart," Dev murmured into her hair, pressing kisses between his reassurances. "Daddy's here. Daddy has you. It's okay."

My heart felt like it was going to implode. It was the first time he'd referred to himself as "Daddy," and I was pretty sure he didn't even realize he was doing it.

Police cars with sirens and lights came screaming into the lot.

Susanna pulled Dev farther off to the side as clinic personnel came flooding out of the front doors to see what was going on.

Pastor Scott was blustering, but thankfully, Brock seemed to realize calming down his client was the first step toward mitigating the potential criminal situation. I overheard Susanna ask Dev if he wanted to press charges, but she added a warning that criminal law wasn't her forte. "I can call my brother Tomas, who's a criminal defense attorney, to advise us."

Dev nodded. "I'd like some help figuring out the best course of action. I can't think straight right now."

Kenji stood calmly at Dev's elbow, handing him a muslin cloth from the diaper bag to help wash the tears and snot off Lellie's face. "I can call the firm in New York, too," he said quietly. Dev nodded again, spurring Kenji to pull his phone out and walk away.

Susanna seemed ready and willing to throw herself into the ring bodily to protect Lellie. "At the very least, we should have them held for attempted kidnapping while we consider our options. We can always dial it back, but it's harder to get more aggressive after being lenient."

"Agreed," I said in a voice too low for Orris to hear. He was watching me carefully from where he stood near Brock, and I expected any moment to get pulled into a conversation with him in which he demanded that I pressure Dev into "being reasonable."

Susanna walked over to speak to the law enforcement officers. Brock and Orris promptly joined them.

Mrs. Scott had somehow pulled herself together and was saying in a loud voice that it was a misunderstanding and that all she wanted was to get Lellie out of the heat for a few minutes.

Dev met my eyes over Lellie's head. "Do you think they planned this?"

I shrugged. "Hard to say. If so, they should have backed into the parking spot. If they had, I wouldn't have reached them in time."

"Thank you," he said in a rough voice. "Thank you so much, Tully."

My jaw ached with suppressed emotions. I was trying my hardest to keep it together, but I was rattled. Were my actions today going to cost me my job? Did I overreact?

Did I care?

"They had a car seat," I said, glancing back at the van. "They obviously planned something. Maybe they were just optimistic about getting a visit with her. Maybe it was an act of desperation when you didn't agree."

"That's the thing, though..." Dev said. It was clear he was having the same problem keeping his emotions under control. "I did agree."

TWENTY

DEV

I could tell Tully was shocked by my words. "You did?"

My throat was sore from swallowing down the tears I was desperate to shed. Watching that woman take my daughter had taken years off my life.

"I told the Scotts and my parents that I would be open to fostering better relations with all of them for Lellie's sake. That it might take time, and neither Lellie nor I was ready for them to take her today, but that I understood they were her grandparents and loved her."

"That's... awfully generous of you," he muttered. I could tell he meant *too* generous. And maybe he was right, but right now, I was actually glad I'd made the gesture. I felt like it somehow proved I was the better person. I'd been willing to work with them rather than refusing them access to Lellie.

And this was how they'd repaid me. They hadn't shown me or Lellie any respect.

They'd scared my daughter to death.

I cupped her face and tipped it up. Her hazel eyes were still wet, but she was no longer actively crying. "Why don't we find Trigger, okay? I think he might like to come out and get a little fresh air."

Kenji was on top of it as usual, stepping forward and proffering the stuffed horse without taking the phone from his ear. I was happy to see Lellie's lips turn up.

"Foss."

"Yes, baby. Here's your horse. You're going to pass out on the way home, aren't you?"

I glanced at Tully. His shoulders were up around his ears, and his lips were tightly pressed together. He was watching the group of people speaking to the officers. When I remembered one of them was his boss, I realized what a precarious position he was in.

"Hey," I said softly. "You can go be with your boss and do what you need to do. You don't need to feel pulled in two directions."

He glanced back at me in surprise, and his eyes softened. "Thank you. For thinking of that. For caring. But no, I..." Movement from the other group caught our attention as an officer stepped away and approached us.

The man was older, maybe in his mid-fifties, and looked as appropriately intimidating as many Texas law enforcement officers did. "Which one of you is Devon McKay?"

I raised my hand. "I am. And this is Tully Bowman. An attorney involved in the custody situation," I added, gesturing to Tully. "And this is my daughter, Eleanor Scott. Lellie."

Lellie's head popped up from my shoulder at the sound of her name. She held her stuffed horse out so the officer could see it. Surprisingly, his stoic face shifted immediately into a warm smile.

"Nice to meet you, darlin'," he said. "What a mighty fine horse you got there."

He glanced back to me. "I'd like to hear what happened from your perspective, if you don't mind. Your attorney gave us the gist of things, the recent custody change after the mother's passing. I'm very sorry for your loss."

I thanked him and explained my version of events, gesturing to

Tully when explaining how we stopped Mrs. Scott from succeeding in her attempt to take Lellie.

"Alright, then I'll need to get a statement from you as well," he said to Tully before glancing back at me. "Do you intend to press charges today? And before you answer that, understand that it is not always up to you, especially considering this involves a minor. It may be that the courts decide to proceed with or without your consent."

"I understand. At this time, I do want to press charges. Against Mrs. Scott for taking her, the driver for whatever part he had in it, Franklin Scott if he was involved in planning it at all or had knowledge of it, and anyone else over there who might have known this was going to happen." As the words poured out of me, I realized just how angry I was. It was no longer fear but jaw-cracking rage.

As the officer finalized his notes and shifted his focus to Tully, I took the opportunity to confer with Susanna, who'd followed the officer over and had remained a few feet away where she could listen but not interfere unless warranted.

"Did they admit to planning this?" I asked in a low voice.

"Unfortunately not. And I'll be honest, Mr. Scott looked upset and surprised. He claimed that his wife was simply overcome and wanted to take a moment alone with Lellie to calm down. Unless he's a good actor, and I can tell you he's not, he had no knowledge she was going to do this. Maybe they came here with the car seat fully expecting you'd agree to an overnight visit, and when you didn't, she panicked."

Lellie struggled to get out of my arms, so I set her down in the grass nearby. She toddled toward a tiny fallen tree branch and set her horse on top of it. As soon as Tully was finished giving his statement, I wanted to get the hell out of here. Circle the wagons and go. If it hadn't been for having a toddler with us, I'd want to fly all the way back to Wyoming.

"Devon?"

My mother's voice was hesitant. I glanced up at her warily but didn't speak.

"I want you to know we had no idea she was going to try anything like that. We would have never condoned taking her without your permission."

I glanced at my father, who surprised me by nodding. "Pastor Scott asked us to help persuade you to allow us some time with her, not to do anything hinky."

"I don't understand why you went along with him. Why not just contact me directly when you learned I had a daughter? Why not reach out and try to mend fences? You know how badly I tried to talk to you back..." I swallowed hard. "Back then. I would have answered the phone. You had to have known that. I just... don't understand."

My mother looked to my father, who sighed. "They told us you were into some bad stuff and that from everything they'd learned, you were living off on your own in the middle of nowhere. They were afraid if we did anything to upset you, you'd just take off with her. We wanted a chance to talk to you in person. To make you understand that we were sorry."

His words caught me off guard. Was he apologizing for cutting me off? For blaming me for Matt's death? "Sorry? Sorry for what?"

My father shifted on his feet. "Well... sorry for not realizing you had a family, for one."

My mother could barely take her eyes off Lellie long enough to look at me, but she spoke, too. "And sorry for you not feeling like you could call us and tell us we had a grandbaby."

Anger coiled inside of me, white-hot and snapping like oil popping in a hot pan. "Maybe I'm misunderstanding you. You're sorry because of Lellie. Not because of anything that happened after Matt's death."

My father's face lost any trace of warmth at the mention of my brother's name, and my mother sucked in a breath. Even after this long, their grief still had sharp edges.

I pushed against them until they cut.

"Are you sorry for blaming me for Matt's death? Do you still think it's my fault? Do you still wish I'd died instead of him?" My words rocketed out of me like the rat-tat-tat of a machine gun with deadly aim. I saw Susanna move Lellie farther away in the grass. Tully must have finished his statement because he came and stood beside and a little behind me like a handsome fucking angel perched aggressively in my blind spot.

I didn't stop. "Are you hoping to reconcile with me, to get to know me again, to see how I live and love, or are you mostly hoping to get access to your granddaughter?"

I felt the warm press of Tully's fingers as they slid against my lower back. Because of the way he was standing, no one else would know they were there.

But I did.

So when my parents stood there, my father with a firm jaw and my mother with a watery, resentful stare, I knew there was no more need for words.

"Right," I breathed. "Okay."

Even Susanna had heard enough to look at me with a face full of kind empathy. I swallowed past the lump in my throat and strode for Lellie. "Come on, sweet girl. Let's go home, okay?"

I kept my eyes away from Pastor Scott, his abductor wife, their snake attorney, and Tully's boss as I beelined it to the Range Rover and began buckling Lellie inside. I knew she probably had a wet diaper, but I couldn't bear the thought of sticking around for one more minute where I could be put upon again by entitled assholes and risk being too fucking nice like always.

Raised voices alerted me to Pastor Scott's attempt to stop us from leaving, but the officers didn't let them approach the vehicle. Instead, the officer who'd interviewed me came close enough to confirm we were allowed to leave.

Tully's boss approached him at the rear of the vehicle, where Tully was loading up the diaper bag and exchanging a few final words with Susanna. I didn't hear what he said, but I could see the conflicted expression on Tully's face.

When the older man finally walked away, Tully climbed into the driver's seat.

Kenji and I exchanged a look.

"I'm sure we can find our way back to Katie's with navigation," I began. "If you need to go with—"

"No."

He didn't say anything, simply waited for us to load up. Kenji and I exchanged places without speaking. He immediately began entertaining Lellie in the back seat while I slipped into the passenger seat next to Tully.

The first part of the drive was quiet. Traffic was high since it was rush hour, and Tully seemed focused on the road. I wanted to say something... ask him what his boss had said, apologize for embracing him earlier, or just plain thank him again for keeping Mrs. Scott from taking Lellie. But I sensed he wanted time to think.

After several more minutes, I couldn't stand it anymore. I reached out and rubbed the muscles of his neck and shoulders. "I'm stressed just looking at you," I murmured softly.

He glanced over at me, the Gulf-blue eyes both familiar and intoxicating. "My boss said he expects me in the office for a meeting first thing."

"You in trouble?"

His eyes returned to the road. "Trouble? No. I haven't technically done anything wrong. And he seems to appreciate the fact I'm spending all this time 'keeping an eye on you.'" He let out a breath. "But he didn't repudiate what Mrs. Scott did, and it's clear he still wants to support their custody challenge."

I huffed out a laugh. "I can't imagine today's events are going to help their case. That's the one good thing that will come from getting the cops involved."

He nodded. "Right. So why can't he see that? Why is he still trying to help them? I mean... I know the answer. The Scotts are one of the firm's biggest clients. I'm just incredibly disappointed to see him acting in his own best interests instead of the best interest of a minor child, even after I told him what a good father you were, what a great life you could give Lellie."

My stomach flipped in a good way. Tully's faith in me meant... a lot.

I moved my fingers into the hair at the nape of his neck and kept rubbing his tight muscles as he drove us home. The sound of Kenji's soothing voice speaking to Lellie assured me all was well in the back seat.

"He probably still thinks the Scotts *are* the best choice for her, Tully," I admitted. "Most people would. Especially more tradition-ally minded folks who have ingrained ideas of what a proper family looks like."

"Why are you so f-freaking reasonable?" he muttered, stopping himself from cursing. It was something I was still doing a shit job of, but I appreciated him keeping Lellie's delicate ears in mind.

I shrugged. "It's easier for me to believe that it's not personal—that he thinks the Scotts would be best because they fit his idea of a heteronormative, two-parent family—than for me to think he has something against me in particular."

Tully glanced at me again. "You're the best choice, Dev. I hope you know that."

Kenji made a soft sound of agreement in the back seat before reaching out to squeeze my shoulder.

I sighed and sat back in my seat. "Well, let's just hope the courts agree. At least we're a little closer to proving it now."

When we got back to the house, Lellie was dead asleep in her car seat. I carried her inside and changed her diaper before putting her in the crib in her room. Thankfully, she was good at transferring and stayed asleep. Unfortunately, the late nap was most likely going to seriously fuck up our night.

When I made my way back downstairs to the kitchen, Kenji was seated at the table, typing away on his laptop while Tully was unloading a grocery delivery. He'd kicked off his shoes and was bare-foot in his suit pants and Oxford shirt, which made my stomach tighten with desire. My city boy looked amazing in his suits, but I would always think he looked better when he unbuttoned a bit.

My breath caught. *My* city boy? Maybe it shouldn't have felt so right to think of him that way, but it did.

He glanced over and caught me staring at him. "I told Kenji we're taking a two-hour break from discussing the situation at the clinic and its related issues. Instead, we're going to swap embarrassing childhood stories. I vote Kenji starts."

"I'm ignoring you," Kenji muttered without looking up from his screen.

I winked at Tully but spoke at Kenji. "That's okay. Your grandmother has told me enough of your stories that I can take over for you in telling them."

His dark eyes came up and pinned me with a glare. "Reconsider your actions, McKay. Choices have consequences."

Tully's laughter made my entire body feel lighter. I joined him in putting away the groceries by telling him the story of how Kenji's grandmother had used chess as a punishment without realizing that Kenji loved the game and would do anything to be able to stay in the Florida air-conditioning instead of being forced to go outside and play with the other grandkids in her retirement community.

"I played for money in college," Kenji added. "Paid my entire tuition at UMBC by fleecing other students. Don't tell me my Baa-Baa wasn't proud then. She still takes full credit for my degree."

"What about you, Dev?" Tully asked. "You got a scholarship to Yale, but what did you do for money while you were there?"

"Mucked stalls, of course. As soon as I arrived on campus, I found the nearest equestrian center. I thought if I could establish a rapport at a barn, they might cut me a deal on boarding, and I could try and bring up the mare I'd ridden at Delmar and Biddy's ranch." I shrugged. "It was a pipe dream. Even if I could afford the board, I couldn't afford to trailer her all the way to New Haven. And that's if Katie's grandparents had meant what they said about letting me have her."

"When did you get Trigger?"

Kenji snorted and went back to working on his laptop. I ignored him. "That mare that I left behind, the sweetest best friend a shy gay kid in Texas could have besides Katie, ended up giving birth to a stallion who went on to father several incredible additions to their ranch. They were so happy I'd encouraged them to breed her they were willing to give me one of the colts several years later as long as I agreed to let them use him to stud from time to time. The last time I brought him down was when I met you."

Tully's eyes met mine across the small kitchen. Memories from that night two years ago were stronger than ever and filled the room with the good kind of tension.

Kenji's voice broke the moment. "Ask him what happened to Trigger's foals."

"None of your business," I said with a surprised laugh, embarrassed by the fact I'd tracked them all down and offered obscene amounts of money to bring them to Fletcher Ranch this past year. "Did I ever tell you about the time Katie showed up to cheer for a football game after sneaking half a box of Franzia wine with the other girls on the squad?"

Tully's eyes danced as he plucked a carrot stick out of a bag and snapped a bite of it in the side of his mouth. "How many horses, Devon?"

"What? Nothing. So they go to do the pyramid, right? And the girl who's supposed to be on top—"

"Twelve," Kenji said. "I'm sure you've met them in Majestic. Silas calls them Dev's Dozen. Way calls them Dev's Emotional Support Herd."

I busied myself folding paper bags into a tidy stack. "There was no way to know if they were being properly cared for. Now I can be sure they are."

Tully tilted his head at me. "If you're that rich, why don't you have more help on the ranch?"

Kenji's entire face lit up. "Here we go. Now you're talking. I think I need to dial in the guys."

"Do not dial in the guys," I warned.

"Even if you weren't rich," Tully continued, "I'd still wonder why you have so little personnel caring for such a large ranch. It makes no sense."

"Agreed," Kenji said gleefully, typing away on his keyboard. I knew what was coming.

The familiar chime of a video call preceded my groan. "Seriously?"

Landry's voice was the first one to come through Kenji's laptop speakers. "Did they arrest those bastards?"

I shot a look at Kenji. "How does he know already?"

Surprisingly, Kenji's cheeks took on the barest tinge of pink. "Yes, but I'm sure they won't hold them," Kenji explained, ignoring my question. "They'll book them and then release them."

"Book and release who?" Bash asked following the chime of his addition to the call. Kenji turned the screen so I could see their faces as each member of the brotherhood appeared. I noticed Rowe seated in Bash's lap on the sofa of their house in the Hamptons.

Silas frowned from his little square on the screen. "Tell me Zane didn't get arrested again." Zane's face popped up in time to hear enough of Silas's question to get defensive. Kenji tried to calm them all down by explaining what happened at the clinic.

Tully raised an eyebrow at me, but I could tell by his grin he wasn't intimidated by this motley crew.

"Guys," I said, interrupting. "This is Tully Bowman. Tully, this is the guys. That's Bash and his barnacle, Rowe, this is Landry, you obviously know Silas, and the guy with the Jesus hair is Zane." I pointed to each window in turn.

I watched Tully as he greeted them. All of my friends were sexy as hell. One was a literal model, and another was a famous rock star. Any one of them would be a better catch than I was.

He waved and smiled before reassuring them Lellie was safe and in good hands with "her daddy." The words sounded surreal.

"Thanks to him," I said, reaching out to put a hand on Tully's shoulder. "He was her hero today."

A chorus of *aww*'s and cheers came from the speakers, causing Tully's cheeks to darken more than Kenji's ever did. Before everyone could calm down, Kenji broke in.

"Tully wants to know why Dev hasn't hired more help on the ranch."

The cheers turned into loud agreement, pointed barbs, and laughter. "Because he's a controlling asshole," Silas accused. I could hear Way in the background trying to defend me.

Landry chimed in. "Never get between a man and his horseflesh. That's why."

Bash kept a straight face. "Money, probably. Employees are expensive."

Everyone burst into laughter. I was tempted to go over there and slam the laptop closed. Instead, I reached for Tully's hand and yanked him out of the room while telling my friends to fuck off.

When I got Tully alone in the guest room, I closed the door and pulled him into my arms.

And shocked both of us by promptly bursting into tears.

TWENTY-ONE

TULLY

Dev collapsed against me, hot tears soaking my collar. My heart ached for him.

"Let it out," I murmured. "It's okay."

I wanted to tell him I loved him, that he was, in fact, beloved. But I also knew this was not the time. I could show him without saying it in words.

I held him tightly. The sandalwood scent of what I'd come to learn was his hair product was familiar in my nose as I brushed my face against the dark waves of his hair. The usual tinge of horse and hay was absent, and I found I missed it. Dev didn't smell like himself without it.

"Sorry," he said in a ragged voice, trying to get himself under control. "Sorry."

"For what? Jesus, Dev. Today was fucking rough. I'm amazed you held it in this long." I could hear the clog in my own throat as I tried to stay strong for him and failed. Tears stung my eyes. "I'm the one who's sorry."

He pulled back a little and met my eyes. His were red-rimmed and wet, his lashes dark and spiky. "What for?"

"For the bad hand you were dealt by your parents. You deserve better. I mean... I understand their grief and that loss can have devastating effects on people, but you deserve parents who love you unconditionally."

"We all do," he murmured. "That's just not reality."

He leaned in to kiss me. It wasn't sexy and provoking but loving... comfort-seeking. We kissed for a long time, simply holding each other in the middle of the room. Finally, Dev pulled away again. "Thank you for being there. Not just for Lellie... I can never thank you enough for that... but for me. For supporting me and just... for being there."

Where you go, I will follow.

My mother had taken advantage of the childcare program at our local church when I was growing up, and I remembered a colorful Bible verse on the wall. Little cardboard sheep pranced around the quote in a way that frequently drew my eye. It wasn't until much later in my life that I'd learned it was Ruth speaking to Naomi, one woman offering fierce, unconditional love to another, that was behind the simple words.

Where you go, I will follow.

I felt the words in my stomach. In my solar plexus. Down to the soles of my feet. For the first time in my life, I understood the desperate need to attach myself to someone, forsaking all others.

It was shocking, this realization. Because there was so much I still didn't know about Dev. How could I feel this soul-deep need to be with him, to comfort and love him, when I'd barely scratched the surface of knowing him?

"Dev," I breathed against his mouth. Emotion clogged my throat again, leaving my words shaky and unsure, exactly the same way I was feeling. "You deserve to be loved. You... I... I..."

I couldn't say it. I couldn't risk scaring him off this soon with words he couldn't possibly be ready to hear. His life was a jumbled mess, and there was already way too much pressure on him from other directions. I didn't dare add to it by giving him one more monumental thing to deal with right now.

"I'm glad you have your friends, too," I finished lamely.

But there was something knowing in Dev's eyes. Something soft and accepting, affectionate and sweet. But he was also exhausted. I could see the effort it was taking him to remain standing.

"You should lie down," I said, pulling back a little. "Rest before the beast emerges from her cave and wreaks havoc over our evening."

"We're screwed, aren't we?" Dev smiled, but I could see the reminder of Lellie's sleep situation had tired him out even more.

"Remember the day I arrived? That was a late-day nap..." I leaned in to peck him on the cheek before whispering in his ear. "But this time, I promise I won't pretend to sleep."

He grabbed the back of my head to keep me from pulling away and turned his face to kiss me hard on the mouth. "I knew you weren't asleep, but I'm glad you kept your eyes closed so you didn't see me staring at the bulge in your shorts."

I walked him closer to the bed and nudged him down on it before following him and pressing him into the mattress. His arms came around me and held me firmly against him. I could feel the length of his hardening cock against mine and arched into him.

"I want you," I murmured against the skin of his neck. "But you need to sleep."

Dev's hands made their way into my hair. "Sleep with me."

Just the words made my dick harder. "Pfft. That's the best way to guarantee neither of us will sleep."

"Fuck me, then."

I wanted to. Desperately. But I knew we would be interrupted. "After we get Lellie to bed tonight," I promised.

He rolled his eyes. "At 3:00 a.m.?"

"At 3:00 a.m." I grinned at him before kissing him long and hard on the lips. "And not a minute sooner."

I forced myself off him, reached out to give his cock a nice firm stroke over his pants, and groaned before walking out of the room.

After taking a moment to calm down, I made my way back downstairs in time to hear a familiar voice in the kitchen.

"Renata," I said with a big grin when I saw Lellie's beloved nanny. She came over and gave me a tight hug. Her dark hair was in oversized Bantu knots, and her giant gold earrings pressed coolly against my warm skin. I was overwhelmed with nostalgia and loss, wishing Katie was here with us.

"I saw activity over here and got excited. Hope it's okay I came unannounced. Mom and Dad sent dinner."

"Of course," I said, swallowing past yet another lump in my throat. "Did you meet Kenji?"

He smiled and nodded. "I've heard a lot about you from Katie through emails, at least. It's nice to finally meet you in person. I know Katie appreciated your friendship."

I was touched by Kenji's kindness in focusing on their friendship rather than Renata's employment. It was true what they said about being able to judge a person based on their friends. Good people surround themselves with other good people.

Renata thanked Kenji for his kind words before turning back to me. "Where's Lellie?"

"Napping."

Her eyebrows winged up. "Are you serious? You've got to get her up, or she won't go to bed at a decent hour." She rubbed her hands together. "Let me at her. As soon as she sees me, she'll drop the grumblies."

"As soon as you wake her up, she'll become Frankenstein's monster," I corrected.

"Cut up an apple while I go get her. She'll be putty in my hands, and you'll thank me later when *you* get to go to bed at a decent hour, too."

She didn't wait for me to respond. Instead, she skipped up the stairs to Lellie's room. When she came back down a little while later, Lellie was a strange mix of cranky and happy. Not even the apples made a dent in her mood.

"What about PB&J?" I asked, remembering how quickly she'd devoured one on the plane.

She stopped whining and blinked. "*Peej.*"

By the time Dev came down half an hour later, Lellie was happily babbling in her toddler chair while eating a second peanut butter sandwich and repeating her new word over and over while a small stack of steamed broccoli I'd added out of guilt at the last minute sat neglected on her plate.

Renata was catching me up on how her semester had finished and what classes she was registered for next semester. It was obvious she was avoiding asking me any details about Dev or Lellie's future, which surprised me.

Only until Dev showed up.

As soon as I introduced them, she began interrogating him.

"Are you keeping her?"

He blinked at her. One half of his hair was smushed flat, while the other side had two or three wayward waves sticking out in the wrong direction from his nap. "I'm, um... what?"

"Yes," I said, shoving my chair back so I could get him some caffeine. He usually drank a soda in the late afternoon, so I was pretty sure a Coke would be a good idea right about now.

"In Wyoming?" she added.

Dev glanced at Kenji with an adorably befuddled expression before looking back at Renata. "That's where I live, so... yeah?"

I set the glass of icy Coke in front of him before returning to the kitchen to bring out the huge grilled chicken salad Renata's parents had sent. There was a basket of rolls with butter and honey to go along with it. Kenji stood up to help me pass out bowls and utensils.

Dev leaned over and kissed the side of Lellie's head. "Mmm, broccoli is my favorite. Remember the wolf in the forest likes broccoli, too, doesn't he? Because broccoli helps him stay healthy and run fast with his friends."

I saw Renata's intense stare soften before her eyes flicked up to me. I gave her a "told you so" look before sitting down and serving a giant pile of salad into a bowl for Dev before serving one for myself.

Renata helped herself, and then Kenji did the same. Renata didn't stop her interrogation, but she tempered it. "Will you bring her back here for visits? I'm going to miss her like crazy."

Dev considered her question while he finished chewing and swallowed. "I'm happy to fly you out to see us on the ranch. You can meet my friends and get to know where she lives. The people in her life."

It wasn't an answer to her question, but it was kind and generous.

He added, "I'd love for you to remain close to her if you'd like. You're one of the few people who's been in her life since the very beginning, and I think that's important. Katie would have wanted that."

It was the first time I'd heard him making any claim on knowing Katie well. Up to now, he'd acted like he hadn't even deserved to know her well, though I knew how much they'd meant to each other. I was happy to see him changing and owning that relationship again. *That* was what Katie would have wanted.

"I'd like that," Renata said with a soft smile. "I've always wanted to go to Yellowstone."

Dev returned her smile. "We live at the eastern gates to the park near Three Daughters. It's gorgeous."

I chimed in to tell her about the views, about Majestic, and about how friendly everyone seemed to be. We went on to tell her about the ranch and the horses, and when I told her about the "real" Trigger, she seemed to melt.

The evening passed quickly, and after a walk to the park for a quick visit to Lellie's favorite climbing playground, we returned home and let Renata do the bedtime routine one more time.

Unfortunately, Renata wasn't, in fact, a miracle worker, and the night turned from good to bad very quickly after her departure. Kenji offered to help, but we sent him to bed in Katie's old room. Thankfully, the house cleaners had already been through to make sure the room was made up with clean sheets and Katie's personal items had been packed away.

Dev and I stayed up, taking turns trying to get Lellie to settle in her crib before the two of us finally fell asleep with her snuggled between us in the guest bed.

When I awoke the next morning, I felt the warm press of Lellie's foot on my neck and turned to see her head resting on Dev's chest. His large hand cupped the back of her head, his fingers tangled in her messy dark curls.

My heart skittered toward him and slid to a stop, safely encased in Dev's own chest, while I forced myself out of bed. Orris was expecting me in the office first thing this morning, and I needed to stop by my apartment first to pick up fresh work clothes.

When I finally arrived at the office, everything seemed normal. On the way over, I'd braced myself for the stern talking-to I was going to get about being a "team player" and helping the firm by "doing the right thing" in helping the Scotts get custody of their granddaughter.

Which was why I was completely shocked when Orris didn't even mention them once in our meeting.

"Good morning, Tully. Thanks for coming in so early. I could really use your help with a client situation."

I blinked at him in surprise. It wasn't uncommon for him to pull me onto a bigger case, but it was unexpected right now, considering he'd asked me to stay with Lellie to keep an eye on her. "Of course. What's the situation?"

He explained that the adult son of one of his clients was interested in creating a revocable trust. "One of my clients has an adult son who is aging out of his family's large trust and needs to set up his own estate planning. The young man has the money from his trust, continuing family financial interests, a business, and multiple rental properties."

As he continued to explain the details, I wondered what I was missing. It didn't seem particularly complex. It was more... labor-intensive. It meant going through a laundry list of assets and determining the best way to draw up the legal language to make sure he was well protected.

Yes, it would mean plenty of billable hours, which was great, but it was also the kind of assistance that could be done by any attorney at my level. While I'd never minded helping Orris with his clients, and I always looked forward to organizing an estate with this many facets, I wondered why he didn't have someone else take it over while I was still working on Katie's situation.

"Should I assume you'd like me to release Lellie into Mr. McKay's custody?" That wasn't quite the right language since we both knew Lellie was already legally Dev's without any kind of release. Katie had made sure in the case of her death, he had prima facie custody. If he flew away with Lellie today—and I was pretty sure he planned to—he'd be well within his legal rights to do so.

I clenched my fingers into a fist where he couldn't see it. This was it. This was the end of my time with Lellie.

With Dev.

Acid burned in my throat as I remembered last night. Sitting around the table and laughing. Watching Lellie pick up each tiny piece of her broccoli between her little pointer finger and thumb after Dev finally convinced her to eat it. Listening to Dev tell Renata about introducing Lellie to the real Trigger. Seeing Kenji sneak a photo of the entire scene and send it to Way and Silas.

Falling asleep together like a little family.

"I think that would be for the best," Orris said. "Your talents are better spent elsewhere, and I've scheduled an appointment for you with the gentleman for this afternoon."

I gathered my thoughts, doing my best to bite my tongue. It didn't work.

"With all due respect, sir, why bring me in on this case instead of having Jim or Louise handle your client's needs?"

He leaned back in his chair. "He's not my client. Not formally, anyway, though I've known him for years. The truth is, I have a full docket at the moment, so I suggested Miles hire you. It's up to you to close the deal. He'll be here at four."

I stared at him. He was handing me the opportunity to sign a seemingly wealthy client with little to no effort on my part?

What the hell was the catch?

Orris continued. "I had a long talk with Miles and his father and assured them both that you were the best man for the job. I smoothed over any concerns Joe had—which were mostly about your age—but Miles himself seemed willing to meet you on my recommendation. Apparently, you also have a mutual friend. I can't remember who, but I'm sure you'll talk about it when you meet."

"I... I don't know what to say, sir."

Orris smiled slightly. "I think the words you're looking for are 'thank you.' I think you and Miles will really hit it off. I told him that you, in particular, are a firm believer in client first, firm second." He shot me a look that was clearly meant to chastise me for my behavior on Katie's case.

I kept my mouth shut. This client was a gift I couldn't and wouldn't refuse.

"I'll do my best," I promised. "And I'll obviously take good care of him as a client."

Orris nodded and shook my hand. "I have no doubt. You're a solid attorney, Tully, and you work hard. If you can help us retain this client, it'll reflect well on you when partnership decisions are made."

After thanking him politely, I made my way back to my office and closed the door.

I needed to call Dev and tell him I wouldn't be flying back to Majestic with them.

My hands shook as I pulled my phone out of my pocket.

"Hey, how'd your meeting go?" He sounded happy and light, like he'd ended up getting a decent amount of sleep despite the rough night.

"Hard to say. I mean... good in that I got a lead on a wealthy new client..."

"Wow. Excellent. But...?"

I tried to figure out how to tell Dev I was being pulled off his case. "He dangled a big fat carrot to get me out of the Scott business," I admitted.

There was silence for a beat on the other end of the line. "Does this mean you're not coming back with us?" Before I could answer, he muttered, "Of course it does. What was I thinking?"

I wanted to jump in and reassure him. "I... but of course I'll..." The truth was... there wasn't a reason for me to return with them to Wyoming. My life was here, and his was there. He was doing great with Lellie and no longer needed my help. He had friends there if he needed support.

He didn't need me.

"I guess I'm... I guess this is it, then," I finished, not appreciating the way the statement ended like a question.

Dev surprised me by letting out a rumble of laughter. "This isn't it."

"It's... not?"

"Not unless you want it to be. I do want to get back to Majestic to check on Trigger and two of my breeding mares, so I'll bring Lellie by later to say goodbye *for now*, but... I can have Kenji arrange to fly you out to Majestic in time for Zane's concert in a couple weeks. That is... if you're interested?"

He acted like this was no big deal. Like we were already together and simply discussing logistics.

"Yes," I blurted, my heart doing an embarrassingly happy jig. "Of course. But I can buy the ticket myself. Kenji doesn't have to—"

"He'll send the plane for you. It'll be quicker than connecting through Denver or Salt Lake."

I could hear the sound of Lellie fussing in the background while Dev told Kenji what was going on. When he came back on the line, he sounded more serious. Intentional. "I'll be okay."

I wasn't sure who exactly he was trying to convince.

Me or himself.

Either way, it definitely didn't feel like it would be okay. It felt like we were papering over a fault line that was about to rupture.

TWENTY-TWO

DEV

I'd woken up with Lellie's warm, pajama-clad body in my arms and the scent of Tully in my nose. When had I ever felt so content and complete?

Unfortunately, I'd forgotten about his need to be at the office early, so when I got Lellie up and brought her downstairs, I was disappointed to find him gone.

"Is he coming back with us to Majestic?" Kenji asked. His hip was propped against the counter by the coffee maker as he took a sip from a steaming mug.

Bam, right to the heart of it. It had occurred to me last night, while I'd been enjoying the easy company and stories of Katie and baby Lellie, that there would be no real reason for Tully to return to Wyoming with us when we went.

And I was ready to go.

Not only did I feel uncomfortable leaving Trigger while he was still recovering, but I had two mares in the final stages of high-risk pregnancies. I knew Way would take good care of all of them, but I itched to be there myself.

And Lellie deserved some stability. She deserved a new normal instead of days in which her schedule was completely fucked like it had been yesterday.

"Dunno," I admitted. "I'd imagine not."

Kenji studied me across the top of the mug while he took another sip. I pretended to ignore him and settled Lellie in her chair before handing her the cup of milk Kenji had already prepared.

"Your ass looks nice in them jeans."

The exaggerated cowboy swagger didn't come out of Kenji's mouth but out of Foster's. I whipped my head around and saw his face on Kenji's laptop screen. He was crowded into the same little window that held Way and Silas. Bash and Rowe were in another, and the final one had Landry and Zane in it.

"Fucking Christ," I said, clutching my chest.

Landry's lazy voice *tsk*'d. "You should probably learn to use cleaner language now that you're an old man."

"What are you all doing up at this hour? Way, how're the horses?"

While they reminded me that New York was an hour *ahead* and ranchers woke up early, I moved to the fridge to grab food for Lellie. It was comforting hearing their voices while I put together a simple breakfast for her. Foster finally couldn't take it and intervened.

"How're you gonna convince that city boy to come back home with you?"

I stared at him until Lellie flung greek yogurt at me. Kenji snickered and handed me a paper towel.

"He's not coming back with me," I said. "He lives here. His career is here."

Silas's face was pinched in thought. "More rich people moving into Majestic every day. Ask me how I know."

I rolled my eyes. "I can't imagine there's enough work for him in trusts and estate law, Silas. Even you, me, and Way wouldn't be able to give him enough work to keep busy."

While Foster didn't know about our billions, he knew enough to know we had enough money to need looking after. Once Silas had turned up, Fletcher Ranch had never seen another dollar in debt after years of struggle. And he also knew that I'd bought a hundred acres of prime acreage and was building a house with a sprawling footprint on it. Even his mother would know I couldn't afford that on any ranch hand's salary.

"Everyone needs a will," Landry said, allowing his serious side to emerge in a rare moment of vulnerability. "You never know when shit's going to happen."

"Language," everyone warned, causing him to shoot his middle fingers at the camera.

"He'd have to start his own firm. That takes mon..." My voice trailed off as I heard how ridiculous that sounded.

"Huh," Silas said, tapping his chin with his forefinger. "Wonder where he could find an investor. Or five."

"Six," Rowe said with an impish grin. Even though it had been a year since he'd turned his business idea into gold, he still wasn't used to having money to burn.

Foster waved his hand dismissively at Silas and Way. "I may not have any money to invest, but even a lowly sheriff needs a will. And there's plenty of contract law around here if he's willing to get familiar with ranches and agricultural stuff."

"His dad was a rancher," I said. "The man's from Texas, for god's sake. I'm sure half his clients are related to agriculture or oil." Before anyone could pipe back in and argue that I was proving their point, I held up a hand. "That doesn't mean he wants it. He hated growing up on a ranch."

Kenji's soft voice interjected. He usually kept fairly quiet when the rest of us were together. "He hated growing up on his *father's* ranch. Don't assume that means he hates ranches in general."

Thinking of Tully watching the sun set against the peaks of Three Daughters and showing Lellie the horses, I knew Kenji had a point. But we'd gotten off track.

"We're not even dating," I reminded them. "We barely know each other. And Tully's smart. He's cautious. He's not going to uproot his life and move to small-town Wyoming so he can watch a guy he barely knows stumble through single parenting. That would be... foolish."

"Beyond foolish," Kenji agreed. "If that's what he was doing. Personally, I think there are good reasons why Tully might want to move to Majestic, but I'm not sure he's aware of all of them. Have you even explained that it's an option?"

Again with the *options*?

Landry leaned closer to the camera, making sure the angle was still complimentary, although the man didn't have a bad angle. "What Kenji's trying to say is that Tully might as well be the father of your child, Devon." His eyes flicked. "Tell him, Kenji."

I turned to see Kenji, who still stood by the coffee maker. His cheeks were a little pink, possibly from the heat of the coffee, and he huffed out a frustrated breath. "No, that's not what I'm saying," he argued. "The point I was trying to make was something altogether different. But... it's true that there are some things you should see that might help you understand things better, Dev."

"Wait, what?" Landry asked. "What point were you trying to make, then?"

Kenji ignored him. He met my eyes and tilted his head toward the tablet lying on the kitchen counter.

"Kenji?" Landry asked again. "You know I hate it when you ignore me, damn it."

I squinted my eyes to see what was on the tablet, but the screen was dark. Kenji used his tablet for everything, but nothing about it was related to Tully or Lellie.

Oh.

Except the messages from Katie, which I still haven't read.

"We'll see how it goes with Tully," I told the others, turning back to the laptop screen and trying to smile. "Right now, I need to finish feeding Lellie and get her dressed. We're heading back to Majestic today, so I'll see you soon, Silas and Way. And the rest of you... I'll see you at the AdventureSmash concert in a couple weeks."

Before they could talk me out of it, I walked over to the computer and ended the video call.

Without a word, Kenji picked up the tablet, swiped to unlock it, clicked an icon, and handed it over. "I'll handle Lellie. Take all the time you need."

I hadn't wanted to do this right now. Quite frankly, I hadn't wanted to do it anytime soon.

But if there was a key to the Tully situation in the messages from Katie, I had to find it. She was one of his closest friends. Even if she didn't mention anything relevant to Tully's career dreams, maybe I'd learn something in here that would give me some indication of whether he might want a serious relationship one day.

I moved through the house to the tiny study in the back corner. It had old wood-paneled walls and an antique desk. But it also had a light pink overstuffed chair and matching ottoman right next to a box of Kleenex.

Perfect.

There was no way I would get through any message from Katie without shedding a few tears.

Fifteen minutes later, I gasped for breath and realized I'd drastically underestimated the waterworks.

Katie's messages ranged from short and sweet "Doc said baby is the size of an ostrich egg. How TF am I supposed to know how big an ostrich egg is?" to long, narrative passages more like a diary entry in which she worried about the pain of childbirth, wondered if she was doing the right thing, and waited patiently for the next stage of her journey. There were photos of pregnancy tests, ultrasound images, cute maternity clothes with a barely noticeable bump, and swollen ankles. And then there was an actual video of her face the moment she delivered. The camera was moving around enough to make me seasick, but when I heard the sound of Lellie belting out her first complaints, I couldn't believe I'd missed it.

I'd missed all of it.

Every milestone, from her first steps to the first time she called

Katie "Ma-ma." Learning she hated peas but loved green beans. Watching her figure out how to push a plastic lawn mower and seeing her little tongue stick out in concentration.

I knew I would get to see so many more of Lellie's milestones than Katie ever would, and the realization stole my breath. The sheer loss overwhelmed me, both for my sake, since I wouldn't be able to share the joy of our daughter with her, and for her sake, for missing all but fifteen months of Lellie's precious life.

There were messages that made me feel seen as a single parent.

It's me again. Today was a good day. I managed to get out of work early and surprised Lellie with a walk to the playground before dinner. She played so hard with the other toddlers that she fell asleep in her high chair before she finished her dinner.

Nights like these leave me with mixed emotions. On the one hand, it's nice to have quiet time alone at home where I can sit in my pink chair and lose myself in a book. But on the other hand, I miss her when she's sleeping and I'm awake and available to be with her. I feel guilty sometimes that she doesn't get enough of me, and I wonder if I'm doing the right thing by continuing to work. Between your money and mine, I could choose to take the next several years off to be with her full-time if I truly wanted to. Am I selfish to remain in my job? To want to continue to grow and nurture that part of me?

But then I imagine her as an older child, then a teen, and a young adult. What does that young woman need to learn from me? Wouldn't I be a better example to her by showing her that a woman can pursue a fulfilling career and also be a loving and committed parent? Or am I falling into a cultural trap of thinking women need to "do it all"? Sometimes I wish I had a partner to talk these things through with.

I can talk to Renata, but she's so young still...

As I clicked through the messages, photos, and videos, I completely forgot the reason Kenji had sent me away to read them.

Until I got to the one about Tully.

There had been many casual mentions of him in other messages. Photos of him in the hospital, holding Lellie awkwardly. Anecdotes about him bringing pork chops and asparagus for dinner one night when Lellie was four months old and innocently assuring Katie there was enough "for the baby to share." A video of a Labor Day cookout, where Katie panned the phone camera to where Tully held Lellie on his hip while talking to someone else. She was reaching for his glass of wine, and he was holding it comically out of her reach while she continued to grab for it.

But then there was the email with a subject line that simply read: *Tully.*

Sometimes I watch him at work. He's incredible at his job—smart, hard-working, and dedicated to taking care of his clients as if they were his own family. I love that about him. He also makes time for me and Lellie even though I know he'd much prefer to go to the clubs on a Saturday night.

It's weird though. Something changed with him right around the time I got pregnant. I asked him about it, afraid motherhood has somehow put distance between us. He insisted it hasn't. He told me how much he appreciates being part of Lellie's life and how he couldn't imagine his life without her.

He's a good man, Dev. The best. I'm so lucky to have him in my life and in our daughter's.

He told me about you... about that night. He didn't mention any details, but he said the two of you had hooked up. I didn't press him on it, but there was something different about the way he talked about you. Softer? Was he blushing? I don't know. Maybe he was just hot since it's August in Dallas for ~~fuck's sake~~ the love of Pete.

(That's me trying to get a handle on not using so many cuss words. It's not easy cleaning the eff-word out of my vocabulary! I can just imagine Lellie showing up to school one day after the Cowboys lose and repeating bad words she learned watching the game with my co-workers.)

I wish I could set you and Tully up properly. I think you'd really like him, Dev.

I stared at the screen where she'd attached a photo of Tully asleep on the sofa in a living room I didn't recognize. A fat-cheeked baby Lellie was asleep face down on his chest with her head tilted to the side over his heart. There was a giant wet spot on his shirt where she'd been drooling. His arms were around her, with one of his large hands sprawled across her back. Her knees were drawn up under her, pushing her little rounded butt in the air.

There was another one. This time, he was tickling her nose with a buttercup, and she was laughing with her eyes squeezed shut. It had to have been taken recently, within the last few months.

Seeing the two of them with flowers piled between them at the ranch hadn't been the first time they'd done that.

There was something sweet about it that gave me a sense of gratitude, which was obviously what Katie had felt. But it also showed his constancy, which was something my parents hadn't shown me.

I wiped the tears off my face and shut the tablet down. I hadn't gotten through all of the messages, but I'd gotten through enough that I thought I understood what Kenji had been trying to tell me.

Tully didn't just care about Lellie because she was Katie's daughter and he wanted to do right by her. He'd been part of her life —an important part—from the beginning, and he'd want to stay in her life as much as possible.

Now, I just had to convince him there was a way for him to stay in *mine*, too.

Thankfully, Renata and her father came over a little while later and volunteered to help us go through Katie's personal belongings to determine what to keep for Lellie and what to donate.

Renata told me that while Katie loved her house, she didn't have the kind of sentimental attachment to it that would make it worth keeping for Lellie down the road.

"You'd be better off buying a beach house with the money and having someplace fun to take her during school vacations in the next twenty years," Renata's father had said with a wink. "Young women aren't nearly as excited about Dallas real estate as they'd be about a place in Padre."

We spent several hours rotating between caring for Lellie and packing up Katie's things. It was easier for me than Renata since I didn't have memories here and hadn't been as close to Katie in the past several years as she had. Kenji arranged for a real estate agent Tully had recommended to list the house, and by the time midafternoon rolled around, Kenji, Lellie, and I were ready to go.

We said a tearful goodbye to Renata and confirmed her plans to come to Majestic for the hot-air balloon festival later this summer. "Take care of her and send me pictures," she insisted with a brave smile.

When I'd checked in with Tully, I'd learned about his firm's plans to keep him busy and distracted from Lellie's case. It wasn't a surprise, though the thought of returning to Majestic without him made my chest ache. In less than a couple of weeks, he'd become a part of my world there.

He'd become a part of my world, *period*.

And even though I understood why the separation was necessary, that didn't mean I had to be happy about it. Or stop racking my brain to find a way to work out a different plan.

After loading up our suitcases for the return trip, the driver Kenji had arranged made her way through the crowded city streets before pulling up to a tall, mirror-bright building downtown. I unbuckled Lellie and held her on my hip as we left the stifling heat and entered the cool, quiet lobby of the sky rise. Professionals in dark suits walked quickly past us with the rapid clip-clip sounds of high heels and wingtips.

Lellie's eyes were big as we entered the glass-sided elevator and whooshed up above the atrium with its green plants and decorative trees in planter pots. When the elevator stopped at Tully's floor, the people down below looked like flies buzzing around the base of the tiny trees.

"Welcome to Dunlevy, Pace, and Trumble," a receptionist said from behind a long desk. "How may I help you?"

"We're here to see Tully Bowman, please."

Before she had a chance to notify him, the man himself came striding into the lobby, his hair perfectly styled and his suit perfectly pressed. I found my mouth twisting up in a grin. Tully looked sexy as hell in his business clothes. The suit pants looked like they'd been tailored with the express purpose of reminding me what his ass and thighs felt like in my hands.

He laughed as he said something to the person walking along beside him—a city boy like Tully, whose suit was impeccably tailored and whose eyes were fixed on Tully's face with a kind of heated interest that bordered on fascination.

I resisted the urge to growl *Mine* and claim Tully right there in the lobby.

Lellie had no such compunctions. "Tuh-wee!" she called happily. "Tuh-wee!"

Tully turned instantly, and his face lit up with a big smile. "Hi, baby!"

For a split second, I thought the endearment was for me, but then I realized he was addressing Lellie as she threw herself out of my arms and into his.

I glanced at the other man to gauge his reaction. It was obvious he was tall and good-looking. A small spike of envy twisted inside me as I realized this man, a complete stranger, would continue to have easy access to Tully after I was gone, whether he was a coworker or client.

"Tully, is this your daughter?" the man asked in surprise.

"Hmm? No, no," Tully said, still making a silly face at Lellie. "This is my friend Katie's daughter, and Dev here is her father."

The description was accurate, but it still stung. He hadn't said, "This is my friend Dev's daughter" or "This is Lellie and her father, Dev, who's a good friend of mine." He definitely hadn't said, "This is Lellie and her father, Dev, the man I've been sharing a bed with for a week."

I exchanged a polite smile with the man, who seemed to look relieved to discover we weren't Tully's family, and then the man turned to shake Tully's hand.

"Thanks for taking the time to meet with me today, Tully. I look forward to working closely with you in the future." His smile was a little too warm, and he emphasized the word *closely* and held Tully's hand a beat too long.

The guy was laying it on thick if you asked me.

But nobody asked me.

Tully hitched Lellie on his hip and tilted his head toward the doorway he'd come through. "Let's go to my office. Where's Kenji?"

"Waiting in the limo. He's catching up on work and told me to take my time." With the other guy's overly warm smile still fresh in my mind, I couldn't stop myself from blurting, "I think he likes you."

Tully shot me an adorably confused frown as he led me into his office. "Who, Kenji? Aw. I like him, too. He's very—"

I shut the office door, grabbed Tully around the waist, and pulled him against me, pressing a seeking kiss to his lips. He came readily, eagerly, pushing me back against the office door while taking care not to crush Lellie. He sweetly pulled her to the side with one arm while fisting my shirt with his other hand.

Lellie giggled, thinking it was a game.

The kiss was over almost as quickly as it had begun. "That," he said breathlessly, "was a hell of a goodbye."

I gaped at him with mouth open and chest heaving. "I told you, it's not a goodbye unless you want it to be." *Please don't want it to be.*

But I didn't know what to say to convince him. So, instead, I pulled him back into me. "More," I breathed.

Tully leaned in and kissed me once more, this time teasing and soft. I followed his movements until he turned his head and pressed a smacking kiss on Lellie's cheek. She giggled again.

"Silly goose," he said, tickling her side. "Are you going to take care of your daddy for me in Wyoming?"

The reminder was a sharp pain that cut through my Tully-clouded brain.

"Dah!" she said, patting at me with a smile. Her attempt to say "Dev" had always sounded like "Dad" anyway. I wondered how long it would take her to say "Daddy."

I shook off my sentimental thoughts and tried to focus. Kenji *was* waiting, and Lellie was bound to get squirmy before long.

"Hey, ah, do you think you can help me with a real estate thing?"

Tully blinked but gave me a polite, professional smile as he moved farther into the office and gestured for me to take a seat in one of the chairs opposite his desk. He sat in the other and set Lellie down so she could toddle around. "Katie's house?" he asked.

I shook my head. "No. I spoke to the agent you recommended, and they're taking care of it. Renata and her parents offered to help, too. This is about my parents' house. It's in Lellie's trust, and I want you to transfer ownership of it to my parents."

Tully's eyebrows creased. "You want to give it to them, free and clear?"

I could tell he was holding himself back from adding, "*After what they did to you?*"

"Yes," I said. "I don't want to have any more contact with them, and this will make it easier."

Tully shifted in his chair. "Uh... technically, Dev, that asset isn't yours to give. I mean, legally, it's in Lellie's trust, and the trust is meant to be used for Lellie. The trust has a 'HEMS' provision, which means while she's a minor, the assets should be used for her health, education, maintenance, and support."

"Aren't I the trustee? Don't I get to decide?"

"Yes and yes. But you would have to determine how gifting a large asset like that to her paternal grandparents, people she will not have a future relationship with, will serve one of those categories." He paused before continuing. "There are other options, though. The trust is allowed to sell assets and reinvest that money in another way. Devon McKay—or any legal entity you own—could be the buyer, and then that legal entity could gift it to the McKays. So you could set up a revocable trust, if you don't already have one, purchase the home at market value from Lellie's trust, and then sign a quitclaim deed…"

He continued to talk through various suggestions until I realized I was too busy admiring his legal competence to understand the complexities he was trying to explain.

I held up a hand. "Can I just hire you to make this happen? Maybe work with my existing firm to figure out the best way?"

He dipped his chin. "Of course. I'd love to help. I can have my assistant reach out to Kenji."

I took a deep breath. "Good. Thank you. I'll feel better if I sever that final connection."

Tully tilted his head at me. "Have your attorneys been working on a new estate plan now that you've decided to keep Lellie? Remember, I'm happy to look over anything they come up with, if you want. Trusts are my specialty."

I saw this unexpected opening and seized it.

"They're working on it, but actually… I really wish there was a trusts and estates attorney in Majestic. It would be much easier to work with someone local instead of my old firm in New York."

I tried to play it cool.

It didn't work.

"You know," I continued, as if just now thinking of the idea. "You should consider moving there. It's a great place to live, and there's a noticeable lack of trusts and estates attorneys in town."

Tully's eyes were calm, a glass-smooth Gulf on a hot summer's day, but his lip twitched. "You don't say."

"And Majestic is growing," I said, clearing my throat. "With the multiyear deal to bring in AdventureSmash races, young people are coming in for work and outdoor adventure. The town is getting a ton of national attention because of it."

"Mm. That's great," he said. "For all of you."

"And if you worked in Majestic, you could spend your days

helping hot cowboys instead of Wall Street bros like that guy." I thumbed over my shoulder toward the reception area.

"That guy?" His forehead crinkled. "Oh, you mean Miles?"

"*Miles*?" I scoffed as if the name was disgusting. Because it was. Who named their child after a unit of measurement?

"Miles Dumas is the heir of one of the largest oil companies in Texas," he explained. His grin widened. "If you're trying to convince me I'd enjoy writing wills for ranch hands and sugar beet farmers more than working on trusts and endowments for a billionaire, you're facing an uphill battle."

I opened my mouth to spout off about the number of billionaire clients he'd sign his first day in Majestic, but then I snapped my mouth closed. That wasn't how I wanted to convince him. And I wasn't allowed to share that information with him.

Yet.

Because there was one condition under which the Billionaire Brotherhood could reveal our true wealth and the story behind it, and that was if and when we found our life partner.

I was becoming more and more confident that I'd found mine, but Tully's easy smile suggested he wasn't having nearly as hard a time saying goodbye as I was.

"So Miles is your client?" I asked.

"Mmm. Looks like it." Tully leaned back in his chair with an abstracted little smile on his face, his gaze tracking Lellie as she tottered over to the floor-length window and babbled at herself in the reflective surface. "He's the new client I was telling you about. The one Orris handed me to distract me from the Scott business and the fact that I'm not with Lellie anymore," he said wryly.

"And will he?" I demanded. The words came out rougher than I'd meant.

Tully's gaze shot to mine. "What?"

"Will this Miles guy keep you too distracted to think about those things?"

To think about me?

"Obviously not." Tully scowled now. "You know I adore Lellie. I'm going to miss her terribly. But you said you'd fly me back to Majestic in a couple of weeks, didn't you? You said... you said it didn't have to be goodbye—"

"That guy is interested in you," I said flatly. "What I want to know is whether you're interested in him, too."

To my surprise, Tully didn't pretend to misunderstand what I was saying. He didn't deflect with some excuse about Miles not being interested. Instead, he gaped at me, lips parted, as an angry flush climbed up from the crisp collar of his shirt, over his neck, to suffuse his cheeks. His eyes positively flashed with temper.

"Are you... are you f-*flipping* kidding me?" he spluttered. He darted a look at Lellie, checking to confirm that she was still engrossed in her own reflection, and in two seconds flat, he was around the desk, standing between my knees, his finger jabbing my chest accusingly just as he'd done a few days before.

"I was in your bed last night, Devon McKay," he hissed. *Poke.* "And the night before that, and the night before that, and the mother-flipping night before that." *Poke.* "Did you *actually* come into my office and try to insinuate that I'm sizing up replacements? Huh?" *Poke.* "Want to know how many men I've actually dated in the last two years, Dev? None. *None.* Because you're not the only one who knew nothing could be better than our hookup two years ago. I *tried* to forget. I tried being with other guys. It didn't work. I never forgot you. And I..."

His hand had gone from poking me to gripping my shirt, his eyes from burning with anger to burning with... something else. Something I didn't want to try to interpret in case I got it wrong.

I lifted my hands to cup his face. "Okay," I said softly.

"It's *not* okay," Tully insisted. "You're..."

"A jealous ass," I finished for him. "And I'm sorry." I grabbed him around the waist and pulled him down to sit on my lap.

I was sure we made a strange sight if anyone were there to see us. Tully was too tall to fit comfortably in that position, especially given the small chair, and I knew his suit was getting wrinkled to hell, but I wrapped my arms around him anyway. The urge to hold him was more powerful than any discomfort.

Clearly, he felt the same because he wrapped his arms around my neck and clung on.

"I hate leaving you here with a bunch of other hot city boys. I'm going to miss you every minute," I confessed.

He exhaled a shuddering breath against my neck. "Yeah, well, meanwhile, I'm sending you home to *Foster*."

I snickered. "Tully, I've told you—"

He pulled back to shoot me a dirty look. "Don't you dare remind me you're just friends," he said. "If you get to be irrationally jealous of my freaking client, I get to be irrationally jealous, too."

I pulled a frown and pretended to think about it for a second, then nodded. "Okay. Deal."

Tully nestled against me again. "I was trying to be calm because I didn't want to upset Lellie, but..." He shook his head. "I'm going to miss you both," he said quietly. "What if she forgets how to say Tuh-wee in the next two weeks?"

I ran a comforting hand over his shoulder. "How could she, when we'll call you every night?"

He sighed. "Yeah. And I guess... it's only actually a week and a half or something until the concert, not a full two weeks. I'll see you both then."

"You'd better." I smoothed his tie. "Because you owe me."

"Owe you?" He frowned. "For what?"

"I was promised a 3:00 a.m. date last night," I reminded him. "And it never materialized. What's my legal recourse here, counselor? Surely there's some kind of breach of contract when one man says he'll rail another into the bed and doesn't follow through."

Tully laughed out loud, exactly as I'd hoped, and this time when he sat up to look at me, his bright, beautiful smile was firmly in place.

"No need to engage an attorney yet, Mr. McKay," he teased softly. He pressed a too-brief kiss against my lips. "It may take longer than I hoped... but I always pay my debts."

TWENTY-THREE

TULLY

Even though I knew I'd see them again in ten days, saying goodbye to Dev and Lellie was awful.

It was the end of our time as a little trio. From here on out, we would only ever see each other in quick visits, snatched here and there in moments cobbled together from two very busy lives. I wasn't sure how long Dev would be content with that before he decided it wasn't worth the trouble. I wasn't sure what I'd do if he did.

Over the next week, I threw myself into work. Learning the client Orris had given me was none other than Miles Dumas had been a shocking revelation. He represented a staggering sum of money, which meant if I could earn his loyalty, I could pretty much guarantee my shot at making partner when the time came.

It was exciting, and if I had to be separated from the people I cared for—okay, fine, from the people I *loved*—then I was happy to have challenging work to lose myself in. And if Dev's words about moving to Majestic and practicing law there not only fed my dreams at night but also popped up with increasing frequency during my waking hours, too... well, I would just have to get over it.

I couldn't possibly give up everything I'd worked so hard for in my career to hang my shingle in a tiny town in the middle of nowhere just because I fancied myself in love with a man I barely knew.

That would be ridiculous.

How would I pay for Nolan's tuition if I were scraping by in Majestic? How would I pad my emergency fund and make sure I had plenty of retirement savings so I'd never wind up like my father?

And for all that Dev had floated the idea of my moving, he hadn't said *why* he wanted me to move. Was it for Lellie's sake or for his?

I'd learned enough about Dev to realize he wasn't the happy-go-lucky drifter I'd let myself believe he was two years ago, but the reality was far more complicated. It seemed Dev had been keeping the whole world at arm's length for years. The chances he'd want to leap right into something long-term with me were vanishingly low.

And if there was one thing I knew for a fact, it was that the more time I spent with Devon McKay, the more I wanted him. One small taste had ruined me for two years. I didn't think I could do "casual" with him.

"Shall we finish this conversation over dinner? It'll give me an excuse to try the new steak place at Bishop Arts that Tomas recommended. Besides, I wanted to ask you about an idea I have for a charitable trust."

I blinked up at Miles, who was sitting across the small conference room table, having just signed a stack of documents while I was distracted.

"Oh, uh... yeah. Sure. I guess it's getting to be that time, isn't it?" I glanced out at the warm, hazy glow of early summer evening. It wasn't the same crystal clear sky that Wyoming boasted with its cool evening breezes. Dallas's summer nights were like a steam room cranked up to its hottest setting, the air still and stifling. A nice air-conditioned restaurant with a cold cocktail sounded just about right, especially if it would help distract me long enough for Dev to get through Lellie's bedtime and his final check on Trigger and the new foals.

After that, I knew I would finally be able to hear his voice instead of swapping quick texts here and there as time permitted during our busy workdays.

I gathered up my laptop and the stack of signed documents before securing them in my desk. As I led Miles toward the reception area, I saw Orris stepping out of his office. Thankfully, he was too far away to engage with me, but he was close enough to recognize Miles and give me an approving nod.

I wanted to roll my eyes. The more I'd spoken to Miles, the more I'd realized there was no chance Miles would have continued to use the same attorney as his father, especially not if that attorney was Orris Dunlevy. Miles had turned thirty and inherited all the money from his family trust, which meant he could finally separate financially, and he'd wasted no time in doing so.

Orris hadn't gifted me a client; he'd done his best to pair Miles with someone in the firm who was young enough to have a shot at keeping the business in-house. Miles had very progressive ideas that were not at all in line with his father's or Orris's traditional views. Had Orris paired him with anyone else at the firm—with the exception of Katie, if she'd still been there—we would have probably lost his business.

As we made our way down to the parking garage, Miles offered to drive me to the restaurant and bring me back for my car. "I'll just leave it," I explained, still distracted by thoughts of the political situation at work. "I live close enough to walk to work tomorrow."

He drove a Porsche Taycan. Just when I was prepared to compliment his choice of driving an electric vehicle, he said, "If I'd known you were going to ride with me, I would have brought my sports car."

"Oh. This is plenty impressive for me," I said with a laugh, appreciating the sleek interior of the expensive car.

"No, I meant because you'd be sitting closer," he added with a wink.

Oh. *Ohh.*

Dev had been right.

The thought made my chest ache with the need to call him and tell him so. To hear him tease and reassure me.

I let out the expected huff of laughter out of habit, but I realized that this was the first time in a long time I had absolutely zero interest in the beautiful single man flirting with me. None.

Meanwhile, the simplest thought of Dev's wavy, dark hair and the sun-streaked laugh lines next to his eyes that reassured me he still smiled sometimes, even though he'd been carrying the guilt of his brother's death for so long, made my heart race and my breath hitch.

I was so *gone* for the man.

When we arrived at the restaurant, I was pleasantly surprised to run into our mutual friend. Tomas was with his sister, waiting for a table. After greeting them and exchanging pleasantries, I could tell Susanna wanted to ask about Dev and Lellie, but she wasn't sure if it was an appropriate time to ask.

"I'm going to Majestic this weekend for a concert," I said. "Any news yet on the case... *results?*"

She shook her head. "I expected to see them already. Should be anytime now. I'll let you know as soon as I know." She smiled and squeezed my arm. "Have a wonderful time, and tell Dev and Lellie I said hi."

After promising to connect with Tomas for lunch or an early morning run in the park soon, we separated and were seated in different areas of the restaurant.

Miles shot me a sheepish smile. "I'll admit I'm glad you didn't invite them to join us. I like Tomas; he's a great guy. But I was looking forward to having you to myself."

His flirtation made me uncomfortable, but it wasn't blatant enough yet for me to confront him about it directly. "I know you wanted to discuss your idea for a charitable trust, and I love a professional challenge."

He nodded and agreed, and for a while, I thought that was it—that he'd received my message without my having to speak more frankly about it.

We ordered dinner with a bottle of wine and began discussing Miles's charity goals. He was generous and intelligent and had clearly been thinking about his charitable plans for a long time.

"It was one of the reasons I was anxious to get my hands on my share of the trust," he confessed. "I'd like to get these initiatives started, but I wasn't sure what kind of legal structure would allow us to also fund some political lobbying. If we're going to try and make it easier for LGBTQ+ folks to adopt from the foster system, we'll need to change hearts and minds in Austin."

As he continued to expand on his plans, I thought this would be a charity endeavor Dev would want to support. And with big money behind it from Miles Dumas, Dev and his wealthy friends' addition could really make an impact.

Would Dev ever consider moving back here if there was something like this to work on? Something that sparked fire in his chest and helped him forget the things he didn't love about living in Texas?

The answer was obviously no. Not only were his parents here, but Dev would never move Lellie back into the Scotts' orbit again. It would make it too easy for Mrs. Scott to pull something like she had at the clinic.

Miles apologized with a smile. "Sorry to keep going on and on. I was hoping to get to know you as well. Tomas told me you run and you're a killer poker player. That's about all I know besides your excellent reputation at the firm."

I let out a small laugh. "Tomas only says that because he's a terrible card player. It makes him feel better to think he only loses to me because I'm that good."

"Sounds about right. So what else do you do for fun? Do you like to dance? Go to the clubs?"

"Yes, definitely. I like to travel. I enjoy swimming and fishing if I can get away long enough. I read... about fifty-fifty nonfiction stuff and sci-fi. I can't stand legal thrillers because they're both unrealistic and too realistic, if that... if that makes sense."

I hesitated. Nothing I'd said was particularly personal, but in light of his earlier flirting, I felt like I'd crossed a line and agreed to treat this as a date.

I quickly backtracked, adding, "And I love my work. I'm on the partner track, which means most of my waking hours are spent at the office. But I don't mind because I truly do like what I do, and I work with some fantastic people."

He waved his hand dismissively. "You don't have to sell me. I already signed the engagement letter, Tully. You're obviously a great fit for what I have in mind as far as the legal work goes. And I hope I'm not crossing a line if I admit I'd like to see you more than just professionally."

His smile was self-conscious but kind, not to mention alluring as fuck.

And it did absolutely nothing for me.

"Miles." I shook my head. "I'm..."

Miles's smile fell a little. "Involved? Not interested?"

I shrugged and exhaled. "I'm not sure what I am, but I know I'm not available. If I were..." I smiled at him. "I'd throw cash down right now and ask for a ride in your sports car."

He threw back his head and laughed easily, letting me know I hadn't jeopardized our business relationship with my rejection. "Fair enough. I understand."

Miles took another sip of wine before suddenly asking, "It's not Tomas, is it?"

"No," I said on a laugh. "God, no. Although we did hook up in law school. We're just friends now."

"Do you want to talk about your situation?" His eyebrows lifted. "Shit. It's the guy in the reception area that day, isn't it? The one with the baby. Is he married? Is that the complication?"

"Not married," I said quickly. "But he lives in Wyoming, and I live here."

"Ahhh. I see."

"Yeah."

The server brought our bill. Thankfully, Miles understood the firm would be paying for it and didn't argue when I handed over my company card.

He took another swallow of wine. We'd been so busy talking we hadn't finished more than half the bottle between us. "You going to leave me as soon as I've engaged you as my attorney?"

"Of course not," I said, trying to reassure him.

He lifted his eyebrow. "It would be okay if you did, Tully. Life's too short to make big decisions based on a job that will never love you back."

"Says the guy with millions," I said, feeling comfortable enough now to be casual with him without giving him the wrong impression.

He nodded. "Agreed. And if you'd said Antarctica instead of Wyoming, I might have worried about your ability to earn a living there."

He had a point. And it stayed in the forefront of my mind all the way to Friday when I finally, fucking *finally*, boarded the jet to Majestic.

———

As soon as I stepped off the small set of airplane stairs and onto the tarmac Friday night, I inhaled deeply. Sage-scented air filled my lungs, and an early evening breeze cooled across my face. The giant sky blazed deep blue with clean pink-white clouds moving lazily by. The peaks of Three Daughters stood stalwart in the distance, and a Fletcher Ranch–branded pickup truck was visible through the fence between the tarmac and the small parking lot by the private aviation building.

Unfortunately, Kenji's slender form was the one standing next to it instead of Dev's muscular frame.

I threw the strap of my computer bag over my shoulder and yanked up the handle of my rolling suitcase. Even though Dev and Lellie weren't there, something about being back in Majestic felt like coming home to me far more than landing in Dallas nearly two weeks ago had.

The weight of my firm's expectation, of the grief of losing Katie, of the singles' scene, and of the unpredictable expectations of my own family back home all faded away, at least temporarily.

"Hey," I said, flashing Kenji a big smile. "It's good to see you. Thanks for coming to get me."

"It's even better to see you. Dev's been in a funk since our plane took off last week."

His words should have worried me, but I was too selfishly happy that I hadn't been the only one upset by our separation.

The drive to town was pleasant. My eyes took in our surroundings hungrily while Kenji caught me up on plans for the weekend.

"Dev would have picked you up, but he and Landry are at the concert venue meeting some of Zane's crew. Silas is helping Way with mayoral duties related to the summer's first AdventureSmash race. Tonight's concert is part of the kickoff for the event."

As we got closer to town, I was shocked by the crowds. Tourists swarmed the streets, and cars were parked everywhere. Colorful event banners were strung across Poke Street, and flower baskets hung from the decorative streetlight poles.

Majestic looked maj—... well, I wasn't going to say it.

It looked amazing. Warm, inviting, vibrant, and fun. Everyone was dressed casually, a mix of summer dresses and adventure wear.

I could see why people loved it here, and I was happy to imagine Lellie growing up in such a charming place.

"Dev wasn't kidding when he said the population swells in summer," I said.

"It's even busier now than it was last summer. Silas and Way worked hard over the winter to prepare. They got zoning approval for two new hotels, but only one of them was finished on time. The other should be ready before the GrandSmash at the end of the summer. Foster and Way managed to lure several state government meetings and conferences here over the winter, which will help fill the rooms this first year. Then I think Way will finally be able to hire an event outreach coordinator."

While I cared about Majestic and about the success of this great place, right now, I didn't want to hear about any of it. All I cared about was seeing Dev... and Lellie, of course, but Kenji had mentioned Jo Blake was keeping Lellie overnight at the Fletchers' big ranch house to avoid the concert noise and crowds in town near her own place.

After stopping to give our information to a security guard, we pulled down a dirt road that approached the back of an enormous white concert tent on a large parcel of land just outside of town. We parked in a dirt lot with several semitrailers and pickup trucks before heading to find Dev.

The pavilion was already full of concertgoers, with more streaming in. It was early enough that no one was rushing frantically. Tons of people were wearing shirts and hats with the distinctive black-and-red ZB logo for Zee Barlo. I still couldn't believe Dev was friends with a famous singer.

While Zee Barlo had only been well-known for a couple of years, it had been two years of skyrocketing fame thanks to his attractive face, fit body, and approachable, boy-next-door social media presence. He seemed to have the magic ability to evoke the influences of Johnny Cash, Taylor Swift, Bob Dylan, and Harry Styles all at the same time, which meant he had rabid followers from a wide swath of the musical spectrum.

We went behind a barricade and approached a kind of portable building acting as a backstage area attached to the stage. Silas called out to Kenji from nearby, asking a question related to the race, so Kenji quickly took his leave. "Just go in the trailer and find the dressing room with Zane and Dev in it. If you don't find them, ask someone to point you in the right direction."

It took my eyes a moment to adjust to the darker interior from the sunset outside. Before I could focus, I heard a shout and was forcibly held back from continuing inside by a man taller than me and about twice as wide in the shoulders—or at least he appeared that way in the darkened corridor.

"State your name."

I blinked. "T-Tully Bowman. I'm here to see Devon McKay. He's friends with—"

"*Dev*," the security guard barked, keeping his eyes on me. "What did I tell you about keeping me in the loop? For fuck's sake, where's Lou?"

Dev hurried out of a narrow doorway, muttering his apologies. "I told you he was coming about ten times, Ryan, but I didn't think he'd get here until after eight." He met my eyes and grinned widely. "You're early."

The man let me go, and I lunged into Dev's arms, embarrassingly shaken up by the confrontation with the security guy.

Sandalwood mixed with hay surrounded me as Dev hugged me with his whole self. I melted against him and inhaled a ragged breath.

"Fuck," Dev breathed against my ear. "I needed you."

For an instant, I thought he meant he'd needed me for something specific, that there'd been a situation like lack of childcare or a legal issue. But then I realized he'd meant it the way I would have meant it if I'd dared to say it out loud.

"I'm here," I murmured.

The words *for now* remained unspoken but very much present.

He turned his face to kiss me, and my heart thundered as his mouth possessed mine and his hands came up to cradle my face. I ran my hands up and down his back, over his ass, and into his thick hair, reacquainting myself with the feel of him.

An annoyed throat-clearing interrupted us. The large bodyguard narrowed his eyes at us. "Believe it or not, this is a place of business."

"Ryan, Jesus." A man poked his head out of the doorway Dev had come from. I recognized the swing of his sun-streaked brown hair as he leaned out and waved us toward him. "Come in. I don't have much time, and I'm dying to thank you in person for saving Lellie."

The bodyguard made a disgruntled sound in his voice. "You're supposed to be resting, Zane."

I glanced at Dev, worried we were intruding. Dev shook his head. "Zane's just in the middle of an exhausting tour, and his medical advisor wasn't happy about adding in this show at the last minute."

"It was hardly the last minute," Zane said before grinning at me. "Ignore Ryan. It's his job to keep me safe, and for some reason, he thinks that includes protecting me from heat stroke and exhaustion. Which is ridiculous since I'm *fine*."

He angled this last part toward the bodyguard and made sure his voice was loud enough to carry.

Dev took my hand in his and held it tightly as we moved down the narrow corridor to the small dressing room. Thankfully, there was a small love seat for us to sit on and remain out of Zane's way after exchanging pleasantries.

He was a lovely man, more beautiful in person than he appeared in the media. I shouldn't have been surprised to learn he was personable, but I was. He definitely wasn't stuck-up or too important, and he was surprisingly not surrounded by tons of people fussing over his hair and wardrobe. He wore jeans with a faded red T-shirt with a scripted *Majestic Rocks* on it over an outline of Three Daughters.

He must have caught me looking around in surprise because he laughed. "This is much quieter than normal. Rowe and Bash haven't arrived yet, Landry wandered off to find Silas and Way, and the security team is feeling a little squirrelly, so they're keeping me isolated from everyone else."

Ryan's voice came from outside the open dressing room door. "Protected," he corrected in a mutter. "Isolated, my ass."

"Fine," Zane snapped. "*Protected.* From people and, you know... fun."

"Or danger," Ryan muttered in a lower voice. "Puh-tay-toe, puh-tah-toe."

Zane rolled his eyes and turned back to me. "Anyway, ignore him.

There's some stuff going on that has his hackles up, but I'm sure it's fine."

"*Fine*," Ryan muttered again. "Jesus fucking Christ."

I glanced at Dev, who just shook his head as if to say, "Don't ask."

As soon as Zane took a seat on the stool in front of the mirrored table, an older man came bustling in to begin applying makeup. He was noticeably silent and behaved like he was more of a set piece than a team member.

"I met Lellie earlier today when we arrived," Zane said. "She's adorable. I told my manager to block out some time over the holidays to come play Santa. Dev can't be trusted to do it right."

He winked, which sent the makeup guy into a round of soft curses.

"Do you have many more tour dates between now and then?" I asked, unsure of how to get to know one of Dev's friends while he was moments away from performing in front of thousands of people. Small talk seemed a bit awkward under the circumstances.

"Oh yeah. We're heading to Europe next week for a bit, then we'll be back doing some recording in the studio. The Shaky Knees festival is in October in Atlanta, which I'm excited about because I'm from Georgia and still have family there. Lots of my friends from high school will probably come and say hi." He turned to Dev with an affectionate smile. "I was hoping the guys would come and join us there, too, to say hi to my Gran, but now that Dev has Lellie, I'm not sure how much travel he'll want to do."

"As long as I have a nanny by then to help out, I can probably swing it," Dev said. He hadn't let go of me, and I tried not to hyper-focus on the feel of his thumb stroking the back of my hand.

"You should come, too, Tully," Zane said with bright eyes. "I'll get Kenji to arrange it. If you can stay a few days, you can come out to my family's place in the sticks. We've got plenty of room."

Ryan made a disgruntled sound from outside the doorway, but Zane pointedly ignored it. The makeup guy left and was replaced by a younger person who started adding product to Zane's hair while he seemed not to notice.

"We can go to the Varsity for a frosted orange. Have you ever been to Atlanta?"

I shrugged. "I went once a few years ago for a legal conference, but I didn't see much other than the scene in Midtown."

Zane groaned. "Ugh, so good. Piedmont Park and the gym at Ansley Mall. Fuck. Sooo many sexy guys. Our friend Kayzo from Yale lives there. Dev, we should see if he wants to come backstage at Shaky Knees. Or maybe we can plan an after-party like we used to."

Ryan leaned his head through the door to glare at Zane. "Are you doing this on purpose? Are you *trying* to bait me?"

Zane waved his hand in the air. "It'll be fine. I'm sure the current... situation... will resolve itself by then. Once we're out of the country a couple months, they'll drop it. Don't worry so much."

I glanced at Dev, who shot me a look that promised to explain it later. Ryan disappeared from the doorway just as Kenji breezed in with Silas and Way.

The following few hours both flew by and seemed to last forever. Zane was amazing onstage, especially from our location in a roped-off section right up front. He charmed the crowd, alternating between high-energy choreographed numbers and heartfelt ballads sung while propped on a stool with his guitar in hand and fingers teasing the frets and strings.

Through it all, Dev's hands never stopped touching me. He held my hand or stood behind me with his arms wrapped around my waist. He threaded his fingers into my hair or leaned in to press a kiss against my ear while whispering something. It was heaven and hell.

By the time he took me back to the ranch, it was late. The cool night air breezing through the windows chilled my sweat-damp skin as old country classics crooned softly through the speakers.

We didn't say much on the drive, simply held hands when Dev didn't need his for the steering wheel and glanced at each other from time to time.

Words remained unspoken as we got out of the SUV and made our way into the barn and up the stairs to Dev's place.

The hush of his apartment was a welcome change from the noise of the concert and crowd. Dev pulled me into his bedroom and closed the door before pressing me up against it with a kiss. His hands moved quickly to the hem of my shirt and yanked it over my head.

Within moments, we were both naked and writhing against each other, kissing frantically. The warm pressure of his body against mine, the soft rasp of the hair at his chest, groin, and legs... the sound of his hitched breaths, and the beer-tinged taste of his tongue in my mouth all drove me out of my mind with need.

"Dev," I begged, cupping his ass cheeks and pulling his hips closer so I could feel his cock against mine.

"What do you want, sweetheart?"

The endearment swooped into my gut and twirled, sending goose bumps skating across my skin.

"I want to be inside of you. I have a debt to pay."

This was a shallow version of the truth. What I truly wanted was to be soul-deep inside of him, permanently etched like an exquisite tattoo of intricate and loving words wrapped around his heart.

We moved into the bedroom, kissing and touching until he was on his back in the middle of the bed, with my slick fingers teasing his hole and my mouth trailing kisses around the hardening peak of a nipple.

Dev's fingers tunneled into my hair, blunt nails scraping lightly against my scalp. I took his nipple into my mouth and tugged. He sucked in a breath and arched up, giving me the opportunity to slip a finger inside of him. After teasing both of his nipples, I moved down and began doing the same to his cock, using my lips to toy with his foreskin the way I knew he liked.

His channel clenched around my fingers as I continued to stretch him out. Dev's usually hazel eyes looked all brown and piercing. I couldn't look away.

"Missed you so fucking much," he said in a voice almost too low to hear. "Need you."

I took a last deep suck of his cock, running my tongue along and around the shaft before pulling off. A groan rumbled in his chest as I moved up to kiss him on the mouth. His warm hands moved across my back and ass as he murmured against my mouth for me to get inside him.

By the time I moved between his open thighs and pressed my cock head against his hole, I was overwhelmed with emotions. How was it possible this was happening? That he felt the same way I did?

And more importantly... was that enough?

I watched Tully's face as his cock began to stretch me open. His expressive face hid nothing. I could see his effort to hold back, to keep from ramming into me and hurting me. I could see emotion flooding him as he locked eyes with me, but he kept his words to himself.

I shouldn't have been grateful that he was holding back with me, but I was. If he'd said any of the words that floated unspoken between us, I wouldn't be able to bear it. Because I also knew that he wasn't ready to give up his life in Texas to come be with us.

And I completely understood.

Katie's grandmother had once told me that sometimes the wrong people came into your life at the right time. I was angry at my father and cursing while cleaning tack in the barn. Biddy had overheard me and counseled me on realizing that sometimes life just stunk, but there were lessons to learn from it.

"And the opposite is true, too, of course," she'd cautioned. "Sometimes the right people come into your life at the wrong time. They teach you lessons, too, and you'll thank god for the gift of them, even if they can't stay forever."

I felt that truth tonight, bone-deep. *Right person, wrong time.*

Tully was the partner I wanted. The man I didn't deserve but craved. He was perfect for me in every way, even though it wasn't quite our time to make something of it.

While he thrust in and out of me, gasping praise against the hot skin of my neck and pressing a kiss after every exclamation, I decided to let go of fear and worry.

Tully was truly a gift.

This might not be the right time for us, but he *was* the right person.

And I would wait for him.

I love you.

The words drifted from my soul to his, unbidden, carrying my heart along with them.

If I'd been in control of my own heart, I wouldn't have been able to let it go. It was too bruised, too beaten down and cast away by others, to risk handing it into someone else's care.

But I wasn't in control, and my heart had happily leapt away without my consent.

What would it be like when Tully took it away again at the end of the weekend? When he moved back into his regular life in Texas, carrying my heart in his chest?

"Tully." My voice croaked, and I felt the warm slide of a tear down into my hairline.

Tully lurched forward to take my mouth in his as he continued to fuck in and out of me.

I held him as tightly as I could and tried not to notice when my tears mixed with his.

We didn't speak. The feelings were too much and words not enough.

When we finally came, gasping and shuddering in a tangle of sweat-damp limbs, my heart did something I didn't know was even possible.

It soared as it cracked wide open.

Unfortunately, the following morning, it broke cleanly in half.

———

I awoke sated and happy. Tully's arms and legs were wrapped around me like a spider holding on to a twig in a strong wind, but his voice was more like the hissing tease of the snake character from the *Jungle Book* movie.

"Devonnnn," he hissed softly. "Devonnn, wake up. I want to go see the babyyyy."

For once, I didn't agree. I didn't want to see Lellie nearly as much as I wanted to see thirty more minutes of Tully in my bed.

"Still sleeping," I grumbled, pulling him more tightly against me.

"You've had her every day. I haven't seen her in forever." Tully's tone might have been whining if it hadn't been spoken with a knowing grin. "Imagine if you hadn't seen her in two weeks."

"It's been twelve days," I corrected. "Not two full weeks."

He laughed and pressed a kiss to my shoulder. "Was someone counting?"

I rolled him over and pinned him down before staring at his crinkled eyes. "Yes. Someone was counting. My dick was counting." I ground down into him, our cocks already hard.

It took about three minutes of sleepy wrestling, kissing, and jacking each other off before we both came. Tully glanced over at me from where he'd thrown himself onto his back on the rumpled sheets. "I like your friends."

I reached over and ran a thumb along his stubbled jaw. "They liked you. But I'm not loving the fact you're thinking about my hot friends after you just came in my hand."

His smile creased the corners of his bright eyes. "I seem to recall you giving me the third degree about my pretty new client recently."

"Mpfh." I tried to block the guy out of my mind, but I remembered seeing him in the lobby clear as day. "Hot and rich. I can give you one or the other, but expecting both is just selfish."

Tully rolled over to straddle me. "You're both, *and* you ride horses. Lellie's not old enough yet, but one day, she'll tell you that's the real jackpot. And she'll be right."

He kissed me quickly before pushing off me to head to the bathroom.

I imagined my daughter grown up enough to care about cute boys. The thought of it made me groan into my pillow.

Tully chuckled from the bathroom. "Shake a leg. You've got horses to micromanage, and I've got babies to cuddle."

If he was offering to share the shower with me, I wasn't about to say no.

By the time we made our way up to the ranch house for breakfast, Lellie was seated in a booster chair at the big farmhouse table while Jo made pancakes on a griddle. Surprisingly, Landry was the one keeping Lellie from throwing her cut-up strawberries all over the kitchen, but I also noticed Kenji was nearby, keeping an eye on both of them.

Tully went straight to Lellie. "There she is!"

When she saw him, her face lit up. "Tuh-wee!"

Zane put a hand over his heart and gazed affectionately at the scene while Way and Silas exchanged a knowing glance. Meanwhile, Jo turned to me and tilted her head at Tully as if to say, "He the one?"

I didn't nod.

But I wanted to.

Instead, I went over and kissed her on the cheek. "Thanks for watching her last night."

She grabbed me and gave me a tight hug. "Grammy's privilege," she said. "I've decided that's my grandma name, so all of you can start using it now instead of waiting for Sheridan's baby to arrive."

I'd only been back in Majestic for a few days when she'd gotten the whole story from me about Lellie's near abduction by the Scotts and my parents' subsequent rejection of me. Again.

She'd been incensed and had immediately claimed me as her own child from here on out, telling me that when the time was right for me to call her "Mom," she would be ready for it. Jolene Blake was good people. The best.

I poured and doctored a coffee for Tully before taking it to him at the table. He'd pulled Lellie out of her booster seat and into his lap, where he was trying without much success to clean her red, sticky hands.

"Thank you," he said in pleased surprise when I handed him the coffee. He set it out of Lellie's reach when he realized it was still too hot to drink.

As I turned to make my own coffee, the shrill sound of my phone ringing pierced the gentle hum of family and friends chattering all around me.

I glanced down at the display, surprised to see Susanna's name on the screen. A call from my Texas attorney on a Saturday morning? I felt a sliver of unease in my stomach.

"Hey," I said, answering it quickly.

Tully looked over with furrowed eyebrows. So did the others.

"Hey, Dev. Got a sec?"

My body began to tremble at the careful tone of her voice. "Of course. What is it?"

"The paternity results came back. And Dev... they show Lellie isn't your biological child."

Black shadows rushed in around the edges of my vision. "That's ridiculous."

"I know. Dev, I know. It may be a lab mix-up, or it may be... something else. The results came in last night, but I didn't check my mail until this morning. I wanted to tell you first thing and let you know not to worry yet."

Yet. She said not to worry *yet.* As if there would come a time for worrying soon.

As if I could simply stop worrying that I might lose my daughter.

"Baby," Tully said, startling me by grabbing my arm and trying to guide me to a chair. "What's wrong? Who's on the phone?"

My hands shook as I tried to figure out whether to hand him the phone or try to find the words to explain that this situation had suddenly taken an unexpected and horrific turn.

The kitchen was silent as everyone stared.

Tully didn't wait to get a response from me. He grabbed the phone and held it to his ear. "This is Tully Bowman. Who am I speaking to?"

The temporary relief in his voice only lasted a moment until Susanna explained the situation. But then his tone was one of anger, not shock and disappointment like I felt.

"That's fucking ridiculous," he snapped before lowering his voice. "Anyone with eyeballs can see this child is Devon McKay's flesh and blood. Hell, Susanna, she looks more like Dev than Katie. What the fuck happened?"

I stared at Lellie as if studying her features would give me some kind of reassurance. I remembered the first moment I saw her—Tully standing defiantly among the crowd at Final Night with her propped on his hip, her little head lifting up from where it had lain on his shoulder, her eyes so instantly familiar to me.

Tully was right.

My rational brain knew there was no possible way she wasn't my daughter. Not only did she have my eyes, but I knew Katie. Tully knew Katie. Renata knew Katie. And all of us knew that Katie was asexual. She'd planned her fertility journey carefully and had selected me because she knew me well and was comfortable with me.

But the less-rational part of me, the part that had learned the hard way that life was a series of plot twists and fuckups, reminded me that mistakes happened in labs, and there were probably plenty of sperm donors with hazel eyes. That part of me believed every bit of Susanna's news because it had tapped into my worst fear.

I was going to lose another beloved family member, only this time, the family member was closer and more important to me than Matt had ever been. More important even than my own mother and father.

My daughter was the most important human in my life, and I could not, would not, lose her.

"Tully?" I croaked, trying to blink away the shadows at the edges of my vision.

He murmured something to Susanna before squatting in front of my chair and grabbing my hand. "Yeah, baby?"

"Tell her we'll go down there and take the test again. It has to be a mistake. I'm not giving Lellie up, so we have to... we have to..." I suddenly realized I couldn't risk it. Returning to Texas meant putting custody of my daughter in jeopardy. Without proof I was Lellie's biological father, Katie's wish to leave her with me was barely worth the paper it was printed on. Not up against a man as powerful as Franklin Scott and the lawyers he had behind him.

I glanced past Tully to my friends, the brotherhood. Silas and Bash both shook their heads frantically behind Tully's back. I glanced over to Kenji, who was frantically tapping on his phone. He looked up when I went silent and also shook his head at me with a meaningful glance at Lellie.

They were right. I couldn't take her back to Texas. At least without serious thought and legal consultation. But I also couldn't ask Tully to be a party to anything that might be illegal or that could get him fired from his job at the firm.

I cleared my throat. Suddenly, my path was clear. "Tully. I need you to go back to Texas and see what you can find out about our options."

This was a lie. I didn't need him to figure out my legal situation— I had Susanna and a huge team of attorneys back in New York for that. What I needed was for him to leave so I could speak freely and make a plan to protect and keep my daughter without creating a conflict of interest that might jeopardize the job he loved.

Tully's eyes, so full of kindness and affection and trust, met mine. "Of course. I'll figure this out, Dev. You know I will."

He reached up and stroked my cheek with his hand before leaning forward to press a kiss to the corner of my lips. Then he stood up, all business, and began to arrange a meeting with Susanna for the following morning in Dallas.

I glanced over at Kenji, who nodded and began arranging for the plane to be ready.

And then I got up and crossed the room to take Lellie out of Jo's arms. I held her to my chest and pressed my lips to her wispy curls. "I love you, sweet girl," I murmured. "Daddy's got this."

Becoming a parent was a steep and unforgiving learning curve. I finally understood that lying played a critical role in protecting your children.

I did not, in fact, *got this*.

But I would figure it out.

No matter what.

TWENTY-FIVE

TULLY

There was something I hadn't told Dev, something that made this situation a thousand times worse.

When the Scotts' attorney had insisted on using their lab to run the paternity test, Susanna and I had arranged for a second set of samples to be sent to a separate lab for processing.

And those had *also* come back showing Lellie was not biologically related to Dev.

I didn't know how it was possible, but I also knew that two different labs wouldn't have made the same mistake.

When I boarded the jet to return home Sunday, after a blur of desperate hugs and promises to fix everything that felt hollow as hell, all I could think about was how I was going to tell Dev that he wasn't actually Lellie's father if it turned out it was true.

It shouldn't matter whether Dev was Lellie's biological father since Katie had named Dev in her will... but it did. A biological parent had a prima facie status that a non-biological parent didn't. It meant he would be the legal default parent, to a certain extent, which would make it more difficult to challenge his right to custody. Without that, it would be much easier for the Scotts to challenge him and win, especially when I happened to know the judge assigned to the case was likely to be favorable to a trusted, long-term Texas resident and well-known Dallas pastor over an unknown single gay man from rural Wyoming.

The Scotts' attorney would dig up every sordid detail of Dev's sexual past, any break in his employment history despite his wealth, and his provable lack of interest in Katie or Lellie for the past two years.

It wouldn't look good.

My palms began to sweat as I tried not to think about the moment a judge would proclaim the sudden end of Dev's short fatherhood. I felt sick, but succumbing to my fear wouldn't help the man I loved.

So I pulled out my laptop and began to strategize. I'd gotten where I was in my career because I had a sharp legal mind.

And I planned to use every bit of it to save Lellie from being taken away from her father.

———

The following morning, I decided to stop by Katie's house to do one last walkthrough before letting the real estate agent take over. Renata and her parents had done a good job cleaning it and staging it to sell, and seeing it so devoid of Katie's personal touches was heartbreaking.

I wandered idly through each room, pulling open drawers and peeking in closets to check for overlooked items.

You're stalling.

Katie had made a lot of good memories in this house, and I'd been there for many of them. It wasn't easy to say goodbye to the place we'd binge-watched *Gilmore Girls* and *Ted Lasso*. The place we'd taken a plaster cast of her giant pregnancy belly and joked about taking a cast of my dick at the same time to share on Grindr. The kitchen we'd destroyed with our attempt at making chicken tikka from scratch and where we'd interrogated Renata after her first date with her boyfriend.

The place I'd brought her home to from the hospital with a tiny little Lellie-shrimp curled up in her baby bucket car seat.

When I opened the small closet in Lellie's nursery, part of me wanted to sit down inside it and close the door behind me. Wrap my arms around my knees and sob in the darkness for all the moments Katie had lost... and all the ones Dev might still lose.

Instead, I forced myself to close the door. And that's when I saw the hairbrush on the floor behind the dresser.

When I got to the breakfast cafe, Susanna had already gotten us a table. Her brother was there with her.

"Hey," she said, tilting her head at Tomas. "Thought I'd bring along another smart attorney to help us figure this out."

I gave Tomas a hug. "Thanks, man. We could use the help."

After taking a seat and asking the server for a cup of coffee, I turned back to Susanna. "I brought a brush with Lellie's hair. Can't they get a sample from that? We can find another lab."

I knew I sounded desperate, but it's because I *was*. And I didn't know how else to help.

Susanna reached across the table and took my hand. "First of all, yes. We can definitely try that. But I..." She hesitated as if unsure how to proceed.

"Speak freely," I said, trying not to sound annoyed by her caution.

"Brock Lois is shady as fuck," Tomas said. "Susanna is trying to remain professional, but fuck that. The Scotts are represented by a snake, and I wouldn't put it past him to have fucked with the results."

I glanced at Susanna, who appeared to agree with him. "But that's why we got a second set of samples," I said. "Right? I mean, how could he have interfered with both labs when one was reporting directly to you?"

Susanna let out a breath. "I don't know. But I've heard of two of his cases where similar stuff has happened. So I was thinking... Is there a way you could ask Orris?"

"What, just ask if he knows if Brock Lois, the guy he probably recommended to the Scotts, is a criminal co-conspirator? In what world would he admit it to me if he did?"

Tomas shook his head. "You'd have to be sneakier than that."

We talked through how that kind of mix-up could possibly happen when it involved two different labs, and it was Susanna who finally said, "What if it was the witness?"

I remembered the quiet man in the brown suit. A young member of Brock's team who'd been allowed to witness the sample collection. He'd been in the room, standing unobtrusively in the corner.

"But there's no way..." I was getting ready to say he hadn't gotten anywhere near the samples, had only stepped forward to view the signatures on the form, watch the sample collection, and sign the witness forms afterward.

But then I remembered there'd been that moment when Lellie had tried to escape into the hall. I was pretty sure that had happened *after* the sample collection but before the samples had been sealed. For two critical seconds, Susanna had been out of the room, and Dev and I had been distracted. The lab tech must've been distracted, too, since he'd gotten a lollipop for Lellie from somewhere.

Could the witness have switched the samples? How the hell was that possible? Would he have created a distraction if Lellie hadn't provided one? Would the Scotts truly sink to that level?

Maybe. But Brock Lois definitely would.

"Okay..." I said, trying to figure out how to get the truth out of a complete stranger who definitely wouldn't want to lose his job. I attempted a lame joke. "Which one of us is going to try and seduce the third-party witness?"

Tomas was a criminal defense attorney. He was known as a shark. When he made eye contact with me, all traces of my flirty friend were gone, and only the sharp-toothed predator remained.

"If you really want to get to the bottom of this... you're going to lie to your boss."

After stopping at the gym to sweat out my anger and frustration, I let myself into the cool air-conditioning of my apartment. It was quiet and clean. The modern furniture was sleek and minimalist, the way I'd always liked it.

There were no sticky handprints on my coffee table or diaper supplies stashed in several convenient locations, and there were zero brightly colored plastic objects in sight.

And it was so sterile it felt like an operating room in the world's most boring hospital.

I wandered through the empty apartment, aching for the silence to be broken by a sudden squawk of discontent that the green beans that were so good yesterday were completely unacceptable today. Or the low hum of Lellie's white noise machine. Or the periodic whickers and whinnies of horses outside the window.

Tomas's suggestion had been bold. Stupid, too. He wanted me to initiate a conversation with my boss in which I confessed to seeing the witness switching the samples. "Tell Orris you were secretly relieved that the DNA results took it out of your hands."

In other words, blatantly lie to my boss... and risk losing my job in a way that would virtually guarantee no other respectable firm would hire me.

It was ludicrous. Something I would never consider doing.

Under normal circumstances.

But the more I thought about it, the more my gut churned with unease when I considered the possibility that my boss, my very own firm, could be complicit in something so unfair and fraudulent.

And the very fact I was suspecting them told me a lot about how much trust I'd lost with the firm since seeing their reaction to Katie's will.

I walked over to peer down at the view I had of a small city park. The heat had tapered off temporarily, so the park was full of people enjoying a Sunday afternoon.

Families with kids on scooters, in strollers, and racing ahead of their parents on the sidewalk. Couples hand in hand, holding dog leashes with their other hand. A woman in a backward ball cap, covering her mouth while she giggled at her phone.

I'd loved living here in the city. I'd imagined a full life here in Dallas with interesting friends, sexy men, and a fulfilling career.

But now, my closest friend was gone. The sexiest man I knew lived a thousand miles away. And my career felt like a promissory note written on counterfeit paper.

I'd wondered what I'd do if it came down to a choice between acting in Katie's best interest or in my own. Now, my priorities had realigned themselves—or maybe just aligned themselves properly—and I knew exactly what I needed to do. I felt the rightness of it in my bones.

My phone buzzed with a call from Dev, and my chest tightened as I answered.

"Hey," I said.

"Hey, beautiful."

His voice was low and slow, lazy in a way that reminded me Wyoming ran on a completely different kind of time than we had here in the metroplex.

My heart thundered in response to his voice. "Hey," I said again. This time, my voice was soft, and even I could hear the affection in it.

"Did you sleep last night?"

My jaw ached with his kindness. Instead of asking about the case, about the lab results, he asked how I was.

"No. You?"

"Mmhm. But only because the guys got me shitfaced."

"You're kidding?" Dev was the least likely of anyone I knew to turn to alcohol in times of crisis. I was surprised he'd let them push drinks on him.

"No. It started with Landry suggesting a whiskey would take the edge off, make me less likely to spout off my anger around Lellie. But then Jo put her to bed in the big house again, and I was still pissed. Silas told me to finish my drink if I was going to be an asshole. I found out later it was a fresh pour. Then, after that, they kept sneaking refills in and convincing me I hadn't had as much as I'd thought."

I let out a laugh. "You must have been really upset. You're not easy to fool."

"I was. Obviously. I was distracted and angry. Hurt. I still can't fucking believe the Scotts did whatever the fuck they did to screw with the results of the test."

"You believe it was malicious now? That she's really your daughter?"

He let out a beleaguered sigh. "Yeah. The guys talked me down and reminded me of the things I'd told them about Katie. There's no way she'd have used a different donor without telling me, and the chances of the clinic making a mistake are infinitesimal."

"Good. I want you to take Lellie to the nearest court-approved lab. Susanna's sending you the information. We'll get another test underway as soon as possible."

"Yeah. I already talked to her. She called a little while ago." He sucked in a shaky breath. "Said you were upset."

"Jesus, Dev, of course I am." I was annoyed he'd doubt it.

"Baby," he began. "I need you to stand down and let me handle this with Susanna. I don't want you to do anything to jeopardize your job, okay? Promise me."

"Dev—"

"No, Tully. Promise me. I need you to take care of *you* because I'm not there to do it, okay?"

His words were so fucking sweet. So reassuring. How long had it been since someone wanted to protect me?

"I can't promise you that."

I heard the smile in Dev's voice. "You can, and I'll tell you why. You love me. And I'm asking you to let me love you right back, Tully Bowman."

I closed my eyes and tried to keep breathing. "Yeah?" It came out as a croak.

His warm rumble of soft laughter rolled across the line. "Yeah. Now, promise me."

I sucked in a breath and lied my loving ass off. "I promise, Dev."

He breathed out a sigh of relief.

As we moved on to talk about how Lellie was doing, how Trigger was faring, and when I could come back to Majestic for another visit, my heart rate calmed.

Every word he shared about life back in Majestic was like twisting the little stick on a pair of cheap window blinds. The sun began to slant in a little bit more until a breathtaking view appeared.

My life, and every single thing I wanted in it, were not here in this vibrant city.

They were there in the sleepy, sage-blown town of Majestic, Wyoming... and I knew I would do anything to make them mine.

Even put my entire career on the line.

TWENTY-SIX
DEV

It took less than two days after Tully's departure for me to realize my new little family would never be complete without him in it.

I was down in the barn, checking on one of the new foals with Lellie safe in her new favorite carrier on my back, when I saw Indigo stroking Trigger's nose over the stall door.

"He likes you," I said, tilting my chin up at him in acknowledgment.

The poor kid had obviously been scared of me ever since the incident with Trigger. Despite everything going on in my life, I owed him an apology.

"Nah. He's just, like, obsessed with peppermints." His eyes widened. "But don't stress, dude. I swear, I only give him one in the morning and one at night. Gotta keep it balanced. Gotta keep his energy aligned."

Surprisingly, I found this almost intelligible. "I appreciate you, ah... looking out for his energy," I said soberly.

Lellie squawked in my ear when she saw Trigger, so I headed over that way and let her pet him. Indigo's face lit up when he saw how happy it made her. "Dudette's a natural. Got the horse bug for sure. Gonna be a big rider, just like her dad. No doubt."

"Hope so. But then again, I'll go gray early. Riding can be dangerous."

"Dude, say less." Indigo rolled his eyes. "I was flexing in a polo match once 'cause I had a girl watching, you know? So when I hit a tail shot—epic shot, killed it—you know I had to turn around to see if my girl'd seen it. Ended up twisting myself right off the pony. Total wipeout, bro. Bruised all to h-heck and took a mallet to the face by their number two just for some extra humiliation. Almost got trampled. Polo's no joke."

"And yet you got back on the horse."

"'Course I did," he said. He added in a fake-snooty accent, "'A polo handicap is a person's ticket to the world.'"

I grinned at him. It had been a long time since I'd met a fellow polo-phile. "Winston Churchill."

"Uh-huh. My first coach called polo the great equalizer," he said. "No matter your size, you're all the same on the back of a pony."

Indigo was not only friendly and approachable, great with horses, and even better with my daughter, but he was smarter than I gave him credit for. I'd misjudged him almost as badly as I had Tully. "I owe you an apology," I began.

He looked surprised.

"I made assumptions about you from the very beginning," I admitted. "Which is unfair. It's something that happened to me when I was growing up and made me angry as hell. You deserved better. I would never want anyone to treat Lellie the way I treated you, and I'm sorry."

Indigo's eyes widened as I spoke. "Whoa, dude. That's, like, totes unnecessary. But thanks. And no worries about the Lellinator. With all these bros around her... *pfft*. No doubt she's gonna shine."

He shook her little socked foot that stuck out of the carrier on my back. "Studies show that positive guidance—like nurturing your kid's potential through consistently positive interactions—in early childhood helps them feel safe and secure. Doesn't have to be overly permissive. But positive. Love and encourage her like crazy, dude. She'll do okay."

I stared at him until he started laughing. It set Lellie off with a case of the giggles until Trigger snorted in my face, which only made the two of them laugh harder.

When they finally caught their breath, I met Indigo's eyes. "Will you stick around after this summer and help me with Lellie?"

His smile faded. "You serious? Like, a *job*-job?"

I nodded. "I know you wanted to work with horses, so you can still—"

"No, dude! I want to work with *kids*. I took the horse thing because no one was hiring for preschools or daycares around here."

Way and Silas, and even Tully, had tried to tell me, but I hadn't listened. Now, it was time to trust the people in my life. Trust that I had a family who cared about me.

Who cared about Lellie.

"Then I'd like you to consider coming to work for me as Lellie's nanny on a trial basis. The trial period is as much for you as for me," I warned, "because I will probably be an unbearable person to work for. I'm a new parent who doesn't know what the fuck I'm doing."

Indigo's lips had curved up in a pleasantly surprised grin. "Well, if my new boss isn't opposed to some gentle and positive guidance... might I suggest finding age-appropriate language to use around her? Language development is fascinating at this age. She's likely to start to mimic the words she hears most often. We should focus on those being words like Dada, right? Maybe not so much with the uk-fay."

Heat bloomed in my cheeks. "It's a hard f-freaking lesson to learn, Indigo."

"No shi*p*, bro. Nooooo ship."

I reached out my hand. When he took it, I felt the promise of a new beginning, one in which Lellie had yet another guardian angel of sorts. Someone who would look out for her and help her grow and thrive.

"Thank you," I said.

I let Indigo help Lellie feed Trigger a peppermint. Thankfully, Trigger remained unaffected by her exuberant noises. My ears were not so unaffected.

"You know another word we should keep working on with her..." Indigo said after a few minutes.

"What?"

"*Tully.*"

I could feel the heat of his stare on the side of my face while the beloved name swirled through the air and came to rest on my heart.

Then I turned to him and smiled. "I imagine you're right."

He nodded. "Nice."

"Does that mean you'd be okay with a little travel until I can figure out where the three of us are going to settle down?"

He pretended to consider it before pumping his fist in victory. "Private jet, here I come. Hey, you got leather seats on that thing, my dude? I might have to snap a few selfies for the 'gram."

As usual, once he got started talking, Indigo didn't stop. And Lellie loved every minute of it. Tully had been right when he'd said I was surrounded by support, and for once, I was going to take advantage of it to get my life back on track and create the family I not only wanted but deserved.

But first, I had to figure out how Tully and I were going to keep our daughter.

"Indigo, would you mind watching Lellie for me right now? I need to ask the guys for some help."

———

"Whatever you need, Dev, we're in," Landry said before I'd even finished sketching out the situation.

Kenji didn't look up from his laptop at the kitchen table. "*You're* not. You're due in Milan tomorrow for the Valente runway event. And Zane already left for his show in Milwaukee."

"Fuck," Landry muttered. "I'm in for moral support. What's the plan?"

He sat on one of the stools at the kitchen island, popping grapes in his mouth while Way finished drying a few dishes and Silas poured himself a fresh cup of coffee.

"I'm not running away from this," I said. "I can't just take off with Lellie—"

"You *could*." Silas lifted an eyebrow. "It's not like you don't have enough money to go someplace no one will ever find you."

I ignored him. "—so I need to prove she's my daughter. I told you Susanna wants me to find a lab near here and get a new paternity test done. I also talked to Tully yesterday, and he agreed. But I don't know if the results from one lab near my new hometown would sway the judge. I think maybe we should find two or three places, just to be safe—"

"Oh, I think we can do better than that," Kenji said. He lifted his head and pierced me with his dark eyes. "I'm just putting the final touches on your paternity lab tour of America."

"What does that mean?" Silas asked. Way patted his leg and softly reminded him to shut the hell up and let Kenji speak.

"It means you have plenty of money, so why not overwhelm them with results from reputable labs all over the country? A Texas judge can't possibly discount positive results from well-known labs in Denver, Salt Lake City, Portland, and LA. I've also thrown in Houston for good measure. All different lab owners. By the time we get to Dallas, we should have results from at least the first two or three labs."

"Won't they say we cheated it? That maybe the sample didn't come from Lellie?"

Kenji tilted his head at something behind me. I glanced at the door as Foster strode in and tossed his empty travel mug at Silas. "Fill 'er up. I've been awake since four."

"You say that like it's special," Way scoffed. "Try being a rancher."

Foster shot him a look. "Try searching for AdventureSmash wannabes getting lost halfway up Maude Peak Friday night, responding to a DUI crash at three in the morning on Sunday, and then getting a text from your Girl Friday before dawn today that I need to pack a bag and get out to the ranch because Dev needs my help on my day off."

I glanced back at Kenji, who smirked. "Foster's coming along on the paternity tour. No one would dare question the integrity of those lab samples if they were video recorded and witnessed by a sheriff."

I blinked at Foster, overwhelmed. "You'd do that?"

His smile was soft and affectionate. He really was a true friend. "Of course I would. I know how much family means to you, Dev. And you need to know that we're part of yours. And family supports family."

"Your mother is making you do this, isn't she?" I teased.

"Jolene gets what Jolene wants," he drawled. "And the rest of us fall in line. She doesn't know about this yet because she's been busy at the cafe, but you know she'd be completely on board with whatever it takes to keep that girl."

I sucked in a big breath and let it out. "Okay then. I guess we're doing this. Is the plane ready?"

Landry cursed under his breath. "If you're using the jet, I guess this means I'm flying commercial. *Motherfucker.*"

"*Whatever you need, Dev,*" Kenji teased, repeating Landry's earlier words in a credible impression of Landry's deep voice. He went on in the same tone, "For you, I will make the noble sacrifice of flying first class on a commercial flight, even if it means the caviar served at my whim is... gasp... domestic."

Landry pouted. "Hey! I didn't say I wouldn't do it. It just means I'm going to have to head out even earlier. Like, *tonight*. Which means you and... um..." He cleared his throat. "Uh. Nothing. It means nothing," he added quickly when Kenji gave him a narrow-eyed, warning look I couldn't interpret.

Kenji turned back to his laptop with a satisfied smile. "Mmhmm. Careful, Landry, or you'll also be flying coach."

Landry gasped and clutched his chest. "You wouldn't *dare.*"

Judging by the tiniest uptick of the edge of Kenji's mouth, I thought he very much probably would.

TWENTY-SEVEN

TULLY

My hands shook as I knocked on Orris's office doorframe. "Good morning. Dawn said I could grab a few minutes of your time today..."

He looked up from some documents and peered at me over his reading glasses. "Sure, Tully. Come on in." He leaned back and pulled the reading glasses off. "Did you hear the latest on the Scott custody case?"

I nodded, closing the door behind me and moving to the seat in front of his desk. "Yes, sir. And I have to be honest." I exhaled and let my shoulders drop. "I'm relieved in a way."

I was relieved to finally have something solid to pin on the Scotts... if I could just get a confession of some kind.

"You're not the only one. Now it's just a matter of getting the judge to make the ruling, and we'll be able to get the local LEOs to help us retrieve her and bring her back where she belongs."

"I will definitely feel better when she's safely with the people who love her best and it's no longer up in the air," I said, speaking from the heart. "I think Katie would want it to be settled quickly."

He gave a solemn nod, as if honoring Katie was his top priority.

I shifted nervously in my seat before glancing back at the closed door and lowering my voice. "I just needed to ask your advice on how to handle something related to the case." I twisted my hands in my lap and hoped I wasn't overplaying my nerves.

His forehead crinkled. "Sure, son. What is it?"

"Orris... the witness from Brock's office switched the samples right after they were taken. There was a distraction in the room, and he... he switched them out. I wasn't sure at first, but when the results came in... I mean, anyone can see that girl is related to Devon McKay. So how do we..." I let the question fade off in hopes he would jump in.

I wasn't disappointed.

"Tully... I think maybe you didn't see what you thought you did."

I shook my head. "No, I did. I'm very sure of what I saw." It wasn't a lie. I was sure I saw nothing more than Lellie wandering off and a room full of adults trying to make her stop.

"But you said you were happy about the results..."

I lowered my voice even more, as if I was part of the conspiracy and didn't want anyone else to overhear. "It's just... I need to know how trustworthy that guy is. I'm uncomfortable with Brock putting the Scotts' integrity on the line unless the witness is rock solid, you know? What if he winds up telling someone...? I know these young lawyers. Hell, we all do. They go out drinking and brag about their accomplishments. Who's to say this guy doesn't end up doing that? It could put the Scotts' custody in jeopardy."

Orris sighed and rubbed at the glasses marks on his nose. "We have to trust Brock. He's done this before. Remember the Howard case a few years ago? The one with the actor and the hotel maid who tried to sue him for paternity?"

My stomach turned, but I managed to look surprised and pleased. "He switched the samples on that one? But the housekeeper won custody, didn't she?"

He shrugged. "She ended up getting custody, but it was due to an unrelated assault case the actor pled out on. The DNA results weren't to blame. Brock came through on those."

I tried to school my outrage. "Isn't he afraid of getting caught?"

Orris tilted his chin down and peered at me over his desk like I was a first-year law student. "Tully. Even if he was caught, what exactly do you think would happen to him? He's worked with the judges in this town for dozens of years."

I sat up straight and blew out a breath. "So Brock arranged to switch out the samples, but he did it in a way we can trust."

Orris nodded. "You don't need to worry. Just keep your head down and let him handle it. He has a call in to the judge now to see if he can get the decision moved up. If so, the Scotts may even be able to travel to Wyoming before midweek. Now... something you can do is to keep tabs on Mr. McKay. I'm sure his legal team will try to have the tests redone before he gets nervous enough to run. But he won't be able to run far since he'll lose access to the money."

Orris obviously didn't know Dev had plenty of his own money.

"What's the situation with the kidnapping charges against the Scotts? Could that affect their ability to get custody?"

He shook his head. "It's easy to prove Franklin was unaware of his wife's plans, so there's no reason to withhold custody from *him* regardless of what happens with Paula. And I'm sure the charges against her will be dropped. The prosecutors know how impossible it would be to convince a jury that a soft-spoken, demure woman like her is a criminal mastermind. She runs vacation bible school at the Church of Heavenly Victory, for god's sake. She just wanted to make sure her granddaughter was safe."

He was right. Ladies like Paula Scott didn't go down for kidnapping. Instead, they were seen as dedicated mothers only out to save poor, innocent children from evil men.

Orris leaned back and studied me. "Tell me how it's going with Miles Dumas. I know he signed the letter of engagement, but have you been able to get a scope of the work?"

I nodded and proceeded to discuss Miles's needs in the broadest and vaguest terms possible.

After surreptitiously turning off the video that had been recording in my shirt pocket the entire time.

———

It took me another few hours to meet with Tomas to determine how best to proceed without putting Susanna in a precarious position as Dev's attorney.

Thankfully, Tomas had friends in high places and managed to get me an informal sit-down with one of his favorite law professors, who immediately sketched out the appropriate plan of action.

The following twenty-four hours were a whirlwind. I hadn't known it was possible to deliberately implode your entire life in such a short period of time, but I'd done it.

I'd hired legal representation at the law professor's recommendation, and they'd taken charge of everything. They'd tendered my resignation at Dunlevy, Pace, and Trumble before accompanying me to a meeting with the Texas State Bar's Chief Disciplinary Council's office. Once my attorneys got approval from them, they would determine what I could tell Susanna and when. I was under certain confidentiality agreements with Dunlevy, which meant I had my own legal situation to manage as well as Lellie's.

If the approval didn't come through soon, I would burst. It was killing me not to be able to tell Dev what had happened in Orris's office, but I didn't want to do anything to jeopardize the case or risk my legal license. I would try to be patient and get proper permission before telling anyone else involved, even the man I loved.

In the meantime, I was anxious to get back to Wyoming... and back into Dev's arms. My assistant had hooked me up by having a stack of moving boxes delivered to my apartment, so at least I could keep busy while I waited for word from the attorneys.

While I packed, I imagined Dev's reaction to my news. I was nervous that my moving to Majestic would be too much too soon for him. He already had enough upheaval in his life with Lellie's arrival, and I didn't want him to feel responsibility for my happiness, too.

But at the same time, I didn't want to wait to be together. My plan was to move to Majestic and open a law practice. To tell Dev that I'd rent a little place of my own while I started my firm slowly. I'd have to apply for admission to the Wyoming Bar and take out a business loan to get started, which was a bit scary, but after careful consideration of my finances, I knew I could make it work. I'd been socking away money for years, and while it didn't come close to making me a millionaire, I had enough saved to pay the balance for Nolan's final year of tuition after his scholarships *and* to keep me afloat while I got my practice off the ground.

In the meantime, maybe it wouldn't hurt if I got a part-time job in town to help meet people and establish trust with the locals. I couldn't imagine folks in Majestic would trust an outside attorney easily, but maybe I was wrong. Maybe the fact I had big-city experience would work in my favor. And I did have a few ranchers as clients who would most likely be willing to give me business recommendations. I was pretty confident Way, Silas, and Dev would give me personal recommendations, too.

And I could help out with Lellie. It wouldn't be easy for her to trust new people, so Dev would appreciate having another babysitter on hand he could trust.

I could almost hear her now, happily calling my name.

"*Tuh-wee!*"

I grinned as I yanked the packing tape across the folded ends of a box.

"Tuh-wee?"

It almost sounded like she was here in the apartment with me...

I whipped around and saw Dev standing in the open doorway of my apartment with Lellie on his hip. Susanna stood behind him, grinning.

Dev quickly set Lellie down before she launched herself out of his arms. She came trundling toward me on drunken baby legs with her arms outstretched and her dark curls flopping in tangled wisps.

"Babygirl!" I cried, swooping in to grab her and hold her close. She smelled like warm graham crackers and lemon-scented hand wipes. Her chunky little body felt like perfection in my arms, the best feeling in the world.

The best... with one very notable exception.

I glanced at Dev. Hope thundered like rabid mustangs in my chest. "What are you doing here?"

His grin was easy, as if he wasn't on the verge of losing everything and breaking his heart for good. "This is where my heart is."

For a split second, I thought he meant his heart was in Texas. It was where he was from, after all, and his parents were still here. But then I realized he hadn't meant Texas.

He'd meant me.

"Dev," I whispered.

Lellie struggled to get down, so I leaned over and set her on the ground next to two big empty boxes. She immediately began sliding them around on the hardwood floor. Automatic toddler bait.

"We came to get you, Tully Bowman," Dev said, moving closer as if he had all the time in the world. I glanced behind him to see Susanna hanging back but grinning from ear to ear.

"You didn't have to come all this way," I told him, stepping forward and running my hands up his chest to his shoulders. "I have tickets to Majestic booked first thing tomorrow."

His eyes lit up. "Yeah? You were coming to visit us?"

I tilted my head toward the half-packed living room and the empty boxes. "Little more than a visit, cowboy."

Dev leaned in and kissed me slowly. I vaguely noticed Susanna talking to Lellie as she led her to the kitchen to give us some privacy.

"I love you," I said shyly. I was unsure if he was ready for that, but he needed to know I was all in on building a life together. I already knew he was it for me. I wanted it all. Him. Lellie. Majestic.

Dev's hands came up to cup my face until he forced me to meet his eyes. "I fell for you the night we met, Tully. But I wasn't ready for you yet. I am now. I'm ready to tell you how much I love you. How much I *need* you. And how much I want to share my life with you. Come home with me and help me build a family for Lellie. A family we can be proud of."

My eyes filled and overflowed as I nodded frantically. I swallowed around a lump in my throat. "She's your baby, Dev. Biologically. I have proof—"

Dev kissed me to shut me up and then pulled back and grinned. "I know she's mine, and I don't need proof. But your lawyers called Susanna an hour ago and told her everything that happened with Orris. They've started an investigation into the witness at the clinic. And meanwhile... well, meanwhile, Susanna now has DNA tests from six clinics all over the country that prove Eleanor Kathryn Scott is my daughter." He paused. "I hope one day very soon, she'll be yours, too."

"You want to share your daughter with me?" I whispered, overcome.

"I want to share everything with you, baby," Dev said. "Jesus Christ, you were willing to give up your dream career for me and Lellie—" He shook his head.

There were a lot of realizations I'd come to that I wanted to share with Dev eventually: that I'd focused on career success because I'd wanted to never feel powerless again, and I'd almost lost myself in the process; that the sense of rightness and peace I felt about my choice made it no sacrifice; that I didn't feel like I'd given up a dream, I felt like I'd gained one.

But instead, I focused on another truth. "I made the best choice for all of us because that's what family does." I grinned up at him. "That's what *our* family will do anyway."

"Yeah, we will," he agreed. He kissed me, a brief brush of lips that left me wanting more. "Besides, Lellie is already your daughter. She might have her Daddy's eyes and stubbornness, but she has her Papa's argumentative streak. You should have heard her babbling at

Jo the other night, trying to convince the woman to take her to see the horses even though it was bedtime. Fortunately, only her fathers actually understand her."

I laughed. We were in for a world of trouble once she actually learned to speak.

And I was so here for it.

"Now, do I have to get Lellie in here to convince you to come home with us?" Dev demanded. "You still haven't answered me."

Like there'd ever really been a question.

I threw myself into his arms and held him as tightly as I could. "Yes. Please. I want that. I want that so much. I... Dev, fuck." My words were strangled and raw. It was impossible to get across just how strongly I felt about him. About *us*.

His arms were tight around me, his large hands moving confidently up and down my back. "It's going to be okay, sweetheart," he murmured. "We're going to have an amazing life together. We're going to give Lellie all the love we didn't get."

We kissed and cried and laughed until Lellie let out a frustrated shriek from the kitchen.

Susanna popped her head around the doorframe and shot us a sheepish grin. "Sorry. Time's up on your love fest. She clearly wants *something*, but I don't speak toddler, and I don't have parental ESP, so—"

Dev and I exchanged a glance and a grin.

"*Peej*," we said at the same time.

EPILOGUE
DEV - SEVERAL MONTHS LATER

"Georgia reminds me of Texas," Tully muttered, holding his hand over his eyes to block out the setting sun. While it was definitely going down, the temperature was still hot as fuck in the park, especially with tens of thousands of music fans in attendance. "It's like they didn't get the memo that October is supposed to be comfortably cool."

I glanced at him as I shifted Lellie's sleeping form from one shoulder to the other. Thankfully, the giant headphones Kenji had gotten her had worked to block out the noise of Zane's music, and she'd been zonked for the final forty minutes of his performance. "You think you're hot? Try holding a furnace against your neck."

Tully grinned at me and reached out to take her. I scooted out of range so he couldn't disturb her. "You crazy?" I hissed. "Don't wake the beast. You were the one who made it a family rule, in case you need reminding."

Tully's eyes brightened with laughter. "I was just trying to help. Besides, she transfers fine. Once she's down for the night, she's down. Even if it's at a concert with thousands of screaming fans, apparently."

I cuddled her closer to me. "She's too sweet when she's asleep. I have to enjoy it while I can."

The truth was, she was sweet when she was awake, too. Ever since we'd all moved into the new house at the end of the summer and settled into a routine, she'd begun to thrive. Jo had warned the reprieve was only temporary since toddlers generally rotated easily between asshole and angel, but for now, we were loving every minute of it.

She was admittedly spoiled rotten. Not only did she have Tully and me, but she also had Indigo wrapped around her finger practically full-time, and she had Way, Silas, Jo, Sheridan, and her husband, Bo, at her beck and call, too. When she'd pointed at one of the foals born this summer—a pretty palomino with a golden coat that shined in the sun—and declared the horse *Peej*, not a single soul had disputed it.

The other guys from the brotherhood made it out to see us when they could. Nearly every week, Landry sent some small item of what he called "baby couture," Zane had worked Lellie's name into one of his songs, and Bash and Rowe had recently been caught murmuring about plans to buy property in Majestic for a second home so they wouldn't miss seeing her grow up.

I hadn't thought it possible for my friends and me to be closer than we were, but somehow, Lellie's presence in my life had managed it. She'd cracked my heart wide and made it impossible for me to hide from the world. Now, I was rooted firmly in the sunlight and thriving.

Things were good. More than good. And I kind of wanted to get back home and continue enjoying it.

Kenji came hustling through the crowd, stopping at the barricade to give the security guy a dark look before being allowed backstage with the rest of us.

"Where's Ryan?" he asked, thumbing over his shoulder at the guard checking ID.

I shrugged. "He followed Zane into the dressing room after he came offstage and barked at us to wait out here."

"Never mind, I just heard from Susanna. She tried to get you first, but you didn't pick up. Guess whose law license was suspended in Texas?"

"Don't say mine," Tully said, reaching over to take Lellie from me. The resulting fresh air against my neck and damp shirt was a relief.

"Hank Kinard," Kenji said. "The poor bastard thought keeping Brock Lois happy was more important than keeping his license. No surprise Lois's firm threw him under the bus."

"If only they'd been able to pin anything on Brock," I muttered, shaking out my arms. "Any news on Paula Scott?"

Kenji nodded. "She accepted the agreement. Finally. She and Franklin signed an acknowledgment that Lellie is your biological child and will sign away all future claims to her and her estate." He waved his slender fingers. "I don't remember the legal explanation, but essentially, it's over. There was one little surprise, though."

Tully pressed a kiss to Lellie's messy curls. "Good surprise or bad? We've had a great night. I'd hate to ruin it."

I stepped closer to him and slid my arm around his waist. "What is it?"

Kenji met my eyes. "Your parents reached out to Dunlevy, Pace, and Trumble and asked if they can put their house in trust for Lellie after they pass away. They plan to leave their estate to her."

It wasn't a bad surprise, but the reminder of my parents was a sour spike on an otherwise sweet night. "Considering she's their only freaking heir, that's not the generous flex they might think it is," I explained.

Tully leaned over and pressed a kiss to the side of my face. "Not true, baby. *You're* their heir. They're passing you over, which—" He shook his head when I began to interrupt. "No, listen. Which is a good thing since it would only be taxed if it came to you first, and you don't need it."

"They don't know that," I sighed. "But fine. I refuse to let them ruin my night. It's fine."

Kenji huffed out a laugh. "Now you sound like Zane."

I couldn't help but smile when I realized he was right.

Kenji's phone squawked with a ringtone of Nelly Furtado's *"Promiscuous Boyyy."* "Fucking Christ," he muttered under his breath. "What now?"

"What did he mean about you sounding like Zane?" Tully asked after Kenji turned away to take Landry's call.

He was rocking gently from foot to foot, holding Lellie against his chest and stroking her back lightly. The movement reminded me of a night two weeks ago when the weather had turned cold and Tully had insisted on building a fire. I'd had plans to put gas logs in the large, stacked-stone fireplace, but Tully had begged me to leave it alone.

"If I'm going to move to the cold hinterlands of the north, there'd better be woodsmoke and fluffy snow," he'd insisted. *"Hot chocolate and fuzzy blankets on the sofa."*

I'd just finished getting the blaze going when the sound of Lellie's cries blasted through the baby monitor.

"Your turn," I'd insisted with a cackle. I'd made a big production of throwing myself down on our deep sectional sofa and crossing my feet on the ottoman.

He'd cursed me the whole way back down the hall to Lellie's room. Twenty minutes later, he'd stood in front of the fire, rocking her in his arms and singing "Goodnight, Sweetheart." It was one of his favorites, and hearing it sung soft and low in his deep voice made my skin prickle and my dick swell.

"Babe," he said, lifting his eyebrows and flashing me a sexy grin. "You're looking at me with an expression I happen to know well, and I have to say it's highly inappropriate right now, considering our location."

I stepped in front of him and put my hands on his hips to pull him in gently. The warm bulk of our sleeping daughter pressed between us as I leaned in to kiss him with light, teasing brushes of my lips against his. "I can change our location," I whispered against his lips. "Just say the word."

The dressing room door slammed open, and Ryan stormed out, cursing under his breath. His eyes were dark, and his hands were curled into fists. After taking three long strides, he stopped, groaned, and pivoted back to the open dressing room door, yanking at his hair. "I'm done trying to reason with you, Zane. We're doing this my way, and that means wheels up in sixty minutes. Do you understand?"

Zane's voice was muffled like he was pulling a shirt over his head, but I could still hear the thread of unease in his words. "I think you're forgetting who's in charge here. I told my family I was coming in time for Sunday supper tomorrow. We're not going back to LA until after I've had my aunt Rinny's tomato corn pie and cheese grits. I've waited months to see my family, and I'm not letting some bullshit *prank* take that away from me."

Kenji stepped back up to us quietly and tapped Tully on the shoulder before tilting his head in the direction of the open dressing room door, where Zane was still ranting.

"And besides, how many times do I have to tell you... I'm *fine*!"

Tully bit his lip against a laugh. He shot his dancing eyes at me, and I felt my shoulders drop.

As I let myself slip cool and easy into the crystal clear waters of the Gulf and float happily into the future with my precious family.

ZANE'S EPILOGUE

I hadn't even felt the stamp this time. The best I could tell, it had happened when I'd been jostled to the side by a stage tech rushing past during the set break. Immediately afterward, Carlo and Kim, the makeup and hair duo, had stepped forward for a quick touch-up, and Kim had quirked her head and asked why I had red ink under the collar of my shirt.

There hadn't been time for the words to even sink in until I'd taken the stage. But there, in front of a hometown Atlanta crowd, I'd realized what she meant.

I'd been marked with another red bull's-eye.

Another target.

Another time someone had proved they could get to me by pressing a tiny rubber stamp onto my skin with permanent ink.

As soon as I'd realized what had happened, I hadn't been able to help glancing over at Ryan in the wings. My bodyguard had been waylaid by my previous manager, who was there representing another one of the performers at the music festival. Wanda had tried several times to speak to me, but Ryan had made it his personal mission to keep her away, especially before I was due onstage.

When he'd seen my face, he'd known immediately that something serious had happened. Ryan always had the ability to see through my attempts at hiding my emotions... and it drove me up a wall.

He'd already taken a large stride in my direction before someone stopped him, gesturing wildly to the tape on the ground indicating the sight line for the backstage area. Ryan's square jaw had flexed, and his eyes had darkened. I'd forced myself to look ahead into the tens of thousands of screaming fans at the Shaky Knees festival. The crowd here in the park was pumped, the weather was unseasonably warm, and the sun had been setting in golden peaches and pinks across the concert venue.

It would have been glorious...

If only I hadn't been ice-cold inside.

Thankfully, the set had gone by fast with all of that energy. I'd allowed myself to get lost in the music, to let it comfort me and help me to forget my troubles, as it always did.

At least until I came off the stage and Ryan yanked me past everyone into the dressing room before barking, "*What*."

It wasn't a question but a command.

My hands shook, and my skin began to tingle with encroaching numbness as the reality of the situation sank in. "It's fine," I said automatically. "Really. F-fine."

His eyes narrowed, but he didn't speak.

I tried to keep my voice steady. "I think..." I gestured to the collar of my shirt. "Um... behind... over my..."

Ryan stepped behind me and pulled at my collar. When he sucked in an outraged breath, it made it all real. My legs wobbled, and his arm banded around my front. The strong warmth of his touch never failed to make my breath catch, which caused my head to feel even floatier.

I hated feeling weak, hated causing concern and more work for others. And I especially hated the idea of Ryan thinking I was some kind of fragile diva who needed protecting from the big, scary world.

So I shoved him away and took a breath. "I told you, it's fine."

"Say that word to me again," he said in a low voice. "I dare you."

I closed my eyes and tried to focus. "I'm not hurt."

"Take off your shirt."

A huff of humorless laughter came out of my nose. I'd fantasized about my personal bodyguard many, many times in the past year. Fantasies in which he'd said exactly that phrase, among many others.

Never had I imagined it would carry so little lust.

Instead of arguing with him—which I knew would be pointless—I yanked off my sweaty tee and dropped it over a nearby chair. I kept my back to him so he could investigate the stamp, but I watched him in the dressing room mirror.

His face was a full storm. A hurricane band swirling around and around, picking up strength as it circled. His large hands came up to hold my shoulders, one thumb smoothing over the patch of skin just over my shoulder and out of my own sight range.

"Is it the same?" I asked softly, trying to ignore the prickles of awareness from his gentle touch.

He grunted confirmation.

Silence filled the room with jagged tension before he spoke. "This is the third time, Zane. We need to get back to LA and call in a—"

"No," I said emphatically. "No way. We're due in Barlo tomorrow morning to see my family for a few days, and I'm not canceling it."

"We're canceling it. This is the third time some psycho has gotten their hands on you, Zane, and I'm not allowing you to—"

I whipped around, shaking his hands off me in the process. "Not *allowing*? I'm not your child, Ryan. I'm your principal, as you remind me on a regular basis. You work for me, remember?"

His eyebrow winged up, and there was the barest hint of a smirk at the edge of his mouth. "I actually *don't* work for you." He paused before casting my own words back at me. "*Remember?*"

I pressed my lips together in frustration. "Fine. You work for the label. But you're here for me, for my protection. And the label doesn't get to decide that I can't visit my family. I've been looking forward to this trip for months, and you know it."

"I do know, and I'm sorry. Genuinely. But it's not safe. We need to figure out how this keeps happening and come up with a new personal protection strategy to—"

I held up my hand. "No. I know what you're going to say. You want the label to bump up the detail and put a fucking army of people on me. That's not happening, not when there's no proof the person or people doing this mean me any harm."

He shot me another look. The man had an innate ability to read my mind, but I did my best to keep my emotions locked down. If he realized just how freaked-out I was by this situation, he'd burn the whole world down to get me home to LA and shut me up tight in my Malibu home.

He'd threatened to suspend the tour to "reassess our security strategy" more than once, but thus far, I'd always managed to convince him to do the reassessing while keeping the tour going. Canceling shows meant costing the venues revenue and costing their workers jobs, not to mention costing the fans lost time and money.

Ryan knew how committed I was to following through on my promises, to providing jobs and bonuses to the people on the team who busted their asses to make these performances the best they could be. He knew how devastated I would be if our team's decision caused even one penny-pinching preteen to be disappointed.

But this time... this time, I was almost tempted to let him take over. To curl up in a ball and ask him to ferry me away from the crowds and the fear of the unknown. The only thing stopping me was the thought of missing a long-awaited visit with my gran.

There was no place I felt safer or more loved than in Barlo, Georgia. In Barlo, nothing would be able to reach me. There, everyone knew me and loved me. Everyone would gather round and keep me safe. For at least a little while, I'd be able to forget about Zee Barlo and simply be...

"Zane." Ryan's voice was like whiskey poured over gravel. "Someone stamped a literal *target* onto your fucking skin."

I sucked in a breath. "Yes, a stylized target. The same target as the one on my first album cover," I reminded him. "It's not a threat. It's a... a... I don't know. A prank. A dare, maybe. Or they have a weird obsession with the album. Or the target icon. Or they think they'll seem cool if they can get close enough to me to..." I didn't have the words to describe what I was trying to say, and I could tell that my arguments were only making Ryan more angry. I added hastily, "My point is, there's no proof they intend harm. So we're not going to over-react. You and Lou can handle it in Barlo. It's a tiny town, for god's sake. And everyone knows me there. And then we'll head back to LA and figure out if there's anything to be concerned about. But I can already tell you there won't be."

"Need I remind you there is a contract stipulation about your safety that indicates..."

I stopped paying attention to the lecture since it was nothing new and instead focused on Ryan's face as he spoke—on his intense eyes and chiseled jaw, on his strong hands that always touched me so gently, on the broad shoulders and barrel chest that made me feel safe and nervous all at once.

"Zane? Are you even listening?" Ryan demanded.

I winced. "Uh. Yes?"

"Jesus Christ," he muttered, storming out of the room. He paused and turned when he got to the hall.

"I'm done trying to reason with you, Zane," he barked. "We're doing this my way, and that means wheels up in sixty minutes. Do you understand?"

I firmed my jaw and forced myself to sound unaffected. "I think you're forgetting who's in charge here. I told my family I was coming in time for Sunday supper tomorrow. We're not going back to LA until after I've had my aunt Rinny's tomato corn pie and cheese grits. I've waited months to see my family, and I'm not letting some bullshit *prank* take that away from me."

Seeing Ryan lose his cool always made me nervous. I swallowed and tried to get us back to normal, to the way things were supposed to be. "And besides, how many times do I have to tell you... I'm *fine!*"

"Sure you are, Zane. You're *Mr.* fucking Fine. Keep telling yourself that."

As soon as Ryan stormed off, I closed the dressing room door behind him and locked it before leaning my back against it and sliding to the floor.

The tears came instantly. I'd been holding them off for hours just to try and get through the final set.

And now here I was, on the floor, face swamped with tears of exhaustion, fear, and a desperate, bone-deep need to go home and see my family.

To forget that someone had touched me without my knowledge. Had managed to pull aside my shirt and ink my skin. Had tried sending me a message of some kind without explaining what the fucking point was.

I let out a shaky breath and tried to get control of my emotions.

I was the king of good fortune, I knew that.

In the grand scheme of things, my current hardships were small potatoes, and I had no right to complain.

Not only was I a megastar, one of the rare unicorns who'd dreamed of being a rock star and had actually made it happen, but I was also part of an incredible family, a priceless brotherhood of life-long friends, and a rags-to-riches story even *before* I'd started my music career.

My life was comfortable and easy. I was living my dream. And by living my own dream, I was able to help others reach theirs. That was a privilege as well as a responsibility.

So yeah, I *was* Mr. fucking Fine, as Ryan called me. And I damn well should be.

I damn well *had* to be.

Too many people were counting on me for me to be anything else.

So even if I was scared, even if I was freaked-out and violated and outraged and wanted nothing more than to curl up in a ball under the covers, I was going to remind myself of how freaking lucky I was. Then, I was gonna smile and get on with the show.

And I did...

Until the emails started.

———

Need to know what happens next with Ryan and Zane? Click HERE to preorder Protecting Mr. Fine → *https://readerlinks.com/l/ 4346475*

If you'd like to know what happened That Night *two years ago, click here to sign up for my newsletter and download a bonus scene → https://readerlinks.com/l/4323180*

Curious how Bash and Rowe got their HEA? Prince of Lies *is now available here → https://readerlinks.com/l/4179577*

For Silas and Way's accidentally-married-in-Vegas story, Marrying Mr. Majestic, *click here → https://readerlinks.com/l/4159323*

LETTER FROM LUCY

Dear Reader,

Thank you for reading ***Inheriting Miss Fortune.***

Special thanks to Amanda Boes for helping me with Trigger's colic and to Andi Privitere for suggesting Landry's ringtone. I love sharing this passion with readers, and getting help from all of you makes my job way more fun.

Up next is Zane and Ryan's story. I love a rockstar/bodyguard trope and can't wait to dive into my favorite hurt/comfort, possessive, and protective themes in *Protecting Mr. Fine.* Check it out here →
https://readerlinks.com/l/4346475

Be sure to follow me on your favorite retailer site to be notified of new releases, and look for me on Facebook for sneak peeks of upcoming stories. You can also join me on Patreon for exclusive content and behind the scenes glimpses.

Please take a moment to write a review of *Inheriting Miss Fortune*. Reviews can make all the difference in helping a book show up in searches.

Feel free to stop by www.LucyLennox.com and drop me a line or visit me on social media. To see inspiration photographs for all of my novels, visit my Pinterest boards. The Pinterest board for *Inheriting Miss Fortune* can be found here → https://www.pinterest.com/lucy_lennox/inheriting-miss-fortune/

Finally, I have a fantastic reader group on Facebook. Come join us for exclusive content, early cover reveals, hot pics, and a whole lotta fun. Lucy's Lair can be found here → http://www.lucylennox.com/l/1437683

Happy reading!
Lucy

ABOUT LUCY LENNOX

Lucy Lennox is the USA Today bestselling author of over fifty gay romance titles including the GoodReads Hall of Fame winner Wilde Love. Born and raised in the southeast USA, she is finally putting good use to that English Lit degree she earned before the turn of the century.

Lucy enjoys naps, pizza, and procrastinating. She stays up way too late each night reading romance because it's simply the best.

For more information and to stay updated about future releases, sales and audio news and to grab some free and bonus reads, please sign up for Lucy's author <u>newsletter</u> on her website at <u>LucyLennox.com</u> or to stay in the know, join her exciting reader group, <u>Lucy's Lair</u> on Facebook.

facebook.com/lucylennoxmm

instagram.com/lucylennoxmm

amazon.com/Lucy-Lennox/e/B01N0IOYPT

bookbub.com/authors/lucy-lennox

patreon.com/lucylennox

pinterest.com/lucy_lennox

ALSO BY LUCY LENNOX

Get my <u>New Release Alerts</u>

Join me on Patreon

Follow me Everywhere Else

Read my books:

<u>Made Marian Series</u>

<u>Forever Wilde Series</u>

<u>Aster Valley Series</u>

<u>The Billionaire Brotherhood Series</u>

<u>Standalones</u>

<u>Novellas</u>

<u>After Oscar Series</u> (with Molly Maddox)

<u>Twist of Fate Series</u> (with Sloane Kennedy)

<u>Licking Thicket Series</u> (with May Archer)

<u>Champion Security Series</u> (with May Archer)

<u>Honeybridge Series</u> (with May Archer)

Visit my website at <u>www.LucyLennox.com</u> for a comprehensive list of titles, audio samples, freebies, suggested reading order, and more!